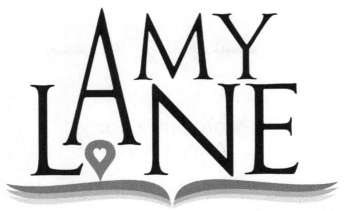

Choose your Lane to love!
Readers love the Johnnies series

Chase in Shadow

C0-BOG-277

"I would expect nothing less from a book by Amy Lane… For all its pain and strong emotional content, I found this to be a beautifully moving story of forgiveness, acceptance and love."

—Smexy Books

Dex in Blue

"For Amy Lane fans this is a satisfying addition to the canon, and I highly recommend it… For those who aren't already fans of hers, I think this could be a good book to start with…"

—Reviews by Jessewave

Ethan in Gold

"Amy Lane is brilliant. She knows how to weave a story that pulls on all my emotions and makes me feel like the characters are my family, my friends. I felt honored to be able to review this…"

—Live Your Life, Buy the Book

Black John

"Amy Lane fans will probably love this book, if you aren't a fan you need to be."

—Love Bytes

More praise for
AMY LANE

Fish Out of Water

"…I will promise you this, you WILL be left with one hell of a book hangover."
—Rainbow Gold Book Reviews

"*Fish Out of Water*… really captured my attention and kept it. This book is gritty and urban. It's suspenseful and I found myself gasping more than a few times."

—Diverse Reader

Red Fish, Dead Fish

"The passion in her words of love and family somehow come through like no other author I know."

—Paranormal Romance Guild

"The suspense is done so well, and the relationship between Ellery and Jackson is really engaging."

—Joyfully Jay

Beneath the Stain

"Amy Lane at her best and yes there is lots and lots of angst!"

—Prism Book Alliance

By AMY LANE

Behind the Curtain
Beneath the Stain
Bewitched by Bella's Brother
Bolt-hole
Bonfires
Christmas with Danny Fit
Clear Water
Do-over
Familiar Angel
Food for Thought
Gambling Men
Going Up
Grand Adventures (Dreamspinner Anthology)
Hammer & Air
If I Must
Immortal
It's Not Shakespeare
Left on St. Truth-be-Well
The Locker Room
Mourning Heaven
Phonebook
Puppy, Car, and Snow
Racing for the Sun
Raising the Stakes
Regret Me Not
Shiny!
Shirt
Sidecar
A Solid Core of Alpha

Tales of the Curious Cookbook (Multiple Author Anthology)
Three Fates (Multiple Author Anthology)
Truth in the Dark
Turkey in the Snow
Under the Rushes
Wishing on a Blue Star (Dreamspinner Anthology)

CANDY MAN
Candy Man • Bitter Taffy
Lollipop • Tart and Sweet

DREAMSPUN DESIRES
THE MANNIES
#25 – The Virgin Manny
#37 – Manny Get Your Guy
#57 – Stand by Your Manny

FISH OUT OF WATER
Fish Out of Water • Red Fish, Dead Fish

KEEPING PROMISE ROCK
Keeping Promise Rock
Making Promises
Living Promises
Forever Promised

Published by DREAMSPINNER PRESS
www.dreamspinnerpress.com

By AMY LANE

JOHNNIES
Chase in Shadow • Dex in Blue
Ethan in Gold • Black John
Bobby Green
Super Sock Man

GRANBY KNITTING
The Winter Courtship Rituals of
Fur-Bearing Critters
How to Raise an Honest Rabbit
Knitter in His Natural Habitat
Blackbird Knitting
in a Bunny's Lair

TALKER
Talker • Talker's Redemption
Talker's Graduation

WINTER BALL
Winter Ball • Summer Lessons

ANTHOLOGIES
An Amy Lane Christmas
The Granby Knitting Menagerie
The Talker Collection

Published by Harmony Ink Press
BITTER MOON SAGA
Triane's Son Rising
Triane's Son Learning
Triane's Son Fighting
Triane's Son Reigning

Published by DREAMSPINNER PRESS
www.dreamspinnerpress.com

AMY LANE
BOBBY GREEN

REAMSPINNER
PRESS

Published by
DREAMSPINNER PRESS

5032 Capital Circle SW, Suite 2, PMB# 279, Tallahassee, FL 32305-7886 USA
www.dreamspinnerpress.com

Bobby Green
© 2018 Amy Lane.

Cover Art
© 2018 Reese Dante.
http://www.reesedante.com
Cover content is for illustrative purposes only and any person depicted on the cover is a model.

Trade Paperback ISBN: 978-1-64080-256-8
Digital ISBN: 978-1-64080-257-5
Library of Congress Control Number: 2017913957
Trade Paperback published February 2018
v. 1.0

Printed in the United States of America
∞
This paper meets the requirements of
ANSI/NISO Z39.48-1992 (Permanence of Paper).

To everyone who has a V in their life.
To those who made it work and those who couldn't.
May the world get better,
may we learn to do more for the Vs in this world—
and for those of us who care for them.
We've got nowhere to go but up.

Prologue
Digger's Dilemma

REG KNEW this room—had used it a number of times in the past. Had engaged in sex for entertainment on the bed, had bent over the dresser, had even come on the closet mirror once or twice, for effect.

He'd been comfortable here, with the smell of antiseptic, sweat, and old jizz. This was his work space, and he'd had no problems at all forgetting about the smell and engaging in the body of his partner, male or female, and participating in sex on camera for money.

No problems until now.

Now he cuddled his coffee like it was December instead of a hot and humid late July.

"Dex," he moaned softly. "Dex, no. You can't... I can't."

Dex had stunning blue eyes, innocent as a baby's, so innocent it was hard to remember he had as many, if not more, porn films under his belt than Reg did. Dex didn't do that anymore, though. Hadn't since last October. Not since Chance—wait, *Chase* Summers, Reg always forgot—tried to kill himself.

Suddenly Dex had quit modeling and started bossing, and quit pining for his useless druggie ex-boyfriend and started living with Kane, who had stopped modeling too, and then they'd gotten married and adopted Kane's niece, and now Reg was the oldest living porn model and all his friends were daddies.

Reg wasn't sure if that was the exact chain of events, but then he was often muddy on cause and effect. He was really much better off in the now.

But right now sucked.

Dex looked up from his computer screen and turned those innocent eyes on Reg.

They were filled with nothing but compassion.

"Reg—I mean Digger—"

"Reg," he said, because the Digger thing had been a day late and a dollar short and it didn't matter now.

"Okay. Reg. You said it wouldn't be a problem."

"He's...." Reg swallowed and darted a furtive glance across the room. The kid standing there in jeans and nothing else was drinking water, just like Reg had told him, hydrating with no sugar, because fucking for money was a strenuous occupation. His sandy-brown hair hung layered around his long square-jawed face, and his eyes—brownish-green, whatever the word was for that—were wide and friendly. He had pillow lips and a ten-inch cock, which made the wide and friendly eyes almost like a trap. Yeah, you could fall for this kid's wide-eyed farm-boy routine, but watch out. He could suck your balls through your cock like a straw and then destroy your asshole with a few good strokes.

He was tall—six foot five now, because he'd grown two inches—with a long torso just waiting to fill out *completely* at the shoulders when the kid passed twenty-five. Or, oh God help him, twenty. Reg was almost ten years this boy's senior, and he couldn't even look the kid in the face. "He needs to find somebody else," he said, taking a sip of his coffee and wishing it was laced with something stronger.

"For the shoot?" Dex clarified. "Or for real life?"

"I wasn't supposed to be on the shoot, remember?" Reg asked bitterly. "I was supposed to be out of it. You said I could be out of it, and then you asked if I could fill in and I—"

Dex was looking at him like he was waiting for Reg to get something, but Reg wasn't seeing it.

Of course, Reg didn't see a lot of things. Reg was pretty goddamned stupid, but Dex was always nice enough to not say that.

He just waited, lush mouth slightly parted, eyes not quite as wide as the kid at the end of the room, but just as patient.

"What?" Reg asked, miserable. "What am I not getting?"

Dex shook his head. "Look, Reg? You undress down to your jeans, and then I'm going to leave the room for a sec. You two need to talk."

Reg started to obey immediately, not sure why undressing was part of talking or why Dex would leave the room before a shoot. He often had one or two guys doing lights and other camera angles too—they weren't there today, and Reg didn't know why and frankly didn't care.

He had one job to do. Get hard and get laid. He wasn't smart, but that much he knew.

So he obeyed orders. He was good at that, even when he topped. It's why he didn't mind when the director made him start fucking or stop fucking or told him more tongue or less or when to come.

Orders meant direction.

Reg needed direction.

He looked up at the big kid in the corner and swallowed. Bobby had given him orders. Good ones, like "Let's clean the house and go out" or "I'll cook if you go buy these ingredients."

In bed he'd been insatiable, had made as many of the decisions as Reg could stand, and Reg could stand a lot.

Or he could with Bobby.

Dex left, venturing into the hallway of the small office complex that Johnnies called home. This room had been outfitted to look like a bedroom—there were a couple here, so they could shoot more than one scene at a time. But the front office had a reception area and offices for John, the owner, and one for Dex, who did most of the editing, and now one for Reg, who didn't fuck for money anymore but arranged public appearances and things.

Until now.

He'd taken off his shoes and shirt, folded it neatly, and set them on a shelf in the corner with his shoes. There were locker rooms for clothes, but sometimes a director would decide he wanted different things for a shot, so always be prepared, right?

Also Reg had a place to keep his coffee, which was a plus. He should have brought water, like what Bobby was drinking, but he'd forgotten.

He hadn't done this in a couple of months.

He stopped fidgeting with his stuff and then walked to where Bobby stood, arms crossed over what was already a magnificent chest, the recent scar still healing across his ribs and stomach notwithstanding. He stared at Reg with a no-bullshit expression that made him look years older.

"I'm sorry," Reg said, not meeting his eyes. "I didn't know it was you, or I would have made Dex get someone else. I'm sure I'm the last person you want to do a scene with and—"

"Reg, stop talking," Bobby said sharply.

Reg looked up at him in surprise. He usually let Reg finish rambling—was, in fact, one of the few people who could stand to listen to Reg talk at all.

3

"Bobby?" His voice sounded broken to his own ears.

Bobby took two steps forward, looming over Reg's five foot ten without apology. "You look like shit," he said. "You haven't been taking care of my boy."

Reg bit his lip, miserable. "I told you to fuck off," he whispered. "Twice."

"Changes nothing."

Reg still couldn't look at him. "I... I can't—"

Bobby reached out, and for a moment Reg thought he'd touch him tenderly, brush his cheek with his knuckle or hug him, and the thought made him want to cry.

Instead he grabbed Reg's hair and tilted his head back slowly, until Reg had no choice but to look him in the eyes.

"You listen to me, Reggie." He sounded angry and sad at once, and his mouth kept working, like he was having a hard time not letting his face crumple and cry. "We're not here to fuck. That's not why Dex put you in here."

"But—" Reg gestured. "The scene!"

"You want to do a scene?" Bobby yanked him forward until their bare chests touched, and Reg's body lit on fire with want. "Fine. We'll do a scene. But you need to think about this right now, Reggie. If we do a scene, we're not doing it for the camera, and we're not doing it for money. We're doing it because we're together, and I'm not letting you push me away one more goddamned time."

He was so close, his mouth soft and threatening, his arms locked around Reg securely.

Oh God, Reg felt safe.

He never felt safe in his life—unless he was right here.

He never felt wanted, just right here.

But he was too old. Too old and too stupid, and this kid... this kid here... he needed someone with promise. Someone he could regard as an equal, right?

Reg swallowed hard and thought about pulling away.

Bobby lowered his head and stayed poised, a breath away. A kiss away. A lifetime away.

"C'mon, Reg," Bobby whispered. "What's it going to be?"

Vernal Bobby

Fifteen months earlier…

VERN ROBERTS flailed for purchase against the hay bale and tried not to let his knees buckle. Goddammit, it was like this *every single time*.

His girlfriend's brother gave the most delicious head, and in spite of Vern's protests, Keith Gilmore wouldn't leave Vern's cock alone.

"Keith," he panted, stars exploding behind his eyes. "Keith, I'm gonna… oh fuck… I'm gonna come…."

Keith pulled back, breathed on the head of Vern's dick, and grinned. "Then come," he taunted before sucking Vern down again. He could only get halfway down, but that was two inches farther than Keith's sister could, so Vern wasn't going to argue. And something about Keith's grip, his stubble, the dirty way he smiled at Vern when Jessica wasn't looking—it always made the blowjob ever so much more amazing.

Keith squeezed Vern's base hard and then tugged on Vern's generously sized balls. It wasn't actually the ball-tugging—that was okay—it was the forbidden way Keith's little finger brushed up against Vern's asscheeks that did it—sent Vern right over, pumping hard and hot into Keith's sucking mouth.

Keith gagged and swallowed and swallowed more, finally backing off when Vern was still milking the dregs out of his own cock, because this here—the coming forever—was about the one thing in the world Vern could do right.

But only with Keith.

"Whoo!" Keith chortled, falling back against the straw and wiping his mouth on his bare shoulder. "Damn, Vern. That's like a party trick. You should do that on the internet and get paid!"

Vern rolled his eyes. "Yeah. I think that's called porn, and your sister would kill me." He bit his lip self-consciously then, tasting Keith's come in his mouth all over again, because it had been Vern's turn to suck first. "Not that, uh, she'd be any happier about what we're doing now," he said delicately.

Keith just smirked at him, completely naked, sweating in the heat of the hay barn. Vern blushed and pulled his jeans up from around his ankles, positioned his briefs, and buttoned up. He checked the neck of his T-shirt self-consciously, hoping none of Keith's jizz had spilled out of his mouth, but Keith didn't come for as long as Vern did, so it wasn't a problem.

"Yeah—and my girlfriend would probably gut us both with hay hooks," Keith said affably. It was true, though—Carla was a little bit, uh, *psychotic* and *jealous* were the words Jessica used. "But that don't mean we're gonna stop." He winked—and Vern recoiled.

"But Keith—you and Carla—you're getting *married* in a couple of months."

Keith had sandy-brown hair and gray eyes in a farm-boy tanned face. When he smiled, he looked bright and wicked and alive, but times like this, when he looked blank, Vern suspected he really didn't have a lot going on upstairs.

"So?"

Vern stared at him. "Keith—you're getting *married*. This… I mean, it's bad enough what we're doing here—but *married*."

The blowjobs hadn't been Vern's idea. He and Keith worked for Keith's dad in the summers—baling hay, driving it to feed stores around the county, feeding Mr. Gilmore's stock. Two years ago—right after Vern hit his growth spurt at sixteen and passed six feet tall—they'd worked a long summer's day and ended stripping off their jeans and hosing each other off behind the barn. Keith had taken one look at Vern's equipment through the wet cotton of his briefs, shucked the briefs down to Vern's ankles, and blown him, right there in the mud. Vern hadn't been going with Jessica yet—but Keith had been with Carla for more than a year.

When Vern said something—as he remembered, it had been along the lines of "But… but… you've got a—omigod, I'm gonna come! Girl—Jesus yes!—friend!"—Keith had grinned up at him, those appealing crinkles in the corners of his eyes.

"Cool your jets—just boys playing around." And then he'd sucked on Vern again, and Vern had come in his mouth.

But now—now with Keith and Carla getting married and Vern and Jess talking about it—this thing they were doing didn't feel like boys playing around anymore.

It felt like cheating.

Vern discovered he didn't like this feeling much.

Keith stood up fluidly, the lean muscles in his twenty-one-year-old body stretching and flexing as he did.

God, he was pretty.

Vern felt like a fag for thinking it, but Jesus—Keith Gilmore's body was made for more than blowjobs. Vern felt a little cheated, actually—here they were, doing this thing that could get them caught, screw up both their lives, and ruin their relationships, and he hadn't even been allowed to run his hand down Keith's back, just to feel his muscles and his skin.

"Stop looking at me like that, faggot," Keith taunted, rolling his eyes. Vern looked away.

"We can't do this after you and Carla get married," he said in a small voice, and for once, Keith's perpetual smirk fell away, and he looked a little lost.

"What? Why the hell not?"

"'Cause it's not right," Vern said, walking to the sink in the corner so he could wash the come off his mouth. "You may not think this is cheating, but I bet Carla won't feel that way—"

"So we don't tell her!" Keith laughed as he came up beside Vern and grabbed a cup from the ledge to start drinking from. Vern flashed to when he and Jessica had been washing dishes at his mom's house the night before, when she used the opportunity for closeness to bump his hip, nuzzle his shoulder, touch his back.

He found that he craved these things from Keith even more than he'd wanted them from Jess, but he knew the second he even tried for them, Keith would laugh and call him a faggot or sweet pea or something obnoxious.

They'd had each other's *dicks* in their mouths, but touching a hip or a shoulder or even a goddamned kiss was somehow worse.

Why the hell was that?

It was starting to piss Vern off.

"It's not right," Vern said quietly, standing his ground. "I like Carla." So that was a bit of a stretch, but still. "Doing this behind her back—it's not respectful."

"Well, it's not like we're *in love*," Keith retorted scornfully.

Maybe not you, but I could be.

7

The thought made Vern catch his breath and fight tears. He buried it—buried it so far down, it took a few more months and a whole lot more dicks before he could unbury it and see what he might have killed.

"But you're in love with Carla, and this ain't right," Vern said, his chest achy and his throat swollen.

"Are you saying I'm some sort of fairy?" Keith asked, like he was getting angry.

Oh, God forbid. "Look, Keith, Carla gives you head. You don't need me. You and me, we just keep doing what we do. We just leave this part of it out, okay?"

"Carla gives lousy head," Keith snarled, and while Vern missed the part where that was *his* fault, he tried to smooth things over.

"Well, you know, practice. All I'm saying is if somebody catches us, we both won't be getting no head from our girlfriends, and living in this pile of horseshit will be even fucking harder."

They lived—quite literally—in Dogpatch, California. Population 200. Of course, there were a bunch of tiny towns in the same fifty-mile radius up in the Sierra Mountains, but the one on their addresses and college applications and driver's licenses was Dogpatch.

Vern was well aware that after he graduated from high school and hay-baling season was over, if he didn't find someplace to work through the winter, he and his mom might not even be able to afford rent on the tiny shack in the back of Frank Gilmore's property.

He couldn't afford to piss off Keith Gilmore. But dammit—*dammit*—this just wasn't right.

As if to prove he didn't know what right was, Keith sneered. "You think living in Dogpatch is hard *now*, asshole, just think of what it's gonna be like if I tell everyone I saw you sucking Dirk Hogarth's dick behind the fuckin' Frostie last week!"

Vern stared at him, mouth opening and closing slowly. Dirk Hogarth was the high school English/history teacher, a slight little man who lived alone with his cats and his sweater vests and his bow tie. Everyone knew he was a fairy, but because he was so mild-mannered, such a sweet little person who never bothered anyone, nobody gave him shit.

All the mothers in the town adored him, and even the students were kind, but that didn't stop the jocks from making fun of him behind his back, daring each other to go suck the guy's dick when they got riled or didn't like their grades.

For the first time, Vern thought about Mr. Hogarth and the rude, stupid shit people said about him behind his back, and felt bad. Mr. Hogarth had been nothing but nice to Vern, and here this redneck cheater was using the guy as a threat.

A credible threat.

"What are you saying?" Vern asked quietly, trying to get a bead on this sitch. "Say it very plainly, Keith. I want to hear you say the words."

Keith had the grace to look ashamed. "Just... you know, Vern. Keep doing what we do. Don't make a big moral deal out of it and everything'll be fine."

Vern's mind raced—although he'd never really been accused of being a brain trust before.

"So if I don't agree to keep blowing you, you're going to spread rumors that I'm blowing someone else," he said slowly. "Like, blackmail."

Keith's jaw thrust out and his lower lip trembled. He looked ready to cry, and for the first time, Vern got maybe an inkling of what was going through his mind.

"Yeah," he said, pretending to be cavalier but achieving instead a sort of pathetic bravado. "That's it. I'm a blackmailer. Making you do something you goddamned enjoy."

Vern nodded. "*Enjoyed.* Past tense, Keith. I'll do it if I have to. I need the job, and your dad don't give jobs to fairies. But from this moment on, I *enjoyed* doing it. I don't enjoy it anymore."

With that he turned around and grabbed his boots, which stood at the open doorway. He paused for a moment to slide them on and then kept right on walking. He and Keith had another two hours of work to do in the goddamned baler, and by God, he didn't want to be here one more minute longer.

THAT NIGHT he went home to the tiny bathroom he'd newly tiled and took a shower, scrubbing at his body—his genitals in particular—until the water ran cold. When he came out of the bathroom, he put on his sleep shorts and joined his mom in the cramped, yellowing kitchen. She was hunched over the beat-up wooden table, tapping on the laptop furtively, like when Vern's father had still been there, afraid every keystroke would be the one that spun him into a rage.

"Looking for recipes?" he asked, because she sure did like to cook.

"Cross-stitch," she replied promptly, smiling. She had an entire *library* of floss now that his dad had split. He looked at her fondly, her lined face and graying hair too old for her actual age. She was, what? In her early forties?

"You should be looking for a cruise," he said, suddenly wishing bitterly he could send her on one. "A place you can read all your romances by the pool and come back all tan."

She laughed, obviously pleased. "Oh, Vern—that's sweet, but we don't have the money for a cruise."

He sighed. "Mom, I don't think we'll have the money for rent this next year if I can't get something to do besides baling Frank Gilmore's hay."

Soberly she looked up from their aging laptop. "There's not much you can do here," she said, but she didn't look happy about it. "And you know, my job at the insurance agency—you never know how many hours."

She worked in Truckee, about an hour away.

"I know," he said softly. "I... I think I need to maybe look somewhere else."

She swallowed unhappily. "I... baby, you're not even eighteen."

Something in his chest loosened. They hadn't spoken much, him and his mom, not before his dad left and not in the five years since. But he'd always known she loved him.

"I know," he said, giving her a watery smile. "And maybe it's time I went down into the big city and maybe found something to do."

She took a breath and rubbed her palm under her eyes. "After graduation," she said huskily. "I... you know. Have a present for you."

He knew. She'd been saving up for a truck—it was one of the reasons she was on the laptop, looking up free cross-stitch patterns. She didn't want to spend money on the ones she could buy at the store.

"I can't wait," he said. From somewhere—somewhere near the bottom of his toes—he pulled a reassuring smile. God. His mom deserved more. More than an empty house. More than empty promises from a drunk with a mean temper. More than to send her only family off into the world with a used truck she'd get cheated on at Frank Gilmore's brother's dealership.

More than a cocksucker for a son who was leaving her alone so he didn't have to give head to a guy he'd trusted with his dick but not much more.

A MONTH later, after graduation, he managed to find a job at a construction firm that was willing to train him up, provided he had some basic skills. At the end of August, he loaded his clothes, his paperback books, and a new pair of work boots into the cab of the fifth-hand Toyota truck his mom had managed to buy him. He'd complained bitterly to Keith—who was speaking to him like they were friends now that Vern was blowing him without question—about how Keith's uncle was screwing his mom over on the car payments. Three days later, Desmond Gilmore had shown up during their regular hay-baling "break" with an unpleasant gleam in his eye.

The fucker didn't wash his cock, and his come tasted like he drank goat piss for breakfast, but at least Vern wasn't leaving his mom with a shit-ton of debt as he went. He had a construction job lined up, and with any luck, he'd never have to see another dick up close and personal. Or a penis neither.

He'd told Jessica he was looking for a way to make money for them.

God help him, he'd hinted at marriage.

"You think you can get a job down there?" she asked, mouth slightly parted, pale blue eyes alight. "Like, maybe get us an apartment and everything?"

For a moment Vern was caught by her, by her big eyes, by her innocence. No, she wasn't a virgin, but she believed in happy ever after. She *didn't* believe in boys giving blowjobs behind the barn, and she *didn't* believe it wasn't cheating if it was another boy.

But you were getting something you weren't getting from her. Something you wanted.

He didn't know how to answer that voice, so he buried it down where that strange tenderness for Keith had gone to die and smiled.

"Sure, babe—we'll have to see. I mean, I've got a job, but I don't know if it's going to be all wine and roses."

She squealed like he'd just given her a marriage proposal that included a trip to New York as the honeymoon and threw herself into his arms. He held her for a moment and then kissed her, like she wanted him to.

They had sex then, in his bedroom, before his mom got home from her job. He was careful about cleanup after, throwing away the condom and washing the sheets, because he was trying to be respectful of his mom's feelings.

And because he didn't want it—the kiss, the sex, the lie—to be any closer to his skin than it had to be.

The day he left, Keith and Carla came to see him off, and Keith laughed and joked with him like he had all the time they'd been bailing hay when they *hadn't* been sucking each other's cocks. Vern waited for something— some sign, some breath, a lowering of eyes, *anything*—that said he meant more to Keith than just a mouth on his privates.

At the end, when he was hugging everyone, Keith said, "You'd better be ready to suck me double when you visit" into the shell of his ear, and Vern pulled back as though stung. He turned to Jessica and gave her a long, wet lip-lock, the kind of thing she'd probably been dreaming about from him since they'd started kissing but he just could never bring himself to give her—until now.

She melted into his arms, and he pecked her on the cheek and then turned to his mom.

"I'll be back in a month," he said softly. "I promise. I'll call when I can."

She nodded. "You sure you have the address of the flophouse?" she asked, voice quavering. Apparently a bunch of guys who worked for the company all stayed in a trailer. The guy hadn't sugarcoated it—a bunch of guys sleeping on cots with a shower—but then, what did Vern really need if he wasn't moving there for good?

At least that's what he'd told them.

Because he didn't want to run away.

Because he felt like enough of a coward already.

"Yeah, Mom," he said quietly. "I got it."

She smiled at him, her eyes—hazel like his—troubled, and nodded after cupping his cheek. "Take care of yourself in the big city," she said, her mouth quirking because they both knew Sacramento could be a lot bigger.

But he also knew it wasn't Dogpatch either.

"I promise, Mama," he said, drawing out his fake-Southern drawl. "I won't let those big-city slickers corrupt your little baby boy."

She smiled and patted his cheek. "You just might be wicked enough to beat them all," she said affectionately. "I look forward to seeing you try."

And that was it.

He got into the truck and drove down to Sacramento. Every mile he put behind him as he wound through the mountain roads to the foothills was a load of stone off his shoulders.

No more Keith Gilmore.

No more sucking guys off when they wouldn't give him the time of day.

No more queer shit, period. He was done with all that, because he had a girlfriend, and he was going to try to do right by her.

He really was.

THREE WEEKS later, he drove a nail through his thumb.

"Fuck," he said dully, staring at it as the blood welled out.

The guy next to him turned around and threw up, but Vern could hardly pull his head out of the haze of exhaustion that enveloped him. The "flophouse" the company provided was seriously a bunch of guys on mattresses on the floor of a trailer—with no air-conditioning and windows that barely cracked. It was early September in Sacramento during a heat wave. That thing was like a convection oven, and the only guys getting any sleep were the three who could fit on the roof without it buckling. Vern had taken twenty dollars of his savings to buy himself a cheap sleeping bag—on sale—so he could at least stretch out in the bed of his truck. He slept a little better there, but not much, because he was sleeping with only a layer of his clothes between him and the hard bed of the truck, and his body hurt more every damned day.

"Dammit, Roberts!" Collins, the supervisor, yelled from across the site. "Stop playing around there!"

Vern blinked hard and caught the nail in the claw end of the hammer, yanking it out before his brain could even register what he was doing.

He stared at his thumb, complete with brand-new hole, and thought stupidly that he could probably push a stud through it like a piercing, when the pain penetrated the fog of exhaustion and he collapsed sideways, letting out a slow-boiling wail that felt like it would cripple his stomach, his balls, and all the other things he was screaming from.

Then God was really merciful to him, because he passed out.

HE WOKE up in the foreman's trailer while someone bandaged his left thumb and someone else shoved a pen into his hand.

He ignored the pain because he had to and asked, "What in the fuck am I signing?"

"An affidavit that says you got your last check," Collins said flatly, his pale blue eyes and sunburned face impassive and disgusted.

"Where's my last check?" he mumbled.

"Right here." Collins shoved it at him, and Vern grimaced. He'd gotten the first one, for a week's work, the week before. This was for two weeks—and it was a lot, compared to what he made baling hay, but he'd seen prices down here in the city, and it might buy him parking for a month, with some gas thrown in.

"You're firing me?" His brain felt like it was expanding and shrinking in his skull. "How's that right?"

"This is your second time getting hurt," Collins muttered, pointing to the bandage on Vern's thigh. He hadn't seen the brackets screwed onto the ends of the lumber in the pile, and he'd misjudged where to turn. He'd ended up with a puncture in his thigh the shape of a blunt, short blade.

"Yeah. It's hot. We're not getting much sleep," he defended.

"Rest of the guys don't bitch." Collins smiled meanly. The rest of the guys were illegal immigrants working to send money home to their families. Even if they felt like risking deportation, they spoke very little English and weren't aware that they were supposed to be protected, immigrant or not.

"They're afraid you'll turn them in," Vern said. "Which sucks."

Collins glared at him as he held his hand poised over the affidavit. "Sign the fucking paper," he snarled.

But Vern was ready for this—he hadn't sucked Frank Gilmore's brother's dick without a contract either. "Give me the check," he snarled back.

Collins shoved it off the edge of the desk, making Vern pick it up with his good hand. Once he got it back, he folded it in half and tucked it in the front pocket of his jeans.

He stood up then, half turning to make sure he had a clear way out to the door, because he didn't trust Collins not to pay guys to beat him up and take his money as he left.

"I'll come back and sign the paper when it's deposited," he said decisively.

"You'll *what*?" Collins yelled.

"You heard me." Vern stood his ground. "Look—I'm not signing shit until I get this thing to the bank. I'll come back to collect my tools."

Collins shook his head. "You leave now, don't bother coming back."

"Then I'll bring my tools with me," Vern said decisively. "I don't trust you, and I need the fucking tools."

"You got your money, you little prick." Collins reached into his desk drawer and pulled out a gun. The guy next to Vern—Vasquez, who had been putting the bandage on as Vern tried to pull his brains back into his ears—put both hands over his head and backed up so fast he upended his folding chair.

"I do," Vern said, hoping this worked. "Look, you can't shoot me. My mom knows where I work, she knows I got hurt, and I told her about this little operation here. You shoot me, she sends the cops here. Let me get my tools, and let me get the fuck out of this hellhole, and you and me are done. I'm gonna find someplace legit."

Collins lowered the gun and spat. "You go ahead and try, you dumbass cocksucker. I'll make sure no outfit in the state'll pick you up. Not a greenhorn like you. No certification, no training—what in the fuck did you expect for eleven bucks an hour?"

Vern's thumb throbbed viciously. "A boss who wasn't a scum boil on a rotting snake's ass," he replied, just loopy enough with pain to say something that awesome. "You have a lousy fucking day, you hear?"

He backed out of the room then, sparing a thought but not a look for poor Vasquez, who had tried to be a decent guy. He backed down the stairs and turned to run through the site, going to the house in the project he'd been working on when he'd nailed his thumb.

To his surprise, his tools were all gathered in their chest, and it sat on the edge of the foundation. He looked around miserably at his coworkers, who mostly had spoken to each other but not to him because they didn't speak the same language, and they were all too tired to try.

"Uh, thanks," he said to the listening air around him. He looked up and caught Gomez's eye and smiled faintly through the pain. Gomez was a young guy, Vern's age, who had a really sweet round face and the beginnings of a mustache.

"*De nada,*" he said with a sad little smile.

Vern got slammed in the gut with a protective streak he didn't know he had. "You can come with me?" he asked, wondering if these words at least would translate.

"No," Gomez said, shaking his head. "Mama... Mama needs money." He grimaced again and gazed at Vern with the same sort of look Vern had seen in Keith's eyes—but, oh God, with the tenderness Keith had always lacked.

Oh. Well, hell. Those nights in his truck, and....

You could have cheated on your girlfriend and taken advantage of a guy without power too, you bastard!

But it wouldn't have been like that, would it?

"Take care," he said softly. "Gomez, just... don't let this guy beat you down."

Gomez nodded and shrugged, turning back to his job.

THE FIRST place Vern went was the Y for a shower and a chance to wash at least one load of clothes. The next place he went was a coffee shop. Then another. Then another. Then another. Then McDonald's. And Carl's Jr. And Round Table. And Jamba Juice.

Most of them told him he had to apply online—but he'd left the computer with his mom, and his phone wouldn't update enough to fill out the app, so he'd suckered an actual pen-and-ink application out of the day managers and at least put his name on a piece of paper that said he wanted a fucking job.

He slept in his truck that night, visited the Y the next morning, and tried again.

And again.

At the end of the week, he went home to lie to his mom.

She fussed over his thumb and clucked that he was getting too thin. All she had in the house was spaghetti and butter. He ate the last of it and hated himself. Jessica and Keith came to visit, and for a moment, Vern let himself fall into Jessica's warm and willing hug and dream. Dream of safety and soft mattresses every night, dream of a small town where you never went hungry, and where if your boss pulled a gun on you, you could at least tell the cops and get the guy investigated.

Jessica wanted to stay the night.

Vern told her that he had to use his mom's computer, and she said that would be fine—she'd wait up.

Oh God.

Vern had dreamed about nothing but Gomez and his sweet brown eyes and his yearning, and the way he'd saved Vern's tools for him. Jesus God, Vern didn't want to touch Jessica with that yearning on his skin.

He spent hours on the computer, filling out an application for every fast-food chain in a twenty-five-mile radius from Sacramento—anything, anything but to come back to Dogpatch again.

He crawled into bed and felt up a sleepy Jessica, knowing it was his duty. He got it up—because that thing never stayed quiet long—but as he moved inside her, the satin of her body squeezing him tight, her soft cries urging him on doggedly, he was thinking of Gomez and the yearning in his eyes.

THE NEXT day Jessica had to work at the Frostie, and Keith said, "That's okay. Vern and me, we can hang."

His almond-shaped eyes went to half-mast when he said this, and his even white smile, that made all the girls want to spread their legs for him, cranked up a notch.

"I need to leave early," Vern said desperately, but his mother teared up.

"Oh, honey—my check went through. I was going to make something special tonight. Can't you wait until this evening?"

He looked at her helplessly, wanting a meal his mother cooked more than anything in the world.

Apparently more than he *didn't* want to suck Keith Gilmore's dick, because "hanging out" meant going to the stables and going down on Keith while he grabbed the back of Vern's head and knotted his fingers in Vern's hair and tried to choke Vern on a six-inch cock.

He finished and Vern swallowed, and for a moment, a brief moment, Keith pressed Vern's head against his stomach and the tight grip on his hair relaxed, turned into a caress.

"I missed that," he said softly. Then he let go and pulled his pants up while Vern went to rinse out his mouth.

17

Vern didn't anticipate the heat at his back, Keith's warm body draping itself over Vern's shoulder, the gentle hand at his backside—or the cash pressed into the back pocket of Vern's jeans.

"Eat something," Keith said, his voice low. "Your mom may buy that you're okay, but you look like shit warmed over."

Vern closed his eyes then and fought off the shaking that threatened to take over his body. He swallowed the last of Keith's spunk and nodded.

Even when he was back in his truck, driving back down to nowhere, hoping for a goddamned job, he couldn't have said what that moment was.

On the one hand, it was all the tenderness he'd ever dreamed of.

On the other, it was another step to whoring his ass out for food.

IT TOOK him two more weeks to get a job waiting tables at a little smoothie café called Hazy Daze. He wasn't making a lot of money, but after a week or two, a few people there let him flop on their couch and use their shower for ten bucks a night.

He still had to go home and sleep with Jessica once a week. And suck Keith Gilmore's dick.

It was almost to the point where the thought of driving home made him want to vomit, but at least he got an employee discount on food that didn't make him break out.

He must have been looking particularly rosy and clean-cut then, because some of the guys who wandered into the place started to check him out.

Particularly when he came out from behind the counter.

"Hey, Dex—check it out!" The guy speaking looked like a dark-haired, brown-eyed gorilla with supermodel face implants and a soul patch. His fake whisper sucked.

The tall, blond, blue-eyed, angel-faced, pillow-lipped country boy with him obviously thought so too.

"That wasn't creepy at all," he drawled. He didn't sound like California country, but Vern could hear the sound of someone who hadn't seen a lot of city in his youth either. "C'mon, Kane—you'll scare the poor guy."

"Yeah, but, you know. You said you're looking for guys who do girls."

"*You* do girls, moron. We don't have to work that hard."

"Boys pay more," Kane said, taking a philosophical pull on his juice. An *actual* juice, not a smoothie, something with lots of protein powder but no food. "But, you know. He's kinda hot. And *look*."

Vern had to smile at the long-suffering expression on the blond guy's face as he swung his head around and, without shame or subterfuge, checked out Vern's crotch.

And widened his eyes in appreciation.

"So?" Kane asked, looking from Vern's package to his friend and back. "C'mon, Dex. Tell me I'm wrong."

Dex grunted. "You're not wrong." There was a buzzing in his pocket, and he pulled out his phone, frowning. "Shit."

"If it's him, tell him to fuck off," Kane said, an edge to his voice.

"It's not him. But Ethan and Chase are there for the shoot, and we're late."

Kane's disappointment was palpable. "Damn. How's that happen? We work out, we have juice—just goes so fast."

The expression on the blond guy's face was fond. "I got no idea. But here. I'll give him John's card. Couldn't hurt."

He walked up to Vern, who had given up pretending to ignore what they were saying.

"Kid, c'mere."

Vern had been bussing the small store and was about to walk around the counter to take the tubs in to wash. He paused at the entryway and turned around to face Dex, the blond guy, who had been friendly when he ordered and kind to the big gorilla who just didn't seem that bright.

"What can I do for you?" he asked formally, because damn, he needed more hours, and his manager, Courtney, was eyeing him with suspicion from behind the counter.

To his surprise, Dex looked vaguely embarrassed. "Look, kid—if this offends you, do me a favor and forget we talked. I like this store, and it's near my house and my gym, and it would really suck to have to change where I get my cleanse, okay?"

Vern nodded bemusedly, wondering what this guy could say that would piss him off. "Not a problem," he said. "This convo never happened."

Dex smiled appreciatively. "Solid." He reached into the back pocket of jeans that looked too fancy to be jeans and pulled out a slick red leather wallet. "Look, this is the card for the company we work for. It's not... uh, a PG-13 kind of place, but if you look at the website, you'll see we're, uh, equal opportunity. And it may be, uhm, up your alley, and it may be, well, not—but if it's up your alley. At all. And you feel like maybe it's something you're interested in. And you don't want to sue me for harassment, here." He pulled a pen from the jar by the register and wrote a number on it. "This is *my* number, and I can set up an audition for you."

Vern got a hit of aftershave and clean male sweat and swallowed against a wave of want he'd never anticipated.

"Uh, sure," he said, thinking he'd call that number no matter what just to get another *smell* of the furiously blushing Dex.

Dex nodded, seemingly in relief. "So, uh…." He squinted at Vern's name tag. "Uh, Vern. Do people still name their kids Vern?"

"Means 'spring,'" Vern said, feeling foolish and off-kilter. "My mom wanted to go to college—likes to read fancy books."

Kindness sparked in Dex's blue eyes. "Of course. Well then, it's a good name. But you've got your hands full, and we both have to bail. I'm going to tuck this card in your front shirt pocket—shit. You don't have one. Okay, don't take this as being fresh or forward. If you turn around, I'll tuck this into your *back* jeans pocket, and you can look at it at your leisure. Is that okay?"

Vern nodded dumbly and turned around, presenting his ass, as it were. "Yeah. Sure. Thanks."

Dex winked. "Don't thank me yet. Right now I could be just some pervert who's hitting on you 'cause you're hung like a fuckin' bear."

He could feel Dex's fingers pull the pocket back and push the card under the flap of worn fabric. The movement was executed smoothly and was over before Vern could even imagine the feeling of those hands sliding tenderly over his backside and squeezing his asscheeks with intent—but that didn't mean his body didn't jump to conclusions.

"What was that about?" Courtney asked as Vern shuttled his body back to the sink. "Was he hitting on you?"

Vern swallowed back a vehement "I wish!" He had a girlfriend. "I'll have to look up his website and see," he said gamely, but he remembered the way the two guys had checked out his body—checked out his package. Remembered Dex's grim and practical discomfort when talking about "equal opportunity" and "*not* PG-13."

He had an idea.

And he was pretty sure it was the sort of thing that would be blocked on the computer back in the manager's office too.

LIBRARY COMPUTERS block porn—so do internet cafés.

Vern looked at the card on his break, though. It featured an artistic line silhouette of a shirtless man, and he knew exactly what he was getting into. He looked at the card again, which read simply *Dex@Johnnies.com*, and wondered who he could flop with that night and if they would mind if he used their laptop.

Then he noticed that the card had an address on it.

One right there in Sacramento.

And he had the next day off.

THE PLACE looked... respectable. A little one-story office complex that appeared to be designed around a courtyard, since there were trees growing out of the middle. Solid. The girl behind the counter looked like a handkerchief in a hurricane, with flyaway brown hair and a sleeveless flannel shirt, and she stared at the phone like maybe it would bite. The thing rang, and she fumbled the receiver, then pushed a pulsing button with extreme trepidation.

"Uh, Johnnies? Kelsey speaking? How can I help you?" The voice on the other end spoke, and her elfin face lightened fractionally as things seemed to work. "Okay, yeah. I'll hook you up with John. He can help you." She stared at the phone and jabbed a finger at the board again. Raising an eyebrow, she muttered, "And I hit *this* to hold, and *this* to transfer, and—"

There was a solid tread in the hallway. "Oh, Kelsey...," a voice sang, sounding like a man at the end of his patience.

Kelsey grunted. "Sorry, Dex. What'd I do this time?"

"Well, I got a real earful of the new girl getting an ass full. Was that your intention?"

Kelsey gave a weak smile. "Well, at least this time it wasn't on speaker."

Dex let out a weary laugh and massaged the back of his neck. "An improvement," he admitted, then sighed. "Okay—show me who you were trying to transfer. Let's try this again." He looked up and saw Vern there, and some of the weariness eased up. "I was hoping for an email, but I got a

21

visit," he said with a bright commercial smile. "That's even better. Give me a sec and we can talk."

While Vern was waiting, he looked around, thinking the office looked so… normal. So pedestrian. Boring, even. With the exception of some kitten posters behind Kelsey, saying things like "Hang in there, baby!" and "Today's going to be a great day!" most of it was beige. If Vern hadn't heard something about the new girl getting an ass full, he never would have guessed porn.

While he was staring around the space and wondering if anyone had ever sat on the copier bare-assed naked, the bell above the door rang.

The guy who walked through didn't *look* like a porn star. Not like Dex or Kane, who were muscular and waxed—down to their eyebrows, Vern was pretty sure, or Kane would have had a unibrow. This guy had scalp stubble dyed an obvious blond. His pale brown skin had the remnants of childhood acne on the cheeks, with cheekbones that made the league minimum for handsome and a short jaw with a pointed chin. Vern might have written him off completely in the looks department, but he had friendly almond-shaped blue eyes and a smile with a sort of pureness—like Keith Gilmore, but without the cunning or the self-awareness of being a douchebag.

He paused as he saw Dex and Kelsey working on the phone and waited until he caught Dex's eye.

"The schedule in the office?" he asked, pointing to a door leading to what looked to be a conference room on the right.

"Yeah, but it's a mess," Dex muttered. "Tango's off, probably for good, so gimme a minute, Reg—I mean *Digger*," he said determinedly. "We might need you more."

Digger—who was apparently also Reg—smiled sunnily, unfazed by the gaffe of his name. "Okay, Dex. I'm here."

He turned to Vern and held out his hand. "Digger. Are you new?"

Vern shook his hand, wondering at that sunny smile and those guileless blue eyes. Was this guy hiding something? Keith's good-ol'-boy smile hid an opportunist who thought forty bucks for a blowjob made him Mother-Fucking-Teresa, but this guy didn't seem to have an angle.

"I don't have a computer," he said apologetically. "Dex there offered me an audition, but I wasn't sure for what."

Digger nodded. "Porn," he said simply, wiping the mystique away with one pass of a battered, fine-boned hand. "You've never heard of Johnnies?"

Vern shook his head in apology. "Sorry. No. I don't even know what kind of porn it *is*."

Digger's shrug seemed philosophical. "Mostly gay, but they're trying to get girls now. Like branching out." He smiled that easy bolt of sunshine again. "I like girls. I mean, guys are good, but I started with girls, and sometimes it's nice to trade off."

Vern's brain sputtered and sparked. Such an easy way to think about it, right? But who did that? Who just said, "Yeah, I'll do either one. They're both nice"?

"So," Vern said, trying to get his brain wrapped around the concept, "like bisexual?"

Digger's frown made him look like a puzzled baby. "But isn't that like gay? I'm not sure I'm gay."

This conversation was officially the strangest thing Vern had ever done with a stranger. "Well, bi means you like both," he said patiently, and embarrassment crossed Digger's open face.

"Yeah. I knew that." He shook his head. "Sorry—I'm not always… remembering stuff good."

Oh. Vern got that. "No worries," he said, smiling with all the reassurance he could muster. "I mean, it's not like I'm an expert."

And Digger chewed his lip, a sort of pained sorrow crossing his face. "I've been doing this for ten years," he said in a stage whisper, like this was a confidence. "I just forget shit."

"But you never forget to come in for your schedule," Dex said, straightening up from the phones and giving Kelsey an absent pat on the shoulder. "That makes up for a whole lot of ills in my book."

Digger gave Dex a comfortable wink. "You just say that 'cause you're shorthanded."

"Yeah." Dex's grimace was not nearly so comfortable. "I don't think Tango's coming back." His voice sank low—this made him sad.

"You'll still visit," Digger told him. "Kelsey told me folks set up shifts in his room. We'll take care of him." Vern glanced at him sharply. He didn't know who Tango was, but there was something childlike and trusting in this guy's voice. Couldn't Dex hear it? He thought this porn shop was full of grown-ups.

"Yeah, but Chance isn't doing too good either," Dex muttered, then shook his head and smiled determinedly at Vern. "I'm sorry—you caught us on sort of a shitty day. Come on back with me into the office. I'll get Reg—*Digger's* schedule, and we'll talk." He squeezed Kelsey's shoulder and stepped from behind the desk. "Sorry, Digger."

"I should have picked a name when I started," Digger said with a shrug. "I'm not that smart."

"Well, John was new too then," Dex said kindly. "We have more of our shit together now. C'mon back."

The back office was just as ordinary as the front office, except the back office had framed watercolors on the walls. There was one picture—a bunch of shirtless, built guys in jeans, standing in a courtyard, arms around each other's shoulders, smiling—that caught Vern's attention. Dex was one of the guys, and Kane stood right next to him, both of them looking carefree and not particularly posed. It was almost like someone said, "Hey, let's do this!" and it had turned into a publicity shot.

Maybe it had.

Digger was on the end of the line of guys, looking a little small in comparison. It wasn't that he wasn't ripped—and not obviously short. His body was tight and compact, every muscle group defined, but he was just not as tall or as bulky as the other guys in the shot, and Vern sort of liked him more for that. He was just… regular. Not a god. Just a guy.

So was Vern.

"That was a good day," Digger said from the little utilitarian desk in the corner of the room. "We were all there for head shots, and John wanted to get a candid. He's a good guy."

"Yeah, he is," Dex said, clicking at a laptop from a standing position. "And here he is!"

A slight thirtyish ginger-haired man walked into the office and smiled almost shyly. "You rang?"

"Yeah, John—look, I gotta go visit Tommy. I mean Tango. Fuck *me*. We're getting guys to spend time with him, if that's okay—"

"What about…." John looked at Vern and grimaced.

"Yeah, well, we can't do anything about him." Dex sighed. "Look— I'm printing out Digger's schedule—"

"Who in the fuck is Digger?" John asked blankly, and Vern got a good look at Digger grimacing. Dex threw John a meaningful look, and John clapped his hand over his face. "Sorry, Reg. Digger. Sorry, Digger."

Digger's smile held no rancor. "Sort of my fault," he said sunnily. "I should never have tried to change it."

"Anyway—I'm getting his schedule, and then I need you to talk to Vern here and maybe film his audition. Trust me, it'll be worth taking time out of your day."

Vern shifted uncomfortably and offered a game smile. "I'll do my best?"

John laughed and shook his hand just when Dex said, "And here we go, Digger."

The printer spat out a sheet of paper, and Dex grabbed a highlighter from a coffee cup on the corner of the desk and scanned through it quickly. "Here, here, here, here, here, and here. You're on a lot in the next two months—I hope that's okay."

"Girls?" Digger said, sounding delighted. "That's exciting. I didn't know if that was gonna last."

"Yeah, well, you can get it up around 'em. You're a natural."

Digger grinned with pride. "Oh, hey—Ethan in a couple weeks. That's great! Haven't shot with him in a while."

"You should give him a call—everyone likes a friend," Dex said, and the kindness in his voice told Vern this was something he'd reminded Digger of before.

"Awesome!" Digger sighed then, his shoulders drooping. "Okay—I guess that's all—"

"No, wait!" John frowned like he was thinking. "No, Digger, no. Actually, if you can wait out with Kelsey for a minute, let me talk to Vern here. If he's up for an audition, I may need a light man. I can pay you."

Digger brightened. "Very cool. Something to do today! I'm down!" He practically skipped out of the office, and Vern watched him go, utterly bemused.

"Digger," he said philosophically.

"Yeah." Dex shrugged gamely and stood up, offering John the desk chair. "I'm glad you came in, Vern. Talk to John here, and hopefully I'll see you around."

John accepted the offer and sank into the desk chair. "Thanks, Dex. Give Tommy my best."

He turned to Vern and smiled slightly. "So, now you've met Dex, and you've met Kelsey and—"

"And Kane and Digger," Vern supplied.

25

"Good!" John gave a fond glance out the window at Digger. "Digger's a good guy. Not bright—but a real good heart." John looked up at the group photo. "They're all good guys," he said with decision. "Or most of them." A brief scowl, and Vern wondered who up there John didn't like. "The thing is, we try to make this a good place to work." A blink and a sudden realization. "You, uh, *do* know what we do here, right?"

Well, if he'd had any doubts before he'd walked in, he sure didn't *now*. "Porn?"

John nodded. "We *just* added girls to the mix, so we're not sure how profitable it will be. Now, people think porn is easy and great—it's just fucking for the camera, right? Yay spiffy! Let's fuck! But there's more to it than that. You up for the spiel?"

Vern's turn to nod. "Hit me."

"Okay, first of all, you've got to get it up and keep it up, and you've got to do it while we've got a camera guy, a light guy, and someone to run the board. Sometimes we can do it with just one guy, but not if we want it to look great, and we want to make great porn. You've got to take care of your body—work out, keep clean, don't eat crap all the time—and you've got to have your mind in your work. We're selling fantasy, so if you can't fuck while you've got your body stretched one way and your dick in someone you met five minutes ago, you should probably rethink this, right?"

Oh. He hadn't thought of that. "I, uh—I'll be honest. I'm not sure. I think I could do it, but guys talk all the time. My, uh... you know. Little Vern—"

"Well, we hope he's not that little," John said matter-of-factly.

"Yeah—that guy. Anyway, he doesn't seem to actually give a shit who's doing what. If sex is on, he's on. So I think I could do this."

John bobbed his head, longish ginger hair flopping as he did so. Vern decided he liked John. He wasn't as warm as Dex, but he was... well, dreamy. Involved, but dreamy. Vern could handle that. John was the kid who had other things to do in school besides school.

"Okay—good," John was saying. "Now, we usually have a solo audition, followed by testing."

"Like, uh, a written exam?" Vern asked, confused, and John laughed like a little kid.

"HIV testing, you precious little pumpkin, you. The testing is a big deal. You're tested three days before, you're tested on set, you're tested three days after. You sign a contract that says no sex—alone or with a friend—three days before the shoot. Part of that is to make sure the tests are good. Part of that is to make sure you've got plenty to shoot, if you know what I mean. But in a month I want all my shoots filmed bareback, girls or boys, and we want to make sure everybody's safe."

Vern blinked and tried to tamp down on the roiling in his stomach. He'd never thought of testing when he was sucking Keith Gilmore's cock. It probably wouldn't matter. If he and Keith were only sucking each other, that was fine. But Keith didn't think of it as sex. What if he'd been "not" having not-sex with a thousand other guys?

"That's fair," he said.

John tapped his pen affirmatively. "A clean boy is a happy boy. Now, about girls or boys—I'm not going to ask who you like best. I'm not even going to ask about your history, but you can tell me if you feel like it. It makes good copy. I'm just going to put it out on the table that guys pay more and ask you if you're willing. And I'm not going to do it now. First let's see if you can get it up and make it work in front of me and Reg—goddammit, *Digger*—and then we'll go from there."

Vern swallowed. "Right now?" he asked, thinking *Wait, I'm going to go masturbate in front of strangers?*

John shot him a look as level as it was unwavering, and Vern realized this was where shit got real. "You can do it in a room or a courtyard. Is that going to be a problem?"

A vision flashed behind Vern's eyes of being naked in the sun, with his fist around his cock, as he showed this pragmatic dreamer and his sweet, more mortal buddy exactly what it was he could do.

He'd be the center of their attention. He'd be the star of the show.

Unsurprisingly, the vision made him hard.

"Outside would be fine," he said without blinking.

John grinned. "Solid."

IT TOOK John and Digger ten minutes to set up. Vern was half-hard before he was even in front of the camera. John talked to him at first, asked him if he'd ever done this before in front of strangers, asked him if it made him hot.

"Yeah." Vern half laughed. Getting his knob waxed by Keith Gilmore had apparently been training for this moment—who knew? Taking his shirt off was second nature. It's what country boys did in the sun, and he smiled up at the sky, eyes closed, as he sat on a chaise lounge and ran his fingers over his chest. He used to jerk off like he was going for a record in high school—he knew what he liked.

"Hard on the nipples," Digger murmured, and Vern nodded, keeping his eyes closed.

"Yup…," he hissed and pulled harder, arching his hips. Oh, this was nice. The courtyard was just big enough to catch a little breeze, and he was sitting under a tree—a little bit of shade but not enough to make him chilly. This was a good place, and he wondered how many other guys had jerked off here for the camera.

The thought brought his cock from half-hard to all the way hard, and he slid his hands under his waistband to make himself comfortable.

He heard Digger's caught breath, the unmistakable sound of anticipation as Digger held a light over a reflecting board aimed at him, and he slid his jeans right down to his ankles, and there he was, in full view of God and everyone.

He didn't care much about God, but boy, for a guy who thought he'd live and die in a forgotten corner of the mountains, it was a fuckin' *charge* to be there in front of everyone.

"Holy wow," Digger breathed, and John made a little grunt of affirmation.

"That's some piece of equipment you got there," John said appreciatively. "You know how to use that thing?"

Vern kept his eyes closed and grabbed himself at the base, squeezing hard and stroking up. And up. And up. "I'll take pointers," he purred. Both of them had worked here. Both of them. They'd been with guys. There was no shame here. He spread his legs and planted his feet so he could cup his balls.

"Fingers in your mouth," Digger said, suddenly sounding authoritative and in charge. "'Cause you know where you want 'em, right?"

Yeah. Oh yeah. Vern knew what he was saying. Keith wouldn't touch him here, but Vern knew that's where he wanted to be touched, and out here, in the open, being admired and spurred on?

He sucked on his fingers hard and kept right on stroking his cock.

Fat and long—he'd measured nearly ten inches when he was sixteen and did that sort of thing. But he knew it was big—Jessica seemed to like it. Keith thought it was worth blackmailing for. But here, under the sun and the observation, he could be proud of it. This thing felt *good*, and it was beautiful, and oh! Oh! It ached! It hurt so sweet, he'd squeeze it some more, and the whole rest of him wanted touch too.

He rolled to the side, and while his top hand kept stroking, playing with his bell, skating across the head in the precome that drooled from the top, his outside arm reached back until his spit-slickened fingers brushed up against his asscheeks, went searching for....

Ah! Just one brush, that's all it took, and he started to convulse. He rolled to his back again and shook, putting both hands on his cock and jerking hard... so hard... oh God....

"Ah!"

He let the word rip just as his come fountained up like a geyser, shooting over his head for a minute before splatting back down on his chest. And again. And again. A strip hit him across the face and another one across his chin. He couldn't seem to stop coming, and when he did, Digger was there, stroking his hair back from his face, grinning.

"Holy fuckin' wow," Digger said, awestruck. "That was real fucking impressive. Just think—I might get to ride that pony one day."

"That's not a pony," John said good-naturedly, putting the camera down. "That there's a stallion." He walked to Vern with a towel and a fluffy white bathrobe in his hand. "Here, kid. Get dressed. Digger'll show you where to wash up. I'm going to edit this. Then you and me, we'll talk business, deal?"

Vern nodded at him dazedly, reluctant to leave his sprawl under the sky.

Only Digger's hands—rough, short-fingered, nails clipped to the quick—stroking through his hair kept him rooted to the world at large.

Blinded by the Bright

WHEN REG had first come to work for Johnnies, John still had the auditions and filmed the porn in his house. Reg had sort of liked that. John kept a nice cozy little home; everything was in good repair. He'd felt safe there. He hadn't had sex with a guy before, but he'd done lots of girls, and he had no problem jerking off for the camera.

That first day—the day of the audition tape—John had asked him if he wanted a porn name.

"I didn't have a family pet," he said, because that was how the joke worked, right?

John stared at him, perplexed. "Reg, this isn't the joke thing. This is having a name to protect your identity."

"But, you know. I'm Reg, the famous porn star. Why wouldn't I want people to know?"

John had red hair and green eyes with blond lashes. When his eyes got really big, it looked like they were bugging out of his head.

"Reg, do you want people to know this about you without your permission? What about your parents—?"

"Mom split three years ago," Reg told him without self-pity. He'd been sixteen, after all, and his other sister, Queenie, had left the year before, with her twins and her new baby. Queenie had a boyfriend, and their mom just had to leave. "Just me and my sister."

A small furrow appeared between John's eyes. "How old is your sister?"

"She's older—she's thirty. But I take care of her." Reggie had frowned then, probably getting the same line between his eyes John had. "There were papers that showed up when I turned eighteen. They said I was in charge."

John's eyes got even bigger. And a little haunted. "You're in charge of your sister? Your thirty-year-old sister?"

Oh shit. Reg gnawed on the cuticle of his thumb. "There were papers," he said seriously. "She showed me how to sign them." He smiled conspiratorially. "Actually, I signed them as my mother when I was sixteen. But don't worry. We do okay." He grinned then so John couldn't see that they only did good when she took her meds. If Reg forgot—spent a night at a girlfriend's house or didn't show up for breakfast, maybe—she'd lie and say she took them. They weren't okay then. They got really bad sometimes. So he didn't do that much anymore.

"Where do you live?" John asked, looking at the address Reg had put on the application.

"There," Reg said. "You know, Carmichael. Mom left us the house. Some money. I just gotta save money for taxes, right? And I could sorta do that at McDonald's, but then, you know." He grinned. "I was surfing porn, and there was your ad. I mean, fucking on camera—way better than McD's, right?"

John shook his head, staring at the application and then staring at Reggie like he was trying to make a decision. Finally he took a deep breath.

"Reggie, do you have a driver's license?"

Reggie nodded. "Yeah."

"Are you registered to vote?"

He shrugged. "No. Do I have to be to work in porn?"

John looked surprised then, and he let out a puzzled little half laugh. "No. No, you don't. And I'm losing sight of my goal here. A name, Reg. Do you want a different name when you work here?"

Reg had grimaced and scratched the back of his head. He'd worn his hair long back then, in thick brown curls. "I'm not that bright, John. Seriously. If someone calls me by another name while I'm fucking, I'll lose my boner looking to see who they're talking to."

John's mouth opened and closed, then opened again.

Then closed. He mumbled something to himself that sounded a lot like "I don't know which one would be worse."

Reggie's eyes clouded. "I did okay, right?" He'd jerked off. His body was the smartest thing he had—responsive, decently endowed. John had said something about working out, because he wasn't very buff, and he figured if his job was fucking on camera, he could work out plenty. "I mean, I didn't suck at jerking off." He stood up and started to unbuckle his pants before shoving his hand down the front and working himself again. "I could do it again right now."

And John, who had just spent half an hour telling him he had a cock like a god, turned bright red and held his hands out in front of his face like he'd never seen a naked man before.

"No! No! Reg, time and place, okay? You're great at jerking off! You rock at it! If you can fuck in public, you've got the job—"

"I've got the job?" Reg was so excited he forgot to do up his fly. He pulled his hands out of his pants and waved them over his head, jumping up and down. "That's awesome! Woot! I'm a porn star!"

"A gay porn star," John said carefully. He'd said something about this before, but Reg hadn't really registered.

"Does this mean I have to have sex with men?"

John's left eye started to twitch. "Yes? We talked about this? It's, uh, a requirement, Reg."

Reg nodded, remembering this. "Okay. Yeah. You're right. I can do that." He gnawed his lip. "What if my boner melts?" And suddenly a little bit of his desperation seeped into his voice. "McDonald's sucks, John. They yell at you there. It's loud. People get mad. I had a lady yell at me because I got her drink wrong. She was awful—I had to shut the window. Why people gotta be like that?"

John shook his head, green eyes dazed. "I don't know. I have no idea. Don't worry, Reg—we'll take care of you. There's things you can do if the boner, uh, melts. As long as you want to work for me, I want you to work. I promise."

Oh, that was nice. Reg hadn't gotten a lot of that since his mom had taken off and he'd had to find jobs. Veronica had looked the jobs up on the computer—Reg wasn't good with them. He'd been taking workability classes in high school, not computer classes, and Veronica got awful when she was trying to teach him how to do things. He could surf the net, end of story. If he hadn't been watching porn on his own laptop, this opportunity would never have fallen into his lap. So having someone be nice about a job—that meant a lot to Reg. He didn't want to let John down.

"Okay, then," Reg said trusting this nice man with the camera. "If you can help me out, I'll do whatever you need me to." He nodded, remembering some of his nicer teachers. "I'm dependable. I'll do whatever you ask me to. I promise."

John closed his eyes and nodded back. "God, it's a good thing I'm already going to hell."

"You'll go to heaven," Reg said, because good guys did. His mom had taught him that much. "Just don't make me take another name."

John had heaved a sigh and conceded, and Reg thought everything was going to be fine.

Everything was rarely that easy.

The first time a guy went down on him, he froze.

His sister's words had rung in his ears—not from when she took her meds, but those other times, when she didn't take her pills and her blue eyes darted and she did the junkie tap on her computer desk. She shouted at the computer then, shrill words about fags doing each other and how her brother better not be a little faggot. Reg had been fine during the kissing and the touching part. The guy had laughed, and his body had been nice. Smooth tanned skin and muscles were fun to touch on a girl or a boy. Reg hadn't known.

But as soon as he was naked and the guy's mouth was on his cock, his boner just melted. John didn't have girls then—which might have helped. Instead Reg had stared at John helplessly, not wanting to voice that promise John had made, that he'd have a job no matter what.

John had called "cut," given Reg a robe, and taken him quietly into the bathroom and given him a little tablet he called Silver Sword. It worked fine—in fact, it had given him a boner he was practically feverish to get rid of. He'd managed to fuck the guy—long since retired and gone from Johnnies—until his eyes had rolled back in his head and he'd dry-come into the bed.

John had a long talk with Reg after that, about being kind and taking other people's cues. He said it was like working at McDonald's. People wouldn't yell at him, but he had to remember that he was touching other people's bodies, and he had to be respectful.

Reg had nodded and remembered as much as he could. But he hadn't taken an enhancement again. Seems he didn't really need it once he knew that being with a guy didn't mean he was a bad guy—just meant he could fuck guys, and that was okay.

Didn't mean he was gay. Didn't mean he wouldn't keep looking for a girlfriend. Just meant, well, his job was a little unusual. Given that he'd had to take a special class in school just to figure out how to fill out a job application and balance his bank account, Reg was sort of proud of that. He had a job skill, one not many people could claim.

Ten years later, he was still proud of it.

He'd caught on to the reason for the porn name, though.

Girls saw him on the website. He had no idea girls watched gay porn.

The first time a girl had seen him at the gym and called him Reg, he just thought he'd met her somewhere and forgot. Medium height, brown hair, muddy-colored eyes—she looked like a lot of other girls, and his memory, not always the best. She'd been aggressive at the gym, touching his biceps, his ass, and he'd thought, "Yes! A girlfriend!"

His last girl had left him when Veronica had gone off her meds. That was a whole other story.

He'd been excited—and willing. She'd gotten into his Camaro with him and started giving him head, right there in the gym parking lot. Her mouth on his cock was decent—he had to admit, he usually got the best head at work—but then she'd stopped and gazed at him dreamily.

"I bet this would be great if Tango were here," she said, licking her lips. "Could you call up Tango so we can have a threesome?"

Reg had gaped at her, for a moment trying to figure out if he'd met her with Tango, whose real name was Tommy, but he hadn't known that then.

And it hit him. "Uh, Tango and I only do that at work."

She pouted. "But… but you guys are *hot*. And you're friends! You were working out together!"

Well, that day they had been. "Yeah, but we're not boyfriends," he said. At that point, he'd been in the business long enough to not care if people thought he was gay. He hooked up with enough Johnnies guys off camera, just because a friend in need was a naked friend who gave good head.

"But you fuck," she said, getting upset. She sat up in the seat and pulled her jogging bra back over her boobs. He sighed. They were nice boobs—pert and bouncy with big raisin-colored areolas. He'd *really* liked it when she hit on him.

"Yeah," he said, trying to be kind like John had been to him. "We do. It's a job. I like him—he's a friend. Like… where do *you* work, Leona?"

"Leora," she snapped. "I'm a receptionist at a law firm."

Oh God. She was smart. Why had this smart woman seen his picture on the computer and thought he'd be smart like her? "Well, that's a real good job," he said sincerely. "And I bet there's guys there you like to talk to. You may even see them on weekends or go to the movies and shit. But you don't sleep with them—they're just guys from work, right?"

She nodded, the furrow in her brow reminding him of John's the last time Reg had gotten help with Veronica's papers.

"So, it's like that. Except when *I* go to work, I fuck guys. And we work out together and see movies and shit. But I don't fuck them unless I'm at work. 'Cause fucking guys is my job." He tried a smile then, because it was sort of funny, right? He wasn't quick—not like Dex or John or Tango or even Ethan, who was actually damned clever although he said he wasn't.

Leora didn't smile back. "So you're not gonna call Tango," she said, sounding bitchy.

"No," he told her. "Tango went home to paint his house. I told him I'd come help when we were done here."

"You'll paint the guy's house on the weekend but you won't wax his knob?" she asked, eyebrows doing that weird jumpy thing people's did when they were reasoning shit out.

"Tango tries to have boyfriends," Reg told her. "That would just make shit complicated." He didn't tell her that yeah, sometimes he hooked up with Johnnies guys because girls were thin on the ground. He just didn't feel like he owed her that much information.

She shook her head. "*You*," she said succinctly, "are a disappointment. Damn. Porn stars—not what you think." She grabbed her workout bag from the back of the car and went to get out.

Reg pulled his pants over his cock and said, "So, uh, will I see you around the gym?"

She shook her head. "Are you kidding? After this I'm doing the women's-only gym across the street. Jesus, what a letdown."

She slammed the door, and he adjusted himself before turning the key and making his way to Tango's. That day, as he and Dex and Kane were painting Tango's trim a really unusual shade of blue, he asked Dex, "Hey, is it too late to have a porn name?"

Dex had blond hair and blue eyes, so not like John at all—not even any freckles—but he still got some of the same looks on his face when Reg talked. Reg wondered if they were brothers.

"No," he said, drawing the word out like he was buying time. "Why would you want a porn name now, Reg?"

Reg shrugged. He didn't want to talk about the girl and the sort of weird and subtle way she'd hurt his feelings. "I dunno. Just, maybe want to be someone else for a little?"

He smiled gamely and pulled on his thinning brown hair. He tended to have it cut different once a month, because it wasn't thick and he liked to hide that, but it had grown out a little since his last do. "I could, you know, cut it. Dye it. It would be like a whole new me!"

Dex shrugged. "Yeah," he said. "Why not? You get your hair done, and we'll take some new pictures for the site when we're doing your next shoot. Replace the pictures, replace the name, keep the stats…." He wrinkled his nose. "Do you mind if we keep your backlist? I don't know if people will link the two, but you've made a *lot* of movies in the last nine years, Reg. You still make money off them. I'd hate for you to lose that."

Reg shrugged. "It's not like people can't figure it out," he said. "I just want to be able to say, 'No, you got me mixed up with that other guy' and mean it."

Dex let out a laugh. "So, what do you want your new name to be?"

"I'll have to think about that," he said, shoulders slumping.

"Should be Digger," Kane said, walking by and not even bothering to pretend he hadn't listened in. Reg liked Kane. He was simple.

"Why Digger?"

Kane grinned at him. "'Cause last time we fucked, it was like you were digging in my ass with a four-by-four. I couldn't walk for three days!"

General laughter then, and Reg laughed too.

"Digger," he said. "I like it."

Dex was staring at Kane with a sort of awe. "It's like genius," he said, shaking his head. "But… *not*."

"Totally genius," Reg said. "I mean, *total*. I'd totally give him a blowjob for that, but that guy's not ever hard up."

Dex grunted. "You shouldn't be either." He shivered then. "Hey, Tango—it's gonna rain here. Maybe finish the home improvement in the spring, you think?"

Well, early November got pretty cold in Sacramento, even on a nice sunny day like this one.

"Dammit! I was hoping to finish before I flew to Florida!" Tango was a good-looking guy—dark hair, snapping black eyes, pale skin—but he kind of snarled when he talked, and he moved so much it made Reg nervous. Reg liked him, but he tried not to be too stupid around Tango, just on general principle.

"You going to Florida?" Reg asked wistfully. John had offered to fly him out there to do location shoots, but Reg couldn't leave town that long.

"Yeah," Tango said, coming by and taking Reg's paintbrush and little paint can from him. "You got that pole real good, Reg. Sorry you can't come to Florida with us, though."

Dex grunted. "Yeah—I'd love to get you out of this city, just once, you know?"

"Well, I can go," Reg said. "Just on day trips. You know, so I can—"

"Take care of your sister." Dex shrugged and kept dabbing since Tommy hadn't taken *his* paint can. "Reg, I try not to say this too often, but is there any way you could get some help with her?"

Reg swallowed. "I don't want to talk about that," he said. Because Veronica had tricked him this last time, and he'd figured it out, but she wouldn't admit it. The pills made her sweet and all, but she could still be cunning when she wanted, and Reg wasn't smart enough to go up against cunning.

"Okay, buddy," Dex said kindly.

Reg had given thanks that day, because Dex reminded him that people at Johnnies were good to him. He could have been at McDonald's, and he wasn't sure they would have understood quite so good.

He wouldn't have had time to work out either, and his body had gotten *way* better since that first audition with John. He'd declined to wax his pubes, though, not after the first time made him cry. John had soothed him that day, giving him a painkiller and some ice cream—and some ice for his crotch—and they'd never made Reg wax again.

But all things considered, on that bright fall day nearly a year after painting Tango's house, when he sat for a minute stroking the new guy's hair while he recovered from what looked like one hell of a climax, he felt good about welcoming another Johnnies boy into the fold.

The place had treated him real good.

"You okay?" he asked after a few.

The new guy with the giant dick sat up a little and yawned. "Damn. I don't usually come that hard. Doing that in front of the camera was sort of a rush."

Reg grinned. "I'm sayin'. Wait 'til someone else is there—gets even better."

The kid frowned. "I think I can do it with girls," he said softly. "Guys—" He bit his lip, full and soft. Reg didn't usually think of guys as pretty. He thought of them as, well, *guys*—but this one…. His long jaw and soft brown-green eyes were sweet. He had freckles—not like John, but like he was a little kid not too long ago. "Is it weird with guys?"

Reg thought about it, because the kid seemed so vulnerable. "My first guy," he said, remembering the Silver Sword, "I sort of froze. But that was 'cause I had all this dumb shit in my head. You know—you're not supposed to do that 'cause it makes you a fag?"

The boy nodded, wiping his chest down with the towel. "Yeah?"

"Yeah. But a hand on your dick is a hand on your dick, right? And the guys are fun. They play. They kiss—and it's okay. It's like…." Suddenly Reg felt self-conscious. "You know. My hand in your hair. Nothing wrong with it. Just nice."

Kid nodded, and Reg stood up abruptly. *Was* nice—but men didn't dwell.

"C'mon. We got showers and shit—like a locker room in a gym, 'kay?"

Another nod. "I'm down for that. Thanks."

"So," Reg said, to break the sudden awkwardness as he led the way through the building. "What's your name gonna be?"

"You mean my porn name?" The kid—Vern?—pondered for a sec. "My last name's Roberts. I could be Robbie or Bobby."

"Bobby's good. I can remember Bobby if I'm screaming your name in bed."

Bobby let out a filthy laugh, and Reg—who didn't find humor sexy because he never got the joke—found himself getting hard.

"How do you know you'll be screaming my name?" Bobby asked.

Oh. Easy. "Anybody who's got that thing in their ass'll be screaming. Shave around it, it'll look bigger. Mine's only seven inches. You've got the Chrysler Building, and I've got…." He flailed. He'd heard of the Chrysler Building, but he'd never even seen it.

"Yeah, but at some point, a dick up your ass has gotta be like a city skyline, right?" Bobby said thoughtfully. "Yeah, sure, some are bigger'n others, but a fall onto any one of 'em is gonna kill you."

Reg thought about that literally. Thought about all the times he'd bottomed, both personally and professionally, thought about how it hadn't mattered—four, five, six, seven inches—there had always come a time when the size hadn't mattered. In the end it had come down to somebody inside him. A person willing to touch him in such a way that he got off.

"That was supposed to be funny," Bobby said behind him.

"Oh." Reg's face heated. "I'm not smart enough for jokes," he said honestly. "But I thought what you said was real bright. It's true. I mean, guys are gonna be grabbing at ya 'cause you're hung, but if that's the only reason they're grabbing at ya, any dick'll do. If you want a guy not on the set, you're gonna need to find one who wants something besides your Chrysler Building, you think?"

And now Bobby's silence stretched uncomfortably. Reg paused outside the locker rooms, looking for the sign they'd had up the week before, saying there were girls in there.

No sign, so Reg ducked his head in and glanced around. "Empty." He opened the door wider to let Bobby inside. "Can you find your way back to the office?"

Bobby nodded, smiling slightly. Yeah—probably only Reg who got lost that easy. "Sure."

"Then I'm gonna take my schedule and go work out. But it was real nice to meet ya, Bobby. You're fuckin' awesome on camera—you're gonna do great here."

He offered Bobby a hand to shake, and Bobby—after wiping his hand a couple of extra times on the towel—took it.

"Thanks for the advice," he said, thoughtful. "So, I'll see you around?"

Reg grinned. "We'll be bumping into each other's uglies eventually. I mean, I do everybody, right?"

Bobby laughed. "Yeah. I was just gonna start with girls, but—"

Reg shrugged. "Most guys say that. Don't know why. I'll be seeing you around."

He left Bobby in the locker room and trotted up to the front desk. He stuck his head into Dex's office to make sure Dex didn't need anything else.

John was sitting in Dex's chair, head tilted back, utter exhaustion on his face.

"Uh, John?"

He startled, like he'd almost fallen asleep. "Yeah, what? What is it? What do we need?"

"Nothin'—just making sure you don't need me for nothin'."

Even John's tired smile was impish and a little crazy. "Dex gave you the schedule with all the shoots on it, right?" he asked, making sure.

"Yeah—that's looking good. You need a light guy or anything?"

39

John thought about it for a minute before printing out another schedule. "Yeah. Sure. Here—all your shoots are Tuesdays, but Thursdays are usually pretty busy. I'm going to say come in every Thursday and I'll put you to work. How's that?"

Oh, awesome. An excuse not to go home. Reg loved this guy, he really did. "That's great. Happy to do it. Thanks, John!"

"Thanks for asking. It was nice of you, Reg."

Reg's heart always warmed to praise—both John and Dex were real good at making him feel not stupid.

"I think the kid's gonna be good, you think?" he said so John didn't have to go back to feeling tired.

"Yeah," John said, waking up enough to be enthusiastic—and less careworn.

"He picked out a porn name," Reg went on. "He decided on Bobby. Which, like, couldn't fit him any better, right?"

John laughed. "Vern Roberts, Bobby Green—he's pretty quick."

Reg couldn't manage the bolt of sadness that passed through him then, so he put it in the dark place in his head where all his secrets went. "Too quick for me," he said, meaning it and grieving it and forgetting it, all in one sentence. "But I can't wait to see him on camera. Gonna be great!"

He left on that line, because he had to go home and put his schedule in his phone and then stick it on the refrigerator or Veronica would get jumpy. It was time to take her to the doctor's soon—he knew it—because she was getting twitchy way more than she had six months earlier. But he couldn't get her to tell him when exactly it was on the schedule, which meant he needed to sit down that night and call people.

With a sigh, he made a notation in his phone, because Dex had taught him that, and it had really helped. Small steps. He took small steps every day to try to be as grown-up as the guys he worked with.

Mostly, it worked.

"VERONICA! I'M home!" He always called out before he opened the door. Bad things could happen if he didn't.

She didn't answer, so he paused for a second and looked with despairing eyes at his rotting porch. He should ask Dex or John how to fix it—he'd have to replace boards and stain the new wood, he was sure, but he didn't have so much as a hammer in the garage.

"Veronica?"

"Come in!"

He pushed the door open and peered about. The dishes had been done and still sat in the rack, and the table was clean as he'd left it. The floor—cracked and peeling linoleum and all—remained swept.

On the one hand, it was good because everything was peaceful. On the other....

"V, you need to eat."

"There's nothing in the fridge."

"There's spaghetti. And I fried up a big batch of bacon for you yesterday. And hot dogs. And carrots." He'd made a list of things she would eat, so when he reminded her, she could come down and have meals. He couldn't always be there for them—he had work, and working out, and Jesus God getting the fuck out of the house and hanging with his friends—but she always had food.

"You made the bacon wrong. It's poisoned."

Reg took a deep breath, reached into the fridge, and pulled out the Rubbermaid container. "See? Not poisoned." He ate the whole piece and reached in for another, but she snatched the container out of his hands.

"I'll have carrots and potatoes too," she snapped, and he pulled out a bag of carrots and walked to the sink to make her some potatoes. Her eating extra carbs was a worrying thing—the balance of meds she had right now usually limited her appetite. If she was skipping them, she might want extra potatoes.

"So," he said casually, scrubbing potatoes the way she'd taught him to when they'd been kids, "you take your meds today?"

She crossed her arms and glared at him, her ratty pink cardigan falling loosely around her shoulders and sloppily down over her faded teddy bear pajama pants. She was wearing one of his high school gym shirts under the cardigan, and it screamed a garish green and black under the faded pink. She hadn't brushed her hair in a few days, and the brown mess draggled down from a clip at her crown, a few of the strands a bright, corkscrewed gray.

"Yes," she said quickly. Too quickly. "All of them. You want to count?"

41

He looked at her sideways, wondering how big a thing it would be if he counted them. He kept track in his phone after every count, and the date. He knew how many of each pill she should have, but letting her know he didn't trust her could make things difficult.

"No," he said. "But bring them out so I can see if we need a refill."

"I can tell you," she said, arms crossed defensively.

"I need to see," he said, keeping his eyes open wide. "You know I can't remember good if I hear. But if I see, I'll figure it out and remember." He was not, in fact, that bad—he'd know if she told him she only had five of the one and ten of the other. But she was trying to hide from him, and she knew how expensive the pills were, so she wouldn't flush them down the toilet.

If she was going to be cunning, he could pretend to be stupid. It was a terrible game but one he'd been playing for eleven years, and the price he'd pay for losing would be dire.

"Fine. I'll bring them down." She glared at him, blue eyes that could be wide and ingenuous or narrow and plotting—it all depended on what the chemicals were doing in her brain. "But it's not right. You're just taking money from the doctors. Everything I've done for you, and you're getting money from the doctors to give me pills. You know the doctors. They don't like how smart I am. You're taking their money to keep me in a fog. I hate the fog."

"I'm not," he said, more afraid of her paranoia than of the argument. "See? I put my schedule on the fridge. I'm working extra, so you'll know when I'll be gone. My friends are doing things—I'll tell you then."

"You bringing any home?" she asked suspiciously, and he thought *Well, not* now! When the medication was working and V was all copacetic, she'd stay in her upstairs bedroom and bathroom, and he'd use the one downstairs. He'd had girls over and boys too—just told them to stay out of the upstairs. It worked better if his girlfriend or hookup had a place of their own, but he could make it work with V most days.

Unless she was like this.

"Not right now," he said easily. "You know I don't like to upset you."

"I'm not a fuckin' baby!" She screamed it, spittle coming out of her mouth and everything, and his stomach dropped and twisted at the same time.

"V, go get your medication, okay? I'm going to call your doc and make sure you got the same stuff."

"I don't need that goddamned poison," she snarled, and he took a deep breath against tears. Oh Jesus, this was worse than he thought.

"V, honey, just do it for me, okay? I haven't signed the papers in a while. I might not be able to sign them next time they show up, not if you're like this."

"You fucking asshole! You'd send me to one of those places? The places that stink of pee and have rapists in every corner? You're my fuckin' brother! I took care of you!"

"Honey, I don't want to. We just need to make sure you're taking your pills, okay?"

"I hate my pills, you fucking moron. Why would I take them to make you happy? Can't you just make sure I have food in the house, or are you too fucking stupid to even do that?"

Reg swallowed against his temper and put the potatoes in the microwave—four of them, because he liked potatoes too, and, well, he had bacon. "V, please—don't make me go get them myself. We agreed I'd respect your stuff, your space, okay? But if you don't go get them yourself, I need to—"

"Fine!" On that word, she whirled out of the kitchen and stomped up the stairs. He listened carefully for sounds of the toilet flushing or water being run, but he didn't hear them. Before he could get suspicious himself and investigate, she came stomping down, four bottles in her hands. She threw them at him, literally pitched them at him from across the room, and the lids burst open and the pills scattered across the floor at his feet.

"Oh fuck." She was on social security, and that paid for her medicines, but what was left for Reg to pay was still a big chunk of his paycheck. He kept telling himself he'd check those papers he signed every year to see if maybe he'd pay less if he turned her over to the state, but he couldn't bear the thought of sending her to one of those places.

He'd never been to one himself, but her sheer terror of a state-run health facility made his own hands sweat with fear like he'd caught the disease of it.

"V," he muttered, sinking to his knees and sorting the pills. "V, just calm down. Let me pick these up, you can take the pink one, and then we'll talk about the rest." The pink one was a sedative—very mild—and it was the one pill she usually had no objection to. Once she had the pink one, he could reason with her, remind her of what would happen if she went off the rails, remind her of her fear of institutions and of ending up somewhere unfamiliar. He made sure all the pink pills were rounded up first and was going after the capsules with the red ends that she hated the most when, out of nowhere, her foot swung up and into his jaw.

He wasn't a little guy, but his sister was solid, and she was fueled by anger and buckets full of crazy. He went toppling backward into the detritus of pill dust, then scrabbled to his hands and knees so he could get her in a three-point restraint.

The ripping pain across his shoulder blade was a surprise.

"Holy Jesus, V!" he shouted, rolling sideways to keep his face and neck protected. "Where'd you find the fuckin' knife!"

"You think I don't know where you hide them?" she taunted as he came up dodging backward. Oh God, she'd found the stash. One goddamned cooking knife—one—in the whole house, and he kept it in a shoebox in the top of his closet. Other boys might keep their spank material there, but not Reg. He'd learned how to use his phone, and he hid the kitchen implements in the dark.

"Well, I didn't until *now*!" he yelped. She didn't know how to hold a knife, he thought dimly. He'd seen enough action-adventure movies, where the heroes were jacked and the villains were stupid. She was shorter than he was and stabbing downward, and he just had to wait until the blade was pointed toward her and—

He grabbed her wrist *hard* and squeezed until the knife clattered onto the ground with all the pill dust. While she was still keening, he pulled her hand around to the small of her back, reached around her shoulder, and pulled her other wrist back too. She thrashed, but he used the pain of the wrenched shoulders to wrestle her to the ground into a three-point restraint, thanking God for the self-defense class Dex had made him take a few years back, when incidents like this were a regular occurrence.

"Let me up!" she sobbed, and he kept one hand locked around her thin wrists and used the other to scrabble on the floor. Pink pill, pink pill, pink pill....

He found one and shoved it in her mouth dry. He kept his finger in the back of her mouth, scrubbing the pill on the sides of her molars until it disintegrated. In one smooth motion, he pulled his finger out of her mouth and used the heel of his hand to clamp her jaw shut, holding her still until he felt her swallow.

Then—because she could take two, the doctor had said that—he grabbed another one while she sobbed and swore at him, and repeated the operation. She was down to sobs, her thrashing mostly for form, as he grabbed the red-tipped capsule he knew was the strongest antipsychotic and shoved it into the back of her mouth.

"No," she wailed. "No, no, no, no, no…." She said something else—the taste, probably—but his shoulder ached like fire, and he had blood running down the back of his arm and off his elbow. He needed to find someone to stitch that up, and he couldn't afford to fuck around. He shoved at the pill until it exploded in her mouth and then held her chin again, trying not to let the sound of her whimpering move him inside.

Of course it moved him inside.

"Sh," he whispered, remembering all the times she'd comforted him in the night. Mom would come home, drunk or high, with a guy or three, and V would hide him in the closet, holding him close, singing softly in his ear. "Take me on," he hummed. "Take on me…." He didn't know any other words than that, but the sound of it was bouncy and happy and something she'd heard on the radio when they were kids. Her whimpers faded to hiccups, and he found the other two pills on the ground before standing up and assisting her.

Her eyes had gone to half-mast—the second sedative had been a little heavy-handed—and he helped her into the nearest kitchen chair before turning to pick up the knife. He put it on the highest shelf—the one she couldn't get to without a chair—and reminded himself harshly to remember it later. He figured it would depend on how many stitches he needed if that worked or not.

He washed the pill residue off his hands—because the doctor had warned about that—poured her some water, and turned around with the cup and the pills, his heart twisting at her crumpling face, the tears just running down, sputtering into space with her little caught breaths.

"Here," he said gently. "Here, V. Let's take them right now. I don't know how many you missed, but I'm going to have to check them morning, noon, and night for a while, okay?"

She nodded numbly. "Sorry, Reggie."

He pressed the heels of his hands against his stinging eyes and pretended the wetness was from washing up. "I know, V." She was always sorry—and he always believed her. The doctor told him about chemicals in her brain and how they whispered things to her. Whispering chemicals seemed like a fairy tale, but he'd heard her talking to people who weren't there, and when they started telling her the pills were poison and Reg was bad, that was usually a sign things were about to go cattywampus.

"The pills are poison. You know they're poison."

"No they're not, sweetheart." Morning, noon, and night. He was going to have to lock the pills up again and administer them like they were food in a zombie apocalypse. No girls, no Johnnies hookups unless he brought them here.

He looked around the house, depressed. Most of the guys didn't seem to judge, but the girls did. He'd put up with the judginess, though, if only he could be not alone here, in this rotting house, wondering when his sister was going to kick him in the balls.

"Poison," she mumbled, still crying. "Reggie, why you gotta feed me poison?"

"So you don't try to kill me in my sleep, V." He'd been one choked snore away from being a nighttime television story before he'd hidden the knives. Time to buy a gun safe so he could eat steak again sometime in the future. With a sigh, he grabbed two plastic bags from the cupboard and bent down again to try to salvage pills. He was good about only saving the unbroken ones—and very aware that he shouldn't let any of the medication get on his skin. The doctor had warned about that, and he'd listened with big eyes.

Something that could seep through his skin scared him to death.

"I wouldn't hurt you, little brother." She gazed up at him then, and through the hair and the wrinkles time had wrought, he could see V—Veronica—with round cheeks and warm blue eyes, the same almond shape as his. She'd been beautiful in her twenties, but the last ten years—illness, anger, even the medications she took—all had exacted a price.

"Not on purpose, V." He squatted in front of her, pulling one of the plastic bags off his hand so he could cup her cheek. "In your heart you're still my V," he said softly. "We still sing together, right?"

She nodded and offered a watery, dim smile. What time was it? He looked around the kitchen and realized it was still only about three o'clock in the afternoon. But she was nodding off—probably because of the two sedatives—and it was just time for her to sleep.

"Come on, V," he said, standing up and offering his arms. She was so small compared to him—and he wasn't big next to the guys at Johnnies. But he worked out all the time, and swinging her into his arms like a child was a lot easier than putting her into a three-point restraint when she was fighting him. He carried her up the stairs, careful not to bang her head, and took her into her room. When he got there, he looked around and groaned.

It was a filthy disaster. He should have known—plates had been disappearing left and right, and she'd been losing weight. All the food was up here, in her room, and oh God, she'd been drawing on the walls again.

He didn't know how to edit what she saw on the internet.

The worst—the very worst—propaganda against minorities, LGBTQ people, God, even against the mentally ill—all of it was filtered through her imperfect mind and found its way onto the walls in Sharpie.

He didn't even know where she got the Sharpie and had a sudden thought to her amazon.com account. He usually gave her money for books—apparently she'd been buying Sharpies too.

In the pile of dirty dishes and fetid clothes, though, her bed stood pristine. He wasn't sure how clean her sheets were, but she made it, every goddamned morning.

He had no idea why.

With a heave he pulled back the covers, settled her between the sheets before tucking them up to her chin.

"Sing me a song, little brother," she commanded.

He looked around the bedroom and thought about all the work ahead, and his shoulder ached—and still bled. But she looked dazed and lost after her outburst, and *Oh, V—I owe you so damned much.*

His mouth twisted, and he began to sing "Puff, the Magic Dragon," which was pretty, and he knew all the words to it. He'd heard from kids at school that it was about smoking pot, but that couldn't take away the purity of the little boy and the imaginary friend Reg had first thought of when his mother sang it to the two of them, or when V had sung it to him.

When he was done, her eyes were closed and she was snoring softly. He stood up and started collecting dishes, thinking he had to have her room and the kitchen clean before he called Dex and asked if he knew anyone who could stitch him up.

IN FACT, Dex knew one of the guys was fucking to get through med school, and within an hour Lance was at Reggie's house, a tall guy with a square, chiseled jaw, blue eyes, an eight-inch cock, and a little first aid kit of purloined supplies under his arm.

"You're not going to get into trouble?" Reg asked after Lance had—blissfully—injected the area with some lidocaine and begun irrigating it. "I don't want you to get into trouble for stealing drugs or anything."

"No," Lance said absently, and Reg felt some pressure against his flesh, which told him Lance was doing things that would ordinarily hurt. "I won't get in trouble because I have a kit for emergencies, and I'm not giving you anything that's regulated. But *you* are going to be in a world of hurt here if you don't go to a real doctor and get yourself some antibiotics. What happened, and why won't you tell me?"

"You know what happened," Reg said, too weary to play with words or do anything fancy. Lance had been here before to hook up. Had met V.

"She went off her meds again," Lance muttered, sounding mad.

"It happens sometimes, but she got really tricky about it. I'm gonna have to watch her close for a couple of weeks. It's okay if I'm gone for short bits—to the gym, to film a scene. As long as I can come home for lunch, I can hold the lights for Dex. But until she gets back online—"

"I get it," Lance grunted, tugging on Reg's back some more. "Can I just say, you would have made my job a hell of a lot easier if you'd called me about two hours earlier? Why didn't you do that?"

Reg thought about all the blood he'd had to mop up from the floor when he'd finished recovering the pills. "I had to clean up first," he said, embarrassed. "I needed to see how many of her pills I could save, and her room was attracting rats." He glanced around again. The paint was peeling off the doorframes, the walls hadn't been washed in forever, and the furniture had been tatty ten years ago. "I mean, it's not pretty now."

Behind him, Lance sighed, and Reg remembered their one scene together. Reg had made him laugh and feel comfortable. It had been Lance's first bottom scene, and Reg had taken charge and done the thing. When they were done, they'd gone out to Hometown Buffet to eat, because they'd both starved themselves for the scene. Lance had cracked jokes like a twelve-year-old, and Reg had gazed into his blue eyes and thought *I kissed that. I hit* that*! How lucky am I?*

It hurt for him to see Reg like this.

But Lance dropped a kiss on the top of Reg's head. "I just want you to be okay, Reggie."

"Digger," he said automatically.

"Sure. This is a long cut—I'm talking fifteen stitches long. I don't care what the house looks like—what are you doing to care for yourself?"

Reg leaned to the side a little, looked up at Lance, and grinned. "I'm having a friend stitch up my owie."

An odd look of pain crossed Lance's handsome features. "Yeah. Okay. There's that. Look, I'm going to call a colleague and see if I can't get some antibiotics for you to take, and then I'm going to stay here and study tonight so you can get some sleep. Is that okay?"

Reg blinked at him, his eyes stinging again. "Would you?" he begged, feeling pathetic and naked. "I'm never sure the meds are taking—not the first night after an episode, anyway."

Lance nodded. "Reg—"

"Digger."

"Digger—I hate to ask, but, are you *sure* you don't want to see about a state care facility?"

Reg shook his head. "She hates them," he said softly, remembering her violence. "Our mom put her in one when I was a kid, and then they let her out and… and she was different."

"Where's your mom now?" Lance asked.

"Who knows," Reg said, staring glumly at the linoleum. She'd taken off a short time after Queenie. "I think she was just as lost as I am."

Lance kissed his temple then, not like a fuck buddy, but like a brother. Reg closed his eyes and realized he didn't know if Lance hooked up with a lot of guys when he wasn't at work, and then realized he didn't care. Lance was a friend right now, and Reg needed one of those so damned bad he couldn't breathe.

LANCE STAYED the night, as promised.

Veronica woke up at around six in the evening. Reg—shoulder comfortably numb, as long as he went shirtless with just the bandage on it—made her dinner, and they sat in front of the television for a while. Then he made her take her medication—all of it—and took her up to her bed and her newly cleaned room.

"I like your friend," she said sleepily. "He's not a fag, is he?"

Oh God. "V, that's a mean word. Most of the words on your walls are mean. I think we need to paint your walls and stop learning mean words on the internet."

"But they're all out to get us, Reggie," she said, eyes suddenly open wide and limpid. "You know that—the fags and the spics and the ni—"

He put his hand over her mouth. "V, that's bullshit, okay? You're looking that shit up, and idiots are spouting bullshit, and you're soaking it up like a sponge. If you don't start looking up nice shit, I'm going to take away your computer, okay?"

"You can't!" she gasped, sitting up in bed. He'd changed her sheets while she sat downstairs, and he felt mildly better about the whole entire world now that he knew she was no longer sleeping on those sheets. "Those people on the computer—they understand me!"

"And some of them are okay," Reg said, remembering the talks John and Dex had given him about reading his fan mail. He'd wanted to respond and get to know people and maybe hook up—and then he'd seen the bad reviews and his feelings had been so hurt! But they'd explained to him about trolls and how some people just frothed in their own jizz (John's words), and maybe it was just best to let computer people stay on their side of the computer. "But a lot of them just…." He couldn't say "froth in their own jizz" to his mentally ill sister. "A lot of them just roll around in their own crap and then try to smear it on anyone who will listen. This shit on your walls, that's someone else's ji—uh, crap. And you wrote it all over your walls and made it your own."

"You're just mad 'cause I called you a fag," she lashed out, but hey— Reg fucked guys for money, had for a long time. He'd been called worse, and he knew that now.

"I wish you wouldn't, but that's not it." He took a deep breath and let his eyes wander around the room. "V, meanness just… breeds meanness." He managed a smile for the girl who used to make him peanut butter and banana sandwiches when there wasn't anything else to eat in the house. "You're my sweet big sister. Sometimes, even if they're out to get you, you gotta forgive them and find another way to be."

"They put the bugs on my arms," she said disconsolately, but he was used to her saying things like that.

"No, they didn't," he told her gently. "Your brain put the bugs on your arms. I wish I could make it stop."

She nodded, her mouth crumpling. "Me too. I'm sorry, Reg. For saying mean things. I shouldn't say them to you. I'm so sorry." Tired tears seeped from the corners of her eyes, and Reg breathed and nodded and waited for her to fall asleep.

He made it downstairs, his shoulder aching fiercely—in fact, his entire body hurting in ways he couldn't even define. He always felt like this after one of V's meltdowns. It was like the fear and the anger and the frustration—and the love—backed up inside his joints and just hurt.

Lance sat at his beat-up kitchen table, textbooks open. He glanced up as Reg stepped into the kitchen, smiling grimly.

"You look like shit, Re—I mean, Digger. This happen a lot?"

"Once a year or so. Sometimes every six months." He shrugged and then called himself retarded because he'd hurt his own goddamned shoulder. "It is what it is." He put his hand out to the doorframe, suddenly exhausted. "It won't bother your schoolwork none if I watch TV, will it?"

Lance glanced up from his books. "TV won't help you sleep," he said. "Wanna fool around?"

Reg grinned suddenly, because he spoke this language. "You got no idea. I helped Dex film this kid this morning—had a ten-incher, if you can believe that."

Lance widened his eyes comically and stood up, sauntering over to Reg with familiarity if not with passion. "Ten inches like a pencil?" he asked.

"Ten inches like a *water bottle*," Reg corrected earnestly, comforted by his friend's smile and the way he was laughing.

"That's fuckin' *amazing*. Think I can get on the schedule with him?"

"You'll have to talk to Dex," he murmured. Lance liked to kiss— he remembered that—and kisses were warm and animal, and even if Reg wasn't gay, he liked them.

"Sure," Lance said, putting his big hands on Reg's hips. "I'll talk to Dex in the morning." He lowered his head and took Reg's mouth, and Reg sighed into his bigger body.

This. This he knew. Could be the only thing he was good at. And even if Lance moved on to practice medicine and marry a tiny blonde wife, right now it was the only cure he had.

Afterward, as he lay groggy with encroaching sleep, Lance stood up to dress, and he found himself thinking about it—about the moment when this smart, nice, pretty doctor boy would move on and leave Reg behind.

"Lance?" he mumbled.

"Yeah?"

"You think you'll remember me when you're off doctoring and being famous, and I'm still here?"

Lance's hand in his hair was gentle, and in spite of what they'd just done in bed, brotherly. "I don't think I'll be able to forget you," he said, his voice raspy and sad.

Reg was going to tell him not to be sad—Lance was going to go off and doctor and that would be awesome—but Reg'd had a hell of a day, and Lance had reamed all his worries away.

He fell asleep instead.

Lance woke him up at four in the morning. Apparently Chance, whose real name was Chase, had tried to kill himself the night before, and all the guys who knew him were at the hospital, trying to see if he'd be okay.

Reg shot up in bed, winced, and fell back down. He remembered Veronica, asleep, but who would be awake shortly and need her meds if he didn't want her to kill him the next time he slept, and how she was going to need him three times a day for the next couple of weeks.

"I can't go," he said disconsolately. These guys were his friends—his brothers, like Lance—and he wanted to be there for them.

"Dex'll understand," Lance said, patting his calf. "Here—go back to sleep. I'll set your phone and lock your door, okay?"

Reg nodded, remembering that Lance had been up all night. "Get some sleep," he said. "Just… you know. Take care."

Lance nodded soberly. "You take care too, Reg. And if you ever want someone to help get her settled someplace else, I can do that."

But Reg couldn't think about that. He could, however, get a few more hours of sleep. He'd take what he could get.

New and Normal

BOBBY'S FIRST shoot was a girl named Trisha, who had dyed black hair and a lot of tattoos along her belly-dancing-skirt line. She was likable enough, but after getting used to posing one way to show off his pecs, and another way to show off his cock, and then a third way so everybody could see his hands on her less-than-ample boobs, the thrill was gone.

He got it up—he always did—and he did the thing.

Dex gave clear directions, made him feel comfortable, and by the time pleasure actually took over and he couldn't stop himself from thrusting his hips into Trisha's willing body, the name "Bobby" fit him like it was the name he should have been born with.

When it was over, Trisha took a deep breath, grabbed some offered tissues to wipe off, and rolled off the bed.

"Damn," she said admiringly. "That thing's huge. I'll shoot a scene with *that* anytime."

"Uh, thank you?"

She laughed self-consciously, pulling on a robe she'd left offscreen. Some of the "fuck-me-baby" armor that had carried her through the scene fell away. "Sorry—that was rude. *You* were nice to work with. If you stay in het, I'd love to work with you again."

He nodded, feeling more human himself. "Thank you—it was a pleasure working with you too."

She dimpled charmingly, like a pretty girl at a dance, swung her sweaty hair behind her, and turned toward the door. "I hope it's okay if I get the shower first?"

"It should be all clear," Dex said, putting away his precious equipment. "Thanks, Trisha. He'll give you about twenty minutes before coming in."

"Thanks, Dex." She gave a little wave and sauntered off, yawning behind her hand. Well, they'd been working that scene for about four hours. Bobby could use a shower and a snack and a nap himself—but not necessarily in that order.

Dex nodded absently and locked up his case. "See you in a few weeks, hon. Study hard." He then gave a tired smile to Bobby. "How you doing?" he asked. "All good?"

Bobby thought about it, but the thinking was easier with the check from his solo burning a hole in the jeans he'd worn that day. He'd managed to find a cheap hotel for the last two nights so he'd be rested and clean, because when Dex had offered him sort of an "emergency shift," as it were, he jumped right on it.

But how did he feel after shooting sex for money—*not* solo?

Soiled? Immoral? Self-loathing?

"I'm *hungry*," he said with passion. "God—I haven't eaten in two days!"

Dex's laughter sounded sincere but subdued. Bobby had gotten that vibe all day, pretty much from everybody. He'd heard "How's he doing?" asked a lot of times, and he figured somebody had been hurt in a car accident or something, but he didn't want to ask.

"Well, good. There's a couple of all-you-can-eat places nearby. Ask Kelsey—she's got a map—and a few gyms nearby, if you miss your workout."

Bobby didn't want to look at his body—he was pretty skinny from the last two months. He figured his cock might have gotten him in the door, but he'd been looking at the other guys walking in. He'd have to step up his game.

"That's awesome," he said, because it was a nice thing to do. "Thank you."

Dex nodded and bit his lip. "Look—think you can shoot again in a week? I know it's short notice, but we're sort of two men down. *I* might end up shooting with you, if that's okay." He paused. "*Goddammit.* We didn't even *ask*—are you up for guys? I could have another girl in here—I mean, I swore I was out of the game, you know?"

Bobby stared at him blankly. A guy. *Dex*, who was sort of giving Bobby the warm fuzzies in his chest already. Could Bobby… do *the thing* with Dex?

In spite of the activity of the last four hours, his cock stirred.

Apparently so.

Trying to salvage some dignity, Bobby found a towel and wrapped it around his waist. When he was staring into space, he wasn't seeing dollar signs—not even though he could make enough to send his mom some while getting an apartment of his own eventually.

Oh—crap. Speaking of....

"I'd love to, but I was going to go visit my mom for a week, and this means I can't."

Dex's eyebrows went up when Bobby could have sworn he was too tired for surprise.

Hell. "I've got a girlfriend, and she doesn't know—and I don't want to tell her right now—not until, you know, I'm settled. But in the meantime, I'm going to burn through all my money on hotels."

"D'oh!" Dex grimaced and smacked his forehead with his palm. "Okay, yeah, I hear you. Where were you staying when you were working at the juice place?"

Jesus, this was embarrassing. "My truck."

Dex closed his eyes and wiped them with his palms. "You guys... this fucking job... eighteen is grown-up. That's the fucking law. Who said? That's what I want to know. Who said eighteen was fucking grown. This whole fucking business needs a goddamned mommy!"

"I got a mom," Bobby said, confused and a little frightened. There was a lot of emotion here that he didn't know how to deal with. "My dad's AWOL, but he was a fuckin' asshole, so no worries."

Dex shook his head and took a deep breath, like he was getting it together. "There's a flophouse—everybody pays into the kitty for rent and takes the first available spot. I'm pretty sure there's only five guys there right now. They've got four beds and a couch—loser gets the floor. But it's better than your truck and not as expensive as a by-the-day hotel, no matter how crappy."

"I usually visit my mom on the weekends," Bobby said, feeling some optimism. "I'd be the perfect roommate."

Dex half laughed, but his voice still sounded thick, like this hurt went way too deep for a little humor. "Then I'll get you that number. Trisha should be done in about five minutes. Come see me when you're done with the shower."

Thank God for Dex. "Dude, I can't even—thank you—"

Dex shrugged and took another deep breath. "Your problem's easy," he said, sounding bitter. "Your problem I can fix. I gotta go. For all I know, Kelsey just put another client on terminal hold. See you up front."

Bobby shoved the clothes he'd worn into his little duffel bag and shouldered it. Then he wandered through the halls in a towel until he found the showers. Trisha was just getting out, thank God, because he wanted to shower alone.

DEX'S LEAD with the flophouse panned out—an apartment in a big complex, but one that had a pool and a weight room and a coin-op laundry. Parking was a nightmare. He usually had to park a couple of blocks away in front of a strip mall or somebody's house, and he slept in fear that his truck would be broken into or vandalized.

But so far so good—his truck was intact, his mom and Jessica understood about the "overtime" he said he had to work, and the guys?

Were a lot of fun, actually. Dex had been right—first come, first serve for the couch, but the guy who didn't get the couch got offered lots of pillows and blankets, and if Bobby slept on the floor by the coffee table, he had his sleeping bag as a sort of mattress. He took some of his first money and bought an actual inflatable air mattress, and offered it to whoever got in last if he got the couch, and was quickly the favorite roommate *ever*.

Someone had a coffee maker, so everybody bought coffee when they were out. Someone had a juicer, so everybody bought veggies and fruit. They kept stuff roughly on spots on the shelf, but if you left a Post-it IOU, people usually forgave pretty quick.

Bobby was so damned grateful to not have to eat out—or sleep in the back of his truck—and to eventually get the shower, that he fell into the crowd pretty easily. The day after he arrived, he signed up for the gym Dex had recommended and was given a Johnnies employee discount, of all things. That was okay. They set him up with a personal trainer, and he spent the next five days getting used to a workout regimen that was, as the trainer told him, almost purely cosmetic. "You've got plenty of actual muscles from whatever work you've been doing. What we're going to start is exercises that will make your muscles pop. Some changes to your diet and you'll be as ripped as the other guys at your work, trust me."

The trainer was a tiny, fit woman in her fifties, with dyed red-gold hair and a sort of pixieish sense of humor Bobby really appreciated. She reminded him of his mom on the days his mom hadn't felt beat down by life, and Bobby drank in Trina's words like they were gold.

The workouts served to tire him out—as did the waiting tables, because he wasn't giving that job up since he didn't have to—but he sure did rest better with an apartment to sleep in. Of course, he hadn't counted on the guys hooking up in the beds, regardless of the full house, but boys or girls, that's what they did. At first he thought it would make him horny—and embarrass him—but one night he was trying to fall asleep on his mattress and saw Billy on the couch wrestling his hard-on, and he fell asleep chuckling.

They were all human animals here. He was just lucky they had enough room to not step on each other in the morning.

And hearing all the sex—and seeing all the beating off—made him sort of ready for his scene with Dex. In fact, more than ready.

He'd spent the night dreaming about Dex's blue eyes, his sweet mouth, and the things that were going to happen to Bobby's body that had never happened before.

He woke up with his hand around his cock, and he had to *make* himself not jerk off. Breakfast was coffee followed by soda water, followed by another cup of coffee, because—as he'd been constantly warned—he was going to bottom, and you wanted your system free and clear when you bottomed, or shit, literally, would get real.

Bobby appreciated the advice from the guys—and the easy welcome. Skylar and Rick were working at the gym as personal trainers or aerobics instructors along with their jobs at Johnnies. Lance, the doctor in training, was maybe Bobby's favorite, but that was mostly because he was quiet. Billy and Trey were muddling their way through junior college, trying to find a calling. All of them were as natural about Johnnies as Bobby had been about baling hay—and about a thousand times more honest and upfront than Keith had been when they'd been baling it.

In spite of all the sex—and God, there was a lot—happening around him on a nightly basis, Bobby got the feeling that if any of these guys said, "That's it, I'm monogamous and in love," it would stick—whether they were talking to a boy or a girl.

Maybe it was that thought that made him just a little more tender than he should have been when he was shooting the scene with Dex.

He couldn't help it. Their bodies were touching, and yeah, a lot of it was lust, because Dex was an expert at touching this spot or that spot or tugging on Bobby's ear or his balls or his hair just when it would really turn his key.

But some of it was seeing the guy's worry the week before, or the way Dex seemed to watch out for all the people at Johnnies. Need something? Have a problem? Ask Dex. If Dex couldn't fix it, he knew a guy who could.

And the "bottoming" thing.

Bobby knew guys who lived in fear of anything up their ass. Keith would have snarled "fag" at him in a hot second if he'd known what Bobby had let Dex do to him.

But… but it had felt good—just as good as being with a girl, if not better. And like being with Trish, he hadn't felt… dirty. Or bad. Or soiled.

He'd felt beautiful. He felt like what he was doing held beauty in it.

He felt even more so after he shivered all over, stroked his own cock, and came.

So in the end, he knew he was looking at Dex with a little bit of his heart in his eyes for their final kiss, the one they had when the camera went dark. Dex kissed him gently and then pulled away. He smiled—sort of a brotherly smile, in spite of the naked bodies and the sex and the room that smelled like jizz.

"Good job, kid," he said and kissed Bobby on the forehead.

Oh. For a moment Bobby was embarrassed. Oh God. He'd almost fallen in love with a *guy* on a porn set! What a sap! What an asshole! Jesus—how stupid could he be?

But as they were dressing and Dex started talking to Reg, who was holding the lights today, about the next shoot they were filming and how he had to run to the pet store after work, he realized something.

Dex had been kind.

He hadn't been condescending or mean. Hadn't laughed in Bobby's face.

Had just told him that sex wasn't always about love, and done it with a kiss.

Well, if anyone knew that, Bobby should, right? Dex was still a good guy, and Bobby had nothing to be embarrassed about. He'd liked the guy with the dick up his ass. There was no shame in that.

"Reg, seriously—are you okay?" Dex's voice, sharp with concern, pulled Bobby to the fore while they were wrapping towels around their waists.

"Got infected," Reg said, and Bobby took a better look at him. His face—usually sort of tan—was red and flushed, and now that the shoot was over, he was shaking, arms crossed in front of him protectively. "A little sick."

"Dammit, Reg—can you call Lance?"

Reg's face went blank. "You're the one with his number, Dex. I didn't want to trouble you. You been so worried."

Dex closed his eyes and nodded, and Bobby realized he could help make this better. "I know Lance. I have his contact number. Here—give me yours and I'll hook you up."

"Thank you," Reg said humbly, and as Bobby drew near, he could see the dark circles under Reg's eyes. Besides being sick, he hadn't been sleeping well either. "I'll call after lunch. Dex, I'll be back in an hour to set up for the next shoot, okay?" He shivered violently, and Dex and Bobby exchanged glances.

"I know you gotta go," Dex said, "but how 'bout you let Bobby take you home? We can skip the shower scene and find someone—"

Reg's face twisted in anguish. "Please?" he asked plaintively. "I... I know I'm sick, but I can do the job, Dex. I... it's my only chance to get out of the house besides the gym. And I've got a shoot next week—I'll be right by then."

Dex took a deep breath, and Bobby stepped up. "Look, Reg? How about I take you to your place to do whatever you gotta do. Then I can take you to the apartment. You can sleep on the couch, and we'll wait for Lance to get out of class. How's that?"

Reg bit his lip. "I gotta pick my car up here and be home by nine," he said. His voice cracked a little, like he was having trouble not just coming unglued.

"Sure," Bobby said. He really did have nothing else to do that day besides stuff his face and stare dreamily into space remembering what total submission felt like. "I'll take you home, we'll go back to the apartment—"

"We can stop to eat," Reg said, smiling a little through cracked lips. "You must be starving."

"Yeah," Bobby said gently. "Look—just let me shower, okay?" He was wearing a towel again. It was almost funny how much he didn't seem to mind being naked after only two shoots.

Reg nodded. "Yeah. Okay."

Dex caught Reg by the arm and pulled him to a rolling stool that Bobby had seen John using during the shoot. "C'mon, man. I'd let you lay down on the bed, but Bobby here shot a ton, and that's sorta gross. I'll get Kelsey in here to change sheets, okay?"

"Don't want to be a bother," Reg said through chattering teeth. "Thanks, Dex."

"Not a bother." Dex ruffled his hair affectionately. "I'll have her bring some water and some ibuprofen."

"I like Advil better," Reg mumbled, and although Dex grimaced, he didn't correct him. Reg leaned back against the wall, and Dex hit the intercom switch next to the door.

"Kelsey? No, sweetheart, don't put me on hold. Dammit." He turned to his clothes, folded loosely on the same shelf Bobby had used, and pulled his phone out of his jeans. As he punched in the receptionist's number, he grimaced at Bobby. "Go shower first," he muttered. "The quicker we get him in bed, the better."

Reg was not too tired to guffaw like a little kid, and Bobby caught Dex letting a smile slip through.

Like a mom.

But not like a lover.

Bobby thought he was starting to get it, but he still had a long way to go.

REG'S HOUSE was a small two-story ramshackle affair off Marconi. The rest of the neighborhood wasn't bad, and the house next door smelled seriously of cat pee, but this place was an eyesore. Bobby grimaced from the cab of the truck as he watched the porch tremble under Reg's weight.

"Stay," Reg said easily. "Eat. You only had one Quarter Pounder—we both know you want the other two."

Bobby munched doggedly, hoping tomorrow he'd get to go to one of the buffet places Dex had recced, and studied Reg's habitat more closely. Somebody needed to do some work on this place before it crumbled down around Reg's ears, but Bobby got the feeling Reg would need a little bit of help with that.

As Reg paused at the doorway, seeming to listen, one hand on the knob, Bobby wondered how many other things Reg would need a little bit of help with. Reg frowned, steadier now that he'd taken some ibuprofen, and opened the door slowly before rushing in. He slammed it behind him, and Bobby, curious, lowered the window and listened.

He heard a woman yelling—and then some thumping and a clatter. He paused, his hand on the door handle, and then everything went quiet. He'd gotten out of the truck and was walking up the drive when Reg stuck his head out the door. He had a blossoming bruise on his eye.

"Give me a minute," he called. "I'll be right there."

Bobby gaped, running to the door, but when he tugged on the handle, it was locked.

Oh Jesus.

What was going on in there?

He stood stupidly, heart pumping, for interminable minutes. His hands shook, and he regretted the half a sandwich on the seat of his cab. Finally the doorknob twisted and Reg came out, sighing gustily and leaning against the door.

"She's asleep," he said, dragging air into his lungs like a swimmer. His face had waxed white, and he had tear streaks under his red-rimmed eyes. "God. She must have spit out her sedative this morning."

Bobby just stared, mouth opening and closing, not sure of what to say.

"Will she be okay *now*?" he finally managed. Bobby didn't even know who *she* was.

Reg grimaced and held up two bruised fingers. "Yup. Almost ripped 'em off, but I got the pills down." He closed his eyes tight. "We're close to the easy part," he said like he was trying to convince himself. "It gets bad like this before she starts taking them on her own. She just...." He looked at Bobby apologetically. "She hates it that she can't be... be *normal*, you know?" Reg shook his head. "No, you don't know. Because I'm making no damned sense."

He wobbled, and Bobby reached around behind him, wrapping an arm around his waist. Reg leaned on him trustingly, obviously grateful for the help.

"Sister?" Bobby hazarded. He'd never had a sister—but for all he thought Keith Gilmore was a skeezy bastard, he knew Keith would go to the wall for Jessica in a heartbeat.

"Yeah," Reg mumbled. God, he was weak. "Sleeping again. She'll sleep until at least eight. I should maybe get here earlier. Eight. So she doesn't get mad, you know?"

"C'mon," Bobby urged. "You got seven hours—let's get some medicine, and you can sleep six of 'em."

Reg chuckled roughly. "You're a good guy, Bobby. Where you goin' when you leave?"

They approached the truck, and Bobby helped maneuver him into the cab. "When I leave where?"

Reg laid his head sideways on the bench seat and looked at Bobby through sky-blue eyes that were both sad and trusting. "When you leave Johnnies. All the smart guys do. Even Dex—today was his last hurrah in the sack. Smart guys don't stay in porn forever, you know?"

Bobby swallowed and shrugged. Something about the question was unutterably lonely. "Just started," he said. "I'm sure I'll figure something out."

Reg nodded and closed those soul-magnet eyes. "Smart boys do."

Bobby shut the door and walked around to the front and got in. "So, what have you figured out?" he asked, unwilling to acknowledge that Reg wasn't as smart as he was. There was just something so fundamentally decent about Reg. Bobby wanted that to be a real thing, not just the consolation prize for being human.

"I'm not smart," Reg said, completely without self-consciousness. "I gave up on being smart in the third grade."

"Yeah? What happened in the third grade?" Bobby started the truck and piloted toward the nest of apartments on Hurley. It wasn't much, but it wasn't a rent-by-the-hour hotel room either, and he'd put down money that his roommates at least knew *of* Reg.

"Took a test to see if I'd be put in the dumb class or the smart class. I wanted to be in the smart class, so I copied off the smartest guy I knew."

"That's good strategy," Bobby conceded. Not exactly honest, but he remembered placement tests. There was a fair amount of pressure there, and third-graders were damned amoral.

Reg laughed shortly. "I picked the wrong kid. I mean, he was smart— damned smart. But he was... what's that word? The one where you fuck up your letters and words and which order they go in?"

Oh Jesus. "Dyslexic?"

"Yup." Reg chuckled. "I got put in the *ultra*-dumb class. But it was okay. I was, like, their star player, you know?"

Bobby's stomach churned. "But you're not ultra-dumb."

"Sure I am. Ask anybody." Reg yawned and curled up a little tighter on Bobby's seat. "I just left my sister alone again," he mumbled. "How stupid is that?"

He was asleep before Bobby could find the words to tell him that it sounded damned smart to *him.*

REG SLEPT for three hours before Lance got home with the antibiotics. Bobby had been right. Skylar and Rick were off shift, and they set Reg up on one of the regular beds, out of the main traffic room, before Bobby even asked them for a pillow. Bobby sat at the foot of the bed, reading a paperback that had been making the rounds of the roommates. This one was by Melinda Leigh and featured a mystery and a boy and a girl who were going to get together. Bobby was a fan, even though he wondered if they had any of these where the boy got together with another boy.

Every now and then Reg would shiver hard or moan in his sleep, and Bobby would make sure he had ibuprofen or water—or a steady arm when Reg had to take a leak.

Skylar sacrificed some of his beloved fruits and veggies to make Reg a vitamin juice, and Rick pulled out some ice packs that he rested on Reg's pulse points on top of the covers. Reg thanked them—half-conscious, he thanked them—but it wasn't until Lance got there that Bobby realized how much pain he was really in.

"You didn't take off his jacket?" Lance demanded, charging into the quiet bedroom with almost obscene hurry.

"He was cold," Bobby said, surprised. "Why? What's under the jacket?"

Lance snarled quietly to himself and helped Reg up. "Reg, I'm sorry," he muttered, sliding the battered leather bomber jacket off his shoulders. "I fucked up. Chase did his thing, and I just totally forgot."

Reg grunted. "Not your fault. Everybody's been sort of off their game," he said, and Bobby held back a gasp.

Underneath the battered leather bomber jacket, Bobby could see a wound—a massive, pus-runny, untended wound.

"Wait," he said as Lance pulled at the hem of Reg's none-too-clean T-shirt. "You just… just *left* him like that? Why didn't you take him to the hospital?"

"No hospitals," Reg whimpered, grabbing Lance by the shirt. "You promised, Lance—you promised me—"

"I know, Digger. I promised," Lance said soothingly. "But I'm going to need Bobby's help here, okay? We need to irrigate the wound and take out the stitches and pump you full of antibiotics. I'm sorry I didn't remember, but man, you can't go back to that house again, not like this."

Reg shook his head, in tears. "But I left her sleeping, Lance. I've got to go back and make her take her pills again."

Lance grimaced. "Digger, look at yourself. You're a mess. Don't you think it's time to let someone else take over there?"

Reg just cried harder, and Bobby couldn't stand it. He sat next to him and wrapped his arm around Reg's waist for comfort. "It's okay," he soothed. "I'll go over. Me and Lance'll go take care of her."

Lance shot him a killing look, and Bobby glared back. Lance had promised to take care of *Reg*, and even though Bobby knew how hard he'd been working—school, counseling the guys, asking all the questions so Chase's boyfriend wouldn't lose his fucking mind—he was still pissed. Chase Summers, whom Bobby hadn't met, had the whole world hanging on his every breath, but Reg—Digger—who seemed to be the genuinely nicest guy Bobby *had* met, had needed someone and nobody had showed.

Bobby didn't want him left alone.

"Will you?" Reg begged him. "Lance, you know her. She'll listen to you. Please?" Bobby had brought in a roll of toilet paper to serve as tissues, and he ripped off some squares and cleaned up the tears and had Reg blow.

Lance shook his head and sighed. "Yeah. Let me get you fixed up first, Reg. We'll go over and give her meds." He grimaced sourly at Bobby. "Junior here can probably work wonders with a three-point restraint."

"Don't hurt her," Reg begged, and Bobby told him he'd try. Inside he was wondering how huge this woman had to be to level a buff guy like Reg, but that was before he saw the festering knife wound *under* the shirt and realized the stakes here were pretty damned high.

Reg followed orders like a pro.

At first Bobby was terrified he'd have to hold the man down, but Lance told Reg to hold still and he did. Bobby stayed for moral support, stroking Reg's sweaty hair back from his face, holding his hand when Lance irrigated the wound and when he gave shots. When they were done, he helped change the sheets and gave Reg one of his own clean T-shirts and pairs of boxer shorts to wear. Reg grinned—a weak, tired grin—and made a crack about Bobby having pretty big shorts to fill.

And then he curled up on the clean sheets and fell asleep.

Bobby stared at him for a moment, his heart as sore as it had been in his entire life.

"He needs someone to look out for him," he said, half to himself.

"Well, *I* obviously suck at it," Lance said bitterly, throwing his supplies into a specially marked bag for hazardous waste. He'd worn gloves and used cleanliness protocols the whole time. Bobby felt a bit of awe for a guy who could do what Lance had just done to Reg's wound.

"You got distracted," Bobby said, letting some of his resentment go. What was going on with Reg had obviously been going on for a long time. Situations like that—you never knew when they'd take a spiral to the left. "My friend's dad, he got injured by a hay baler—had been using it his whole life. Lost concentration for one minute. Life's like that sometimes."

Keith's dad had gotten mean. Was that why Keith hadn't wanted to be tender or real? Was his dad why Keith had never wanted to acknowledge what they were doing, even to himself?

Suddenly Bobby didn't care.

The guy whose hand he'd just held didn't give a shit about gay or straight. He just wanted people to help him when he needed it. He just wanted company in a life he saw as going nowhere.

Bobby's life wasn't going much further. Bobby might as well.

But Lance hadn't followed what was in Bobby's head. "You shouldn't have promised him about his sister," he said unhappily. "You have no idea what you got us in for."

"That bruise on his face told me a whole lot," Bobby retorted. "What medication are we giving her, exactly?" He looked back over to the bed to see what Reg was doing, but he was out. He couldn't hear this conversation or be embarrassed that it was being held without him.

"She's paranoid schizophrenic," Lance said. "And when she got hold of the knife last week, she'd stopped taking a pretty stiff cocktail of antipsychotics. Reg has been trying to get her on it again, but she's damned smart. I think he has to literally scrub the sedatives against her teeth to get her to swallow them, and usually when he's done there, she'll take the rest. But it's not easy, and it won't sit right. You'll be putting a tiny woman into a three-point restraint and shoving shit down her throat. I had to do it during my psych rotation, and I'm telling you, Veronica is as bad as it gets without tying her to the bed and putting a needle in her arm so she has to take her cocktail by IV."

Bobby swallowed but held firm. "Then maybe we should get there by eight so we can get her before the last batch wears off."

Lance shook his head and then told Skylar—hulking, good-natured surfer-blond Skylar—to keep an eye on Reg.

"Yeah," he said seriously, channel surfing from the couch. "I'll make him some more juice and keep an eye on his temp. I'll call you guys if anything changes."

"Do that," Lance said shortly, making to leave.

Bobby couldn't just go. He ran back to the bedroom for a minute so he could squat down by the head of the bed. "We're going to take care of your sister," he said softly. "But that's 'cause you want us to. Not 'cause she's more important than you, okay?"

Reg opened sleepy eyes. "Thank you," he said, smiling slightly. "I totally owe you."

"Naw." And then, because he was in this house where guys fucked other guys sometimes for pleasure and sometimes for money, he leaned forward and kissed Reg's forehead. Reg couldn't call him queer or expect Bobby to suck his dick. He did, in fact, just snuggle down under his blanket and shiver.

"Nice," he whispered. "Bye, Bobby."

"Back in the morning. Ask the guys if you get hungry."

"Skylar's a good guy. Eight-inch cock—but he fucks real sweet."

Bobby let out a shocked laugh, but Reg was already back asleep. He was going to have to get used to Reg reciting porn stats on his friends. It wasn't a way Bobby had ever thought of relating with the world.

VERONICA WAS unexpected.

Lance let himself in with a key, and they found her sitting at the kitchen table, staring blankly into space. A tiny woman with way too much graying brown hair falling in her eyes, she wore old pajamas, stretched and faded thin. Her eyes fell on Lance—tall, tanned, dark-haired, blue-eyed Lance—and something sparked in them, something almost girlish.

"Hi, Veronica," Lance said smoothly. "I hope you don't mind we let ourselves in?"

"Where's Reggie?" she asked—but not rudely. Everything about her was relaxed and tranquil.

Bobby remembered when his father seemed relaxed and tranquil, right before his mom walked in front of him during a big play on TV or made too much noise in the kitchen cooking dinner.

"Your brother's sick," Lance said softly. "He wanted us to come make sure you were okay." He walked to a cupboard and found her medication, just where Reg had told them. He was in the process of pulling the bottles down when she made her move, darting for the depths of the house toward a set of stairs.

Bobby was bigger, taller, and faster—he tackled her before she got to the stairs, and like Lance had told him, took one arm behind her back and then the other, perching his knee in the small of her back while she thrashed.

She was stronger than she looked—and damned determined—but like Trina had noted this past week, most of his muscles weren't for show.

Which made what he was doing feel so much worse.

Oh God.

She was tiny.

Reg wasn't a big guy, and as much as he worked out like the rest of them, he just didn't have the body for bulk. His sister was built like he was, small but solid, and her wrists felt like brittle sticks under his hands.

"Please," he begged. "Please, Veronica. Don't fight like this. Man, we're just trying to help—"

"Poison!" she screeched. "*Poison!*"

Lance walked up steadily, without urgency. "Veronica, I'm going to pry open your mouth and use the tongue depressor to open your throat. Then I'm going to push the pills in while I hold your jaw. It's not going to be comfortable, and I'd rather not do it, but you can stop me now if you just—"

"Ulf!" Bobby grunted as she gave a particularly hard thrash.

"Cooperate," Lance finished, sinking to a squat and following through. Bobby thought about how hard he must have been pushing so she didn't bite down on his fingers and grimaced. God, he must have been bruising the shit out of her mouth.

He didn't realize he was crying until he felt a draft on his cheeks, and then her thrashing stopped.

"No," she wailed, facedown on the dirty floor. "No, no, no, no, no…. No poison. God, Lance, why you gotta see me like this?"

Bobby's heart constricted.

She had a crush. On her brother's friend. Of course. Normal people had crushes; why couldn't she? But this friend had to shove pills down her throat while Bobby put a body lock on her, and the betrayal must have been...

Acute.

She cried some more, and Bobby stood up and helped her to her feet. "Want to come sit down?" he said quietly. "I'll make you some food."

"There's nothing in the fridge," she wept. "Reggie's been sick."

"I'll call out for pizza," Lance said, stripping off the gloves he'd worn during the procedure. "Whole works—salad, soda, meat-lover's special, on me."

Bobby's stomach gurgled, and he knew the hand on Veronica's shoulder shook. "I'll go in halvesies if you order two," he said plaintively.

Lance's eyes got big. "Hey, didn't you work today?"

Bobby gave him a weak smile. "I am *so* damned hungry," he admitted. Lance's chuckle made everything normal then. Most natural thing in the world to walk Reg's sister to the battered tapestry couch in the living room and give her the remote.

A thing he regretted doing not an hour later.

"The Fox News channel?" he asked under his breath as he and Lance cleaned off the table enough to set the pizza on. "Like... the *Fox News* channel?"

Lance shuddered. "She's paranoid, Bobby. She thinks everything is out to get her. Who better to tell her she's right?"

"Oh my God," Bobby muttered. "That's heinous. Reg doesn't own guns, does he?"

Lance dropped the pizza box onto the table from a bigger height than he'd probably planned. "God no. He had to lock up the goddamned knives. Why?"

"Because—they're all screeching about minorities and shit—she's telling me all the brown people—her word, by the way—are out to get her. If she'll attack her brother with a knife, can we not let her have a gun?"

"Yeah—I think Reg is smarter than that."

Bobby frowned. "Of course he is. But if she wanders out of here on her own one day, some asshole will sell her one."

Lance grunted and turned to lean on one of the flaking counters. "Yeah. I know. It's reason number one hundred and twelve why this is a bad situation all around."

Bobby let out a groan and laced his fingers behind his neck. He didn't even *know* Reg. But then he didn't know Dex that well either, and Dex had done him more than *a* solid. Dex had taken care of him the best way he could. Bobby believed in pay-it-forward, but it was more even than that.

Reg was decent. And kind. And cute and funny. And he was sticking with his sister through the bad times when Bobby had cut and run, leaving his mom to fend for herself on Frank Gilmore's property. Not that Frank would be asking the same favors as Keith, but still.

Bobby admired Reg and liked him, and this situation was just not fair.

"You said he was smarter than that," Lance said, cutting into his thoughts.

"Well, yeah. Why?"

"Not everybody sees that in Reg."

Bobby thought about it, about Reg's sad little admission that he'd tried to cheat to stay out of the "dumb" class.

"Schools don't always know," he said, thinking about it. "The kind of smart you are to be in school isn't the only smart there is. My... my girlfriend's brother was top ten in his class. Ten years from now, he'll still be in Dogpatch, knocking up his wife."

Lance's mouth twisted. "Bobby, I gave Reg an IQ test once—and I know they're biased as hell, but he asked. It came back in the low eighties, which isn't technically intellectually disabled, but it's not genius level either."

Bobby grunted, uncomfortable. "What's your point?"

"The only reason I haven't reported this situation to somebody is that Reg is an adult. A fully functioning, equal in the eyes of the law adult. If we start interfering with this 'for his own good'"—Lance raised air quotes, and Bobby felt like shit—"we're saying he's not our equal, he's disabled in some way." Lance looked away unhappily. "I mean... he's my friend. I can't look the guy in the eye or hook up with him or even shoot a scene with him if he's... he's a child."

"I don't see him as a child," Bobby said, feeling sick to his stomach. God. Lance was right. How awful would it be for Reg to be hanging out with all the guys from Johnnies, only to find it was some sort of pity? But it wasn't—that wasn't why Skylar was giving up his bed or his produce. That wasn't why Billy had spent ten minutes crushing ice, or even why Dex had sent the guy home with Bobby to make sure he'd be okay. It certainly wasn't why Lance was here.

Lance who "hooked up" with him.

"Then why?" Lance asked baldly. "You hardly know him."

Bobby looked away. "I like him," he said, voice small. "I just... I mean, I guess you guys are a thing, but... you know. He was nice to me."

"We're not a thing," Lance said dryly. Then he sobered. "You go ahead and like him. Don't mind me. I'm getting protective—because you're right. This situation isn't safe, but I don't know what else to do about it besides be his friend."

Bobby smiled a little, but he was tired, and it fell flat. "Everyone I know lives over a hundred miles away," he said. "If this is what I gotta do to have friends, well, it's a lot less of a pain in the ass than driving back up past Truckee."

Lance's smile was a little dim too. "Have some pizza, Bobby. Sit on the couch and fall asleep if you have to—I mean, you shot a scene!"

Bobby nodded, suddenly exhausted. "Yeah." He yawned. "And I haven't had my man-nap yet."

Lance shook his head and pursed his lips. "Poor baby. Reg was the one who told me to take a long bath and to eat my favorite carbs and basically treat myself on scene days. We haven't shown you much of the good side of the business."

Bobby shrugged. Money in his pocket, friends, and pizza. "Maybe next time," he said philosophically.

"Who you up on the schedule with?"

Bobby smiled. "Well, I got a girl named Rachel next week—"

"But...," Lance asked leadingly, and Bobby flushed. "It's okay, you know," Lance said softly, probably responding to the heat in Bobby's cheeks.

"What is?" But he knew.

"If you like boys more than girls. It's... it's perfectly normal. You know that, right? Sometimes it's boys we like best, sometimes it's girls." Lance smiled reassuringly, and Bobby thought he was going to make an amazing doctor.

"I guess after I do a few more of each, I'll find out," Bobby said with dignity. But he remembered that moment today when he thought Dex held the keys to the world. He remembered that yearning—the *buried* yearning—when he'd wanted to touch Keith Gilmore softly, with sweetness under their skin. He remembered the onerous sense of duty that came with knowing he was going to have to spend time alone with Jessica.

He knew.

Lance knew too, apparently, because he kept his handsome, vaguely exotic-eyed face completely bland when he nodded. "Okay, then. So you've had a girl, a boy, you're getting another girl—who's your next boy?"

Bobby couldn't let it go. Lance—God, so handsome, so put together. And he was gonna be a fuckin' doctor. They all knew that. "Are you?" he asked gruffly.

"Am I what?" Lance folded his arms across a chest someone should be writing home about.

"More, uh, comfortable with boys than girls?" Bobby squeaked.

Lance pursed his lips, almost like a maiden aunt. "I'm gay, Bobby. I got no problems with what I do. Do you have a problem with me admitting I'm not just gay when the film rolls?"

Bobby considered that carefully—because so far, Lance was the only one he'd heard admit it. But Bobby still wanted to be Lance when he grew up, so, "No problems," he said, hoping Lance believed him.

"Good."

And Bobby heard it, a sort of relief. This comfort he'd felt—the easy sexuality among the guys in the apartment, the way Reg copped to sleeping with pretty much everybody in the company—it wasn't all easy. He saw it then, that there were pockets of silence in the banter and secret heartbeats in the healthy bodies.

"So," Lance continued in the beats between Bobby's understanding, "who's your next guy?"

Bobby had to smile—shop talk. It was surprisingly neutral. "Ethan," he said, "but Reg has him first next week."

"Ethan and Reg have shot together—they'll be money." He sobered. "If Reg gets better in time. But that's our job. Anyway, Ethan's a good shoot. You'll like him. He should show you a better time."

Bobby shrugged and got himself a plate full of pizza. He didn't have the words to say he'd rather be back in the crowded apartment, watching

Reg sleep, than having a "better time." After their discussion, he wasn't sure if Lance would believe him anyway.

OF COURSE, he hadn't shot with Ethan yet either. He might have changed his mind if he had—but maybe not.

The night passed without incident. Reg's sister went to sleep when she was supposed to and woke up and took her medication without any ruckus. Lance had to go to school then, so he took Bobby's truck, rolling his eyes at how big it was. Bobby wasn't sure what to do next—besides play on his decrepit phone—and thank God he had his charger. His options were sit in the living room and watch *Fox & Friends* or, well, clean the house.

He picked cleaning the house. By the time Skylar came by with Reg's vintage orange Camaro—Rick riding behind him in Skylar's Prius—he'd gotten the corners of the kitchen floor clean of the greasy, hairy residue that tended to collect there and measured for new tile, as well as for new cabinets, and even started the calculations for how much lumber and nails would be needed to start on the porch.

After taking a leak in the downstairs bathroom and tiptoeing over the dry rot—and worrying that the toilet would crash through the floor along with all the crappy toiletries, thick with a layer of dust—he added *everything* for the bathroom to the list.

God, he could work out in the mornings, do his three-hour shift at the café, and come here and fix shit. He wouldn't be lying if he told Reg it was more for his own therapy than to help Reg out. Working out, hanging at the apartment, shooting scenes—Bobby was used to working his ass off. He could already see boredom sliding down the pike at warp speed on a three-hundred-pound ass.

A part of him bitched about the cost of lumber and home improvement while he was trying to save money for his mom, but a part of him was thinking that he knew how to get lumber wholesale, and he had his own tools and some of his own supplies.

And he had to do *something* with his time, right?

"Whatcha doin'?" Skylar asked, throwing Bobby the keys as he knelt on the porch, doing calculations on an old envelope with the stub of a pencil he'd found in Reg's drawer.

"Figuring out how much wood I'd need to fix this place up," he said without thinking.

Skylar stared. "You can *do* that?" he asked, awe in his voice, and Bobby looked up, smiling into Skylar's surfer-boy face.

"Yeah, I can do that. I came down to Sacramento to work construction. There's not much to do in Dogpatch besides help people fix their houses and maybe build a barn or two."

Rick walked up next to Skylar, both of them wearing black jeans with white stitching and spendy leather jackets in the October chill. Bobby was wearing the same jeans he'd put on after he'd showered when he was done with the shoot—practically transparent 501's—with a T-shirt that had holes in the neck and a sweatshirt he'd had to buy to be on the varsity boys' wrestling team.

"Did he just say Dogpatch?" Rick asked. His face was a little leaner than Skylar's, and he had brown hair with one of those widow's-peak hairlines that would probably start receding by thirty, but his wide-blue-eyed expression was practically identical to Skylar's.

"He did," Skylar muttered, staring at the porch. "Did you just say Dogpatch? Isn't that a neighborhood in San Francisco?"

Bobby rolled his eyes. "It's also a town south of Colton in the Tahoe National Forest. Wow, you guys. I've seen maps. Sacramento isn't the only city in the world, you know."

"Well," Skylar said drolly, "it's not Dogpatch."

He had to laugh. "So few places are." He sobered. "How's Reg?"

"He needs another two days of antibiotics and sleep. Lance wanted to know if you wanted a break. You could drive Reg's Camaro to the apartment—we left a space for it—and stay with Reg."

Bobby nodded in relief. "And next time I come here, I'll have some supplies," he said, feeling enthusiasm in his stomach. Then he frowned. "I can't decide which one I should start with—"

"The bathroom!" the guys said in tandem.

"It's not even a question," Rick said, nodding. "I actually took my morning dump at the apartment on purpose so I didn't have to take it here."

Bobby and Skylar stared at him, but Rick didn't seem to think this was too much information.

"I'm saying—if I was Reg, I'd shoot a hundred and fifty scenes a year, just so I could use the bathroom in the offices all the time."

Bobby's eyeballs were drying out, and he blinked a couple of times to see if he was actually hearing this.

"He'd die," Skylar said seriously. "Think about it—you fast for two days before the scene, you get all fucked out during the scene, and then you eat and bulk up for at least a week, maybe a month, before the next scene. He'd die of dehydration if he shot a hundred and fifty scenes a year. Like, no question. It would kill him."

Oh God. And *Reg* was worried about being stupid.

"Not to mention chafing," Skylar continued. "I mean, remember Kane? He did a scene a week for a couple of months. Dex had to rub diaper ointment on his ass. No way it could happen. The most you could shoot would be, maybe, fifty. But that's pushing it. You'd lose muscle mass."

Rick nodded, conceding the point. "And afterward you'd never want to fuck again. Especially if you're more into girls than boys."

"Yeah." Skylar was looking at Bobby now for confirmation. "Right, Bobby?"

"Oh dear God," Bobby mumbled. "You guys, I'm going to go give Reg's sister her meds, okay? I know it's a little early, but—"

They both grinned at him, straight white teeth practically blinding him. "He's got that look," Rick said.

"The one that says he wouldn't trust us to wipe our own asses—or each other's," Skylar agreed. "Dude, we scared him off, and it hasn't been two weeks."

Bobby shook his head and realized they were yanking his chain. "You both suck—"

"And swallow," they said in tandem. "I mean," Skylar clarified, "it's part of our job."

Oh Jesus. "Yeah, well, you go swallow each other all you want, but stop tugging on my balls," he said, laughing. "And seriously—she needs her meds in an hour. Anywhere I gotta be tonight?"

Skylar shook his head. "We're on for tonight—text us and let us know how Reg is doing tomorrow." He grinned. "I brought groceries! We can feed Veronica health food—she'll love it!"

Bobby nodded, biting his lip.

Sure she would.

"Oh come on," Skylar urged. "Go home and nurse Reg." He looked sideways at Rick and then back at Bobby. "He's been asking for you."

"Really? Why?"

Skylar shrugged. "I think he remembers you being kind yesterday. But he's worried about you watching V—thinks she's going to hurt you, so go back and reassure him."

Bobby smiled, thinking that Reg would be good company. "Do you guys have a deck of cards or anything? Poor guy's gonna be bored shitless."

Rick wrinkled his nose like Bobby had suggested using a Sears catalog for toilet paper. "Seriously? Cards? Our apartment has ultra-cable, remember? And apparently V watches nothing but *Fox News*—he's in heaven!"

Oh. "I'll pick some up anyway." Bobby finished his last notation and tucked the paper in his jeans. "I can ask him how he wants his house fixed too."

"Dude." Skylar shook his head.

"You gotta learn how to slack." Rick nodded in total agreement.

"All this… this *doing* stuff."

"Not good for you. Saying."

The two guys regarded Bobby from wide, guileless blue eyes, and Bobby squinted back. "I think you guys need to bale some fuckin' hay," he muttered. "But thanks for bringing the Camaro—let me get my duffel out of the kitchen and I'll take off."

HE STOPPED on the trip back to get a pack of cards and then thought of a couple of games that would need two decks. And then, on impulse, he bought a game of Monopoly too. It had been a long time since he'd sat down with his mom to play games. He had the feeling Reg wouldn't be letting him win.

Reg was curled up at a corner of the couch, watching a rerun of *Law & Order* with unhappy eyes.

"What's up?" Bobby asked, setting a bag of takeout teriyaki bowls on the coffee table.

"This show moves damned fast," he muttered. "I can never keep up with who they're talking to and why."

Bobby grabbed the remote and turned the TV off. "Yeah, well, I gotta admit, I don't watch a lot of television. Here—eat this. It's good for you."

He handed Reg a bowl of teriyaki chicken with a plastic fork and scowled when Reg just sort of picked at it.

"Don't like vegetables?" he asked.

"Never had this before," Reg confessed. "V eats pretty simple stuff, and I don't like messing with that. And I gotta keep my calories down, so I just eat a little bit of what she's having."

"Well, man, you're in luck. This is chicken and veggies, and as far as we're concerned, it's the food of the gods."

"Yeah," Lance said, coming in from one of the bedrooms and yawning. "Unless you've got a scene in two days."

"Gas," Bobby confessed but Reg gave an impish grin.

"Six days, Lance—can I have it now?"

"Yeah, sure." Lance looked longingly at the bowls—and Bobby had bought four too, because he hadn't known who'd be home. "Bobby, you want my chicken and veggies? I can have a little bit of rice this far out."

"That's the best part," Bobby said, grateful.

When they were done with lunch, Bobby pulled out the cards and dealt out a hand of three-man cribbage, keeping score on a napkin. Reg picked up the rules really quick, and what followed was sort of a magic pocket of time. Lance was funny and quick, and he lost Reg sometimes, but Bobby learned to watch when Reg's eyes glazed over, and he'd insert something to clarify in the middle until Reg perked right up. For his part, Reg seemed eager to be entertained. Jokes, anecdotes, stories from Bobby's misspent youth—all of it was digested and remarked upon and generally enjoyed.

Bobby couldn't remember spending such a simple afternoon with friends. Not before his father left, because why would he bring a friend over to a powder keg, and not afterward because his mom was always so worried about money.

Lance put down his last hand regretfully. "Gotta study," he sighed. He stood up and yawned. He paused as he passed Reg and put a gentle hand on his head. "Buddy, you're ready for some more meds and your own nap. Bobby, could you get him to bed for me?"

Reg grunted, eyeing Lance sourly as he walked toward the tiny round kitchen table where his books sat, still opened. "I can get my own pills," he muttered, but mostly to Bobby.

"Yeah," Bobby said through his own yawn. "But I'm ready to nap too, and I can snag Rick's bed since he's gone."

"You don't want Rick's bed." Reg stood up and wrapped the couch blanket around his shoulders as he shuffled to the bedroom. "He and Skylar had messy sex on it this morning when they thought I was asleep."

Bobby hissed air through his teeth. Rick and Skylar fucked like rabbits, sometimes with Billy, Lance, or Trey—although Billy had a girlfriend he brought over some nights, who apparently thought a sock on the door was a ticket to a soundproof room—but mostly with each other. Bobby had seen them sometimes, crossing paths in the apartment, one getting out of the shower while the other was cooking dinner, and he'd seen a hand hovering over a shoulder and a bit of confusion when a kiss on the cheek or a hand on the back would be the most natural thing in the world.

A little voice in his head was asking how they didn't know they were in love.

And right now, it was asking if he was willing to crash on Rick's bed if they hadn't changed the sheets.

"You can sleep with me," Reg volunteered. "Skylar's got a queen-sized. Just crash next to me, and if I thrash too much, grab the spare blanket at the foot and then go sleep on top of the comforter."

"That'll work." That little voice again, telling him he was happy about this because it meant he'd get to hold somebody—hold *Reg*—without anybody thinking it was wrong or strange. There was such freedom here. It was almost daunting how many things he could say or do in this apartment, with these guys, in this *life*, that he'd yearned to do in his old life.

How much of his fascination with Reg had to do with the freedom to touch, to be kind, that he had here and hadn't had at home?

He made sure Reg downed his medicine and then tucked him in against the wall. He took the edge of the bed, and Reg started shivering as Bobby got him settled. It was the most natural thing in the world to spoon up against his back, the way Jessica always expected him to do but he'd never wanted to do. Until now.

"Mm," Reg mumbled. "This is nice. You're good at the snuggling, Bobby. Anyone tell you that?"

"Not my girlfriend," Bobby murmured on a laugh.

Reg laughed too. "You should do this with Ethan," he said drowsily. "Ethan loves this. I think the whole reason he's in Johnnies is to touch like this."

Oh. A part of Bobby wilted. This was just how you touched when you were at Johnnies. Of course.

"Is Ethan a good guy?"

"The best," Reg said happily. Then, like he was offering a gift: "But I don't know if he ever would have sat with me and played cards like that. I sure did like that, Bobby. I hope we can do that again."

Bobby tightened his hold, fever and all. "Me too," he said softly.

Something he could offer Reg that no one else would. He liked that. He could play cards for years.

Left Behind

REG'S BACK healed up nicely, and Lance was able to take the stitches out before his scene with Ethan. His fever was gone by the fourth day, so he got a whole day of being able to eat before he had to fast for the shoot, and all in all, he was glad to not be sick again.

Going back home was hard, though.

V was real sweet. Apparently Lance and Bobby had put the fear of Big Men in her, and she was right on even keel with her meds, but Reg remembered the peace of sleeping through the night at the apartment, and how there were always fruits and vegetables in the refrigerator, and he missed it.

He missed Bobby even more.

They'd played cribbage, rummy, and Monopoly for three days, and Reg got used to the shy little half smile the kid got when he was about to win. He started rooting for Bobby to win just so he could see it. He liked the way Bobby didn't expect him to know everything but didn't feel sorry for him when he needed an explanation. He said he was used to not knowing things because he grew up in a small town, but he'd had a computer and a mom and a high school education and everything, so Reg thought maybe he was just protecting Reg's feelings.

It worked.

Reg felt safe with him. And protected.

Every night while Reg had stayed there, Bobby had slid into bed behind him and held him tight and close. No sex, which was fine because at first Reg had felt like shit, and then, when he'd felt better, he needed to save it for work, but strong. And warm. And safe.

Reg had never felt safe asleep.

The morning of the shoot, Bobby showed up at Reg's house with that old truck of his full to the brim with lumber and pipes and linoleum and stuff, and Reg stared at it.

"What's all that?" He peered over Bobby's shoulder as he stood at the door. It looked like construction stuff, but Reg didn't know construction.

79

"I'm gonna rip out your bathroom floor and fix the pipes so they don't leak," Bobby said matter-of-factly. "The bathroom on your floor—don't worry, I won't intrude on V's space."

Reg's jaw dropped a little.

"Why in the world would you want to do that?"

Bobby shrugged, that little half smile playing on his lips, the one that said he had something nobody else did. "I worked out already. No shift at the café, nothing to do—don't want to get bored."

"Well, uh, yeah." Reg was still floundering on *why*. "But… dude, I've got a scene!"

"Well, good. You can shower at Johnnies. I'll have this done in a couple of days."

Reg sighed. "Ethan and I were gonna go out afterward," he said, feeling bad. Hooking up was just hooking up, right? And Ethan was one of the few guys who could do it after doing it. All day. "I hate to leave you here while I'm off—"

"Working? Visiting friends?" Bobby shrugged. "You didn't really want to leave V alone anyway, right?"

Reg glanced over his shoulder, but she was in the living room, watching the news. "No," he said under his breath. "But you gotta be careful, okay? No tools where she can get them, okay?"

"Yeah." Bobby nodded. "And if you're bringing Ethan over, you gotta text me. I can be ready to clear out before you get here, okay?"

Okay. Well, that would be… okay. Reg could bring Ethan over, and Bobby could leave.

"Isn't that weird?" he asked, not sure why.

Bobby frowned. "I got no idea. But I…." His eyes moved back and forth steadily, like he was trying to read a book in his own head. "I got a girlfriend?" he finished. Then he shook his head. "Whatever. I'm just being a friend."

Oh. "You'll still cuddle with me if you stay the night, right?" Reg asked plaintively. "'Cause that's the whole reason I hook up with Ethan anyway." He smiled happily. "The guy likes to cuddle."

A look of relief crossed Bobby's face. "Yeah. Good. Cuddle. That's what we'll do if Ethan's not here." He frowned again before Reg could and broke the awkwardness by turning toward his truck. Reg helped him unload before it was time to shower and prep, and then took off. The entire ride there, instead of looking forward to Ethan—big, brown-eyed, Italian Ethan, who drew more viewers with one of his videos than Reg did with three—Reg kept looking back to Bobby and his simple assumption of doing chores at Reg's house.

And how happy Reg had been to see him.

Too bad about the girlfriend, though. Now that Reg was healthy, he'd been thinking about Bobby's lean body, his chest that hadn't started to bulk up, and his guns that were hard and terrifying without looking like big cannonballs. He'd seen Bobby's body, all of it, and had felt him, long and warm along Reg's back. Reg had *wanted* that body. But it wasn't to be.

At least he had work.

Ethan was beautiful to work with. Reg, who always worried about doing something wrong, about touching someone the wrong way, about turning them off instead of on, had been Ethan's first partner, and he'd learned that there was *no wrong way* to touch Ethan. And because there was no wrong way—because every touch brought Ethan pleasure—that sort of made Reg happy about finding all the *super-right* ways to touch him.

And sometimes the right way to touch him was to play tag, like little kids, until Ethan caught him and nailed him to the floor.

Fucking Ethan was a pure joy, because every time you rubbed a piece of his skin not touched by sunlight, he groaned and shuddered. And he loved to kiss.

Today of all days, when Reg's stamina wasn't what it usually was, they actually finished the shoot and had Ethan coming—three times—within the span of two hours. After two hours, Dex called a halt.

"Okay, guys," he said, laughing as they both lay back in the bed, panting. "We're done here. No shower scene—Reg's bandage would need to come off, and I have it on good authority it's gross, so we won't do that."

Ethan grinned at Reg, his blinding smile making everything in Reg's life sunshiny. "Well, gross is bad," he said, winking. "We can shower without fucking. How's that."

"That's good," Reg said, shoving himself up and trying to look like he wasn't exhausted. "We doing anything afterward?"

Ethan grimaced. "I'm selling my car," he said with a sigh. "I've gotta get an apartment, and the car…."

Reg grimaced. "Aw, man. That bites." Ethan had a superspecial MKZ, new and technical and bright red. Reg was jealous. They'd hooked up a time or two, and Reg had fond memories of blowing Ethan in the front of that car while they parked at the river and talked about nothing at all.

"Yeah, well…." And Ethan's grimace went sad. "Got kicked out of the house," he said. He glanced up at Dex, and Dex nodded. Obviously not news.

"This is, like, the *shittiest* fall," Reg said with passion. Tango, Chance, Ethan, *Reg*. "Oh my God! Can, like, one good goddamned thing happen this month?"

Ah, Ethan's grin really *could* make everything all right.

"You can come help me pick out a new car that won't cost so much," he said hopefully. And it was like Bobby had shown up at his house so he could do this nice thing for his friend.

Hanging with Ethan was as wonderful as it always had been. Reg flirted shamelessly and remembered that Ethan called him Digger, like Dex and Lance were supposed to but Bobby never did. But in the end, when Ethan turned down the offer for the hookup, a tiny, secret part of him was almost relieved. He talked a little bit, about how hard it was to find a girl. He wasn't gay, right? Wasn't that what he was supposed to be looking for? A girl?

Then he remembered. "Hey, Ethan!" he said, as Ethan was dropping him back at the Johnnies parking lot. "I just remembered something."

"Yeah?"

"You're gonna be matched with the new kid in, like, a week and a half—did you see that?"

"Bobby?" Ethan frowned to remember. "Yeah? We've got stills to shoot. He must be hot shit, 'cause Dex usually saves the special still shoots for the guys he thinks are gonna make top ten."

Reg floated between the top ten and the top twenty. After ten years, he was just happy to be top anything at all. He told Ethan he was getting too old for this porn bullshit—and he'd said it because he was tired, and he hadn't wanted to admit he'd been sick, but God, all the sadness this month, he could feel it in his bones.

"He's pretty," Reg acknowledged, because how could you not? "And he's hung like a monster, but he's sweet too. Anyway, you're his first bottom, and he sort of got screwed over with the whole 'treat yourself' thing. So, you know. If he gets a chance to go out for dinner—God, anywhere but McDonald's—could you take him? He hasn't really seen us at our best, you know?"

Ethan's smile wasn't quite his brightest, but Bobby wouldn't know that.

"I'll do what I can," he said. "If we can stand each other after two days of shooting naked, I think that'll be something special."

God love the guy—he was awesome. But still, it was nice to come back to the house and find Bobby there, elbows-deep in drywall dust and crumbling floorboards.

"Heya," he said, peering up from where he knelt, a little cushion under his knees. He'd apparently been ripping up the floor around the toilet, big work gloves encasing his hands, the leather worn to a shine. "Good shoot?" The wood near the toilet was brittle, flaking away under his hands, and Reg marveled that it hadn't disintegrated under his own feet as he'd been taking a piss in the middle of the night.

"Short," Reg said gratefully. "We went and traded in Ethan's car afterward—but he wasn't up for anything else." He frowned, remembering why. "God, this month sucked. People getting sick, hurting themselves, getting kicked out. It's like a perfect fucking storm."

Bobby grunted while ripping out a floorboard. "I've never lived through a perfect storm before," he said. "Pretty much glad I'm just along for the ride."

"What you are doing there is magic," he said, full of admiration, mesmerized by Bobby's capable hands making the floor disappear. "Can I help?"

Bobby wrinkled his nose. "It's kind of small in here or I'd let you. If you want, you can take the shitty wood out to the truck and pull the good stuff up to the porch. Sort of swap shit out if you can."

"I can do that!" He had no idea how to *fix* the house, but he was all excited about having something to do to help get it done. Right up until he yawned.

"Don't worry about it," Bobby said, pushing himself up and stretching. "I forgot *you* had a scene today, and frankly, you're looking tired. Did you eat?"

Reg grinned. "Yeah—we went out to Chili's before the car thing. I'm good."

"Fancy." Bobby winked, because it wasn't *that* fancy, but it was dressier than Hometown Buffet. "There's some apples in the kitchen, and I made some of that pasta—the kind with the cheese inside, and the white sauce, in the little bowls? I made that for V for lunch, and there's plenty leftover. So go eat, and I'll clean up here so I can start again in the morning after I work out."

Reg nodded gratefully. "Thanks, Bobby. I can help tomorrow—it's just so nice of you to come over here and do this."

Bobby shrugged. "I like the apartment and all, but everybody has stuff to do this week. I like to keep busy."

Reg looked down and away, registering the construction dust over the cracking white tile of the hallway and remembering the loneliness that had hit him when Ethan had given his regrets for hanging out that night. "You, uh, wanna stay the night? I mean, we don't have to do anything, just… you know."

Bobby frowned, like he was doing complicated math in his head. "Uh, yeah. Sure. Like we did at the apartment. No worries."

Like no sex. Which was fine. Really. Because Reg had just had sex, right? Hours upon hours of sex. Or, well, two hours. But sex. And Ethan was good—Reg always felt *better* when he was done doing a scene with Ethan—like all that happy, real touching energized him.

But still. No sex with Bobby. Even though Bobby seemed to like him. Seemed to want to spend time with him. Didn't even mind sleeping with him. But no sex. Because why?

"You got a girlfriend," Reg said, squinting and hoping it wasn't obvious this was a guess as to why they wouldn't be having sex.

"Yep," Bobby said, dusting off his hands. Most of the floor was up, so he had to balance on the support beams as he walked to the edge of the bathroom. "I'll have to replace some of the beams tomorrow. Think you'll be up to help me?"

Reg nodded, and another damned yawn snuck out, and he realized he was never going to get to the bottom of this mystery if he was nodding off as he stood.

"Go," Bobby urged. "Go nap. I'll clean up, and we can have a good night."

Sure. A good night with no sex. Reg thought that sounded like sort of a trap—like a good day at school, when everybody knew there was no such thing, but he was too tired to argue.

He could get to the bottom of the no-sex thing later.

Heh, heh… bottom!

But nobody bottomed that night.

First they had dinner—just like Bobby suggested—and then suffered through television with V before Reg made her take her meds. This time, though, she popped them in her mouth, took a swig of water, and kissed his cheek before going to bed. A big part of him relaxed—oh God. He could sleep—at least until she started hiding her pills again.

But after that, he and Bobby brushed their teeth and stripped to their shorts and got in bed.

They just lay there and touched—and talked.

Reg heard about his mom, who sounded nice, and his girlfriend, who sounded, well, like a girlfriend, mostly. Pretty, with soft boobs, and sweet. He heard a little about the girlfriend's brother, but Bobby kept a pretty tight mouth about that.

Reg kept going back to the girlfriend.

"I like girls," he said plaintively. "I do. I miss having a girlfriend."

Bobby grunted and rolled over on his side so he was facing Reg but not touching. Reg liked that. He could see Bobby's eyes when they talked and look at his full lips when he smiled in the dark.

One of Reg's few purchases as an adult had been a king-sized bed with matching bedding that he swapped out every year. This year the comforter was a faded chambray blue, and the sheets were a few shades lighter. Bobby must have liked it, because he ran his hands back and forth along the edges as they talked. Something about seeing how John and Dex cared for the sets at Johnnies showed him what he could do with his bedroom—so he did it. He had dressers and a mirror.

He kept things clean, kept his clothes folded, kept stuff dusted, and swapped out the posters on the wall every so often. This was his space, and he loved it.

And seeing Bobby here, lying shirtless on his sheets, was sexier than words.

Even when they were having no sex.

"Why don't you have a girl?" Bobby asked, looking at him like the answer mattered.

"Well, I used to," Reg told him. "But girls find out about Johnnies, and sometimes they want freaky shit—and I tried the freaky shit. Doing a threesome with another guy—that never ends well. I mean, it ends well with the three guys, but never with the girl and the two guys, that's for sure."

Bobby hid a laugh by biting his lip—a habit Reg could forgive him for because it made him look evil in the good way. "Why not two guys and a girl?" he asked, hanging on to Reg's every word.

"Well, it either comes out one of two ways," Reg said, speaking from experience. "Way one, all they want is to see the two guys fuck—and that's great. I do it all the time. I got no problem with that—but I took the girl out to dinner, and I'd like to at least, you know, touch her boob, kiss her, something, 'cause, hey, we're in bed together, right?"

Bobby nodded sagely. "Okay, so that's one way."

"Or the other way is she expects we'll spend the whole time with her, and only with her. So, you know, it's *all* about her and two guys doing all the stuff to her. And sometimes, when you're doing something special, this is nice, but... I mean, *dude*. One of the first lessons at Johnnies is... returning... giving back—what's the word?"

"Reciprocation," Bobby said, pulling out that big word without blinking. Yup, one thing was sure—this kid was too smart to be in Reg's bed.

But anyway....

"Exactly! So, like, you get a blowjob, you give one back. You like to bottom, that's fine. Either find someone who likes to top or learn how to top just for that time. It doesn't matter—you give back. So two guys doing all the things for this one girl—if she's not giving them blowjobs on the other days, it's not... you know...."

"Fair," Bobby supplied.

"Yeah. It's not fair. So that's some of the freaky shit girls want, and it's not as fun as it sounds. Some of the other shit is, like, big orgies, and I did one once, and nobody wanted to wear a rubber, and I was the only one who'd even *seen* an HIV test, and once I realized all these people jizzing all over the place didn't have more respect for themselves than that, I found my keys and my shorts and went home."

Bobby chuckled. "So, no *bueno*."

"No. No *bueno*."

"Have you tried… I don't know, finding a *nice* girl, who doesn't mind—"

Reg grunted and rolled to his other side. "Yeah. And she was okay until V went off her meds. But it's… it's like I can't talk to girls like we're talking here. I miss that when I'm dating girls. It's just plain weird."

"Then why not a nice boy?" Bobby asked, his hand coming up to Reg's brow and playing with the quickly growing scalp stubble.

Reg narrowed his eyes. "I'm not gay," he said.

"You can be, you know, bi."

They'd talked about that. "But isn't that when you fuck guys but have a girlfriend?" Reg asked, feeling stupid.

The way Bobby's big hazel eyes widened and his face went absolutely still didn't reassure Reg on that account either.

Idly, while Bobby was struggling for an answer, Reg reached out and rubbed the super-straight bridge of his nose. Bobby crossed his eyes for a moment and then captured his hand—but didn't release it.

"Bisexual is when you like both. So you could have a girlfriend to come home to or a boyfriend to go out with. You don't have to have them both at the same time to be bi."

Reg thought about it. "But how do you have… you know. A grown-up family if it's only two guys?"

Bobby spread Reg's hand and started drawing small designs on the inside of his wrist, and for no reason at all, Reg started getting hard.

"I don't know," Bobby admitted. "But you see it on TV. People do it all the time."

Reg wrinkled his nose. "We must watch very different TV," he said, remembering V's news program.

Bobby kissed the center of Reg's palm, and Reg watched him, the small flower of warmth blooming in the center doing nothing bad for his hard-on at all. He didn't question why Bobby would do that, or how it was different than hooking up, like, say, with Lance or Ethan or any of the other guys. But something near the pit of his balls said it. *This is different. Guys who just fuck each other don't do that. Why doesn't Bobby know this?*

"Yeah, well, your sister watches the scary kind of television," Bobby admitted. "The guys in the apartment watch sitcoms and action shows and get their stuff off the computer."

Reg grimaced. "V uses the computer. I don't. I kept getting bugs and crashing mine, so I sold it, like, years ago. I could barely fill out the application at Johnnies."

Bobby grunted. "You know, we should get one. Like, go in on it. I could leave it here. We'd learn how to use it so it didn't get buggy. That could be good."

Reg whimpered and rubbed himself against the bed. He thought if he saw one shot—just one shot—of two of his friends locked in the middle of something passionate, spewing spunk from their cocks or swallowing or getting fucked so hard their eyes closed and they couldn't talk—he would probably sympathy-come right now.

"Okay," he said, thinking more about surfing porn than any good the computer would do. "That could be good. Just… oh, geez… tell me when and where, and I'll go shop—Bobby, I'm gonna come from that. Isn't that fucking… *weird*?"

Bobby took Reg's first two fingers deep into his mouth, and Reg imagined… just imagined… those pretty eyes looking at him while Bobby's sweet mouth milked Reg's cock for everything he had.

His orgasm rolled agonizingly through him. He should have been all sexed out, but still it churned slowly, like his brain cells were awakening in all his nerve endings. The realization that he'd been turned on and brought to climax by this kid just from having his fingers sucked made fireworks erupt all over his body.

His penis actually hurt, and his balls ached by the time he was through.

He lay, still facedown on his bed, panting and gazing at Bobby like he was scary magic man. "That was the damnedest thing," he breathed. "I woulda… I didn't think I coulda… how did you *do* that?"

Bobby heaved himself across the bed and kissed his cheek. "I got no idea," he said softly. "But I don't think either one of us could be all straight for something like that to happen."

Reg grunted, too tired to even argue. "I thought you had a girlfriend," he whispered.

"I do," Bobby whispered back. "This wasn't… it was like lying in bed with you when you were sick. Feels natural. Like it's what I should be doing. Doesn't feel like cheating. Isn't that weird?"

Yeah. Weird. Reg whimpered. "You're gonna leave me for your girlfriend," he explained, like Bobby didn't know this. "That's how it's supposed to be."

Bobby *hmm*ed in his throat and pulled his hand through his hair. "Why?" he asked.

"'Cause people don't leave their girlfriends for people like me," he said, feeling patient. Bobby was still looking at him, pretty eyes big and full of disbelief. "It's like nice girls don't date porn models, and nobody wants to live in this falling-down house with my sister. These things are true."

"Hunh," Bobby said. "Does that mean you don't want me to stay the night?"

"But you're fixing my bathroom!" Reg said, confused as hell.

"Yeah—but you don't have to put out for me because I'm fixing the bathroom," Bobby said, laughing. But wounded. Reg could see that in his eyes. Oh hell.

"No," he said, reaching out and capturing Bobby's hand. Ah God, the closeness. This was what he loved about Johnnies—the closeness. The kindness. He'd always paid it back in the coin of sex, but here it was, being offered for free.

He had no currency for that.

"No what?" Bobby asked quietly, squeezing his hand.

"Just... just stay. Talk to me. Be my...." Friend? "I can't think of the word," he said disconsolately.

"Companion," Bobby told him. His voice sounded husky in the dark. "Let's do companion."

"Okay. Let's be companions. I like that."

"Good."

Reg closed his eyes then, because it had been a long day and he was still recovering, but he felt it when Bobby inched closer to him, his body massive and muscular and warm. Bobby was the one who pulled the comforter over their shoulders and settled the pillows under their head, and it was Bobby's breathing that lulled Reg to sleep.

Friends. A companion. Was that really the word Reg wanted?

Lessons in the Interim

JESSICA TEXTED him at least four times a day.

Sometimes it was silly stuff she found on the net, and sometimes it was dream houses, and sometimes it was sample budgets for how much he needed to make to have an apartment for her to move out to Sacramento.

Sometimes it was selfies of herself at her job or with her brother or horseback riding—which was something she loved to do.

When he was done filming his scene with Rachel—who'd been bitchy to the point of making Bobby limp, if truth be told—he found Jessica had left ten texts for him during the six hours of work.

He wasn't sure who he'd been most irritated with by the end of that day—the girl waiting for him in his hometown or the girl who'd said, "Oh, for Christ's sake—that's not a fucking baseball bat. You can stop hitting me in the face with it anytime." Jesus—there was nothing in the sex handbook that said she couldn't hold it with one hand while giving a blowjob, was there? He was busy holding her hair back and opening up his chest so everyone could see her swallow his cock. Improvisation wasn't just for Shakespeare!

But after his shower—and there were a thousand people in the locker room, so he found himself practically falling asleep in the shoot room and resenting the hell out of having to smell him and Rachel in the sheets—he realized he was both loving and hating every ding his phone made from his pocket.

He'd kept his job working Hazy Daze, even after he started getting all the work at Johnnies. The shifts were for three hours, and he only worked two days a week there, but his mom had texted him that Keith's dad was raising her rent. He'd be damned if he let his mother get kicked out of her house because he stopped giving Keith Gilmore blowjobs and couldn't protect her. But he hated waiting tables—and sucked at it for that matter—so he dreaded getting a text asking him if he could come work.

So that was two people he didn't want to hear from.

Then again, it could be one of the guys. Rick and Skylar were funny—and they often got their clients to pose for him. They were good about having not just the eye candy too. The scrawny kid who could now lift five pounds more than he could last week, he got shown to all their friends so he could read all the "Good jobs!" and "Keep goin' little bro's!" that came rocketing back. Skylar had one client who had lost 100 pounds and had 150 more to go, and he told the woman that he'd send pictures to all his friends so they could cheer her on too. She'd declined the pictures—Bobby could have told him that—but she did appreciate the good wishes whenever he told his friends the newest weight-loss news.

Trey—tall, lanky Trey, with a smirk instead of a smile and perfectly coiffed black hair—liked to text his roommates his English professor's quote of the day. Billy—almost as small and compact as Reg, but with pale skin and hauntingly dark eyes—would text *his* professor's geeky vector drawings whenever he went into physics. Bobby kept those. He particularly treasured the one asking about the speed of a monkey that fell out of a tree and got swatted across the river by the elephant's trunk. If his high school teachers had been that funny, he might not have hated school so much.

Lance would text them chores or shopping that needed to be done, but since he usually threw something goofy on the list, like "Cranberries and popcorn to decorate apartment" since Thanksgiving was coming, that was okay too.

Reg had a trivia calendar at his desk. Bobby had seen it on the nights he'd spent when he was working on the bathroom. He'd had to leave the job half done and spend odd hours on it since waiting tables at Hazy Daze, but Reg didn't seem to mind. They locked up the bathroom, and he used the tiny one off his bedroom when Bobby was gone, and on the days Bobby could make it, he was welcomed with a smile and lunch and company.

Reg's smile seemed to increase in amperage and appeal every time Bobby knocked on the door. He'd send Bobby the fact of the day from the trivia calendar every morning since that first time, the time Bobby had made love to his hand, and neither of them had spoken about it. The trivia was an attempt at connection—which Bobby appreciated—and Reg usually added a comment on it.

Condoms only prevent conception 85 percent of the time. Jesus, Bobby, it's a good thing we're in gay porn, or I'd be a daddy.

91

Bobby would remember the trivia just because he loved the glimpse into Reg's mind. And man, did he love getting texts from his Johnnies people—hands down. His roommates were fun and going out into the world to make the world a better place, and even though he was just a guy with a hammer (heh, heh), he felt like he was helping them by providing an air mattress to the last guy in the door.

But still—Reg's texts felt different.

Every visit to Reg's house to fix up the damned bathroom took Bobby a little further into Reg's life—and a little closer to the man himself.

Bobby's fascination with him hadn't diminished in the two weeks since they'd had to care for Reg during his infection.

As much as Bobby liked his bright, mercurial roommates, there was something about Reg's steadiness that he treasured more. As lovely as the other guys were at Johnnies, as muscular and stacked and, yes, hung like elephants as the guys in the catalogue were, something about Reg's compact muscles and bowlegged walk made Bobby almost hunger to touch him.

And the fact that they *did* touch—snuggle in Reg's bed, touch hands, touch faces, casually, tenderly, a brush to the shoulder, a kiss to the inside of Reg's wrist—it filled something fundamental in Bobby's soul. It was like all those times he'd wanted to touch Keith but knew he'd end up with a bloody nose while *still* reeking of Keith's come—*those* moments were healed one by one, every time he and Reg touched freely and no sex was involved.

But Reg was right. That morning, before Bobby's still shoot with Ethan, Reg had texted, *I looked up 'companion,' and it still doesn't seem right. We can buy a computer after Christmas—I keep fumbling my keyboard looking for a better word.*

The text was riddled with spelling errors, and Bobby's heart beat hard enough to crack and flake a little as he thought of Reg *trying* to spell anything so he could figure out what they were.

Friends wasn't covering it—but they weren't lovers either.

No.

Even if they did a scene together, Bobby was learning that didn't really make them lovers.

Particularly after the stills shoot with Ethan.

"God, that was hard," he said over a light veggie platter he and Ethan shared when it was over. Reg had coached him the night before—bring some nice clothes, be ready to go out. Even if it wasn't the actual scene, Ethan was a nice guy to hang with.

Bobby had the feeling that hanging with Ethan was like facing a friend audition.

His chest ached to pass so he could be Reg's friend too.

And Ethan was easy to like. During the shoot itself, they'd been skin to skin, doing weird, hard, twisty things with their bodies while constantly fluffing to make sure their dicks were hard during the frame.

Ethan had kept things light and friendly, and after they'd collapsed on each other in a sweaty, giggling pile of naked after the final shot, going out with him had been as easy as Reg told him it would be.

And then Jessica had texted him, out of the blue, while he'd been sort of losing himself in Ethan's easy conversation.

Whatcha doin', hon?

Eating with a coworker, why?

We just haven't talked in a while, that's all.

Bobby gritted his teeth. No, they hadn't. He'd kept busy—damned busy—with the working out and waiting tables and the working on Reg's bathroom, and he'd done that for a reason.

Helping to fix a friend's bathroom is all.

Don't you want to talk to me?

Not now, Jessica! I'm eating! It was a lie, of course. They had to fuck the next day, and Bobby was already learning that starving was the key to a good scene.

He wasn't sure how many years he'd be able to starve himself before a scene. He'd already realized he had no qualms about sex for money, and he wasn't particularly ashamed of that. But going without food....

He stared at the crisp celery and carrots on their little tray and thought longingly of a hamburger.

"Tomorrow," Ethan said with a weak laugh, and Bobby looked up from his frustrating phone conversation and put the damned thing in his pocket.

"Yeah, I know." He breathed deep and took in the smell of hamburgers from the kitchen, hoping that would sustain him. "Sorry about the texting." He didn't want to tell Ethan that he didn't really *want* this girlfriend far away in Truckee, because that seemed mean somehow to Jessica, and

Bobby was starting to see how being decent to people mattered in the world of Johnnies.

"I get it. People want your attention." Ethan nibbled on a carrot stick disconsolately, like he was trying to think of another polite question to ask Bobby so he didn't have to talk about whatever was weighing on his own chest. Bobby had purposely made light of his time in construction and the awful setup of exploitation he'd escaped while staring down a gun barrel to get out. He'd shown his scarred thumb as proof that he was clumsy and told Ethan the story in a way that made him laugh.

Ethan was putting a good face on what looked like some serious heartbreak—Bobby didn't want to tell him the horrible shit. Who needed to know that about the guy you were working with? Seriously.

As if to confirm Bobby's suspicion that Ethan had great deep, dark things going on in his head, he suddenly said, "Hey—do you want to come with me to get inked?"

Which was how Bobby found himself in a tattoo shop, a place he'd sworn he'd never go into, just because who had the money to suffer for vanity, right?

Ethan wanted a Chinese symbol, something small, in the small of his back near his ass. Bobby didn't want to ask—the look on the guy's full-lipped Italian face was one of fierce penance, and Bobby didn't want to intrude.

He spent the time browsing through the art held in the poster displays around the room, and as Jessica buzzed fiercely in his pocket, he started to think about an image, any image, he'd want inked on his body for all the world to see forever. About all he could come up with was the innocence in Reg's eyes, but hey, he'd only known the guy for a couple of weeks, and he'd always thought tattoos of people's faces were stupid.

"Hunh…." He opened one of the display posters and saw a dragon, all in black lines, vertical and twined around a tower. The pic was beautiful, and suddenly he could imagine this drawing, stretched out over his ribs. He took a picture of it and texted it to Reg.

Think I should get a tat?

I thought you were saving money?

He smiled. *Crap. Yeah. You're right. Maybe after my mom's paid up for the winter.*

Jessica buzzed him again. *So, what you doing?*

He thought about her—she'd love a tattoo, or the idea of a tattoo. She'd gotten a few since they'd graduated from high school, and Keith had gotten a big chain around his bicep since Bobby's last trip up the hill. But he didn't want to share this idea. She'd probably get him something for Christmas, and then he'd have *her* money on his skin. God—at least when he fucked on film, it was his own doing, his own choice.

He didn't feel owned by anybody—not with Trish, not with Dex, not with Ethan taking stills that afternoon. It felt same as carpentry.

Honest work.

What was he doing?

Waiting tables, he lied. *Text you when I get home.* He'd never told her about the miserable trailer with thirty guys on the floor, and he'd never told her he'd quit the job in construction.

He'd mentioned picking up shifts as a waiter—because Billy did that between gigs at Johnnies and school.

He could keep his lies straight because they were the same lies he'd been telling since August—but he'd never felt *bad* about the lies until now. This wasn't a lie to put a pretty face on an ugly truth. It wasn't a "don't worry about me" lie. It was a lie to get her off his back, because he didn't want to talk to her, even about everyday, ordinary things.

He'd rather talk to Reg. Hell, he'd rather talk to *any* of the guys at Johnnies—but really, he'd rather talk to Reg.

Ethan was standing, stretching, then paying and tipping his artist. Bobby noticed him but was still staring at the picture, wondering if he could put a hammer and a saw in the dragon's claws, because those things were apparently a part of him that weren't going away.

"You want some ink?"

Bobby smiled at him, his pretty face and warm brown eyes. Today had been hard work—but tomorrow? Tomorrow, being skin to skin with this sweet guy doing penance in ink? Felt a little like payday.

"Can't afford it," he admitted. "Sending money to Mom, helping Reg fix his place—"

"Oh my God!" Ethan stared at him, enraptured. "You're helping Reg fix up his house? That's *awesome*."

Bobby had to laugh. "You been there?" Of course he had. Bobby was getting the feeling Reg had hooked up off camera with as many guys as he'd fucked *on* camera.

"Yeah. Me and Reg hang sometimes when his sister's feeling okay." Ethan's face fell. "Families. Sisters. They can fuck you up, you know?"

Bobby regarded him steadily, because he knew Ethan had been kicked out of the house, but he didn't know particulars. "No sisters," he said in apology. "Only Mom." He thought of his father and Veronica. "But yeah. I've seen it get dire in other ways."

Ethan nodded. "Your mom? She's okay?" This answer seemed to matter to him, and Bobby wondered if maybe his mom had *not* been "okay."

"She's tired," he said after a thinking moment. "And sad. I wish I could give her more." He half laughed. "I'd fuck a lot of guys to get her the hell out of Dogpatch."

"Hunh."

"Hunh what?" Bobby searched his face, looking for clues.

"Just… you didn't say anything about getting your girlfriend out."

Bobby regarded him steadily. "No. I guess I didn't."

Ethan blew out a breath and smiled sadly. "Well, I am not the person to judge. None of us at Johnnies are. It's just…."

That pause went on so long Bobby could hear the buzz of the tattoo needle in it, and the long, slow exhalation of the twentysomething woman getting her girlfriend's name tattooed on her shoulder.

"What?" he finally asked.

"Living a double life—it's not… it's not good for you. I mean, last guy I know who did it tried to kill himself." Ethan blew out a breath. "Last two guys, really."

Bobby recoiled. "Oh Jesus. No!" He grimaced. "I mean, no on the killing myself. But yeah. I see your point. It's not good." He shrugged then. "I visit her about every two weeks. Used to be one week, but after I started at Johnnies…."

"Got busy," Ethan agreed. "Especially with waiting tables—"

"And fixing Reg's bathroom." Bobby grimaced, absentmindedly touching the poster again, because the dragon was cool. Ethan was stroking the smooth metal frame, so maybe Bobby wasn't the only one who liked to touch. "I think I'm going to bail on the visit this weekend so I can finish that. I don't like the idea of leaving it open while I'm up in Truckee."

"Well, that's a real nice thing," Ethan said admiringly. "And ooh—man, I hope you make your money soon. That's an awesome tattoo. Can you imagine it, mouth over your nipple, the body just riding down your ribs and curling the tail around your belly button?"

Bobby actually shuddered. "Oh damn," he breathed.

"Oh yeah." Ethan shook his head. "I hope you get a chance to get that," he said wistfully—and then winced, probably because his own tattoo hurt. He sighed. "We got a long day tomorrow...."

Bobby nodded. "Yeah. Time to go."

Ethan took him back to Johnnies to get his truck, and after he hopped out of Ethan's little hybrid and started the truck with a familiar rumble, he had a thought.

That should have felt like a date.

That *should* have felt like a date.

Dinner, an activity, time talking together.

But it felt no more like a date to him than having obligatory sex with Jessica when his mom was at work.

In fact, going over to Reg's house, working on his bathroom, and looking forward to a quiet dinner and talking in Reg's bed felt more like a date to him.

God. Bobby was having sex with more people—more *beautiful* people—than he'd ever dreamed of, and he was still more confused about who he should want to be with than he had ever been.

So Many Fish

REG'S THING against girls who liked freaky shit had nothing to do with jealousy, really; it had to do with convenience and effort.

Two people, naked, was a perfect equation in his eyes—touch, reciprocate, touch, reciprocate, touch, reciprocate, happy ending, happy ending, sex had been achieved! He didn't mind threesomes on set, because usually the director gave the whole thing shape: You, Reg, get the blowjob; you, Ethan, give the blowjob; you, Tango, fuck Ethan while he's working. And then change positions. So, again—touch, reciprocate, touch, reciprocate, touch, reciprocate, happy ending, happy ending, happy ending, sex had been achieved!

But the idea that a girl would go off and have sex with someone else if Reg didn't want to have the freaky sex with *her* didn't bother him. The problem was, once a girl did that—or left for a variety of other reasons, including "Man, you're a sweet guy, but your sister scares the shit out of me," she normally didn't come back, not even to have dinner or go to the movies or something.

To be a companion.

More and more, Reg treasured his Johnnies guys to be his companions.

Which was why he didn't really understand the feeling in his stomach when Bobby went off to film his scene with Ethan.

Bobby was Reg's friend, right? He did everything with Reg that the other guys did—hung out, had dinner, helped Reg with Veronica-watch. The only two differences were that Bobby knew how to fix Reg's house and didn't mind doing that, and, well, Bobby wasn't hooking up with him at night.

When Bobby stayed the night, they just… talked. Held hands. Rubbed backs. But they hadn't kissed, and while Reg got aroused—and Bobby did too, for that matter; Reg had seen him adjusting himself—they hadn't gotten naked.

No sex.

It was driving Reg bananas. He was starting to wonder if he'd done something wrong.

Bobby stayed at the apartment with all the guys the night between his stills and his shoot. He admitted that he slept better there, because it was easier to ignore all the sex than it was to keep an eye out for V, and Reg had insisted. But, dammit...

Reg missed him.

And the next night, the night after the scene, Bobby texted to say he was going to sleep at the apartment again. He'd won the coin flip for the bed and just wanted to curl up in a ball.

Reg could relate. When Bobby—or somebody—wasn't there, he just wanted to curl up into a ball too.

Which meant that when Trey texted after Bobby and asked if he could come by because only the air mattress was left, Reg said that was fine.

He knew what he was in for. He got V settled down after her horrible news program—the one that taught her to be afraid but that she was afraid to let go of—and cleaned up the kitchen, and then cleaned up his own bathroom, because it was getting more traffic now. Reg had seen Bobby's careful attention to detail, and he appreciated it, and admired the young man who paid it.

He was not sure why he kept thinking about that while he waited for Trey.

Trey himself was lanky and tall. Not as tall as Bobby or Lance, but when he stepped respectfully through the front door with a six-pack of beer in hand, Reg told himself he wasn't that tall anyway.

He should be grateful for lovers he didn't have to look up to.

He should be grateful that Trey wanted to kick back and drink a beer on his couch.

He should be grateful that Trey was a direct lover—none of this holding-hands bullshit, none of these secret, shy kisses on his shoulder or his cheek.

He should be *grateful* somebody wanted to share his bed, somebody who'd been trained, like Reg had, to give and receive.

Someone who'd been tested multiple times and who knew the score. Knew it wasn't lasting. Knew it wasn't big eyes and sweetness. Knew...

Knew that companions were friends and not lovers and that lovers should eventually be girls, even if that didn't seem the way Reg's life was going right now.

Knew that sex was as straightforward as dogs humping, and as necessary.

Knew there was no reason—none at all—why Reg should feel empty and sad after he'd blown his wad in Trey's mouth. No reason Reg should go to the bathroom to clean up after Trey came in his ass, to sit on the toilet for fifteen minutes, crying soft and silent tears.

THE NEXT morning Reg got a text from Bobby saying he was on his way over while Trey was still in the shower.

Reg stood, frozen, staring at his phone, wondering if he'd done anything wrong.

His eyes were still gritty and his chest still achy from the crying jag the night before, and he was still pondering, in a restless, distracted way, where those tears had come from.

He summoned a smile, though—Bobby was coming.

They were companions. That was good, right?

Still, when Reg opened the door for him, Bobby all fresh and scrubbed clean, his curly hair wet-combed back from his forehead, his long, sweet face lit up to see Reg, he couldn't stop the storm cloud feeling in his stomach that something was heinously wrong.

"Hey!" Bobby said brightly. "Was that Trey's car in front? Is this where he came last night?"

"Yeah," Reg said, trying not to fidget. "He came over and we hung out."

Bobby stepped fully into the house, his eyes tracking everything—V sitting on the couch with her breakfast, the small table full of mail that Reg had been sorting when he'd texted, and the empty six-pack sitting next to the fridge, waiting for recycling.

Trey, coming out of the shower in just his jeans, grinning like a man who'd had sex the night before.

"Hung out," Bobby said dully, and Reg wasn't imagining it. All the bright and shiny faded in his voice, leaving the air around them acrid with things unsaid.

"Yeah." Reg tried to smile and failed. "Like, you know, you and Ethan the night before."

"We shot a scene yesterday," Bobby said, voice pitchy and on edge. "Wasn't too much we could do the night before the scene."

Trey frowned, his heart-shaped, pretty face wrinkling in confusion. "Am I missing something? Bobby, are you mad at me? All the beds were taken, and Reg said I could come stay here—"

"No," Bobby said, but his voice made Reg shiver. Was that just because Reg had heard it warm and in the dark? "No—this is like… I guess this is just Johnnies, right? You forget. I mean, I fucked Ethan yesterday. No reason Reg shouldn't be with you last night. You're right. I just…."

"Sh!" Reg said desperately, looking behind his shoulder to see if V had heard. She hadn't, still immersed in the morning commentary of bigots, frauds, and thieves.

"Sorry," Bobby said automatically, but his face looked like it was made of stone and wood. "So sorry. I'll go get my stuff and finish the bathroom. You won't have to worry about me in the way anymore."

"You were never in the way!" Reg said desperately, not sure how to make this right, or if there was anything *to* make right. "I love having you. You don't have to talk about leaving like you're going somewhere."

"I am," Bobby said, his voice faraway. "I haven't visited home in a while. I need to go see my mom."

"And your girlfriend," Reg said bitterly, surprised at the bloody well of rancor he discovered in his chest. "Don't forget to visit *her*."

Bobby's eyes widened, shocked maybe, because that was almost written policy—you didn't mention girlfriends, spouses, boyfriends, people who wouldn't approve of what they did.

People who'd get mad.

"I won't," he said with a faint lifting at the corner of his mouth. "Thanks for reminding me, Reg. I really need to start looking for a place for her too." He turned around, all the promise that had been in his stride petrified to sullen stone.

"Wait!" Reg said, almost desperate. "Bobby… we, uh, Trey and me, we were going to get donuts. Uh, want some?"

Bobby's chin threatened to crumple, and Trey looked at Reg meaningfully. "Reg, how 'bout you go get donuts for all of us—me and Bobby will—"

"No!" Bobby said almost desperately. "No. I mean, sure. I'll have donuts. How 'bout you two go get them. I'll watch V and haul lumber and you don't have to mind me. I'm hired help. But free. Don't worry about it.

Not a problem. You'll be in the way while I'm hauling lumber anyway." He practically ran out of the house then, slamming the door behind him.

Trey turned to Reg with deep regret written on his pretty face. "Oh, Reg. You should have told me—"

"What?" Reg asked, that surprising bitterness not spitting out of his mouth fast enough. "That he comes over at night and holds my hand? That's all he wants from me. Just… a companion. Not… not a… a… whatever—"

"Boyfriend?" Trey asked sharply.

"Don't you have to be gay to have a boyfriend?" Reg asked, legitimately confused.

Trey wrinkled his entire face. "Oh, baby. I hate to break this to you but—"

"Gay people are nasty," V said, emerging from the living room with precision timing. "They're sneaky. Want everybody to be gay. Want to make us make it illegal to not be gay."

Reg gaped at her, his entire brain feeling like a mouse in a washing machine set on spin. "V, gay people are nice. You gotta not listen to those assholes on TV."

"That's not true," Veronica snapped, before glaring at Trey. "I don't like this one—he smirks. Where's Bobby?"

Trey blew out a breath. "Bobby is outside, waiting for me to go get donuts. Reg, I'll be back in an hour."

Sure he would. After he and Bobby talked like grown-ups and left Reg here in the kitchen to sulk and worry like a child.

Reg's chest hurt, and his breath wouldn't come all the way, stopped up like it did when you were in the pool too long and your lungs were slogging through half a gallon of chlorine.

"Maybe me and V can come with you?" Reg asked desperately. God, he wanted to talk to Bobby alone—that was all. Just explain to him, how Trey was his friend, a quick lay, just a thing, but Bobby was… more. Bobby meant more. Bobby was a *companion*, and Reg didn't want that to end.

Trey sighed. "You and V stay here," he said. "I'll take Bobby to go get donuts. Reg, you and me, or you and Dex or Ethan or someone need to talk. I think you've got this whole…" Trey glared at Veronica, clearly out of patience. "Thing," he spat, "wired in your head wrong. But I can't explain it now, and you and Bobby need to set things right between you in your own way."

Reg's throat ached. "It feels so wrong," he said, and his voice came out thick and broken. "It felt wrong last night—"

"You should have said something," Trey murmured. "Why didn't you?"

"I didn't have the words." Reg sank into the kitchen chair and stared at his hands as they dangled between his thighs. "And I still don't."

From the front yard, they heard a clatter of boards and pipes hitting the ground.

"Well, Bobby's got some," Trey muttered, pulling his hand through his hair. "And judging from that racket, they're all bad. Here—I'm gonna go put a shirt on." He grimaced, the grooves piling up on the sides of his cheeks. "Veronica, what kind of donuts do *you* like?"

"Chocolate ones," she said, her voice mellowing. "That would be real nice. Thank you."

"You're welcome, sweetheart." Trey turned toward the bedroom, and probably to the shirt he'd brought with his shaving kit the night before. "Reg, you sit there and think of some words, okay? I'll try to calm Bobby down."

Trey disappeared, and Reg stared at the door disconsolately. His entire life he'd acknowledged that he wasn't bright. Whatever a brain needed to be good with words or numbers, to be quick with ideas or creative, Reg's brain didn't have it.

But in his entire life, he'd never felt so piss-stupid as he did at this moment here.

Breaks and Fixes

BOBBY COULDN'T look Trey in the face—and the guy was his roommate, and Bobby even liked him.

"Bobby, man—look, I didn't realize it was like that with the two of you, I swear!"

"There was nothing to know," he said numbly. God. There wasn't, was there? Nothing to know. They touched. They held hands. Bobby stroked his hair, his face, held him close. Wasn't sex. Wasn't a relationship. Bobby had a girlfriend.

The thought made his eyes burn more, and he pulled the last of the lumber out of the truck. "Yeah, right," Trey snapped. "That's why you look like I killed your dog."

Bobby tried to pull himself out. "I don't have a dog."

"Oh dear God. *Bobby.* What's it going to hurt to admit you got attached to the guy! I mean, Reg is supposed to be the dumb one—"

"*He's not dumb!*" Bobby snarled, dropping his tool chest and swinging around to confront Trey. A red mist passed in front of his eyes, and suddenly he could see himself waling on this perfectly innocent, perfectly *nice* person who had never wronged him, not really, and certainly not on purpose.

"Okay, absolutely," Trey said, holding his hands up and looking alarmed. "I can see that. Not dumb. He's not. *You* are."

Bobby gaped like a fish and became aware of the violence in his muscles. Oh God. Just like his old man. A mean, bitter fucker who swung first and asked questions later.

"I'm sorry," he said, trying to find his footing. "I... I don't know why—"

"Because you care for the guy," Trey said softly. "Look—man, our job, it can fuck you up about stuff like this, but I've seen you with him. The day he was sick, you were almost frantic. You've been... been trying to be a part of his life."

"He doesn't want that." Bobby ached in every joint in his body. Was this what his mother felt like? Disappointed every day of her life? Was this what made you old? "This?" He gestured to the work behind him. "This was just… to him this is just what friends do. So… I'll be…." A hookup? God. He couldn't go in and hook up with Reg. He didn't want to hook up with *anyone* right now. Wouldn't that be using, the same way Keith used him? "I'll fix his bathroom," Bobby said miserably. "And then I'll go home and see my girlfriend and work Johnnies down here until I can move her down."

Trey grunted and pulled a hand through the longish part of his hair on top of his head. "Bobby…. Man, is that going to make you happy? Is never seeing him again going to make you happy?"

"I coulda hit you," Bobby said, still appalled. "I… I'm not ever gonna be that fuckin' guy."

Trey closed his eyes. "I don't think that's why it was going that way," he said with what sounded to be exaggerated patience. He opened his eyes. "If you feel strong enough about someone to—"

Bobby closed his eyes and shuddered. "See this?" he snarled, showing the bumps on his clavicle. "Broken three times, and not 'cause I loved skateboarding. I've seen what an asshole with a fist can do. I'm *never* gonna be that fuckin' guy."

"Jesus," Trey muttered. "I think you're wrong," he said, voice growing stronger. "I think you're wrong, and I think you're doing this wrong, and I think you're throwing something away that could really be special. We all love Reg, but none of us ever just lay next to him and talk to him. And yes, Bobby, that came up in bed last night. It was like hearing your boyfriend talk about his ex during orgasm, thank you very much, and now I know why."

Bobby felt all the blood leave his face. His breath came up short, and spots flickered behind his eyes. "That… that makes it worse," he whispered, not sure why.

"Because what me and Reg were doing—that was sex. It was athletic, like stretching a muscle or bungee jumping. What *you* and Reg were doing?" Trey's voice broke, when Bobby had been keeping his steady. "That was real," he said. "Jesus, Bobby—don't give up something real because Reg got confused. This shit confuses people *not* in porn. It confuses the hell out of *me*, or I'd be with a guy right now."

Bobby's laugh had blood and glass in it. "Neither of us are gay?" And yes. It came out like a question. Because… because his chest felt ripped open. Because the thought of Reg's compact, sleek body naked in bed with this sweet guy stopped his fucking breath.

"Oh Jesus," Trey snarled, suddenly as angry as Bobby had been. "You fucking deserve to be miserable. How long is it going to take you to put their house back together?"

"Three or four hours," Bobby said, lost and a little scared. "If I haul ass."

"I'll give you five. Fucking haul ass. I'm going to take that poor kid and his freaky-assed sister out to breakfast and then clothes shopping, because everything she owns looks handed down by clowns. Be gone by the time they get back. If you can't get past 'I'm not gay,' you're not ready to take care of *yourself*, much less Reg."

Bobby gaped at him. They were roommates—they kidded, they shared the remote control, they raced each other for the couch. This level of depth—it boggled him.

"I—"

Trey shook his head abruptly. "You'll just fucking hurt him," he said. "Take your truck around the corner—go get your own goddamned donuts. Be back in twenty minutes, and then don't come back here at all." He turned back toward the house and paused, shoulders slumped. "You probably think I hate you," he said, voice softer, pained. "I don't. I like you, Bobby. You're a good roommate, a good guy. But too many of us have been dicked around by guys who won't cop to liking guys. I just... not with Reg. I just can't."

"Yeah," Bobby said gruffly, remembering that last time with Keith, his body draping over Bobby's, the bills wadded in Bobby's back pocket. "Yeah." He had to turn away then because the memory did it for him, and his eyes were swimming with tears. He made it around the corner and to McDonald's for coffee, and was back at Reg's half an hour later.

He finished his work in record time, because the house was empty. There was nobody there to talk to, nobody to "help" him clean up, nobody to help him with his tools, nobody to offer him a break and a beer and a moment to stop and take a breath.

Nobody to hold hands with.

Nobody to whisper secrets in the dark.

Nobody to look at him like he was special, and Bobby and only Bobby could make him happy.

Three and a half hours, and the bathroom looked brand-new. White tile on the floor, new plumbing under it. Bobby left a quart of paint at the closet, with a brush and instructions for how to paint the inside, if Reg wanted to keep his towels splinter-free.

He swept up, loaded the trash in his truck, and drove away.

By the time he got to the Kohl's parking lot about a block away from his apartment, he was sobbing so hard he couldn't breathe. Lance found him there an hour later, still shaking. He made Bobby unlock the cab so he could get in and sit in the passenger seat.

"Trey called me," he said quietly.

"I… I'm not sure how I fucked up," Bobby said, feeling hollowed out. "I'm not sure why this hurts so bad."

"Yeah." Lance grabbed the keys dangling from the ignition. "C'mon. Let's go inside."

Bobby was never sure what happened next. How things went from ice cream to vodka to Lance, moving gently inside him…

Kissing his tears as Bobby whispered Reg's name.

HIS MOM was working overtime that weekend. He told her he'd come up the next weekend for sure, which got them damned close to Thanksgiving territory. He picked up four extra shifts at Hazy Daze and one extra scene at Johnnies without the stills shoot. On the plus side, his "own apartment" fund was growing fatter, and Dex had told him that his video downloads were through the roof, so once he started getting a percentage from those, he'd be able to move out.

Which was good, because life in the flophouse was becoming… tangled.

After his night with Lance, he managed to pretend it was all okay— nothing to see here, just a boy experimenting with his sexuality. He moved through the rest of his days in sort of a void. He would think *Hey, I should see how Reg is doing*—And then his heart would swell and ache, and he'd ask himself *Why? What do I offer him, if I go to his house?* And he'd be headachy and out of it for the next few hours. He waited tables on automatic, did the dishes on automatic, texted Jessica back on automatic.

His heart felt like an aging cardboard box in the rain. Only the memory of what he was supposed to be held him up.

A week and a half after he finished the bathroom—the only way he could think of that day—he woke up to an urgent voice in his ear. "Bobby, grab this."

And he grabbed it. On automatic.

"Mmm… wait—no—keep squeezing."

"Skylar?" Bobby mumbled, facedown on the air mattress. His hand draped over the side, and round and firm in his palm was… well…. "Is that your cock?"

"Yeah. Keep stroking… c'mon…."

Automatic. It was just… so easy. Like having sex with Lance or showing up to work and waiting tables or servicing humans. He stroked smooth and even, letting Skylar's uninhibited moans drive him on.

"Yes… oh my God… Bobby, your hands are great!" Skylar propped himself up on his elbows, and Bobby could see him now, surfer-blond hair tousled, tanned, defined body stretched out on the floor.

"Why aren't you in bed with Rick?" Bobby asked dumbly, but Skylar had just spurted a little bit of precome, and Bobby knew his cue now. He squeezed at the base, then stroked up to the head and teased that.

"'Cause Rick's watching," Rick said from Bobby's other side. He *was* watching—with his dick out, hand stroking happily.

"Oh my God, you two," Bobby mumbled. "Why don't you just stop with the sex games already and admit—"

"Yes! Yes! Oh man! Bobby! Please! Faster!" Bobby complied, too numb and too sad to even ask himself if this qualified as sex, perversion, or just helping out a buddy in need.

"Admit what?" Rick asked, eyes opening and cock deflating at the same time.

"Admit you're in love!" Bobby snapped, just when Skylar moaned "*Yes!*" and jizzed all over his hand.

The silence was almost as painful as Bobby's thickening hard-on squashed against the air mattress.

"We're in what?" Skylar asked, voice in the postorgasmic loopiness phase Bobby was starting to recognize.

"Love," Bobby said irritably. "Jesus, who's got the tissues?"

Skylar took a handful from the box by the TV and passed it to Bobby, who started to wipe off his hand. "What makes you say that?" he asked, and to his credit, he sounded genuinely puzzled.

But Bobby got a good look at the devastation on Rick's face. "Never mind," he said, feeling like ass.

Rick shrugged and turned away, and finally Skylar looked at him. "Rick?"

"I don't know why he said it," Rick lied.

"Wait—wait, Bobby—why would you say a thing like that?"

Bobby saw the confusion, the cluelessness, and his irritation wiped away like the come on his hand. "You guys do everything together. You work at the gym, you see movies, you eat. You talk and screw around, and Jesus—did you or did you not try to get me to go walking in the fucking park with you two days ago?"

"But," Skylar said, looking hurt, "it's Capitol Park. It's nice this time of year—and, you know, it's free."

Bobby nodded. "Yeah, Skylar, but when I couldn't go 'cause I had work, you went together anyway. And you may not have held hands, but I'd put *money* on the fact that at some point in the walk, each one of you wanted to, and you just pulled back. 'Cause I know how that feels. And it's bullshit. It got me where I am now, eating my fucking heart out and going up to visit my girlfriend because I can hold hands with her and not have to change my entire goddamned idea of who I am. But you guys don't give a shit about any of that. You just… just screw everybody in your apartment in the hopes that nobody figures out that who you really want to screw is *each other*. Every day, all the time, only fucking you!"

"Rick?" Skylar asked, voice lost. "Rick—is that…?"

But Rick's back was toward him, his shoulders drooping, his entire body screaming defeat, and Bobby was suddenly a third wheel instead of a valuable cog in a threesome.

Well, he was slowly learning, wasn't he? The difference between sex and love.

"We were having fun," Rick said, voice low and aching. "You know. Didn't want to spoil the fun, because if I spoiled the fun, maybe I wouldn't have you anymore."

Oh God. Bobby wanted to put his face in his hands and howl.

"But…." Skylar pushed up, shamelessly naked in his body, cluelessly naked in his soul. "But you'll always have me, bro. I mean, you and me—why would we split up?"

Bro. Bobby was listening to confessions of love, and Skylar used the word "bro." Laugh, cry, or throw up—he was on for all three.

"Because Bobby's right," Rick said sadly. He turned around and rolled his eyes. "He was a prick about it, and his timing sucked, but he was right."

Bobby shook his head. "You involved me in a kinky threesome before coffee," he said, hating everybody. "I regret nothing."

"Whatever," Rick snorted. "I'm in love with you, Sky. I... I loved you from our first scene. But you were all... free sex! Let's play! And I... man, I was along for the ride."

Skylar started to laugh as he draped himself along Rick's back. "Well, it was fun," he defended. "But, you know. Only 'cause you played too."

"But... *love*. I... I don't know if I can keep playing with you, now that you know I—"

Skylar pulled his chin around and kissed him, so tenderly, so sweetly, Bobby forgot all about the rude awakening and the weird threesome and remembered all the things he used to yearn for when Keith Gilmore was sucking him off.

These guys together—they made Keith look like an ass clown. The give and the take of them, the way Skylar held Rick's chin, the way Rick closed his eyes—it wasn't for a camera or for show.

It was for each other.

"Keep playing with me," Skylar said softly. "And I'll keep playing with you. And only with you. And that's all I need. It's all I ever needed."

"Sky?"

Bobby wondered if that was Skylar's real name, because if it really was, Reg could quit kicking himself for the whole Digger thing that wasn't quite sticking.

Fuck. Reg.

"I love you too, Derrick. Jeez, don't be dense."

Rick turned around, and they started kissing some more, in earnest, stumbling until they made it to the door to their room, slamming it behind them.

Bobby stared after them, confused and heartsick and stunned and still deliriously happy for them at the same time.

"Well, that was the damnedest thing," Lance said from the couch.

Bobby swung his legs over the edge of the mattress and stared at him, running his hands through his longish hair. "Lance, don't take this the wrong way, 'cause you all been really decent to me and I appreciate the hell out of that, but I think I need my own place."

Lance regarded him with compassion. "Things too messy here, farm boy?"

He grimaced. "Sex confuses things," he said and then remembered he was probably going to have to have sex with Jessica, and his stomach cramped.

"Yeah." Lance shrugged, and in the silence they both heard the unmistakable sounds of Skylar and Rick doing what they apparently did best. "And sometimes it makes them really wonderful."

"Haven't had that happen yet," Bobby confessed. The moment of his audition, when he was coming down from afterglow and Reg was stroking his hair back from his face, kept running through his mind. "Maybe once," he whispered.

"Whatever you have to do to get back to that," Lance told him. He stood up and let the blanket fall down his fine athlete's body while he stretched. "You can shower first, I'll make coffee, and then we can go work out before you leave for the hills."

Bobby nodded, thinking that he'd really, really miss this place if he left.

And that he absolutely, positively had to fuckin' leave.

HOME.

The tiny house on Frank Gilmore's property had peeling paint that Frank wouldn't let them paint over, peeling linoleum he wouldn't pay to replace even if Bobby did the work, and plumbing that groaned like an old whore because Frank was waiting for it to rust and explode.

Jessica clinging to him like a limpet when she got off work, grabbing for Bobby's cock the minute they were alone, and planning their wedding and their apartment and their children and their lives, never pausing for breath or giving Bobby a chance to tell her no, no, he couldn't be her knight in shining armor—she was going to have to do what he did and rescue herself.

His mom, trying to cook things for him like chicken Alfredo when a grilled cheese would do, stared at him worriedly, trying to figure out the changes, from the waxed eyebrows to the bulging muscles to the grim look even *he* knew rode his face when he wasn't paying attention.

And Keith Gilmore, blackmailing him into giving a blowjob, every goddamned time.

This time Bobby hit the line. The line where he didn't give a shit what Keith thought of him. He was a *professional* at giving a goddamned blowjob—he knew how to squeeze, how to stroke, and goddammit, he was getting to be an expert at the spit grope. He had Keith shaking and ready to come with two fingers up his ass before he could say the words "Don't do it, faggot!"

This time he moved out of the way while Keith shot come all over the hay bales in his daddy's barn.

"Damn," Keith swore throatily, his knees buckling as he landed on the slide of hay coming off the bale stack. "Jesus, Vern—I shoulda clocked ya for doin' that, but God, that was amazing."

"Thank you," Bobby said, going to the sink to wash up. He had a chubby going on in his shorts, because this was his profession, he guessed, and getting aroused was part of it, but all in all, he felt pretty damned dispassionate about this scene now.

Those moments with Reg, lying in bed, looking to see Reg's eyes glint as they told secrets, held hands, laughed softly—that seemed to matter so much more than going down on his knees in this dusty damned barn.

"You been studying up?" Keith asked suddenly, voice hard. "Sucking other dicks than mine?"

Bobby looked over his shoulder and rolled his eyes. "What's it to you?" He grabbed a hand towel and wiped off his hands and face, then pulled some lip balm out of his pocket to soften the cock burn around his mouth.

He'd had a scene three days before, and sucking a dick for four hours tended to leave a mark.

Keith got up and buttoned his jeans, then pulled his sweatshirt over his head. "What's it to me? You're my goddamned—"

Bobby cut him off before he could take another step, fisting his hands in Keith's sweatshirt and shoving him back up against the hay bales. "Goddamned what?" he growled. "Goddamned whore? Goddamned property?"

He couldn't mistake the hurt on Keith's face, but he was beyond caring. "I thought we were friends!" Keith swallowed. "But look at you— you're all buffed out and waxed—your hair's cut special. Hell, your jeans ain't even worn. You got yourself a sugar daddy down in the city, Vern? 'Cause I won't hold for no—"

Oh Jesus. "Let's get one thing straight," Bobby said, making sure Keith was looking directly at him. "I would have done anything for you once. Yes. Fucking anything. But right now, the only reason—the *only* reason—I just got down on my knees is that my mom lives in this fucking town too. But that's not going to be the case always. So the day I can pack up and move her ass the hell out of here, you will forget you ever begged me for it and we can end our association. Are we clear?"

"What about my sister?" Keith snarled. "Aren't you going to take her too?"

Hell to the fuck no. "Whether I do or not," Bobby told him, relentless, "it has nothing to do with you wanting your dick sucked."

"Jesus, you fuckin' whore—"

Yup. At least Bobby knew what he was at this point. No illusions there. "I am what you made me," he said simply. "You're lucky you got the finger bang for free."

He dropped Keith then—just dropped him—and walked out to his truck. Keith's house was within walking distance of the barn, so he felt no qualms at all jumping in the cab and driving back to his mother's house.

His pocket buzzed as he pulled up the gravel-and-mud driveway.

For a minute he was tempted to ignore it, thinking it was Jessica talking about getting off work. There *was* a text to that effect, and he answered a vague *That's okay—go home and I'll see you tomorrow*, but he had to type every letter twice because he was sweating so badly.

There was another text. This one from Reg.

I miss you. I didn't mean to make you so mad.

Oh Jesus. Jesus. Bobby had just walked away. Had he left as big a hole in Reg's life as Reg had left in his?

I miss you too. I was more mad at myself, and I didn't want to be an asshole.

He stared at the phone, wondering what Reg would do with that.

You can visit again, if you like.

Bobby closed his eyes and imagined what he'd do when he got home. Waiting tables. Fucking guys. Finding an apartment and moving his air mattress in.

Hanging out with Reg?

Could he do it?

Could he come in and have a beer and play video games and talk and not touch Reg's hand? Not rub his back? Not want to....

He did. He wanted to kiss Reg all the time.

Because God, yes. Touching without kissing... he kissed the guys at Johnnies on set all the time. Hell—Lance had kissed him during that hallucinogenic, drunken pity fuck.

Was that what Bobby had been missing? Reg's lips on his own? Had he been working up to that?

Hell.

He was going to type *I can't*. He was.

But he remembered Rick saying "If I spoiled the fun, I couldn't have you anymore."

How long had they been roommates? How long had Rick pretended he wasn't in love, just so he could be next to Skylar, doing things with him? Just so they could *be* together.

I'd like that, he wrote. Bobby wouldn't dick with him. He'd keep his promise to Trey. He would. No touching. No... yearning. They'd be friends. Rick and Skylar had done it. Bobby could do it. He added, *Make sure it's okay with Trey first.*

Bobby and Trey had been civil to each other. They made each other coffee if the other one was up. Bobby offered him the couch if Trey got in late from his other job. But Bobby wouldn't forget that moment when they'd been chest to chest with each other over the man on the other end of Bobby's phone right now.

He said to ask you. Said you were feeling sad.

Augh! God love those guys in that damned apartment.

I was. I didn't want to leave things like that. I'm glad you texted.

Me too. What are you doing now?

Bobby smiled a little. So normal. Like he hadn't been the walking dead for nearly two weeks.

Going in to say hi to Mom. She's making dinner for me. Probably us and the TV tonight.

Is she nice?

Oh hell. Had Bobby not even talked about his mother during those moments of holding him? He must have. Maybe that's why Reg was curious.

She's the best. She loves me. Sacrificed a shit-ton so I could have a truck and go down to Sac and work. I want to get her out of here.

Does she want to go?

That there was an important question, wasn't it?

I suppose I should ask.

That's a good idea. I don't always know what people are thinking even if I see their face. Sometimes I need them to tell me.

Oh, ouch. Fucking ouch.

I'll text you when I'm back in town. I'll come over to watch TV on Thursday if you want. Bring dinner.

That'll be real nice. Thanks, Bobby.

Course.

Bobby scrubbed his face with his hands and tried to fight the burn behind his eyes. Sucking Keith's dick hadn't done it. Seeing Sky and Rick together hadn't done it. Spending the night before with Jessica, watching her shamelessly use him like a ten-inch human dildo, hadn't done it.

A few lines of text from Reg had broken through, shattered that self-protective layer of scar tissue he'd worked so hard to spread over his heart.

Dammit, Reg—how am I going to do this if I can feel shit again?

"VERN?"

Bobby yanked his attention away from the far horizon and focused on his plate. Mom used old china, the kind with wreaths of wildflowers under a crackled finish, when she was serving something special.

"Sorry, Mom," he said, taking a bite. "It's really good. I'm just—"

"About a hundred miles away," his mom said, smiling faintly. "Seriously—I called your name three times."

Ugh. "The guys at work call me Bobby." He grimaced apologetically. "You know, 'cause Roberts?"

His mom recoiled. "Well, *I'm* still calling you Vern," she said, sounding affronted.

Good call, Mom. It would have been awkward to have his mother call him by his porn name.

"That's fine. I'm just thinking… you know."

"No," she said quietly. "I don't know. Explain."

He grimaced. "Do you want to live here forever?"

Her eyes opened. "Do you want to take me away from all this?" She sounded half-kidding, but also a little wistful.

"If I could…," he said haltingly, "if I could get us a nice apartment in Sacramento, someplace near where you could get a job, would you work there? Could we… I dunno. Never come to fuckin' Dogpatch again?"

She didn't reprimand him for his language—but then, she never had. "I wouldn't mind. But Vern, don't you want to save that sort of thing for your girlfriend?"

He groaned. "Mom…."

"You're not breaking up with her, are you?"

"Well, not now," he mumbled. "But… I'm not sure if, well, being in two places is exactly…." *Conducive.* He knew the word. He didn't like sounding too smart in front of his mother. "Good for a relationship. It's… it's hard enough when you're right there with them, across the couch, you know?"

"Vern, do you have another girl?" His mother looked concerned, and he didn't blame her. "I didn't raise you like that."

"No other girl," he said, sighing. She hadn't mentioned boys. Or hookups. Or women who made his penis hard and helped him ejaculate for the job. There had only been two of those—might not ever be more—but he had to think of them in a way that didn't count. "Just… Mom, would you hate me if, if maybe I was a little different than you thought I was?"

"Like smarter than your grades?" she asked grimly. "Because we covered this through high school."

He grimaced. Hadn't gotten the best grades. Swim team, wrestling, partying out by the swimming hole, finding a job—anything sounded better than sitting down and doing math and English when kids like him didn't go to college.

In a million years, he didn't think he would have realized the joy of random paperbacks, passed around by friends, to be read and discussed like television shows that no one had time to watch, but it was too late now to go back and take English again. Besides…

That wasn't what he was talking about.

"I mean… like, settling down with a nice local girl and having babies," he said, because that was a start.

Her expression lightened around the eyes, so much so that she looked years younger, young enough to be Bobby's mother, young enough to go have another life besides this one.

"Oh, Bobby. Why do you think I wanted you to do better in school so bad? I mean…." She shook her head. "My whole life, I thought there was something bigger than hanging in a small town and having a kid. Not that I wasn't happy to have *you*," she hastened to say, "but your dad...." She looked at her hands and swallowed. "Sometimes I think the reason he was so angry, and drank so much, was that he wanted out too. But he just... he didn't want to make the sacrifices, you know?" She closed her eyes. "Making your life work the way you want it to—you've got to give some things up."

"Oh," Bobby said, thinking he understood very much. "So... like giving up the person you care for the most, because they're not who you're supposed to have."

"No!"

Bobby looked up from his dinner—which was still tasty cold, thank God—because his mother was seldom that vehement. "No?"

"No—I'm talking, like giving up a night of beer with your buddies to stay home and be with the person you want to be with more. Fixing your house instead of partying. Working instead of calling in sick. Those are all acceptable sacrifices, you understand?"

"But people?" he asked, wanting to hear it from his mother, because the words might not give him courage, but they'd definitely give him hope.

"People shouldn't be given up," she said, her voice sinking. "Not if they make you happy."

He smiled a little. Okay. He didn't have to give Reg up. He'd go back home, find a place to move his mom, and hang out with Reg again. They could be friends. He could do this, have a friend.

Nobody had to know that he wanted more. Nobody had to know that he dreamed of sleeping with Reg in his arms, like he had when Reg had been sick. Nobody had to know that he thought about Reg's mouth, lean but surprisingly soft-looking, and wondered—now that he knew what a man's mouth could feel like—what would that mouth do on his body?

Nobody had to know but Bobby.

Not even Reg.

That Word Again

"So," Bobby said, kicking back on the couch and smiling, "you ready for me to work on your house again?"

Reg thought about the bathroom, gleaming and perfect, and how the floor didn't crackle under his feet anymore. The day Bobby had left, when they all got back from shopping, Reg had gone into the bathroom and painted the shelf.

His job wasn't smooth and perfect, but the job was his own, and even though he'd been upset—hurt, and sad, and all sorts of things he couldn't put a name to—he'd been proud too.

Bobby had left him a job and trusted he could do it.

Which was why he'd been dying, in little teeny increments, when Bobby didn't text him the next day. Or the next.

He'd fucked it up. He wasn't sure how—he wasn't even sure *what* they were—but he'd fucked it up. It upset him so bad that the next time Trey asked to come over, Reg asked him, somewhat disconsolately, if maybe Bobby could come with him.

Oh jeez, Reg. Do you really want Bobby?

I thought he was my friend. Why won't he even text me anymore?

He was sitting on the couch after dinner, tuning out Veronica's show. Bobby had left a paperback the last time he'd been there—a thriller by some guy named Lee Child. Reg had tried to read it three or four times, but he just couldn't get beyond how much he didn't care about Jack Reacher. He wanted to ask Bobby about it, see if there were any books about people he could care about.

But he was afraid to text him, because Bobby had never texted back.

And now it looked like Trey wasn't texting either. Oh, wait—

I told him not to. I didn't want him messing with your head.

Reg stared at the text, a surprising anger surging in his chest. Of all the....

I'm not a little kid, he'd texted. *Me and Bobby, we still had stuff to work out. He was my... companion? ... friend, and I made him feel bad.*

118

Sorry, Reg.

Reg grimaced—he really couldn't hold a grudge for shit.

It's okay. But is he there at the apartment?

He's out of town. I take it you don't want me to come over?

Reg thought about it.

I think it would confuse things right now, he texted regretfully.

No sex, I promise.

Reg stared at that. Oh God. That was the thing, wasn't it? The thing that was hanging him up about Bobby? Bobby hadn't made a move—sex didn't seem to be on the table. They seemed to be *more* than sex, right? More important?

But did he have to stop having sex with other people to have the *more* than sex with Bobby? Wouldn't he eventually get horny? He knew he was sort of special, down to fuck, all the time, anytime, but seriously—no sex?

Except, thinking about the look on Bobby's face as he walked out of the kitchen sort of shrank his boner anyway.

Okay. At least until I get my head sorted.

Good plan. I'll bring beer.

So Reg and Trey sat side by side on the couch and watched TV. No sex. None of the cuddling Bobby had been doing. Just… watched TV. And Reg thought *Hey! I can do this! I get this no-sex thing! I have sex on set all the time—why do I need to have sex in my regular life?*

He was good with that. He was *great* with it.

And then he texted Bobby, and Bobby said he'd come back, but same thing. No sex. And no touching either.

And Reg wanted to cry at first, because dammit—getting laid was the one thing he could do right! But God—anything was better than Bobby being gone and mad.

So fine. No sex. No touching. For weeks.

And it was driving Reg insane.

"The house?" he said blankly, staring at Bobby's mouth. Was it his imagination, or had that lush, wide mouth grown lusher and wider? He'd been doing a lot of scenes—did sucking cock work out the lips like lifting weights worked out the arms? Reg figured his own mouth must be hella muscular—but not as sexy as Bobby's. Not as red. Not as wide and smiling. Not as pillowy when it was pursed.

"Yeah," Bobby said, smiling slightly. "I mean, I finally found a place to move in—I sign the lease after Christmas, but I paid first month's already—"

Reg wrinkled his nose. "Isn't that bass-ackward?"

Bobby shrugged, looking uncomfortable. "Yeah. Yeah, it is. But I did some work on the place for the apartment—I couldn't really afford it with just my savings. That's why I haven't offered to work on your house until now. I was busy fixing the stove so it didn't suffocate us and nailing all the baseboards down, redrywalling the bathroom, fixing the sliding glass door so it slid—"

"Oh my God!" Reg burst out. "*Bobby*—you're practically building this guy's apartment for him!"

Bobby blew out a breath. "Yeah," he sighed. "I know. But my mom—I mean, not before Christmas—probably not until spring. But I want to try to get her down here. Take care of her until she finds a job she likes. And the apartment is the first step, and then some furniture, and—"

"But doing that while you're working two jobs?" Reg could see it now. The bags under Bobby's eyes, the way the beer seemed to make him really mellow, really fast. "You must be exhausted."

Bobby yawned, hiding it apologetically behind his hand. "Well, yeah. I'm looking forward to having Thanksgiving weekend off," he said, trying to focus after the yawn almost took over his face.

"I'm going to Chase and Tommy's," Reg said happily. "They're having a thing." His face fell. "I can't stay long—I'm coming home with leftovers for V, but you're welcome to come." Veronica's meds had been cruising along, but Reg still waited for the prickle at the back of his neck to tell him that wasn't going to last. It never did with V.

Bobby grimaced. "You know? I wish. Skylar and Rick are going to Skylar's parents—I guess they're coming out and stuff."

Reg shivered. "Scary. They're so brave. Coming out is what got Ethan kicked out."

"Yeah." Bobby sighed. "And he's a good guy too."

"I think coming out is why…." Reg shook his head. He didn't want to gossip about Chase Summers and Tango anymore. It felt disloyal. They were his friends, and now that Chase was going to be okay and Tango was Tommy, they deserved privacy. He'd already learned that privacy was important, even if you showed your naked bits on the internet for the world to see.

"Why what?" Bobby asked, curious. He seemed to be curious about *all* the guys at Johnnies.

"Why Chase hurt himself," Reg said, hating to talk about the fact that he'd done that. It just… it hurt to think of him, tall, easygoing, big jock smile on his face. Reg had been right about him being two people— and apparently the other person had been screaming in pain for his whole entire life.

Reg didn't like to think about that. He wondered if he was strong enough to scream that long.

"Because he hadn't come out?" Bobby asked, nodding slowly. "Yeah—I'd heard that. So I'm glad for Rick and Skylar. They'll come out, and even if Mom and Dad don't know about the porn, you know, moms and dads don't always know everything, so it'll be okay. But Lance is going to his parents'—I guess he has to be Super Good Medical Student for them, so they don't know about the porn or the gay either."

Reg made a hurt sound. "Lance is a good guy," he said softly.

Bobby tilted back another swallow. "He is. And he doesn't deserve that. But Trey's gonna be there at the party, and I think Billy is too. So, lots of people. But I'm going back to Truckee." He let out a big sigh, like he didn't want to, and Reg was afraid to ask.

If he hated going to visit his girlfriend so much, why was she still his girlfriend? Dammit, Bobby deserved a… a… special friend who made him happy. Made him feel bright and shiny, like that was the reason sex was good.

Thinking about sex again made Reg focus on Bobby's throat as he swallowed the beer, on his chest as every breath stretched out the worn T-shirt he wore. His biceps were getting bigger, and his pecs, and the baby fat that had made him seem soft had melted away, leaving only the sweet, wide, smiling mouth.

That could suck cock like a dream—Reg had watched all his videos twice.

Bobby should be getting sex.

It was practically the only thought in Reg's head.

"You don't like Truckee?" Reg asked, because it was the last thing Bobby had said and all his other thoughts were of Bobby naked, of Bobby touching Reg's face, his shoulder, his back, *while naked*.

"I don't like... who I am when I'm there," Bobby said, thinking. "I... I'm just figuring stuff out here. But back home, I have to act like it never occurred to me, you know?"

"What never occurred to you?" Reg watched him lick his lower lip and then sink his teeth into it. Reg chewed his own lip in sympathy, because dammit, *he wanted to taste Bobby's red, swollen mouth.*

"That I'm not... not going to get married and have kids and get a job in fast food or law enforcement or anything else that's available up in the hills."

Reg frowned, distracted for the moment by the conversation. "Not get married?" he asked, the idea sort of rocking him back in his brain. "Why would you think you wouldn't—"

Bobby grimaced. "I'm not...." He smiled a little. "I've had three scenes with guys," he said after a moment. "I... I liked them. Liked them better than the scenes with the girls. And I think about it, and I've felt like that my whole life. What's that say?"

Oh. *It says you should be sleeping with me! It says there is no reason you and I shouldn't be having amazing sex right now. You can kiss my neck and rub my lips with your thumb. You can nuzzle my temple and rub my back. And all those things you did before, except with* sex.

Reg's cock ached in his jeans, and he was afraid if he actually said what he was thinking, he would jump on top of Bobby and *kiss* him. Slowly, intimately, in a way that said he wanted all those things—the sweetness, the touching, and oh my God, Bobby's cock in his ass!

And that might make Bobby go away again.

Because sex had cost him Bobby's company last time, and even when they were just watching TV, the company was so much more important than the sex.

Mostly.

Reg swallowed through a dry throat. "It's... I don't know," he said after a painful moment where—against all nature and most of his life's habit—he tried to beat his boner into submission by the not-awesome power of his not-awesome brain. And in that painful moment of arousal and hesitation, a truth emerged.

"I guess I always thought settling down with a girl was what I was supposed to want—but it's sort of a pipe dream, right? 'Cause I've got to take care of V. Can't have movie night without someone with her. Can't...."

He grimaced. "I mean, I wouldn't be no good kind of a father anyway, but I wouldn't bring a kid here. I… I guess I can keep hoping someone'll want me for longer'n a night, but you know. Not a brain trust. Right now I'm just lucky people still want to see me use my dick, right?"

Bobby's face did something complicated then. "You're kind," he said after a moment. "You're loyal. You are friends with *everybody*, and not just because you put out. You let easy stuff, things we take for granted—like beer, or a warm meal, or something fun on TV—make you happy. You don't judge. You're dedicated to someone who frequently tries to hurt you, and you remember that she doesn't want to be like this." Bobby closed his eyes tight, and when he opened them, they were shiny. "There's a lot more to you than how you use your dick, Reg. I just… I wish I could give you the long-term happy ending. Find a girl for you. Something."

Oh. Oh oh oh. This was not supposed to be about him.

He rubbed his chest, which had gotten all achy while Bobby was talking. He needed something easy to talk about. Something that would make Bobby laugh so his eyes weren't all shiny and he didn't look like he wanted to cry.

"Yeah," he said, giving what he hoped was a smile. "But I can still use my dick pretty good."

"Don't know," Bobby said, and it looked like he tried to smile, but only one corner of his mouth came up. "I haven't seen any of your porn."

And *that* made Reg laugh. "Well, I'm not showing it to you *now*. Find something good on TV, okay?"

"Yeah. Sure, Reg."

Reg had to look at him twice, because something in his voice sounded… wobbly.

But then *everything* in Reg felt wobbly, so he wasn't sure how he could help.

But as fall progressed, foggy and chill, Reg sure hoped *something* could help, because every visit Bobby paid was both wonderful and awful. Reg, who wasn't a fan of the long make-out session in the porn vids, was suddenly made terribly aware of how the slightest expression, word, *smile* from one person and one person alone could send him rocketing from zero to complete arousal in less than a heartbeat.

And he was terrified of letting on.

By the time Christmas rolled around and Bobby left to visit his family, the pressure in Reg's chest was so tight he almost couldn't breathe.

When he dropped the light foil three times in one shoot, Dex called a halt to the scene—which was fine because it was Lance and Rachel, and apparently neither one of them could say who was less attracted to the other.

"You guys, take five." Dex wrinkled his nose. "And Lance, go see if Billy is available. You guys can have a threesome. He at least knows what to do with…." He made a vague all-encompassing gesture.

"Tits," Rachel said dryly. "They're called tits, Dex, and it would be great if someone knew what to do with them, because this guy's trying to adjust the sound and nothing's coming. *Nothing* is coming."

Lance grimaced and grabbed his phone out of his pants, not even bothering to put on a towel. "Deal," he said. "Sorry, Rachel."

She gave him a sympathetic smile and pulled on a robe. "I know, hon. Not really your thing. We just… you know…."

"We got along so well," Lance sighed. "Yeah, that's my whole history with women." His phone vibrated. "He can be here in an hour." Lance frowned. "Half an hour if he doesn't need to douche."

Dex nodded. "We'll let him do oral on everybody, no penetration. Still testing but, you know—"

"Window," Lance and Rachel said in tandem. "Deal."

"Great. Now Reg, talk to me. What in the fuck?"

Reg grimaced. "Sorry, Dex. Just, you know…." He rubbed his chest, because he didn't want to talk about Bobby and the very weird, very *real* sort of conundrum he was facing.

"Stress?" Dex asked kindly. "What are you doing for Christmas?"

"Well, everyone's going places, you know? So just me and V. Bobby and I already picked out stuff for her."

Bobby had left Reg a present too—a couple of them. Reg told him that he didn't want to open them unless Bobby was there, and Bobby said he needed to wait until Bobby got back from Truckee, then.

That was okay.

Even though they'd picked out a small tree together, and put up paper ornaments like Reg had done since he was a kid, it wasn't going to feel like Christmas if he was alone.

But now Dex sighed. "Look—Skylar and Rick can't go back home."

"Yeah—the coming out thing...."

"Not so much, no. I'm pretty sure there's a couple of other guys who don't have much to do. I'll be out of town, but don't worry. Guys'll start calling you up, okay?"

Reg smiled, grateful to his toes. "We can have, like, a Christmas slumber party," he said. "If guys bring donuts, V's down for it."

She was being surprisingly docile right now. Bobby had bought a few more paperbacks to the house, and V dove right in with Reg. She liked pretty much everything Reg *didn't*, but that was okay. What wasn't okay—not really—was how little she had to say about the books. Reg thought it must be because she kept going off her meds, but she used to talk more about books. He was a little disappointed, really. He finally had something to say, like Jack Reacher was an asshole, and she couldn't give him any reason to like that book besides just "I liked it." He seemed to remember that when she'd been younger, she had good reasons for stuff. She used to talk about her English classes all the time. Of course, reading still gave her brain something to do besides obsess at the news she read on the computer, which was always a good thing.

Dex frowned, though. "There's something else—we've done this before, and you haven't been this jumpy."

Oh. This was embarrassing. "I haven't had sex in almost two months," Reg told him apologetically. "I mean, you know, besides sex on set."

Dex's eyes widened. "Holy Mother of God."

"I *know*! I am horny *all* the fuckin' time!" Oh Lord, was it good to talk to somebody about this.

"But Reg! *Why?*" Dex looked genuinely concerned, and Reg didn't blame him. His reputation was well founded.

But Reg didn't have an answer for him either. He just rubbed his chest and shrugged. "Shit," he said thoughtfully, "is changing."

This was true. Chance and Tango weren't working anymore. Dex wasn't starring in the videos anymore. Reg hadn't seen John in a month, and there seemed to be girls *everywhere*.

Reg remembered when he *hungered* for girls to be on the set, and this seemed to be the bitterest of jokes, because now he just wanted to go home in case a *man* showed up, one who didn't even want sex.

Dex blew out a breath and started scanning images of Lance and Rachel's shoot. Most of them sucked, but Dex kept them anyway. You never erased people fucking—sometimes you just couldn't be that picky. "You are telling me. Okay, buddy—for whatever reason you're cutting back on the sex. Don't worry. We still got your back. No Christmas alone for you."

"Thanks, Dex. When Bobby gets back, you know—it'll be better."

Dex paused, his thumb on the Forward key. "Bobby? You and Bobby hanging out now?"

"Well, he took real good care of me when I was sick. And, you know. He likes to come hang out."

"And you don't have sex," Dex said slowly, just to make sure.

"Well, you know. He's straight."

Dex pursed his lips and looked at the computer screen again. "Sure he is," Dex muttered. "Everybody's fucking straight. Except none of the straight people are signing on to fuck girls. That's my life."

Reg wasn't sure what that meant. "I thought Bobby did girls."

Dex shook his head. "Not so much. After Ethan, he said he'd rather not."

Reg grunted. He remembered now. "Maybe it's on count of his girlfriend."

Dex gave him an unreadable look. "Yeah. Sure. You should ask him."

"Oh no." Reg held his hands out in front of him. "Bobby and I get along real well, unless sex comes up. For some reason that's when it all goes to hell."

Dex scrubbed his hands through his hair. "I can't. I can't even. Reg, go check on Lance and see when Billy's coming in, okay?"

"Yeah, sure. Thanks for the help, Dex."

Dex buried his face in his hands and muttered, "I can't. I got nothin'. We get on the plane in a week and I can't even."

Well, yeah. Reg got that. He felt like that most days of the year, not just the ones before Christmas.

So Dex left him with a pretty good plan, but then Christmas came and Dex and Kane got back early from their trip, and Bobby ended up at Tommy and Chase's Christmas night along with the whole rest of Johnnies because he came back early from *his* trip, and then Billy offered to stay with Veronica so Reg could go to the Johnnies thing 'cause Bobby was going to be there…

And the whole thing went to hell.

Hells of Our Own Making

BOBBY PULLED up in front of Tommy's little house in downtown and tried not to cry.

There were a zillion cars in front of the small sky-blue house with trees in the backyard and warm yellow light coming from the window. On the one hand, being around the Johnnies guys, seeing his old roommates, that might be the perfect distraction.

But Reg's car was here too, and Bobby was at a *loss* for how to deal with Reg.

Keith Gilmore had tried to get him alone every second of the last three interminable goddamned days, and every time Bobby had been tempted— just for the sake of expedience—to go down on him, he remembered the look on Reg's face when they were…

Anything.

Shopping for his sister, and he found something that reminded him of her as a child.

Sitting on the couch watching a superhero movie Bobby had personally seen with him at least three times.

Making hamburgers with fixings in the kitchen and mumbling to himself so he'd remember all the ingredients.

Opening the door as he heard Bobby's tread on the porch and smiling— just smiling—because he was glad to see a friend.

Bobby just couldn't. Just couldn't do it. Couldn't go down on Keith Gilmore. Couldn't have sex with Jessica. He'd managed the first night, but… God. It felt like he was doing her a disservice, no matter how much she told him it was awesome. After that he just held her, three nights running, telling her that it was getting weird knowing his mom was in the next room when he'd never cared before.

Truth was, those same pictures of Reg going through his head when Keith tried to get him alone were going through his head double-time when he was alone with Jessica.

He'd opened presents with his mom that morning, and she'd been so happy. A new leather jacket, clothes he and Reg and Trey had picked out, and new leather boots. He'd wanted her to walk around in this pissant town and look good—because *he* thought she was better than anybody else there.

He'd given Jessica a gift certificate to amazon.com. She'd been so excited to get it—the past two years had been an embarrassment of him buying her the wrong damned thing, and this way she could pick out something she liked.

And he *didn't* have to get too personal, because every time he touched her, even if it was just to drape his arm around her shoulders, he felt like he was trespassing or poaching or something.

He had no right to touch this girl if he didn't mean it, and he *so* didn't mean it.

So when he'd texted Trey and Lance and found out that Tommy and Chase were hosting Christmas night at their house, he was thrilled. A few beers, the guys he'd gotten to know—the guys from the flophouse who he missed since he'd moved his air mattress and his sleeping bag into a bare corner of a big apartment—he was down with that.

But then Reg had texted him, and his heart dropped into his stomach.

Being with Reg right now... God! Bobby's emotions were so close to the surface.

He'd moved into that damned apartment, working his ass off for the manager for the right to sleep there while he saved money for the lease, and the result had been a whole lot of time in his own goddamned head.

A whole lot of time to read books and think about Reg.

And Reg was in his head even when he was reading books.

He'd read an action-adventure book, and he was saving Reg from the bad guy. He'd read a romance book, and he and Reg were sailing into the sunset at the end. It didn't matter what kind of book it was, Bobby could find a way for him and Reg to be in the story somehow, even if they were just minor characters, sharing a cup of coffee at the place where all the action went down. Bobby, who used to write one paragraph for a three-page essay and avoid creative writing like the plague it was, could suddenly spin a tale in his head from beginning to end, as long as the sweet guy in the crumbling house with the big grin was a part of it.

It was the damnedest thing.

But Bobby had seen the way guys hooked up with him—had seen the way Reg approached sex in general.

If Bobby "hooked up" with Reg and it was just that—a hookup, sex as trade for a body and a friend that night—Bobby would scream and disappear. Someone would come looking for him in his apartment, and they'd find an air mattress and a sleeping bag and a shit-ton of paperbacks, and a little ball of agony in the center, because in his whole life, Bobby had never imagined how much raw emotion he could focus on one person.

Not his girlfriend. Not Keith Gilmore. Not the people he worked with naked.

Reg.

Bobby turned off the ignition of the truck and closed his eyes. When he opened them, the object of all this sweaty, painful introspection was standing at the open door, waving cheerfully at him like Bobby was the best Christmas gift ever.

Bobby couldn't disappoint him.

He grinned and hopped out of the truck, doing the handshake/chest-bump thing that seemed to make most guys happy.

"Good to see ya, buddy," he said, thumping Reg twice on the back and trying not to dwell on how good he smelled. He used Old Spice body wash—Bobby had seen it in his shower, and it should have smelled dumb and cheesy, but it didn't. It smelled classic.

"Did you have a good Christmas?" Reg asked, capering up the porch stairs like a kid. "V liked the presents you gave her. How did you know to get stuffed animals?"

"'Cause girls just like 'em," Bobby said, shrugging. "Besides—these went with some of the books I've been giving you." *Miss Peregrine's Home for Peculiar Children*. The stuffed animals had been macabre, but V—when she was lucid—seemed to have a sort of macabre sense of humor.

"I liked those books," Reg said, nodding. "They were some of the few books me and V agreed on."

Bobby grinned and looped a companionable arm around Reg's shoulders, trying not to yearn. "Good. Did you open your gifts?"

Reg shook his head. "Nope. Told ya—waiting for tomorrow. You coming by?"

Oh yeah. "Course," Bobby said, trying not to let his voice drop. God. He had to go into his apartment tonight. Aces. It was a beautiful place—a giant front room with two smaller bedrooms behind it, and a kitchen almost larger than the front room *and* kitchen of his mom's place in Dogpatch. Arched doorways, little indentations up near the ceiling—if the kitchen stuff hadn't been installed by a blind lunatic with a contractor's license, it would have been a perfect place. Bobby had discovered so much stuff out of code, if he wasn't fixing the place up under the table, he would have reported it.

"Good." Reg turned a smile up at Bobby's face that made Bobby feel like he hung the sun and the moon and the stars. *Dammit, Reg. I just want to be with you.*

They entered the party, which pretty much the antithesis of the small, cozy dinner and breakfast he'd had at his mom's place. Guys playing video games, guys at the table playing board games, guys in the kitchen eating the spread.

Dex and Kane were there, casually holding hands and talking in the hallway with Ethan.

Chase and Tommy wandered from group to group, playing games, talking to the guys. Lance and Trey were there, playing Monopoly with a few guys Bobby didn't know.

Bobby looked at Chase for a long moment, wondering about how he'd done it, done the porn and the girlfriend, and the being in love with someone and the double life. Bobby couldn't. His heart felt fractured and crumbled, and he wasn't living with Jessica, making a home with her. He couldn't judge Chase—not at all. But he could wonder, maybe, why it had taken the guy a year to fall apart.

Bobby wasn't doing so hot after two and a half months.

But he couldn't just stare at the guy. John was on the couch, watching Rick and Skylar punishing people in *Call of Duty*. Bobby hadn't seen him since his first shoot—and he wasn't looking great.

Bobby's stomach rumbled in unease as John's eyes shifted from place to place while they talked. Meth addiction was a big deal in the hills, and Bobby had seen enough of his old high school people go under to recognize some of the signs.

But John was nice—if distracted—when he talked to Bobby, asking when his next shoot was, being complimentary on the work he'd done so far. Eventually he wandered off, and Skylar asked him if he wanted next.

"Yeah, sure," he said. He didn't play a lot of video games, though. "Better pit me against someone who sucks. I'm not great."

"I'll play you!" Reg said brightly, coming full circle.

"Oh God," Skylar groaned, watching as his character got annihilated. "Reg is better'n any of us."

Bobby looked up in time to see Reg preen. "Reg, I had no idea. Why don't you have a system?"

Reg flushed. "V's not a fan," he said, grimacing. "She kept throwing them away when I was gone—said they were beaming shit into the house that made her crazy. Got expensive."

Oh God.

"Well, let's play here," Bobby said, waiting for Rick to give up his controller.

He did after he finished the event and Skylar pulled him off the couch. "Thanks, babe. Nice of you to kill me and keep playing."

"I didn't kill you, Sky. We were playing with other guys in Tommy's system, remember?"

Skylar shook his head. "I have no idea how that works or how you even know that. Whatever."

Rick rolled his eyes, but he pulled Skylar in for a kiss anyway.

Something about the gesture—an intimate moment in the midst of a sadness Bobby had never seen in them before—made him reluctant to ask how their Christmas had gone.

Sometimes it was just better not to know.

Reg grunted as they wandered away. "We're not gonna play the big group," he said decisively, doing something with his controller. "If you're not good at it, we'll just do a challenge ourselves. Now I'm gonna be the healer, and you're gonna be the point guy. So you run in front and shoot people, and I'll send you healing mojo every time you get hit. But you gotta protect me, see?"

Reg showed him, and he grinned. "You make it really easy," he said, feeling good at this for the first time ever. "Watch out, there—that guy got through!"

"Oops—gotta heal myself there! Get that fucker for me, 'kay?"

"Yeah. Yeah—oh, and that asshole there—got him!"

Oh, this was fun. This was *amazing*, in fact. This was a thing they could do so well together that it was like they shared the same brain. They plowed through the challenge, and the next one, until Bobby looked up and saw Trey waiting patiently for his up. Bobby winked at him, because they were good now, and gave up the controller when his guy bit the dust.

"Trey's been waiting," he said, standing up and stretching. "You guys should compare notes about Christmas."

"He and Lance spent the night," Reg said matter-of-factly.

Bobby's eyes must have gotten horror-show big, because Trey winced.

Oh God.

Oh God—Reg had… he and Trey and Lance….

"I'm sure Trey didn't mind that at all," Bobby said numbly, and Trey looked at him in apology.

"No," he said. "I promise."

But Bobby didn't know what "No" referred to, and it was none of his goddamned business anyway, was it?

"I got no claim." Bobby swallowed, and the misery of that hesitation out in the car came hammering back. He walked away, feeling defeated and sad and like he was hurting the guy he least wanted to hurt in the entire world.

And that's how he was feeling when Ethan sat on the love seat and asked him how his Christmas was.

Oh. Oh God. Ethan.

Who was warm and who got one-night stands and who just wanted to be touched. In that moment all Bobby wanted—*all* he wanted—was to be touched by Ethan, since he couldn't be touched by Reg.

Ethan told him that Dex and Kane had gotten back early, and Bobby, God help him, jumped to the wrong conclusion immediately. And then was mortified. Reeling from the thought of Reg and Lance and Trey, the conversation devolved from there. In his entire life, Bobby had never hit on someone the way he tried to with Ethan in that moment.

Later he would reflect on the miracle that he caught Ethan on the night Ethan would say no.

Ethan had a boyfriend—and one he truly cared for. Ethan wanted to make it work, and that meant no hookups. Work was work and hugs were hugs, and Ethan could take all the hugs people would give him—but not the sex.

Because even porn stars could be faithful.

And he remembered—*he'd* been faithful, in his own way. He'd treated porn like a job, not a lifestyle. He'd moved from girl porn to boy porn—and while part of that had been to address the secret ache he didn't even want to voice now, part of it had been he hadn't wanted to cheat on Jessica. And he'd meant that.

Those things he'd said to Ethan, the crass ones about "Ooh boy, a threesome!"—that didn't have to be who Bobby was. That was Keith Gilmore, or his father, speaking out of his mouth, and he'd worked his whole life to not let that happen.

Bobby had worked his whole life to be the guy on Reg's couch, the dependable one who didn't hurt people for kicks. Being hurt—yearning for someone he couldn't have—that didn't change who he'd worked to be.

So Bobby listened to Ethan, tucked into his arms like the big brother he'd never had, and closed his eyes. Trey got up to go talk to someone, and Kane took his place on the couch next to Reg, and while Bobby was trying to cope with the idea that he was replaceable on all levels, Ethan kept talking and restored his faith in mankind.

Ethan was in love.

Ethan, the guy who'd climbed on his cock and fucked him unmercifully, was going to make sacrifices to make it work.

There, on the couch, talking to a friend, Bobby could make some decisions he hadn't had the strength to make on his own—or looking yearningly at Reg.

When he opened his eyes, still in Ethan's arms, it was like he was seeing daylight for the first time in months. Kane won a battle with Reg and howled, jumping up and down like a gorilla, and Ethan assured Bobby he was the gentlest soul in the world. Suddenly Bobby could see all the Johnnies guys for what they were. Sex might have clouded his brain for a little, but sex wasn't the big deal here.

How they treated each other—*that* was the big deal.

So he and Ethan sat and hammered out plans, and suddenly... suddenly... he could see daylight. Could see a future, different than the one he'd been seeing at home.

When Dex tapped him on the wrist, he stood to get his coat and go, looking around to say bye to Reg first.

He found Trey, glaring at him from across the room, instead.

"What?" Trey snarled, coming in to talk privately as Ethan and Dex went to go say bye to Chase and Tommy. "Who do you think you're looking for?"

"I didn't see him leave," Bobby told him, heart sinking. God, when could they stop being stupid about each other? He needed to talk to Reg *now*, to put an end to the stupid, to the misunderstandings, to the hurting.

"Why would he stay? He heard every word, jerkoff," Trey growled. "Could you have not hit on Ethan while he was right there?"

"Right after I thought he slept with you and Lance on Christmas Eve," Bobby snapped back. Then he held up his hand. "Look—I get it. He didn't. You didn't. My brain just doesn't go from Dogpatch to Pornpatch on a dime, okay? I wish it would. I wish I just *got* the difference between sex and caring and what we do in front of the camera, but it fucking takes a while."

"So you're going to tear him up while you embrace the learning curve?" Trey's voice lost some bitterness, so Bobby gained some faith that he could make this right.

"I was hoping we could find it together," Bobby told him. "Has he left already?"

Trey let out a breath. "I was going to go outside and follow him home." He glared. "And this time, yes—we were gonna do it, 'cause you're not the only one who didn't want to be alone."

Oh thank God. "Well, if this goes wrong, be my guest. I obviously fucked it up beyond repair. But right now, give me a chance to go make this shit right."

He hurried outside into the chill air, noting that the fog had come out in a thick blanket. He saw Reg getting into his car, looking around for Trey probably, and called out, "Reg! Wait!"

Reg paused for a moment, a look of such agony on his face that Bobby almost stopped.

"We can't be friends anymore," Reg said, his throat thick. "I can't do it."

Bobby's heart stuttered. "Reg, I—"

"They spent the night on the couch. They did. And I ain't had sex in two months because you didn't like it, and you just went and hit up Ethan, right in front of me, and that wasn't—"

Oh fuck.

Bobby swallowed. "That was shitty," he said, feeling regret in his bones. "Sorry, Reg. That was... that was a shitty thing to do to you." He took a deep breath. "I was hurt. I... I shouldn't have been, but I was. I—"

"What kind of friend does that?" Reg demanded, and Bobby realized he was crying, faint tear tracks gleaming in the porch light from the house.

"A bad one," Bobby told him back. He held his palms up to Reg's chilled face gently and wiped the tears with his thumbs. "A really crappy friend. But I think that's the problem. That's why everything's felt so awful and wonderful these last two months."

"Being my friend is awful?" Reg asked, the sob in his chest making his voice shrill.

"No, no," Bobby soothed, pulling him close and kissing his forehead. Reg was small but built powerfully. Bobby had a heartbeat to give thanks that Reg wanted to be kissed. "Being your friend is wonderful. I'm so glad—every day I'm glad—that you were in the office that first day. That you got to see me, that you ran your hands through my hair. I'm so grateful. You made me feel so special."

Reg rested his head against Bobby's shoulder. "I want to be mad at you," he said, voice muffled. "But I missed how you used to hold me like this. I don't know why you stopped. I mean, I know it was because I hooked up with Trey, but I don't know why this had to stop."

Bobby held him tighter, and his own eyes burned—and to his mortification, spilled over.

"I didn't understand at first, myself," he said, shaking, he was so glad to be holding Reg again. "But then tonight, I was talking to Ethan, and... and he said no. And I was glad. I was glad he said no. Because I didn't really want to be with him. I just... I couldn't watch you be with someone else either."

"But you got a girlfriend!" Reg snapped—and God, this was justified. Bobby knew it was, but he was going to follow through anyway.

"Not for long," he said with feeling. "I shouldn't have let it go on this long. I don't want a girlfriend. And I don't want Ethan. And I don't want *you* to hook up with anyone else."

"But...." Reg jerked back, looking confused as hell. "What in the fuck, Bobby. What *do* you want?"

Oh, he couldn't have asked for a better line.

"This," Bobby said, grasping his chin and tilting his head up. Reg's mouth was open and vulnerable and ripe for the taking, and Bobby took. Bobby lowered his head and drank from Reg's mouth like a man dying of thirst, and Reg kissed back, eagerly, hard, giving for every kiss Bobby stole, and Bobby kept taking. Ah! Gods! He tasted so good!

And again, and again, until Reg raised his hands to Bobby's hair and yanked tight, urging him closer. Bobby wrapped his hands around Reg's bottom and hauled him up, until Reg wrapped his legs around Bobby's waist and clenched him tight, and still the kiss went on. Reg moaned, grinding against Bobby in frustration, and Bobby pressed him tight, tighter. Reg pulled away and shuddered before burying his face against Bobby's throat and letting out a long groan.

He was jerking against Bobby, hips twitching, and with one last heave, he bit Bobby's neck hard, and Bobby realized Reg'd just come, right there, in his pants.

Bobby groaned and kissed him again, only moving away when Reg's legs started to shake. Gently, Bobby lowered him until his feet touched the ground and then wrapped him tight against his chest.

"I came in my shorts," Reg moaned, sounding dazed.

"Yeah, well, lucky you," Bobby muttered. "'Cause I'm spending the night on Dex and Kane's couch and I didn't. That's gonna be fun."

"Why you spending the night there?" Reg demanded. "Why not with *me*?"

Bobby stroked his hair, hands still shaking. Reg had let it grow out a little this last month, cutting off the dyed blond part. What was left was a rich, dark brown. "Because I haven't broken up with Jessica," Bobby told him, still catching his breath. "I'm not sleeping with you as a hookup or a part of work. When we do this again, it's because I want to be with you, like this. I want to kiss you and touch you and be the only one you do this with—"

"Outside of work?" Reg clarified, and Bobby had to sigh.

"Course. We gotta eat. But I'm moving out of the big stupid apartment and moving into Ethan's tiny crappy one so he can move in with Dex and Kane. I can save more money that way for me *and* my mom and spend more of it fixing up your house."

"You can stay with *me*," Reg demanded, sounding bad-tempered, and Bobby had to laugh. Reg's body aligned so perfectly with his, so warm, so immediate, somebody might have to pry him out of Bobby's arms before he forgot his original plan.

"I might," Bobby said, nuzzling his temple. "Soon. But for now, I'm going to break up with my girlfriend and fix my life. And *then* I'll impose on your life."

"Sex, Bobby," Reg all but wailed. "Jesus God, I get you're all smart and shit, but seriously. I've got a little brain. I want sex. With you. And nobody else. When's that gonna happen? I'm dyin' here. Dex had to make those guys stay at my place 'cause I kept dropping shit, because I couldn't concentrate, because *sex*."

Bobby laughed and whispered in his ear. "Soon, Reg. Soon, I promise. Maybe not tomorrow, but soon. And I'll bring dinner. And I'll spend the night. And I'll make it special. I promise."

"It's already special," Reg grumbled. "I haven't gone this long without since I was in high school."

"I'll keep that in mind," Bobby said gravely. And he would. Because he wasn't going to scare Reg with the big *L* word. Yet. "Just…." He grimaced. "Just tell Trey you'll be by yourself tonight. I promise I will be too."

Reg grunted. "Fine." Then he rolled his eyes and laughed. "I would have felt like shit in the morning anyway. You know—I don't know what's so great about you. You're the first person in the world who made me feel shitty about sex."

Bobby closed his eyes and kissed him briefly, one more time. "Well, you're the first person in the world who made me look forward to it. So hang on. I promise. We'll have it. It'll mean something. Be ready."

Reg nodded and wrapped his arms around Bobby's waist for a hug so tight Bobby almost couldn't breathe. But that was fine. It was. Because the *L* word was coming—Bobby could see it on the horizon already. He figured the hug helped make them ready.

THE NIGHT on Dex and Kane's couch was weird. He could hear the two of them, quietly making love in their bedroom, and it didn't sound dirty. Just sounded intimate. He bet Ethan could ignore them in the same way kids pretended they didn't hear parents doing it. It was just not meant for anybody outside those walls.

First thing in the morning, he and Ethan went to Ethan's apartment to gather up Ethan's stuff. It wasn't much, all told—a garishly colored comforter, ugly-ass yarn dolls that were surprisingly soft, and boxes full of high-end clothing that looked amazing on Ethan but would probably look as pretentious as hell on Bobby's country-boy ass. Bobby helped Ethan unpack and let him show off the reptile cages that belonged to his new roommates. Bobby could still smell the calking and new plaster that had gone into securing the king snake and the iguana in their clear glass habitats, and he assessed the job with a practiced eye.

"This is good stuff," he judged, running his finger down the line between the glass and the wall. "Whoever your contractor is, he knows his shit." The snake batted the glass softly with his head, and Bobby refused to jump back and gasp. "Which is good, because if this guy got loose last night, I'd be the fuck out of here."

"He's got a total hard-on for Dex," Ethan confided, staring at the snake with suspicion. "I mean seriously. I've heard of dogs and cats liking one person more than another, but whenever Dex comes in the room, the snake presses himself up against the glass and drools."

Bobby eyed the animal with a little more compassion. "Well, not that I haven't been there, buddy, but don't ever make a play for my balls, okay?"

The snake flickered his tongue out and eyed Bobby up and down. Bobby figured the vote was still out and decided it was time to leave the room.

"No offense," he said as he entered the dining room, "but I'm sort of more about the mice. I had a pet rat in high school. *He* was my friend."

Kane was in the dining room, making waffles in his underwear. Apparently not giving a shit who saw you in your boxers was something that hallmarked guys living under the same roof. Bobby had to admit, now that he'd lived through Skylar and Rick and spent time snuggling with Reg, he was starting to approve.

It hit him then, the knowledge that he liked the view.

He'd always liked the view. He'd liked looking at Keith without his shirt—and even Keith without his pants, until things got ugly.

The guys at Johnnies were all good-looking and all built—and the best thing about living in the apartment had been getting to *see* them all, muscular calves, thick thighs, flat tummies, tapered waists.

The best part about kissing Reg the night before—besides the fact that he was Reg, and Bobby had never kissed a man before without a camera rolling or heart breaking, and it had been intimate and warm—had been that Reg was male.

All the small things he'd been denying about himself for so long, from this twisted relationship with Keith Gilmore to his willingness to give up girls at Johnnies—even his teeny-tiny sweetheart crush on Dex after their scene—all of it.

He knew.

He'd always known.

Kissing Reg the night before, promising him… promising him a *relationship*—but here, in this house, with these guys in their underwear, he had the words.

"What?" Ethan asked, tousling his hair.

"I'm gay," Bobby said in wonder.

Dex leaned against the counter—also in his boxers—and took his first hit of coffee. "You expect us to be shocked?" he asked after he swallowed.

Bobby shook his head. "Just… just… never said it to myself before." He shrugged and took a deep breath. Yeah—now was the time to do it. "Guys, I'll be out in a bit for breakfast. Thanks for making it—it was real thoughtful."

"Thanks for moving Ethan in," Kane said, flipping a waffle like an artisan. "We didn't want him living alone like that."

Dex frowned. "Speaking of which—are *you* going to be okay alone?"

Bobby didn't know why he didn't tell them about Reg right then. Maybe it was because he'd just figured out the gay thing, and it was still a giant Technicolor explosion behind his eyes. And maybe it was because Reg had belonged to everybody at some point in time. Bobby wanted a little bit of Reg that was just his.

"I'll be fine," he said with a shrug and a smile. "Ethan let me keep the reading lamp—I'm so there." He took two steps down the hall and paused. "Uh…." He was going to ask if he could use Dex and Kane's bedroom, but then he'd heard their night noises and now he couldn't. "Please tell me the snake can't get out."

Dex rolled his eyes. "If he can, I'm suing the contractor. Knock yourself out."

Bobby suppressed a shudder and walked into Ethan's room to plop down on his messy bed. With a sigh he dialed Jessica's number.

"But why?" she wailed after he told her. He looked at the iguana for sympathy and didn't see a lot forthcoming.

"Because, hon. Because when I'm not up the hill, I don't think about you, and that sounds shitty and it is. It's not right. You're a nice girl, and you deserve to be thought of all the damned time, and I don't. I need to make it right."

"But, Vern! How am I going to get out of this damned town without you?" She sniffled, and a small bit of anger flashed in his breast.

"I don't know—but why aren't you down here with me if you wanted to get out so bad?" he asked, knowing it was unjustified but saying it anyway. God—all the damned worry about money and how much it would be easier if he'd had a helpmate in the process. He didn't want *her*, but she hadn't known that.

"But… but you were supposed to pave the way!" she accused. "You're the provider!"

"Well, I'd rather be an equal," he said, and while he knew *he* was thinking of Reg, maybe it would give *Jessica* another way to think about a partnership. "Jessica, look. The breakup is all me, but I'm just saying—it's hard to be a knight in shining armor. Maybe you need to look for a man you can work next to instead."

"Thanks a lot for the tip, Vern," she snapped. "That's really fuckin' wise of you." But he could hear the tears in her voice. However she felt about him, he'd hurt her—and badly.

"I'm sorry," he said into the silence. "I didn't want to hurt your feelings. But I think you'll be able to grow a lot without me."

"What about you? You got any growing to do, champ?" she snarled.

"Yeah," he said, and he heard her surprised gasp on the other end of the line. "Jessica, you got no idea how much I'm learning about myself."

He looked at the snake and rolled his eyes, because he wasn't about to tell the girl he was gay. For one thing, his mom still had to live in that town, and for another? The stuff between him and Reg, or him and any of the guys, that all felt private. He realized that for the last two and a half months he'd been having a crash course on how hard the world got, how weird it got, when you were showing one face to the sun and keeping another for just a few people to look at.

He couldn't help not telling her he was gay—he hadn't even told his mother, and his mother was really the only one he owed the truth to. But he *could* take her out of a position of power in his life, because if he didn't trust her with that, there wasn't much he *could* trust her with.

He managed to end the conversation five minutes later and finished it up with a text to his mother. *Broke up with Jess—she or her brother may be by to get her stuff.*

His mother answered, *Good. Long time coming, hon. Maybe next time you'll stay home longer, you think?*

Oh jeez—*Mom.*

Yeah, sure. Love you, Mom. Happy New Year.

You damned well better call me by then!

It wasn't until he laughed that he realized his eyes had overflowed. Apparently burning bridges and making your life square didn't come without consequences.

Ever.

BY THE end of the day, he and Ethan had moved his pitiful stash of possessions into Ethan's pitiful by-the-month apartment. Standing in the middle of the place, and yeah, it wasn't awesome, but still—he felt like he could breathe for the first time in months.

He kept his sleeping bag on the bed, making plans to buy a comforter and a new pillow, and folded his clothes up in drawers. Ethan let him keep the weird animation posters so it didn't look like a barren hellish wasteland.

Bobby looked around the room after he got settled and smiled a little.

Had his own couch, his own bed, a minifridge, and a television.

Not that the quality couldn't use some upgrading, and the neighborhood was a shithole, but this was as close to comfortable in his own surroundings as he'd been since he'd left home in August.

Well, if you didn't count Reg's living room, it was.

Speaking of…

Guess where I am?

Not here.

He laughed a little to himself. Well, Reg was nothing if not direct.

Sorry about that. I was going to open presents with you this morning.

You texted.

Yeah, but I didn't tell you why I couldn't make it.

I'll bite. Why couldn't you make it?

'Cause I broke up with Jessica.

There was a long pause after that.

Because of me? Bobby could hear the cautiousness there, but he wasn't going to have the "We're gay!" discussion on text or even the "I'm gay and you're bi" discussion.

No. Because of me. Because I'd rather be with you.

Really? Why?

Lots of reasons.

Then why AREN'T YOU?

'Cause I just moved into Ethan's old apartment and Ethan's living in Dex and Kane's guest room.

He waited a moment for the response, and it didn't disappoint.

That is a surprise. Why did we do that?

Bobby thought about it for a moment. Important question.

Because I needed a place in the world. Mine. Before I could come over and invade yours, I needed my own.

Another pause.

But you ARE going to come over and invade me, right?

Bobby swallowed, and his eyes burned for the second time that day. But this time in happiness.

What are you doing tomorrow?

Working out. Grocery shopping. Trying to convince V to for God's sake let me watch a movie instead of the fucking news.

Wanna work out together?

Sure.

We can go grocery shopping together.

Okay.

We can check in on your sister together.

Fine.

And then we can come here and kiss a lot.

GREAT! Why can't we do that here?

Bobby chuckled.

Because I've never done it with someone I cared about, Reg. Not a guy. I just might get loud.

Heh heh heh

Bobby laughed again, and his body tingled. This was good. This was important. He and Reg—they could be the start of something real.

His whole soul felt warm.

An Old Thing Made New

"JESUS, REGGIE! Don't drop that thing on my foot. You'll crush me!"

"Sorry, Trina." Reg adjusted his grip on the weight he was trying to bench. "Sorry."

"No worries, big guy—what's got you spooked?"

Reg grinned at her, because they both knew he wasn't that big. But Trina was five foot nothin' and a half, so maybe to her, he was as big as he needed to be.

"Was just watching Bobby do squats. He's looking real good."

Trina secured Reg's weight before looking up. "Bobby, fix your form or we'll be carting you to surgery!"

Bobby straightened and grinned at the both of them before doing another one—this time with his back straighter.

"Yeah, Reg," she said patiently, rolling her eyes. "He's looking great for a dead man. Why you looking at his ass like that?"

Reg chuckled. "'Cause that ass is gonna be mine," he said, with no self-consciousness at all. Well, Trina knew the Johnnies guys. He was pretty sure they couldn't shock her by now.

Trina cocked her head. "Yeah? You two hooking up?"

Reg gave a little headshake and lowered the weight carefully to his chest, and then pushed it back up. And again. And again. He finished the set and let Trina help him set the weight in the cradle before swinging his legs around.

"No," he said, like she'd just asked. "Not hooking up. Just...." He tried to put it into words. Couldn't. "Kissing. We're planning to kiss. And he swore there'd be sex. So I'm gonna assume the ass is mine."

Trina cackled. "Well, you do that. *Ass*ume away. But why's the kissing a big deal?"

Reg thought about it. "Well, 'cause usually, when I'm trying to have a relationship, it's girls. But when I just hook up, it's guys. But I haven't had a relationship in years, and Bobby says that's what he wants with *me*. So it's gonna be different. I mean, I don't really think of myself that way, but if it means I get to bang Bobby, I guess that's okay."

Trina opened and closed her expressive brown eyes very slowly. "Well, I'm not sure if I can fault your logic there, Reg. But you ever think that maybe you're lucky?"

Reg just gaped at her. "I'm sorry, have you met me?" Of course she had—she'd been his trainer for the last five years, ever since John had gotten their local guys a discount on a personal trainer—which was about two days after Reg pulled his groin muscle so badly he had to cancel two scenes because he couldn't fuck anymore. Trina had literally saved both his life *and* his penis by showing him that sometimes the quality of the lift was more important than the weight.

Reg was grateful to her every day—and he'd been sure to tell John that she earned every penny he paid her.

The other guys who used her as a trainer sort of loved her too, but Reg liked to think he was her favorite. Until Bobby, he didn't get to be the favorite very often.

"Yes, Reg, I've met you," she said, tagging him playfully on the arm. Trina could ride double-centuries on her bicycle—that was two hundred miles in a day. She could probably kick his ass to sundown, like she threatened to do when he fucked up his lifts.

"Not that lucky," he reminded her. He'd had to put off bench presses for a while as his stab wound healed—Trina knew how not lucky he really was.

"Well, no," she admitted. "Some of your life is pretty much the definition of not lucky, but the thing where you're not sure if you want girls or boys—that's a lucky thing."

Reg cocked his head. "Huh. Really?" He wrinkled his nose. "'Cause… 'cause it's confusing. 'Cause you're supposed to want girls—and I do! But you know, all the shit on television and stuff—the news. You're supposed to want girls. And I thought if I was doing boys for money, that was okay, 'cause, you know, money is good too. But…." Oh, he was so not good at thinking inside himself. "But I want Bobby like I'm supposed to want girls."

Trina's mouth was parted slightly, and every so often it would work, like she was going to say something but then couldn't figure out what.

"Look," she said at last. "Reg, I see what you're saying. You were told your life was supposed to look a certain way, and it doesn't. But see— that's just a guideline. My whole family has had congenital heart failure—I wasn't supposed to live past fifty. But I had surgery, and I've lived my whole life fit, I eat right, and I'm planning to be giving you shit for another thirty or so years."

"But I eat like crap," Reg said, feeling a little guilty.

"We'll change that," she told him, and it didn't even break her stride. "What I'm saying is that sometimes the thing they tell you your life is supposed to look like, that's not the thing that's good for *you*." She turned around to where Bobby was doing preacher curls, his biceps bulging satisfactorily with every curl. "I mean, look at him," she said, nodding. "You could have the life they show you in the picture, or Jesus God, you could go home to that. I mean, Reg. You gotta find guys a little bit attractive or you couldn't get it up when you film."

"Oh, I could," Reg said, nodding. Not everybody knew that. "Some of the guys use the stuff that gives 'em an autoboner, but I don't fuck so good when I do that, so yeah. You're right. For me, I like touching guys just fine."

She gave him another slow blink. "You don't... how do you not... oh hell. I can't ask."

Reg looked down, a little embarrassed. "It's like... you ever get a really bad itch? Like, in a place nobody can see?"

Trina stared back. "Like a yeast infection?"

Reg shrugged. "Sure. I don't know. But I guess. Anyway—imagine having to scratch that itch so bad, you don't care if the person you're scratching it on actually likes being a... a...."

"Scratching post?" she asked.

"Sure. But, you know. Shaped the opposite."

"I got nothin'," she said after a long pause. "Well, I mean, I've got a long conversation with my husband that's going to make him put his hands in front of his crotch for a while, but other than that... okay. That doesn't sound pleasant on either end. I'll pass."

"I'm going to do toe lifts," he told her, and she followed him to the small Pilates ball with the platform. These things were *hard*. "Let's see how I can fuck this up."

"Here," she said, holding out her hand so he could balance. "Let's see how you can make this *work*."

Once he was locked into place, his stomach and thighs doing most of the work, he started to go up on his toes and then settle back down, slowly and deliberately. Trina held her hand out so he could grab it in case he lost balance.

"It's not awful," he confessed after the first ten reps.

"What's not?"

"Being on the juice, or being with someone on it."

"Oh," she said, and he had a moment to wonder if he wasn't blowing this poor nice married lady's mind out of the fucking water by talking about fucking, but then she asked, "But is it awesome?"

"No," he said promptly before launching into another series of lifts. Oh, this was rough on his stomach. That damned ball was tough to stand on.

"What's awesome?" She caught his hand for a moment as he flailed. "To you, I mean. What makes you want to be in a relationship as opposed to… I guess, just do it for the camera."

And six and seven and eight and nine and ten.

He grabbed her hand and steadied himself as he went still.

"He likes me." Reg took a deep breath, his stomach aching. "He wants to be with me because he likes… me, I guess. I mean, not just sex, because God knows we ain't had *that* yet. But he likes… the person I am. He wants to make me happy."

"Hm." She held still, and he caught his breath and started on his last set.

He finished, sweating, and she handed him a towel.

"Having someone—anyone—who wants to make you happy. That you could be happy with. And that you don't have to juice up to bone—I think that's an important thing right there, don't *you*, Reg?"

Reg nodded and hopped off the platform.

"Let's see how I can fuck this up," he said, winking at her. She didn't laugh, though. She patted his back, even though he was sweating through his tank.

"Let's see how you can make this work," she corrected. "Just like lifting weights."

He grinned at her. "You're good at this coaching stuff. You should stick with it."

"Yeah, well, I never thought I'd be putting my training license to work by life-coaching porn stars," she admitted. "Let's hope *I* make this work!"

Then she walked him to the ropes and proceeded to destroy him in a good way. He figured she did okay.

LATER HE and Bobby walked down the aisles of Safeway, and Reg watched as Bobby stocked his cart with things like apples and water and brown rice. He bought a little saucepan, and some frozen chicken and some spices too.

Reg watched him woefully and threw things like mac-and-cheese, hot dogs, and spaghetti in his own cart.

"You're eating all healthy-like," he said, wondering what V would do if Reg brought home brown rice. He'd brought home salad in a bag once, and she'd thrown it up on purpose. That had been a fun night. "I go with old standbys."

Bobby smiled faintly. "My mom is always trying to make gourmet stuff," he said, shrugging. "I don't mind, really. She… you know, it's a way she tries."

"Tries to be what?"

"A good mom."

Reg threw some cookies in his cart and tried not to cringe. He gave V two cookies every night after dinner, because everybody deserved dessert.

"I think my mom was sick like V," he said after a moment. "Sometimes she tried really hard, and we were washed and dressed and everything had to be perfect and she'd scream if it wasn't. And then we'd get home from school and the house would smell like weed and she'd be asleep and we'd have to get dinner." He saw another kind of cookie V liked and added that. "V was in high school by then, you know? So she'd get me dinner, and then she'd walk down to the liquor store and buy us cookies. So it's like a tradition. A couple of cookies at bedtime."

Bobby grunted and added his own box—his were Nutter Butters, and Reg liked those too. "When'd your mom go?"

Reg didn't like talking about this. He was usually pretty good about goofing off so girls didn't ask. But this was Bobby, and it felt serious, so he didn't have it in him to start juggling cookie packages or grabbing bags of M&Ms or something just to change the subject.

"I was in high school. We have an older sister, Queenie, but she got pregnant twice and moved out when I was in, like, eighth grade. She sends us Christmas cards but never visits. There's always a new kid. I can't even remember their names."

"Oh God." Bobby half laughed. "But after she moved out, it was you, V, and your mom."

"Yeah. High school was when V started getting sick—started yelling at people on the bus, slapped a lady at the store where she worked. Mom took her to the doctors once or twice, and then…." He shrugged apologetically. This story—not his favorite. "They had this fight that made shoving pills down her throat look like story time at the fluffy-bunny factory. It was…. They took apart the house. Took me a week to clean everything up. Every glass and plate got broke—that's why all we got is plastic shit now." Reg saw some crackers he liked with tinned soup and threw them in the cart dispiritedly. "Mom left, like… before the dust settled, and it was just me and V. And one day—I remember this, 'cause I was cleaning out Mom's room, and there was doctor's pills and ashtrays and syringes and shit—it was bad—V comes to me and tells me she'll finish the cleaning but she needs me to do some homework."

"Homework?" Bobby said the word like he was tiptoeing. Like he was afraid to put too much weight on the word, or something would break.

"Yeah—I've got to do it every year. It's, like, conservation papers."

"What?" Bobby was looking at him oddly. "What are you conserving?"

"My sister. See, I promised her. First I filled out the papers and put Mom's name on 'em—Willa. But then when I turned eighteen, I signed them for myself. And then someone from the state came over and looked at the house and looked at V and asked me about her meds—and I was better at getting her to take them then." He grimaced. "She's gotten wilier about *not* taking them. Anyway, they're the papers that say I'm in charge."

Bobby ran his cart into an endcap of rice cakes, and they both spent a few minutes picking stuff up and stacking it right.

"You're in charge of her," he said, like this was a big deal. "Legally?"

Reg nodded, solemn, like he was in front of the social worker. "Yeah. It was real important—if I wasn't in charge of her, she'd go into a state place. And she, I guess she stayed there a couple of times, before the big fight. I didn't know—they told me she was with friends, but she wasn't. She was in the loony bin, and it was awful." Reg lowered his voice. "They don't feed you real good there—and I remember this, 'cause when she came back from 'visiting with friends' she'd be starving. And she'd smell like cigarettes. And she'd scream at night—it's bad there, Bobby. I don't want my sister there. So I signed the papers when I turned eighteen. She's my sister. I'm in charge."

"But, Reg...." Bobby shoved a rice cake package on the cardboard display. The damned thing fell back down, and Bobby threw it in his cart. "Reg," he said again, standing up straight. "You've been in charge of your sister for ten—"

"Twelve," Reg said proudly.

"*Twelve* years! Without help?"

"Well," Reg said, not sure what the deal was. "I had Johnnies."

Bobby nodded, but he still looked upset. "But... but I can see you not wanting her to go to the state place, Reg. Maybe... I don't know. We've got benefits at Johnnies."

"She's got social security," Reg said, nodding. V had walked him through that too. It was a good thing she was so smart when she wasn't crazy, or the two of them would have been lost.

"Yeah, but maybe there's a better place through the Johnnies insurance," Bobby said, like he was thinking things through. "Like, a place that would make her take her meds, and they'd be nice to her, but they could maybe keep her off the internet so much."

"But I promised her." Of all the things in his life that got hazy and confused, Reg was crystal clear on what a promise was and damned proud of this one. "You don't understand. When we were kids, she kept me safe. Mom would be breaking up the house and screaming weird shit and having knife fights with some guy, and V, Queenie, and I would be in the closet. She'd wake me up and keep us safe. She loves me. Why would I want to send her somewhere else?"

Bobby stopped and closed his eyes and took a deep breath. He opened his eyes and looked at Reg with determination.

"Because she stabbed you in September, Reg. Can you promise that's not going to happen again?"

Reg shrugged and scowled. He scratched the back of his ear and studied the freezer food behind Bobby and wondered if Bobby knew how to cook steak, because Reg loved steak but couldn't ever seem to make it without it being tough.

Bobby watched him impassively for a few moments and finally sighed. "I'm going to take that as a no," he said quietly. He ruffled Reg's hair then, like they were friends, and shook his head. "But I'm also going to take that as the discussion is tabled for the moment."

Reg narrowed his eyes suspiciously. "Does 'tabled' mean 'not over'?"

"It means I think you deserve more of a life than this, Reg, and I think there should be resources out there to help you."

"But that's why I started porn!" Reg wailed. "Because McDonald's didn't pay for crap, and I needed more resources to take care of her!"

Bobby took a deep breath. "But, I don't know. A nurse? A home visit? God, someone to come watch her for you while you go out of town for a day?"

"Where would I go?" Reg asked, and Bobby rubbed the back of his neck.

"Dogpatch?"

"Isn't that where you live?"

"Not anymore," Bobby told him soberly. "I have an apartment here in Sacramento." He turned then and stalked through the meat department, going too fast for Reg to ask him if he knew how to cook steak, but he slowed down around the ham. "Was there something here you wanted?" he asked courteously. "I can't cook much in mine, so if you're getting big-meal stuff, this is your stop."

Reg bit his lip. "Uh… steak?"

Bobby reached for a packet of the thick-cut kind, with lots of fat. "Sure. Do you want something to marinate it in?"

Suddenly the conversation, which had seemed to exist in a black whirlpool for the past ten minutes, grew a bright silver ring. "Do you know how to do that?" he asked desperately. "Because I *love* steak, but I have no idea how to make it."

"Well, I think the cow makes it," Bobby said, putting the package and a bottle of something in Reg's basket. "But I know what you're getting at. Here—we can get some bread and some veggies too. I'll make it tonight."

Reg's breath suddenly stopped jamming up his chest. "That's a good idea, Bobby. Thank you."

"My pleasure," Bobby returned easily. He winked, but he didn't kiss Reg or grab his hand or anything.

151

Reg wondered that he'd want that.

He'd never wanted that with the Johnnies guys before. Ethan would hang on everybody, but that was expected. The guys roughhoused, they slugged each other's arms—their physical space was sort of nonexistent.

But Reg had never wanted… affection from anybody. Not in public.

But he didn't know if Bobby wanted any either.

"C'mon, Reg—let's finish up and get your food to your place. Then we can take my truck to the apartment."

Reg followed him quickly, suddenly all questions about his sister and public displays of affection lost in the promise of the two of them.

But when they got to Reg's house, V had taken apart the kitchen, throwing the plates and the silverware on the floor, the old contents of the refrigerator, the little rack of plants Reg liked to keep—and, oh God.

"Books?" Reg asked, his voice wobbly. "You got me paperbacks for Christmas?"

He must have raided the used bookstore for an entire box full, because his present had been pretty big and heavy—and now they were spread all over the rotting, melting food.

"Here," Bobby said, all practicality. "Let's get the books up and stacked first. You do that, and I'll get the food in a big trash bag, and then we can throw the dishes and stuff in the sink and wash the food off. We can fix this."

Reg nodded, his lower lip not firm at all. This. This was what Bobby had been talking about, and now he was probably going to get all "I told you so!" on Reg and they would never have sex, never be together, and never even hug again.

To Reg's surprise, Bobby looped an arm over his shoulder and kissed his temple. "It's okay, Reg. We can fix this. Get the books stacked and go find your sister. Deal?"

Reg nodded. "Books?" he asked again, because he'd loved reading the books with Bobby and V—but he'd never thought somebody would think *he* was a good bet to give a book to.

"You wanted ones where people treated each other decent. I asked my mom, and she said that was mostly romances, so I got a bunch of those."

"Like boys and girls?" Reg just wanted to understand.

"Well, I'm sure they've got boys and boys," Bobby told him, blowing his mind. "But these are about being nice to each other. I thought they'd make you happy."

Reg nodded and fought the burn in the back of his eyes. "They do," he said gruffly. "That was a really good present, Bobby. Let's save them."

Fifteen minutes later, Reg had stacked most of them in the corner, relieved because they were only a little sticky on the covers and he'd been able to wash that off. He'd had to throw away a few, but they were small, and he made Bobby put the titles in his phone so they could find them again.

Then, while Bobby finished up the cleaning, Reg went and found V.

He knew where she'd be—she was always in the same place.

In her closet, crying.

This time, as Reg looked in, he saw a tiny bag of pills in the corner of the closet, and he wanted to smack his head with his palm like an idiot.

"You hid them?" he asked, hunkering down next to her so he didn't look scary.

"I felt so good," she whispered. "And then… you know. I heard them."

"Voices," he clarified.

"I know they're not real." She turned her face up to him, tracks working their way through the grime. "I just… I wrecked your present," she moaned, wiping her cheeks on her knees.

"Why'd you do that?" Because damn. Bobby had left her something good, and she'd already opened it.

"There were bugs in them," she whispered.

Reg held out his hand. "Give me the pills, V."

She did, docile in her emotional exhaustion. He pulled out a dose and an extra sedative, figuring she'd need the rest and he and Bobby had earned the peace of mind.

"Swallow," he told her, his voice flat. He wasn't going to go get her water either, because he knew that trick. The lock was still busted on the door from the last time he'd had to break it down.

She dry-swallowed and showed him her tongue, over and under. He looked around her room and sighed.

It looked like the kitchen, minus the food.

"Get in bed," he ordered gently. "I'll start picking this up."

"I'm hungry," she begged plaintively, and he fought off a moment of terrible rage.

And swallowed it down, because that's what you did when someone heard voices and was at the mercy of their imperfect brains. You swallowed that anger, because it didn't do a goddamned thing.

"Well, you'll have to wait until Bobby and I pick up the shit you threw on the fucking ground," he said, his voice short but not sharp.

She slapped him—but not hard. "Don't be rude."

"I'm hungry." It was the truth—they'd been planning to make sandwiches. "And I've got another hour or two to go."

She let out a growl, and he had just enough time to dodge backward before she got him in the head with a shoe. He snatched the damned thing out of her hand—high heels, back from the days when she'd take the bus into town and go dancing—and threw it across the room. She wasn't very strong, but he'd seen that movie where the guy got caught with a spike heel in the eyeball, and he wasn't excited about having those in the closet anymore.

"All done?" he asked, his stomach gurgling.

"I hope the bugs eat you," she snarled, and he stood up and hefted her out of the closet and over his shoulder, kicking and screaming as she went.

He reached to the top of the closet, where she couldn't reach and mostly couldn't see, and grabbed the box he'd gotten from the sex toy shop about a year after he'd gotten his job at Johnnies.

He'd *wanted* an actual straightjacket, the kind they used in the movies or in the more hard-core medical facilities, but apparently they didn't sell those retail. What they *did* sell—at least what he was familiar with—was bondage equipment.

The good stuff.

The padded cuffs that went around the bedframe and the anklets that left her helpless.

He hated doing this.

Most of the time, he'd just as soon give her sedatives, but she'd been hoarding pills for a long time, and her medication levels were probably down. He needed to clean her room, and he needed her to not be attacking him with deadly footwear, and dammit, eventually they all needed to eat.

He had a gag—not a ball gag, because those broke your teeth and hurt your neck if you used them for too long—but a basic elastic gag that she couldn't reach after he handcuffed her to the bed.

He hated this. This was worse than the three-point restraint. Every movement was a fight, and he knew, no matter how gentle he tried to be, he was bruising her wrists. He worked out every day, for fuck's sake. She had no chance to overpower him, none at all, and he was just a big ugly fucking bully, locking her in metal cuffs.

When he was done, she stared at him, angry tears rolling down her cheeks, and he shrugged, his own eyes burning and sore. "V—dammit. You tried to blind me with a fucking shoe."

She squeezed her eyes shut and screamed behind the gag.

He sighed and shoved a pee pad under her hips, because if she lost control of her bladder, it was easier to change her clothes than it was to change all the bedding.

After that, he stood and began to clean up. The clothes went back in the drawers; the knickknacks that *weren't* broken went back on the dresser. The broken ones he stacked on her mostly untouched desk.

"I see you left the fucking computer alone," he muttered, ignoring her muffled scream of outrage. "And...." Hell. "You didn't slice up the stuffed animals we got you for Christmas."

He hadn't wanted to tell Bobby that's where most of her stuffed animals had gone when she'd been in her early twenties.

He looked from the stuffed unicorn and the stuffed leopard to V, hands resting by her ears now, body sagging into the mattress. "Well, I love you too," he told her, voice sinking. God, he needed to take the trash downstairs, but first he needed a—

The door opened, and Bobby stood there with two trash bags and two pairs of plastic gloves. Together they picked up the remains of the bathroom garbage she'd strewn about her floor. Reg noted dully that she was on her period. Doctors would know, he thought. Doctors would know if maybe the stuff that went on in her brain didn't fuck with her meds. Doctors would know if maybe there wasn't something they could do when things got too overwhelming.

But doctors would take her away from him.

He looked at her, chained to her own bed with padded handcuffs, and wished he could sink into the floor.

"Hey," Bobby said, putting a hand on his shoulder. "She's asleep. Should we unchain her now?"

Reg shook his head. "I'll chain her to the bedframe and put the other stuff away," he conceded. "She's... she's going to need some of this until she gets her med levels back."

"Okay. Let's do that, then."

They gave her room to move and a bucket to pee in—and some paper to wipe. But Reg had John bolt the bed to the floor years ago. She couldn't get out, she couldn't get to her computer—she just had to lie there, and rest, and chill the fuck out.

It was the only medicine Reg had.

Then Bobby took him downstairs, and Reg's breath caught.

The kitchen was clean—everything. Swept, wiped, gleaming, as much as the battered tile and cupboards could gleam.

"Here," Bobby said, pulling a chair out for him. "I made lunch while you were upstairs. Sit and eat—I'll take her a plate in case she wakes up."

"No forks," Reg reminded him. He had scars.

"I figured," Bobby said dryly. He set down a sandwich with some fruit on the plastic plate and added a cup of milk. Then, while Reg was looking at it in naked gratitude, he disappeared up the stairs with one on a paper plate for V, as well as a bottle of water.

By the time he got back down, Reg was still staring at the sandwich, just flummoxed.

"Reg? Is it any good? It's just meat and some pickles and—"

Reg shook his head and wiped his eyes, because his vision was blurry. "It's great," he said, and his voice cracked, and Bobby was there. Just *there*. Not kissing or groping—just *there*, holding him while he cried.

He had no words for what it meant. Not just the help, because he'd had that before. But the aftercare, the quiet support—from a guy who might want sex, but who had been there, in Reg's life, steady as a clock, and who hadn't complained once that they hadn't had it.

The tears dried to hiccups, and Bobby wiped his eyes with a napkin, then bent and kissed him on the cheek. "Eat, Reg," he said quietly. "Obviously, I'm staying here tonight. We've got time."

Reg nodded and looked away, feeling... God. Young. He felt young. He felt like a little kid, lost among the great and terrible grown-up things that were happening around him.

He couldn't look at Bobby as he ate—but Bobby was sitting next to him, eating his own sandwich too.

After lunch Reg went upstairs to clean up V's meal and make her take her night meds. She'd finished her sandwich, but she threw the plastic plate at him as soon as he walked in the door.

He thanked her for it cordially and declined to escort her to the bathroom. She had the bucket. If she wanted to use a toilet so bad, she could not be so damned awful.

When he got back downstairs, Bobby had lunch cleaned up, and Reg realized it *was* lunch, and only three o'clock in the afternoon.

He sighed and flopped onto the couch. "TV?" he asked, feeling drained.

"Sure," Bobby said, a little smile on his face that seemed to be saying something the opposite. Reg started flipping through the channels listlessly, feeling as though his entire day had been ravaged. All the good times the two of them had been planning had been taken over and destroyed by his sister's mental health issues, and he dreaded Bobby bringing up the subject again.

So he was really surprised when Bobby didn't sit next to him on the couch.

Instead Bobby grabbed a cushion and threw it on the ground between Reg's spread thighs and sank slowly to his knees, regarding Reg with a tiny quirk to his lips.

"What's this?" Reg asked, bewildered and stunningly aroused.

"Just kick back," Bobby said, his lip quirk growing into a playful smile. "I haven't done this for fun before. Let me play." He went after Reg's belt and the riveted buttons on the 501's with great concentration.

"Pl—ay?" Reg's voice shot up when Bobby grabbed the waistband of his jeans and tugged down. Reg was sitting on his own couch, bare-assed naked.

"Yeah," Bobby murmured, kissing the insides of his knees. Reg sucked a breath in through his teeth.

"Why play?" he asked, his voice gravelly with sudden, surprising want.

"'Cause you need to play," Bobby said, his eyes sober as he pushed up to kiss Reg's inner thigh. "I've been taught to kiss here and touch there and penetrate this way—but I've never had a chance to just... play."

"Ahhh...."

Bobby's idea of playing included using the tip of his tongue to taunt Reg's inner thighs. Reg struggled with the legs of his jeans, and Bobby helped him kick them off so he could prop his feet on the edge of the couch and leave all his body—all of it—spread out for Bobby to play with.

He nibbled. He nuzzled. He tasted.

When he was done with Reg's thighs—enough to leave Reg tingling and squirmy and sweating for something more direct, more aggressive, more arousing, if that was even possible—he placed both his palms on Reg's asscheeks and spread them.

For a moment Reg couldn't catch his breath. He loved a good rim job—he'd showered thoroughly, and he thought... maybe.... But Bobby blew softly and then licked Reg's crease to his taint. Reg moaned slightly and tangled his hands in Bobby's hair, resisting the impulse to hold him there until he tongue-fucked Reg to orgasm.

Bobby was exploring. Reg's job was to be Bobby's playground, to abandon any sort of illusion that he could control what was going to happen and have faith that whatever it was, he'd enjoy it.

Bobby's tongue hit the base of Reg's dick, a particularly sensitive spot that Reg usually pushed at with his thumb when he was stroking off.

Bobby's tongue was a tease, a delirious, tingly, half-kept promise of a tease, and Reg grunted, "Harder... right there... please—oh God. Yes."

He was so good. He wrapped his hand around Reg's cock and stroked, pressing that spot and then teasing his head, licking it a little and blowing on it and licking it, using the faintest hint of his teeth on the bell of it before soothing by taking the whole head in his mouth.

Reg lost words.

It was like he left his body on a glow of sensation and floated above them, Bobby with his green-brown eyes big, fixed on Reg's face, Reg's cock stretching his lips, and Reg, half-dressed, splayed, and shameless on his couch.

He spurted precome just when Bobby was tongue-teasing again, and Bobby caught it across the cheek.

Reg suddenly wanted to lick it off, to taste his mouth, to grind up against him. *No kisses yet. We ain't had no kisses.*

But Reg couldn't voice that—he could only shove his palm in his mouth and scream, bucking his hips. He wanted to be penetrated, wanted his asshole stretched and his taint rubbed, and though he'd never had trouble asking for what he wanted before, this—this was too much. He reached down with one hand and pulled his cheek aside, begging without words, and Bobby's chuckle against his cock reassured him.

"Want something, Reg?"

"Nungh!"

Oh, how embarrassing.

But Bobby rewarded him.

First he held Reg's cock up and out of the way, and then, using his other hand, he helped Reg spread his ass so he could lick—and then drill—with his tongue.

Reg made a sound, gut deep and chest long, welcoming the invasion, the pressure, the everything. He wanted more. He wanted fingers. He wanted cock. He wanted Bobby's mouth on his dick and something up his ass and…

"*Yes!*"

Two fingers, not smooth but manicured, slid right in and scissored. Reg's whole body washed cold, and when Bobby sucked his cock in again, he spurted some more.

"Lube," he managed. "Fuck… fuck me…."

Bobby must have kept the lube in his pocket, but Reg didn't care where it came from. It was warm and silken around his hole, and Bobby—oh!

Reg's eyes widened as Bobby positioned himself, as he remembered Bobby's biggest attraction on the porn set.

"Jesus God," he said in wonder. "I'd forgotten how fucking big you are!"

Bobby grinned at him shyly and then moved back from Reg's asshole and dropped his head to take Reg's mouth.

Ah… spit-sloppy and come-flavored. Raw and animal, Reg suddenly felt very much at home in his own skin, returning that ravenous, all-consuming kiss.

Forever.

That's how long they kissed. Until Reg needed again, like a wound, he ached so bad inside for Bobby's cock.

"Please," he half sobbed, pulling away from the kiss only because he hurt for possession. "Please—oh God. Oh God—keep coming." Because he was huge. Ginormous. He stretched Reg's asshole beyond burning or stretching, into Reg's heart, lungs, and diaphragm. But Reg begged some more, his breath coming short, while Bobby took over his body, like Reg was his other skin.

"Ahhh… yes." All the way. He was all the way inside, and Reg shook from his toes through his heart, just trembled with all the pleasure, all the sensation, all the awesomeness of having this boy, this beautiful boy inside him, driving out sadness, pain, and fear.

"C'mon, Bobby, don't make me beg." Because he needed it. Needed the pounding and the pain. Needed it all.

"Never," Bobby whispered, and he pulled back and slammed forward, so big Reg saw stars behind his eyes.

"Keep going," Reg ordered. "'Cause that—that's fucking beautiful."

Oh God. Yes. Yes. Beautiful. That tremendous, beautiful cock inside Reg's body, until there was no room for anything but the stars and the shaking, the hot and the cold, and his helpless screams into the palm of his hand as his own cock flopped brutally against his stomach and shot stream after stream of white against his chest.

Bobby fell forward, trembling. Reg expected him to pull out then and stroke himself off. That's what they did in the vids—you were taught that. People wanted to see dicks spew stuff—it was magic. But Bobby was rutting inside him, grunting, eyes closed, lush lower lip bitten in concentration. He hit Reg's button, and again, and again, until Reg cried out and convulsed, this second orgasm taking him by surprise, the nerve endings still raw and sensitive from the last one.

Reg contracted hard around Bobby's cock, and Bobby gave a soft "Ah… ah… ah God, yes…" before coming.

Reg groaned.

He could feel it.

Bobby's come. Hot and pulsing, inside him.

He'd never felt that. It always spattered his ass, or his chest, or his open mouth and his face. Even his hookups came on him like porn stars.

But Bobby didn't.

Bobby filled him, warm and sticky, until he finally collapsed, breathless, still mostly dressed in a hooded sweatshirt and tee, on top of Reg's chest.

Reg squeezed against him, still huge and only slightly softened, wondering… oh God. Yes. He was still magical there.

"Stay," Reg asked breathlessly. "As long as you can."

"Okay." Bobby kissed his forehead then, and his cheek, down his jaw, along his neck. Reg wrapped his legs around Bobby's hips and drove his heels into Bobby's ass, his own dick growing hard again. Reg kneaded Bobby's biceps as Bobby pushed himself up, and then began thumbing his nipples, pinching softly, and then a little harder when Bobby threw his head back and groaned.

"One more time."

"Yes," Reg panted. He didn't even care if he came. He just didn't want Bobby's cock to leave his ass, because he hadn't known it, but he'd been empty until now, hollow, needing something in his body, in his *life*, that he'd never thought to crave.

But Bobby didn't fuck in small measures. Bobby pulled that monster back, far, and shoved it in until Reg could taste it in the back of his throat. Again, again, again, harder, slicker, lubed by the come sliding out of Reg's ass, coating his cheeks and the backs of his thighs.

The thought of that—so dirty. Reg, who'd been fucking on a porn set for a decade, felt the wicked thrill of something filthy and sexual, right down in the pit of his stomach.

Bobby rubbed Reg's balls with his abdomen as he thrust, and Reg had to come. He reached between them, grabbed his own cock with one hand while he kept the other on Bobby's nipples, and he squeezed with one and played with the other.

"I want to kiss you everywhere," Bobby chanted. "I want to suck your nipples, and finger your ass, and see your face when you come. I want your jizz in the back of my throat. I want to taste it and swallow it, and lick your balls until you scream. I want all of you, Reg. Every bit. Now come for me. *Come for me!*"

And like his dirty words weren't enough, his voice, commanding, *demanding*, did it. Reg gasped, almost afraid when his gut clenched and his groin clenched and he turned himself inside out one more time for this kid who had just cared for him and loved him and fucked him so sweet he might never fuck again without remembering this moment here.

He didn't want to ever forget.

"*Geeeaaawwwd!*"

Oh, it was exactly as painful and as awesome as he feared, that last orgasm. Everything ached, especially his asshole, as Bobby drove in for the final time and shuddered. Reg's ass milked him, squeezed the last bit out of him, and Bobby collapsed again, this time sweating and shaking so hard Reg would have gotten him a blanket, but neither of them could move.

"Reg—"

"Don't move."

"'Kay."

Reg wondered then—had his sister heard? Usually his hookups in his room were necessarily quiet, but this time….

He couldn't regret it. Even if he went upstairs to check on her and she screamed mean words at him—she'd just have to get used to it was all. He wasn't giving this up for random silent Johnnies hookups in his room.

"Reg—"

"Don't move," he said automatically. His ass was dripping come on the couch, but he didn't care. He'd wash it off.

"Not moving. That was amazing."

"God, yes."

"I mean… I've never done that with someone I cared about before. Not like I care about you."

Reg's eyes burned, and he couldn't figure out why. He wasn't sad. He was, in fact, gloriously happy, in a way he couldn't ever remember being.

"Me too. What does that mean?"

Bobby gave a little laugh. "It means I'm gay. I hope that's okay."

Reg wrapped his arms tighter around Bobby's waist. "Why is that special?" he asked, but mostly himself. "Why is it special if I'm gay or bi and not straight, just having sex? It *is*. I just don't—"

Bobby stopped his maundering with a kiss. When he pulled back, he looked soberly into Reg's eyes. "It means we care about each other the way you keep thinking you'll care about a girl someday, Reg. I planned like that too. I may have sex with guys and like it, or get a blowjob from a guy and like it—but I have to fall in love with a girl and marry her, because that's how you grow up and be happy."

Reg sucked in a breath, dislodging Bobby from his ass, but that was okay, because this was important. "Yes!" he said. "Yes—that's it! That's what I thought—but… but Trina tried to tell me—"

"That's how we feel about each other," Bobby went on—maybe because he had to. Because he had it in his chest, and he needed Reg to hear it, now that they were close and Reg might never have sex with anyone else and know what sex was for. "We feel like we're the future together. I want to plan with you. I want to make my life fit you. I want us to be family. I even want you to meet my mom. This idea that we can fuck around with any guy we want but our hearts will one day belong to a girl—that's not us. I mean, some of the guys at Johnnies may leave the set and go home to girlfriends, and that's okay. But that's not me. And I'm really…."

He bit his lip, and Reg realized—truly realized—that he wasn't nineteen yet. He turned nineteen in May. Reg was almost thirty.

"It's not me either," Reg said, trying to pull his weight. "I… until, maybe… until maybe you kissed me at the car, I thought it was. But… but I don't want you to go nowhere. I want… I want you to stay. I don't imagine a girl anymore, home when I get home, making me happy. I imagine you."

Bobby kissed him again, short, tender, and then slid to the side.

"We should clean up," he suggested unwillingly, but Reg knew what he meant.

"You take the shower first—I'll clean the couch."

Bobby pushed off the couch and offered his hand up. "Deal."

But once Reg was standing, he felt compelled to pull Bobby down for a kiss. "That—I've fucked a lot, Bobby. All over the place. That there on my couch, with you. That was my best time."

Bobby grinned tiredly. "Mine too."

"Do you need to have more sex to figure out if it's still your best time?" Reg knew he asked that wrong, but it was just now hitting him—he was older. By a lot.

"No," Bobby said, voice gentle. "I know my best time when I have it. Let's clean up and watch some TV, and I'll go through your books and see if there are any that didn't get thrown away that I might still be able to replace."

Suddenly Reg felt a wholly childish moment of glee. "You'd do that?"

Bobby looked at him, brows drawn together. "Of course. I wanted to read those books too. I thought we could go through the bag together."

Oh. Of all the…. Reg ducked his chin and blushed. "That sounds like a real good idea," he said softly. "I like that idea." He swallowed. "Do you think I should bring V a book when I check on her?"

Bobby grimaced. "She needs to be nice to them," he decided. "If she wrecks one, we're going to have to make her earn it back."

"Like with taking her pill without fighting?" Reg asked hopefully. "And not throwing stuff when she's mad?"

"Yeah. That's good." Bobby seemed to brighten. "Here—let me hit the shower. Operation 'Buy V's Love with Books' is about to commence."

V WAS asleep after Reg got out of the shower. He left her a book with a soggy cover, since he and Bobby were going to have to replace it anyway. He figured they could have the book talk when she woke up.

He paused for a moment at her doorway, looking down at his sister for an honest minute.

She was lying on her side, the hand with the padded cuff tucked under the pillow, her head on top, and her spill of graying mousy hair covering her eyes.

She was getting old.

The thought shocked him a little, because *he* didn't feel old, but then he was pretty much fucking around and getting paid, same as he had been when he was nineteen.

But his hair was thinning on top—he'd let it grow out some, but he could see his hairline going back a little. He was going to have to cut it short or shave it, pretend he'd never had thick curly hair, if he wanted to stay on film.

But you could still see the down-to-fuck nineteen-year-old he had been in his eyes. Could you still see Reg's savior, his beloved older sister, in the face of the sleeping giant?

He closed his eyes and remembered her as a kid, and when he opened them and looked at her, he could see that person in her again—the girl who had protected him and showed him how to cook when their mom was gone. He saw the girl who'd taught him how to read and who used to buy him cookies and who used to use coat hangers and tinfoil to find cartoons on their old tube TV.

He saw the sister he loved.

How often did he see that person these days?

He had to ask himself that. He *had* to. Because Bobby, not once, had said, "I want to be your guy, but you got that crazy sister." He'd gotten to Reg's house—to a disaster area—and had buckled down to help clean up.

No bitching or moaning, just practical to the bone, that was Bob—Vern. That was Vern Roberts.

Reg knew his real name, and that made him proud.

But Vern or Bobby, that boy had stepped up, and Reg realized that asking him to step up to V's mess was a lot to ask. Today he did it without question. Could he do it tomorrow? The next day?

Five years from now?

And it wasn't fair of Reg to expect it of him. Reg knew that. And Reg knew that if Bobby walked away because he got tired of sleeping with one eye open all the time, that would be on Reg's head, for keeping a promise he'd made when he'd been still in high school, to a woman who wasn't the same today as she'd been back then.

And Reg might lose him—the one person who'd ever offered to stay.

Dammit, that wasn't fair either!

Reg's breath was coming faster in his chest, and he wondered what was wrong with him, that he'd be crying now. Today. How was it that he had such a wonderful thing happen in his life, but he felt like he could cry for hours?

He must have heard Bobby's tread on the stairs, because his hand on Reg's shoulder wasn't shocking.

"Whatya see?" Bobby asked quietly, near his ear.

Reg turned and shut the door. "My sister," he said simply. "She's not a monster, but she's not easy to deal with either."

"No," Bobby said, pulling Reg close so their bodies touched. "Not easy." He still smelled fresh from the shower, and his chest stretched the hell out of Reg's old T-shirt, the same way his cock threatened to hang out of his old basketball shorts. The results were sexy as hell, but for once, Reg'd had his fill of sex and needed to do some talking.

"But she's part of my life," Reg said, like maybe Bobby hadn't figured this out in all the time he'd spent at Reg's house, *not* being a boyfriend, just being a friend.

"I know it."

"You'll get tired of it quick," Reg told him, wanting to be honest.

"But not tired of you." Bobby kissed his forehead, and Reg remembered when his sister used to do that for him. It was a sweet thing—a thing that didn't ask anything from a person, just gave all the reassurance possible.

"Good." Reg rested his head against Bobby's chest.

"Ready for some TV *now*?" Bobby's arms tightened around his shoulders.

"God yes. And some dessert—we bought cookies."

"Yeah."

The rest of the night was about as perfect as it could get. They lay on the couch, feet in each other's laps, desultorily rubbing because they both agreed that felt nice. They ate cookies and milk and watched a movie with lots of explosions and very little dialog, and then, when Reg started nodding off, Bobby grabbed his hand and pulled him to bed.

It was not a new experience, sleeping in bed with a man—or even with Bobby, for that matter. Reg kept waiting for that moment when he woke up with Bobby's hand on his stomach or his hip or his back, that long, rangy body pressed up against Reg's, and realized that he'd done something irrevocable.

It didn't happen.

Instead they murmured to each other quietly as they fell asleep, talking about the TV show, about their plans for tomorrow—Bobby had to go back to his apartment and get new clothes—and when their next shoot was.

Reg closed his eyes midsentence, talking about how he was glad Scott wasn't on the schedule anymore because the guy would fuck your ear hole if he thought it would get a better shot, and fell asleep.

Sometime in the night he got up to pee and paused in the light from the bathroom to see if it really *was* Bobby, after so many months without.

He slept on his stomach, his head turned toward Reg's empty pillow, arm flung out like he was trying to possess Reg even in sleep.

Reg remembered the times Ethan had stayed over, with his craving for touch, and he remembered rubbing Ethan's back—literally, for hours—but Ethan had never tried to claim him like that. Dex had stayed here a time or two, but Dex had that sweet way of disengaging. Reg had learned a lot from him, actually, about how to sleep with someone without giving them the impression it meant anything. Lance tended to fold over him, but protectively, like Reg was a child. Trey slept in his own corner, arms folded, as solitary as a baseball in a case.

In his mind he flipped through the incredibly long list of guys who had slept here, in Reg's bed, for fun, for company, to make sure Reg didn't have to be alone, and not once did he remember a guy who just possessed Reg, sure and honest.

Bobby's eyes fluttered open, and he squinted against the light. "Come back to bed," he ordered. "That light is skewering my eyeballs like a shish kebab."

Reg laughed softly. "That's gross, Bobby."

The man in his bed grunted. "What are you looking at?"

"You. You're just... beautiful." It wasn't a manly word. Straight men didn't call other men *beautiful*. Reg had certainly never thought of a man that way, in spite of all the guys he'd fucked.

But then, maybe Reg had never been straight; maybe Bobby was right. The thing inside him that could let him picture having Bobby in his bed every night forever—that wasn't a straight-guy thing, not even a straight guy who fucked other guys for convenience.

Bobby blinked those big brown-green eyes at him. "That's sweet, Reg. Why's it sound like you're afraid to say it?"

"You said you were gay." Reg shrugged. "And I'm probably bi. And it just hit me. I think you're beautiful. I want you in my bed. That's... that's real. I'm not going to get hit by a bolt of lightning that says I'm different or you're different or my life has changed. That thing in me, it's always been there." He shrugged, feeling this in his gut. "I was just too piss-stupid to know it."

"Come here." Bobby held out his hand. Reg turned off the light behind him and moved forward, trusting himself in the dark until he felt Bobby's fingers close around his palm. He tugged a little, and Reg tumbled into bed, eyes searching for Bobby until his vision adjusted, and he found himself lying with his head on Bobby's shoulder while Bobby regarded him soberly from just inches away.

"Hi," Reg said, smiling a little and touching Bobby's face with his fingertips.

"You're not stupid," Bobby said. That was sweet—the kid meant it.

"IQ of eighty-three," Reg said. He'd *made* Lance give him that test. He'd heard the word "retarded" whispered about him often enough. He had to know. It was almost like the word "bi"—he had to know the words that defined him so he knew what he had to work with.

"That don't mean nothing," Bobby said, his shoulder moving under Reg's ear as he shrugged. "That means you were afraid through school, so you didn't pay that much attention. It means your mother was losing her shit, and you didn't get enough to eat, and that hurts your brain. It means nobody sat down with you and read, the way my mother did with me. It means you were eighteen and making big fucking decisions about your sister, with no one to help you, and you didn't have time to study all the shit that makes you look smart on paper."

"It means I can't think for shit," Reg said bluntly. "Don't make me more than I am, Bobby. I... I... if fucking wasn't a thing you could get paid for, I wouldn't have no fuckin' teeth. I broke this one here"—he pinched an incisor in the front of his mouth—"when I tripped on my own damned stairs because I was twenty-two and drunk. John had just gotten dental insurance, right? But I hadn't signed up for it—because dumb—so John and Dex, they *forged the fuckin' papers* so I could go in and get a crown. Smart people don't do that shit, Bobby. Just...." His chest ached saying this. "Just don't think more of me than I am."

"Reg, there's a difference between being young and drunk and stupid and not having the smarts to figure that was a bad fucking idea."

Reg sighed, suddenly exhausted. "Well, when you figure out what the difference is, let me know. I seriously need to have that shit explained."

"In the morning, maybe," Bobby said on his own yawn. "But yeah. We'll work on it."

"Mm...." Then Reg remembered something important. "Bobby, do you mind that I don't call you Vern? I know it's your name and all—I was there, remember?"

"Yeah. Christ no. Please don't call me Vern. I hate that fuckin' name."

"Mm... I'm not so fond of Reg, but I couldn't even come up with my own damned porn name, so I think I'm stuck with it."

"Want me to call you Digger?" He said it with a chuckle, so Reg knew he didn't mean it.

"No. You try to call me that when I'm crossing the street and about to get hit by a truck, and I'll die. I didn't remember when guys were fucking me—they'd be like, 'Digger, harder!' and I'd be like, 'Who else is in here?'"

Bobby laughed, low and sweet, and Reg smiled like he'd won something. He'd meant to be funny—that didn't happen often. He was real pleased.

Bobby's mouth closed on his in a gentle kiss, and Reg just opened for him, just long enough for them both to close their eyes. The kiss ended, their breathing evened out, and Reg fell asleep.

Nothing earth-shattering—but as he slept, he knew in his bones that this was different.

He needed it to be.

Home Bird

BOBBY CALLED his mom a few days after that first night at Reg's. New Year's Day meant spending an odd night in his new apartment, mostly because he had a scene on the third, and every time he slept in Reg's bed, he woke up having some sort of surprising and new sex with Reg.

Sex with Reg *always* felt new.

It was almost shocking how much sex with a guy Bobby knew and cared for and wanted to spend time with was different than sex on set with a naked guy pulled off a schedule. Bobby could see how straight guys could do that, if they could get it up—the mechanics were just basic physics. Once you got over "Hey, that's a guy's hand or mouth doing that, and I'm usually attracted to women," well, if you could come in front of a crowd, you could come in front of a crowd.

Sex with Reg was nothing like that.

Suddenly Bobby could understand how people stayed married *and* happy for years and years. He'd never seen it himself, but he'd heard of it happening.

And he knew what an abomination those last few months with Keith Gilmore had been.

God, even porn sex was honest sex. Nobody was *making* him do it. He chose that shit because he had the equipment and the by-God fucking inclination.

But what Keith Gilmore had been making him do for the past six months—every time Bobby'd said no and Keith had used Bobby's reputation or his mother's comfort in town as a reason to face-fuck Bobby until he gagged—*that* was an abomination.

Bobby couldn't do that shit anymore.

He wondered if he could explain it to Reg in any way that wouldn't make him feel like a dumbass. Then he remembered Reg's painful, honest confession about being "stupid."

Reg wasn't stupid. He wasn't a brain trust—Bobby wasn't deluded about that—but Reg had been determined that Bobby know what he was getting, as they lay down in his bed to sleep that first night.

It was Bobby's turn. He was going to have to do it and make sure Reg knew who *he* was, inside and out.

Maybe the best way was to let Reg see where he came from.

And God—wouldn't it be nice to get Reg the hell out of Sacramento?

Bobby still loved the place. Now that he had a little bit of money—and tips over the holidays had filled his pockets more than he'd expected—he'd been asking for recs. Where to eat, where to dance, where to see movies. Trey liked theater—Bobby had three recs for plays in the next month.

He wanted to take Reg with him. He used to go dancing at a local bar with Jessica—one of those places that let you in if you looked eighteen but only served people with IDs. Bobby had liked dancing, but he wanted to try it with someone he really wanted to touch.

He thought there might be untapped potential for sexy in that direction.

Everything—*everything*—he'd ever known about dating now opened up before him in a great vista beneath his feet. Except Reg could only look at the vista—he couldn't go explore.

They needed to find a way for him to explore.

It was with this idea in mind that Bobby called his mom.

"Vern? Good to hear from you, baby! How was your New Year's?"

"Not bad. Me and a friend and his sister hung out, blew noisemakers, that sort of thing." Veronica had been impressed. Bobby brought sparkling cider and cake, and together he and Reg had cooked a small ham and potatoes. She said it felt like a real holiday, and Reg's face, watching her twirl the noisemaker happily—the sweetness there had stopped Bobby's heart.

Dammit, Reg just wanted her to be happy.

"A good friend?" his mom asked. "I mean, you talk about friends there—I just don't hear any names."

Thanks, Mom, for the perfect opening.

"This guy's name is Reggie—we all call him Reg. He's a nice guy."

"What's he do?"

"This and that—he's not, uh, a professional or white collar or anything. And man, he needs me to keep working on his house, 'cause

171

the place… damn, Mom. Falling the hell apart, I can't even lie. I did his bathroom before Thanksgiving, but I think I'm going to have to take on the kitchen next. I hate to do it. I'm still waiting tables, and I can't finish it as fast as he needs to—"

"Well, he's a grown man—he can deal with takeout," his mom said. Well, practical. Of course.

"He's grown, but his sister…." Oh jeez. Anything he said would feel like a betrayal, but he needed to talk to Mom so bad. "She's got some mental problems," he said, hating the way that sounded. "Like, if she doesn't take her medication, she goes batshit crazy and takes out the house. When she's on the meds, she's sweet—just like he is, actually. Just… I think they both needed a mom, and they didn't get one. But if I start redoing their kitchen, that's just…. I mean, there's tools and shit around and—"

"Is she dangerous?" His mother sounded concerned, and Bobby didn't blame her.

"Well, you know. Not when she's had her meds."

His mom let out a long breath. "Does he have any help besides you?" she asked, so steadily he felt like she might almost know what Reg was to him.

"No… I mean yes. The guys he—*we* work with will do about anything for him—"

"Do they know how to deal with someone with her problems?"

Well, they did *now*! "They've picked up a few things." He grimaced. "They've had to. You know—it's just a challenge."

"Vern, if your friend's sister needs to be someplace they can take care of her, there's no sin in that. You know that, right?"

Bobby swallowed. "It's complicated," he said, sorry he'd told her. He'd wanted someone—an adult someone, not a kid fucking his way through college someone, or a porn model or porn photographer someone— to tell him that what they were doing was okay. Because facing Reg with this problem—no. They'd been together for… for a week. Just no.

But moms didn't always do what you wanted them to, and Bobby should have known that by now.

"Okay," his mom said quietly. "Your friend—Reg—how's he deal with all this?"

"With a heart as big as the world," Bobby told her, thinking of all the times Reg had forgiven Bobby for fucking around with his feelings because Bobby hadn't known any better. "He's... he's got the best heart, Mom. I think you'd really like him."

"Mm," she said, as though coming to a conclusion that had nothing to do with Veronica. "Are you going to bring him up sometime?"

"Yeah—I was thinking maybe in a couple of weeks, if the snow isn't too bad." The weather really was a factor. Bobby didn't have chains.

"So early February? I can do that." His mom's voice dropped. "The money you're sending me actually lets me afford heat. I hate that you took that responsibility on, son, but I'm really grateful for heat."

Bobby swallowed. "Someday we'll get you moved out of there," he said softly. "I... I don't like you there alone."

"Well, your, uh, friend Keith comes by a lot," his mom said, sinking a stone in his stomach. "But not in the good way."

Bobby sat up in bed, trying hard to remind himself that the sky had just dumped a frickin' ton of snow in the Sierras and people couldn't get home from Tahoe for work the next day.

"Explain that."

"He's just... odd about it. I mean, he came by, like you said, after you broke up with Jessica, and he was real cordial and all. But he kept saying things like how we needed to get you back up here again, and how you needed to come to your senses and come back. I tried to tell him you liked it down there—that you were trying to move me down there, actually—and he got... he got mean, Bobby. Said all sorts of stuff about me being a shitty mother—"

"I'll kill him," Bobby growled, halfway out the door.

"You'll do no such thing, and you'll sit your ass down and stop posturing like a kid."

Bobby sank into one of the kitchen chairs and winced when it creaked under his weight. He'd been eating a ton of chicken and veggies and bulking up like he'd never believed. It was a good thing he liked to keep busy, or this working-out thing might end up in a very fat Bobby.

"How dare he!" Bobby snapped. "Mom—you've got to tell someone. He's not right, you know—"

"Vern, he's your best friend."

Bobby grunted. "Not really. He was a friend. And then he was an asshole who… never mind. Just don't trust him. Don't let him in. And don't tell him I'm bringing anybody by."

"Don't you want him to meet your new—"

"No. Just… no. I want him to not know I'm there, even when I'm there." Bobby took a breath. "And since I'm not going to be hanging out with Keith or Jessica this time, have a to-do list for me. I can tighten up the house and make it more snug, okay?"

"You did that last year," she said softly, but he remembered.

"Yeah, but I have money for materials this year. I can add more insulation to the roof and add some wedges to the doors to keep the drafts from seeping out. Trust me—we can squeeze some money out of your heating bill. I've been wanting to fix that place up for years."

His mom chuckled fondly. "You never did say why the construction job didn't work out, but I'm glad you seem to have found your niche waiting tables."

"The guy was sort of a criminal, Mom. Just, you know—I'll find another job like that."

He hadn't wanted to look, actually. The foreman's words about blacklisting him still rang in Bobby's stomach. They may have been lies, but the idea of applying to a decent construction place and finding out he could never get work like that again would do a number on Bobby he didn't think he could survive.

He loved working with his hands so much.

He'd been biding his time, waiting for the spring, when most outfits got desperate. If he could buy a computer—and one was coming, it was in the budget—he'd be able to look some more.

"A better one," his mom said optimistically, and he agreed with her for form.

They rang off then, and Bobby moved from the kitchen to the bedroom in three steps and threw himself across the bed. His first instinct was to call Reg and tell him his fears about Keith Gilmore, but then he realized Reg didn't know who Keith Gilmore was really, and certainly not who he was to Bobby. And definitely not about where this sudden sense of danger would come from.

He sighed and settled for texting Trey.

I need a favor—I'll do anything to pay you back.

Will you come over RIGHT NOW and unplug the sink? Rick tried shaving his chest instead of waxing this time. Bad things happened.

Oh my God. Sure—but you'd better do the favor.

Whatever. Get your ass here and ask us then.

Bobby stared at his phone, bemused, and grateful—not for the first time—for the Johnnies network. He texted Reg next, putting on his boots and grabbing his tool belt as he waited for an answer.

I'm going to the apartment—Rick shaved his chest, and they need a plumber.

Heh, heh—I'm not the only one who doesn't like waxing.

Doesn't bother me. Just glad no one's asked me to wax my asshole yet, 'cause ouch.

You don't have much hair back there anyway. Some guys it's like licking a cat.

Bobby read that text twice and ran into the wall dividing the bedroom from the rest of the apartment.

OMG

Heh heh heh—make you laugh?

Gay porn models licking pussies? Absolutely. It was a horrible, crude joke, but Reg started it.

OMG—I DIDN'T MEAN IT THAT WAY!

Bobby chuckled. *I know you didn't. But I'm gonna crack up during the shoot anyway. Thank you for that.*

Welcome.

Bobby got into the truck and checked his phone one more time before he started it up. The next text surprised him.

I think I gotta ask Dex if I can not light your scene. I think that would be a bad idea.

Why? Bobby hadn't thought about it. So many months had gone into identifying "work sex" as different from "heart sex" that he'd completely forgotten Reg would even be there.

'Cause either A. It would make me horny and I gotta wait two more days. Or B. I'd feel bad 'cause you were with that other guy. I know it's stupid. I just know it made me feel bad when I thought about it.

Bobby's heart hit his chest harder than usual.

I never thought about it. It's like I'm a different person on the set. The person I really am only wants to be with you. That guy on the set, he could fuck the world until the oceans ran jizz.

The truck was idling, and he was about to sign off when his phone beeped again.

HAHAHAHAHAHAHAHAHAHAHAHAHAHAHAHAHAHAHAHAHA

Bobby blinked. He hadn't actually meant it to be funny, but if that lightened the moment, he was all for it.

He really didn't want to think about him and Reg and Johnnies. That way lay monsters.

AND THE plumbing situation in the apartment was not much better. Bobby eyed the mess in the big plastic tub he'd brought in with distaste—and dispassion. He'd brought thick rubber/Teflon gloves, and they'd turned out to be one of the best investments of his life.

"You guys, this is bad," he said, looking at the corrosion in the U-joint. He'd switched the water off completely, and with a grunt he turned to the back of the toilet to see if the damage extended there. "Who's been tossing chunks in the sink?"

All four of the guys were gathered around the doorway, and Trey looked away, biting his lip.

And so did Lance.

They caught each other's eyes then, and their glances skittered away like squirrels accidentally climbing the same goddamned tree.

Skylar, Billy, and Rick stared at them in horror. "You guys." "Dudes!" "Ohmygod!"

"But... but *why*?" His eyes watered with more than the stench in the bathroom. "And it's seven o'clock at night—I need to go to a fucking hardware store, or you guys are gonna be pissing in the shower and shitting in the trash."

"That's amazing, Bobby," Billy said, dry as toast. "I didn't think I could get any queasier, but that did it."

Bobby scowled at them all. "Okay. I know this isn't fair, but I need Trey and Lance to come with me to the hardware store." He stripped off his gloves. "And someone else to rinse this shit off in the kitchen."

"Hm," Skylar mused. "Physical vomit or emotional vomit? Pass me the gloves, Bobby. I'm getting off easy."

"I'll go get trash bags," Billy offered, and Rick groaned.

"Great—I'll go get dish gloves from under the sink."

Bobby set the gloves down and scowled at his two former roommates, neither of whom could meet his eyes.

"This is gonna be a treat," he muttered. "Like I can fucking manage my own goddamned life?" They stood, like little kids, and Bobby had a thought.

Holy fuck. They were *all children*. No wonder Dex had seemed so overwhelmed.

"Everybody out to the truck," he muttered. "We've got about five minutes to get to the store before you guys are sneaking into McDonald's to take your morning poop."

Lance and Trey turned on their heels and trotted out, and Bobby turned to the vomit detail. "You guys got any ideas?" he asked, because... because he didn't get paid for this!

"You put the fear of God into them," Skylar said, sober as Bobby had never seen him. "Me and Rick'll get 'em addicted to health food. It's all we got."

Billy grunted. "I know the name of Chase and Tommy's shrink," he said, out of the blue. "I can call him and see if we can make an appointment."

Oh damn. Okay. Backup.

"Great. You guys do that shit, and I'll see what I can fuck up."

The three of them rolled their eyes, and Skylar spoke first. "Dude, you are scary grown-up compared to the rest of us assholes. I mean...." He gestured at the corroding pipes in the plastic tub. "They were literally rotting our plumbing with their problems. Go—fix everybody's pipes. We're there for you."

Bobby shook his head and followed Lance and Trey out the door.

GOD. LOWE'S. Bobby hated it—but he hated Home Depot too. Giant warehouses with *so much shit*. He always felt like he could wander those damned corridors for years and nobody would ever find him. Fortunately, Lance and Trey were super eager to help him find the plumbing supplies and the various pipes and shit, and Bobby wondered if they thought finding plumbing supplies would make it all okay.

But they weren't opening up, so he guessed it was his turn to talk.

"So when I was eleven years old, my dad beat my mom up until he had to take her to the hospital. He left me at home, hiding under the fucking bed, took her to the ER, and took off for I don't give a fuck where."

"Jesus," Trey muttered, and Lance just grimaced. Yeah, well, Lance was hella smart—he probably knew where this was going.

"So I was home for five days before my mom could ask anybody where her kid was, and the police sent someone to get me. And I'll give you ten guesses what happened."

"You ran out of food," Lance muttered.

"You bet your ass I did. The breakfast cereal and milk were gone by the second day, and then the tinned soup and the bread. By the time they sent somebody to my house, I was sifting old oatmeal through a strainer, getting rid of the bugs."

"That's fucking gross," Trey muttered.

"*You think?*" Bobby threw an extra U-joint into the basket he was holding with undue force. "And when I came to Sacramento—you guys saw me on the upswing. 'Cause I spent a month—a fucking *month*—sleeping in my truck so I didn't cook like a sardine with *forty* other poor bastards in the trailer. We had to live off fast food, but we were all saving money, so guess what. That was one meal a fucking day, and if you were loopy as a fucking butterfly by the end of the day, guess what happened."

"I know this one," Lance said, voice dry and quiet. "That's where you got the fresh scars on your thumb and your thigh."

Well, yeah. They'd been together, even if Lance hadn't seen his porn.

"You're damned straight," Bobby snarled, throwing six brackets in his basket, one at a time, hard enough that they bounced around a bit before they hit bottom. "And when I *got fired* from that fucking job, because—and get this—I was *clumsy*, I was living out of the back of my goddamned truck and trying to get a job. I went home and blew my girlfriend's brother 'cause he was fucking *blackmailing me*, and he shoved forty dollars in my back pocket. And you know what I did?"

"Kept it," Trey whispered.

Finally Bobby looked at him, because he sounded near tears. "You're goddamned right I did. I was fucking starving. So c'mon, guys—I don't get it. I don't fucking get it. Why? You're both fucking hot. You're both fucking smart. Neither of you are stuck in porn for fucking ever—you got prospects. So tell me. Help me understand here. *Why?*"

"Because I look in the mirror and I still see a fat kid," Lance said, sounding broken. "I work out, I work my rotation, I do my classwork, I shoot my scenes, and I feel so in control. And I go home, and all I can hear is my parents telling me to do better, and stories about what a fat little kid I was. And how… how much it sucks to be gay. And… I just… food is the thing I can't have. It's the one goddamned thing I can't have and—"

Bobby sighed and pinched the bridge of his nose, part of him trying to remember what else he needed to fix their goddamned bathroom.

"Control," he said, getting it.

"You're good." Lance's tone of voice would have melted the pipes if his stomach bile hadn't.

"I understand control," Bobby admitted, thinking about how easy it had been to fuck for the camera. His body, his call, his idea. Little boy from Dogpatch got to be a god. "I get it. But Lance—" And suddenly Bobby's hurt at the world at large flooded him. "Lance—these guys. They depend on you. And you know better. I mean—you *know* better, right? There's shit everywhere that tells you how bad this is for you—"

"Do you know how many doctors smoke?" Lance asked angrily. "What, I don't get one lousy vice—"

"Get fat!" Bobby snapped back. "Eat it. Own it. Have a fucking ice cream sandwich, for fuck's sake. Don't toss it down the fucking drain, man." His voice wobbled. "Man, Reg looks up to you—do you know how much?" He looked at Trey, who was staring at his hands. "Either of you? He—he's got nothing, but the way he looks at you guys, that gives him something, right? Like guys as smart as you will be his goddamned friends."

Trey wiped his eyes with his palm, one at a time. "You fucker," he mumbled. "That's… that's playing fucking dirty."

"Then talk to me," Bobby told him, his own eyes burning. A part of him was saying *What? You lived with these guys for two months and suddenly you're family?* But most of him was saying *God, I love these guys like my fuckin' brothers. How'd that happen? I didn't know there was that much of my heart to give.* "Both of you—did you know?"

Trey shrugged. "That's why both sets of pipes, Bobby. One night I left the door unlocked, and Lance walked in, and it became our thing."

"You couldn't have bonded over blowjobs?" he asked, hating that idea. "Because seriously—"

"Look—we just knew, okay?" Trey muttered. "And you don't know what it's like. I've looked at your fucking reviews—"

"For what?"

Trey rolled his eyes *and* his head. "Oh my God—your *porn*, Bobby—don't you ever look and see how people like what you do?"

"Why would I care what they say?" Bobby asked, feeling stupid. "I just care that they download it so I can afford to bring my mom down here and get her the fuck out of Dogpatch."

Trey and Lance exchanged a pitying look. "Well, that's great," Trey told him savagely, kicking at the absolutely immovable pole in the center of the aisle. "That's just fucking perfect. You don't even fucking look. Would you like to know what those comments say about me? 'Great smile but a big moon face—lose some weight, porky, and I'll care how you pork.'"

"Ouch," Lance muttered, but Trey wasn't done.

"That one's just clever. I get it all—I get fat face, fat ass, low body tone, concave chest—by God, there's *nothing* those fuckers won't criticize, and I get it, right? I get that you put yourself out there, you gotta expect some blowback, but I'm *killing* myself in the gym trying to fix that shit, and it's just never fucking enough—never. And I need the money, and I actually like the fucking work, but that shit on the computer, man—it just echoes in my head all day, and it's all I can hear and—"

"Sh…."

Bobby and Lance both moved in at the same time, folding Trey up between them, calming him down. He shook in their arms until the intercom sounded, telling them they had ten minutes to get their purchases and get the hell out.

One more second, two, and a final squeeze, and Trey pulled away.

"Sorry," he muttered. "Sorry—I didn't mean to come apart like—"

"You're both too bound up," Bobby muttered. "I mean, we get back and Billy's gonna have appointments with Chase and Tommy's shrink lined up for you guys, but I'm telling you right now—this shit is all…." He used the hand holding the basket to make a circle around his stomach. "Bound up. Like too much meat and not enough fruit. Constipated. It's all constipated in your soul. And you guys—you're living with a bunch of gay guys—"

"Billy's straight," Trey said reasonably.

"Like that fuckin' matters. You think he doesn't love you guys? You're living with a bunch of guys who can fuckin' listen. That's what I'm saying. You're living with a couple of health food nuts who'll turn your bodies inside out trying to make them perfect, but even better, you're living with *friends*." He felt this injustice keenly as he stalked toward the front of the giant musty vault of tiny bits and pieces used to repair the random shit in people's lives. "I mean, I was calling to ask a favor, and Trey didn't even hesitate—and I'm the outsider here, right? I bailed on your little flophouse 'cause...." He sighed. "'Cause sex would be too easy. I'm not wired that way." He swallowed a little, met their eyes, and shrugged. "I already fell for somebody, you know? I liked that person. I didn't want to fuck around with his feelings if I didn't have to."

"We get it," Lance said with a sigh. He placed his hand on the back of Bobby's neck and squeezed, his touch platonic and familiar and intimate all at the same time. This was why—*this* was why Bobby had stayed as long as he could. This was why he didn't want to leave Johnnies unless he had to. All those years living in Dogpatch, thinking he was a freak, letting Keith Gilmore talk him into fooling around when he knew it was wrong— all that was because he wanted *this*. A group. A community. A tribe he could count on.

And who could count on him.

"What do you get?" Bobby asked—but he didn't shrug Lance off.

"You're our friend. A good friend. And you care."

Bobby nodded. "Damned straight." He took a step forward and gave the clerk his basket of stuff, and Trey moved in to pay for it.

"I get a frequent-flyer discount," Bobby said, pulling out his card mournfully, and Trey laughed.

"You're fixing our plumbing for free, Bobby. And apparently trying to fix our lives too. Let us at least pay for our own parts."

"Yeah," Lance said. Then he wrinkled his nose in thought. "And weren't you going to ask us for a favor?"

Bobby nodded and waited for the clerk to bag their parts so they could leave.

As they were walking toward the truck, he told them his idea and how he needed an overnight watcher for Reg's sister.

He wasn't surprised when they said yes—but he was grateful.

"So you're taking Reg to meet your mom why?" Trey asked into the engine-rumbling quiet.

"Because." Bobby was glad he was driving. Trey's voice sounded thick, and Lance had been mostly monosyllabic since checkout. He wondered if this was what an intervention looked like, and if there was always an exhausted calm after the storm.

"And?" Trey prompted.

"Because there's not enough fucking moms here," he muttered. He remembered Dex, trying not to cry. He hadn't known, then, about Dex's best friend, Tommy, about Tommy's lover, Chase—but then Bobby had been dealing with Reg and the guys in the flophouse up close and personal. He was starting to *know* about how badly they needed some frickin' moms.

"Dude, we're grown," Trey snorted, and Bobby shook his head.

"The hell you are. You may think you are, because going home is like going to a hostile country, but you're not. I mean, I turn nineteen in May. I get that I have to register for the draft and I can get convicted for a felony, but I'm telling you! If I ever get arrested or deployed, the first person I'm frickin' calling is my mommy!"

Lance's choked laughter told him he'd hit a nerve.

"I know it's not that way for everybody," Bobby said quietly. "But Dex can't mom the whole company. And I'll do my best. But right now, Reg needs a mom. He needs to know it's not all awful. And my mom lives in a shitty little house because the guy who owns it is an asshole, but you know what? She brings out her best cooking every time I go. And I may not tell her everything—she might never know about the porn. But whether she knows exactly who he is to me or not, I want her to know about Reg. Because it's important, and she's my frickin' *mom*."

He'd left early on Christmas. That thought haunted him. Jessica and Keith—people he'd be happy if he never saw again—had influenced his decision, and he hadn't stayed through Christmas night. Maybe he hadn't felt how much he needed his mom until he saw how hard Reg's life was without his.

"So okay, then," Trey said into the following silence. "We'll let you take Reg to get mothered." He let out a huge sigh. "I think that's one of the most awesome things I've ever heard, actually."

"Think she'd adopt us?" Lance asked, and he pitched his voice playfully, but Bobby heard it. The longing. His stomach cramped with how much awful was in the world he couldn't fix.

But he could do something here. He could make sure Lance and Trey knew that hurting themselves was unacceptable.

It was all he had.

THE GUYS had cleaned up the mess with bleach and everything, so Bobby had no problem replacing the pipes and reconnecting all the clamps. He turned on the water again and flushed the toilet, then ran the water, just to make sure it all worked and nothing dripped. Then he turned to the watching roommates.

"Done," he told them. "But you're gonna rot another hole through the pipes if you guys don't fix yourselves."

Lance and Trey nodded soberly, and then Lance surprised him. "Hey— do you have to go back? You can stay and watch movies or something. We promise—everybody's clothes stay on."

Bobby grinned. "Yeah—absolutely."

He ended up staying the night. In the morning he woke up on the air mattress in time to hear Lance finish making an appointment with someone—Bobby assumed it was the shrink.

Bobby rolled over and saw him in the corner of the couch, arms wrapped around his shins, cheek on his knees.

"That was hard," he said.

"I'm sorry." Bobby felt like he'd made him do it.

"Don't be. It came from the right place. I just… I hurt."

Bobby nodded, thought about Reg at home with his sister. About his mom stuck up in the snow. About all these guys in this apartment, doing the best they could. "I hurt for you," he said. Meant it.

"Reg is a really good guy."

Bobby sat up in bed, surprised. "Yeah. I think so."

"Why didn't you hook up sooner?"

Bobby scrubbed his hands through his hair. "'Cause I was dumb. It's hard, you know? Figuring the difference between sex and love and what you should do and what you really want. I have sex at work, I guess. I make love with Reg. I should date and marry a girl. I really want a guy. Reg. That's as much as I've got figured out."

Lance half laughed. "I don't know if I've ever made love. I get all the sex I can handle. I should date and marry a girl. I don't want a girl. I'm supposed to become a doctor. But I'm so tired. So damned tired."

Bobby got up off the air mattress, grabbed his phone, and made it to the couch by the time Lance lost his shit. Rocking this guy—this guy he looked up to—in his arms and telling him it was all going to be okay made him more aware than ever how ill-equipped he was to be a grown-up.

And how he was the guy Reg depended on.

Navigating Strange Waters

REG WOKE up the day after his scene wondering why it felt like Christmas.

Then Bobby texted.

OMW—bringing a couple changes of clothes and some more stuff to work on the hallway.

And lube?

Didn't we still have some?

We're going to use more. Lots more. Swear.

God, he missed Bobby.

He'd come over during the day for lunch, to watch TV, keep Veronica company, and of course to work on the house. He kept eyeing Reg's cabinets with serious intent, and Reg was starting to get scared. There were canned goods in the back of those cabinets that predated Reg's twenty-first birthday. He honestly had nightmares sometimes about what would come out of those cans if opened.

But that didn't mean Reg didn't look forward to the rattle of Bobby's pickup as it pulled up next to Reg's Camaro in the driveway. Bobby brought games for them to play at night, and he and Reg were reading the same books and…

And Bobby kissed him at the car before he left. Long, deep, slow kisses, the kind that left Reg feeling breathless and young, like the world was wide-open and glorious and Reg could do anything with his life.

Anything.

And then Bobby would leave him, hard and aching and hating their jobs with a passion, and Reg would remember.

He was a porn model with no education to speak of, and caring for his sister was a full-time job.

Oh.

Oh yeah.

It was almost unfair how easy it was to forget all that with those long, powerful arms wrapped around him.

The night Bobby spent in the apartment with the guys had been interminable. Reg wasn't worried about Bobby getting laid. The whole reason he wasn't at Reg's that night was because he had a scene, and there was an abstinence period.

But he hadn't been with Reg.

The next day, though, he'd been thoughtful and withdrawn—and his kiss at the car had been particularly fierce, leaving Reg wrung out and shaky by the time he was done. He didn't say what was wrong, and Reg didn't know how to ask, but the next day had been his scene.

Reg had done lights in the other room, so he hadn't seen Bobby until after he was done, wrapped in a robe, and on the way to the shower.

He'd smiled tiredly at Reg and held out his hand, like he was keeping Reg far away.

"No kiss," he said, voice sounding rocky. "Not now. Wait until I'm clean, okay?"

And Reg stopped there, right in the hallway, and let Bobby pass, realizing what it meant, for him to be clean.

Somebody else's mark was on Bobby's skin. Somebody else's *come* was drying there. Maybe his voice sounded funny because he'd swallowed too much jizz and it had gone down the wrong tube—happened to Reg all the time.

For the first time in twelve years, it hit Reg. What he did for a living. Like it was brand-new and he was a virgin with no fucks under his belt.

And he was horrified.

That thing he did in the dark with Bobby—even those times they hadn't been naked, when Bobby had just come over and touched him, held him, kissed his neck or his shoulder, or even, once, down the bumps in his spine—those things were *his* things.

Except Bobby had just done those things under the lights, for the camera.

Reg didn't feel any resentment for the other guy in the shot—but dammit. He had so little in life that was *his*. He wanted his things *back*.

It was irrational. He told himself again and again; he knew this job. He knew what that kid brought into his house, into his bed, was special. Bobby wasn't giving the same kisses on the set that he was giving to Reg. He wasn't whispering the same things.

Whether Bobby topped or bottomed was the director's choice on the set, but in close and personal, when it was just the two of them, Bobby took charge. In a way it was almost scary how much Bobby seemed to know about telling Reg what to do, but in another way it made total sense.

Bobby *knew what to do*. He knew when Reg got too excited or just needed to be kissed hard and into the mattress. He liked to touch, sliding big work-roughened hands over Reg's skin like he was covering Reg with his essential person-ness, protecting Reg with a layer of warmth, giving him a thicker skin.

Reg saw Bobby sexed out, looking like he knew he didn't smell great, and he felt some of that warmth seep away.

Reg wanted his things back.

He was still standing there, reflector in hand, when Dex walked through the corridor and bumped him from behind.

"Uh… Reg?"

"Sorry, Dex. Just thinking." For a moment he was embarrassed, but if Dex thought there was anything weird about Reg *thinking*, he didn't say that.

"What about?"

"About… about what I do for a living."

Dex grunted. "Hold a reflector and listen to me say 'Dammit, flash your junk'?"

Reg snickered. Yeah, the last shot had been with a new guy who'd picked the name Harvey, which Reg thought was the dumbest porn name *ever*. He thought making o-faces and waving his wang around made for good film. Dex had needed to stop shooting to say "I know it's gross, but people like to see that thing moving in and out of the asshole, so you're gonna have to lean back. Do some stomach crunches if it's too hard, but it's necessary." And then Skylar, who'd been bottoming for this shot, had cracked up, and Dex had turned on him. "Dude, I know you douched and shit, but whatever protein drink you guys are downing now, it's *rank*. Maybe stick to fruit juice the day before the shot?"

"Aw, dammit, Dex!" Skylar had whined, "Now I've gotta think pineapple juice to get it up again. Do you know how wrong that is?"

Dex just looked at him. "I watch guys have sex day in, day out. If I can do it without smell-o-vision, there's a chance I might get laid myself, so no. I don't feel sorry for you. Seriously—what have you been drinking?"

"Spinach, kale, and this new sort of protein powder that… uh… I haven't tried… uh…."

Dex was staring at Skylar and touching his nose. "Bingo."

"Yeah. It's bad. Sorry."

Dex shook his head. "No worries. Harvey there apparently can get it up in a meat-packing plant. Everybody, break for hygiene and Gatorade. Back in five."

So their jobs were not exactly glamorous, but it was finally hitting Reg why any guy who was hung like a god and could come on command might opt out of porn.

"Reg?" Dex shoulder-bumped him. "C'mon, man. Let's get to the next set—it's just a basic intro video. New guy."

Reg brightened for a minute. "Really? Audition tape?"

"Yeah. This guy's pretty hot. If he does good, we may fly him out from Kansas City and back to film."

Reg sighed. Another guy who got to go places Reg had never seen. Another new face—and new dick—in porn, to replace the guys who had grown out of porn and were now on to the grown-up parts of their lives.

"Well, if a horny teenager awaits," he muttered and walked around the complex to the other bedroom set to film.

THE BOY was pretty—super pretty, actually. He had longish blond hair and a wide, smiling mouth—not unlike Bobby's. Big brown eyes too. Reg had been in the business long enough to know that the way he brought himself off slowly, his face relaxed and happy, arching like a bowstring as he shot, and the almost decadent pleasure he got from licking his own come off his hand—all that would make him a surefire winner at Johnnies.

But Reg felt none of the protectiveness over this one—Kip—as he felt for Bobby.

When Kip was done and collapsed on the bed, laughing softly at his own audacity, Reg shyly handed him a towel and then offered him a robe. The kid took it, but of course all his attention afterward was taken up by Dex and whether or not he'd passed the audition.

Well, duh.

But Reg looked at Dex and got a brief thank-you salute before he went up front and found Bobby chatting over the counter with Kelsey.

"Reg!" she said as he walked around the front. "Hey, buddy—I cut your check today. Do you want it?"

Oh yeah—payday was always good, especially when you'd been working extra days as the light guy.

"Sure. Why'd you cut it early?"

She grinned at him cheekily, pregnancy rounding out her face, but in a pleasant way. She'd been all sharp points and angles before, but Reg liked soft women—round and substantial. Maybe because he'd done enough guys to be worried about breaking the super-skinny girls.

"You're one of the first ten guys on my list," she said with a shrug. "So I print out a batch of ten, and hey, hello…."

"I get paid." He kept a grin on his face because it was a nice thing she was doing, but inside he died a little.

"So mine doesn't come out until tomorrow," Bobby said, but not like he was asking for a special favor.

"Sorry, Bobby."

He winked and waved his hand. "No worries. I got tips to tide me over. But I send most of this check to my mom, so I can tell her when the money's going to come."

Kelsey held her hand to her mouth. "You don't send her money, do you? Like cash?"

Bobby shrugged. "I send her an insured money order. Why?"

She frowned and started writing information on a business card. "Okay—so this is the information I need you to bring me for your mom. Don't worry, I won't look at it, you will. But once we have this from her and this from you, you can—" She frowned again. "You've got a smartphone, right?"

Bobby grimaced and pulled out a *very* dated version of the phone Kane had talked Reg into buying that fall. "Not so much."

Kelsey scowled at him. "Okay—look. I'm going to cut your check right now." She sorted through some numbers on her computer and hit some keys. A specialized printer by her knees started spitting out a familiar piece of paper. "I've seen the numbers—you're getting residuals with this one, and it's way big." She ripped the check off the printer and handed it to Bobby, nodding so he could look at the numbers.

"Damn," he whispered, and Reg watched his face carefully. Not greed. Not "Whoopie, gonna have fun tonight!" Relief. It was a look of sheer relief. Reg got it then, the responsibility for his mom that had been weighing Bobby down the same way Reg's deal with his sister seemed to weigh on him. Maybe that was why Bobby was so good with V.

But Kelsey didn't know any of this. "You need to go out and buy a smartphone—something current. And then I'm gonna show you how to transfer your funds to your mom's account so you don't have to mail shit. And *then* I'm gonna show you how to fuckin' live, kid, 'cause by this time in their careers, most of these bozos have a new phone, a new car, and a new fuckin' leather jacket to show off their new porn bodies. I'm sayin'—you're doing all of the work and getting none of the bennies."

Bobby laughed, taking the rant with easy humor. "Fair enough—and you're right. When I was looking for a job, the phone could have saved me a whole lot of running the truck up to my mom's to fill out applications."

Kelsey nodded firmly. "Well, now you've got a couple of jobs, you can use it for other things. Reg, help him get a phone and a data plan and all that other shit we need here in the twenty-first century, okay?"

"Sure thing, Kelse."

"And then bring him back here tomorrow so I can show him how to use some of that shit."

"Sure thing, Kelse." Bobby echoed.

She rolled her eyes at him. "Are you two a thing?" she asked suspiciously.

Bobby's cheeks went a flattering pink, and Reg found it suddenly hard to meet her eyes. "Uh—"

"I help him fix his house," Bobby mumbled.

Kelsey rolled her eyes again. "Sure. You have a cell phone from the dark ages, and you use your money to help him fix his house. Men. You all suck."

Reg's inner twelve-year-old surfaced. "Well, not all of us. Just, you know, gay guys and bi guys and porn guys—*we* all suck. But straight guys aren't supposed to do that sort of thing."

She clapped her hand over her eyes. "Go away," she groaned. "I love you, Reg, but go away. I'll see you both tomorrow, after you've had sex and you can pretend you're not a thing some more."

"I'm not getting laid, Kelse," Reg said, laughing. "I've got two more days before my shoot—you know that."

She banged her head softly against the counter. "Could you... could you both just not? You're masculine pheromoning all over my nice little desk here. Go away."

"Sure," Bobby said, bumping Reg's shoulder with his own. "We'll see you tomorrow, Kelsey. We love you, Kelsey. You're gonna be a good mom, Kelsey."

"Shoo!"

They laughed and left, and Bobby walked toward Reg's car. "Tell you what," he said, sounding happy. "I'll follow you to your house, and we can check on your sister, then do what Kelsey said and get an iPhone, 'cause she's right. I'm not up to getting the laptop yet, but I understand you can get books cheap on your phone too."

"Wow," Reg said, suddenly seeing the potential of having books in his back pocket without abusing his beloved paperbacks. "You'll have to show me how that works."

Bobby nodded soberly. "Sure thing. See you at your house." Suddenly he grinned, the tiredness of filming the scene seeming to fall away, along with that weird shame that had seemed to take him over in the hallway. "We can celebrate a little," he said softly. "No sex until your scene—but we can have some fun."

Oh wow. Like a date. It had been so long since Reg had gone on a date with someone, he'd almost forgotten that was an option.

V HAD been in a dark mood when they brought her lunch, and Reg had made her take the extra pink pill, just in case. She'd downed it with a scowl and some curse words—but no violence—and Reg called it good.

He and Bobby had opted out of fast food, because Bobby had asked for some recs and found a bistro not far from his apartment in midtown. Reg felt very fancy in a place that served tasters of beer and a special fruit-and-veggie plate. Bobby was starving, so he ordered a hamburger, all the extras, and he carved off a little bite.

"I won't tell," he said with a wink. "You've got two and a half days—it'll be gone by then."

Reg laughed and told Bobby the Skylar's-special-sauce story (as Dex had called it by the end of the shoot), and Bobby chortled, washing down his hamburger with soda, since he was too young to order beer. When they were done, Bobby left a big tip because he said the service was great, and Reg was impressed too.

"I never tried to wait tables," he said, embarrassed, as they walked back to his car. "Fast food was hard enough—always loud and people yelling."

"I just smile a lot," Bobby said, shrugging. "And when I screw up, I try to fess up." His face clouded. "Which reminds me—well, of a couple of things. A good thing and a bad thing, really—but you have to know the bad thing before we talk about the good thing."

Oh crap. "You do know I'm not that bright, right?"

To his surprise, Bobby smacked him on the back of the head. "Stop saying that. Just... just stop. I was being confusing. That was not your fault."

"Okay, fine." Reg squinted at him and repositioned his stocking cap. "Could you maybe be *less* confusing? Just a little?"

Bobby grunted and buttoned up his jacket. Kelsey had been right—warm leather coats were sort of the Johnnies uniform, and Bobby was wearing a denim jacket with a hooded sweatshirt underneath. Reg remembered how, right after Thanksgiving, Kane had come in wearing a really nice warm coat and new hat, because Dex had bought them for him. They had become a couple, and Dex wanted to take care of him.

Reg paused, almost tripping over a crack in the sidewalk. "Do you want a coat?" he asked, baffled by this sudden impulse. But... but Bobby was *cold*. And he was wearing a denim jacket that was coming apart at the seams.

Bobby rolled his eyes. "I've got one. And it's not hardly cold here—it's way colder in the mountains. My mom's up to her ass in snow. I just need a phone."

Reg stared at him, hood up around his neck, his hands—skilled and work-roughened—red and chapped. "You... you need warm stuff," he said stubbornly. "We'll get a phone first. Then Target."

"Not Walmart?" Bobby asked, amused.

Reg shook his head. "The ceiling freaks me out," he answered. "Target has gloves. We'll go there."

"You're driving," Bobby said, bumping their shoulders together. "I can't stop you."

Reg wanted to take his hand—his cold, rough hand—and blow on it, make it warm. Who did that in public? Boys and girls, that's who. Reg shrugged unhappily. "Yeah. Yeah. Then that's where we'll go."

He kept his word too, after he and Bobby spent a long damned time talking about data plans and bandwidth and available apps. Reg got it, because most of the guys at Johnnies had, at one time or another, spent time with him buying a phone. Bobby's eyes were glazing over by the time the sales guy put in the SIM card and activated the phone.

"There you go," the smiling salesman said. He was cute—in his twenties, big brown eyes and pale bronze skin—and had shown off his phone with pictures of his wife and kids as he'd shown Bobby the works. "Now all you gotta do is take a picture of your girlfriend for wallpaper."

One corner of Bobby's mouth quirked in, and for a moment, Reg was afraid he was going to be mean or militant or even just really, really personal in the face of this stranger.

"Reg," he said instead. "Here—let me get a few pix."

Reg saw them, a series of them, when Bobby was done. His mouth open and his eyes wide in surprise, then his teeth biting his lip shyly as he looked away. Finally he was looking directly into the camera and smiling, his nose wrinkled a little, one side of his mouth twisted just a bit higher than the other.

"Those are real good pictures," Bobby said, his voice low and sort of intimate. "I'll put this one as my screensaver."

"That one?"

Reg's chin was pointed away, but his eyes were looking into the camera, and he was biting one side of his lip.

"That's the one," Bobby said, winking before he turned to the salesman. "Here—is there anything else I have to sign?"

"Nope." The guy smiled at the two of them warmly. "You guys have a real nice day."

They left the store, and it hit Reg as they neared the car. "Hey, Bobby?"

"Yeah."

"Do you think he knew we're a couple?"

Bobby shrugged. "I think he might have guessed." He let out a breath. "Target next?"

"Yeah."

Reg started the car to steer them deeper into midtown before Bobby spoke again.

"Would it have bothered you? If he did?"

Reg grunted. "No. I mean, I go in public with Johnnies guys all the time. Some of 'em are... uh... *out* out. Doesn't bother me. Just, you and me, I just... we didn't say anything. Didn't do anything. Didn't hold hands or... you know."

"PDA?"

"Yeah. PDA."

Bobby grunted. He did that a lot when he was thinking, and Reg didn't mind, because it meant neither one of them was comfortable with words. So many of the guys were going to school or just really smart in general. One of the nice things about Bobby was that words weren't toys to him. Like everything else around Bobby, they were strictly functional.

"I used to hold hands with Jessica in public, and I spent a lot of time trying to get away from that. I'd go fetch her ice cream or hold groceries— anything so I didn't have to touch her personally."

Reg grimaced. "That's not friendly."

"No. But... well, there was this guy, her brother, Keith. And we'd...." He looked out the window. "This is embarrassing," he said glumly. "This is, like, the worst thing I've ever done. But we were both going out with girls—I was going out with his sister, for chrissakes. But we, you know. Blowjobs. And that was all it was. He'd give me mine and I'd give him his. And I'd want to...." He sighed. "I wanted to touch him. So bad. You're the first man who let me touch you like I wanted to touch him when we did that. That's why I got so confused, I think. There were the blowjobs, and I wanted to touch him, but if I *did* touch him, I'd be gay. And... the truth was, I just really, really... *liked* him."

"Like you like me?" Reg asked, trying to put this in perspective. Reg wasn't the first guy Bobby liked. That would take some getting used to.

"Well, not nearly as much," Bobby told him as they came to a stop. Reg looked at him sideways then, and found that same shy smile at his lips that Bobby had captured on his camera. He'd had no idea that was in him— prettiest picture he'd ever taken.

"But I didn't know that," Bobby added, looking away. "Light's green, Reg."

"'Kay." Reg pulled through the light and kept going toward Target.

"Anyway, there was no touching. No softness. And I… I wanted that. But he was getting married in a few months—they put the wedding off, but it should have been October. Anyway, I told him no. No more. Wasn't right. We were lying, and it didn't sit right."

Reg had to smile. "That's my boy."

"Yeah?"

He didn't even have to think about it. "Yeah. You make mistakes—but same mistakes everybody else does. You're just super good at learning from them, that's all."

Bobby grunted again, but it sounded like a happy grunt. "Well, thanks. Unfortunately this mistake didn't go away."

"How could it not go away?" 'Cause it was that simple, right? You tell a guy no, he backs off.

"Dogpatch is a small-assed town, Reg. He threatened to spread rumors about me—the kind that would keep me from getting work, the kind that would get my mom treated bad. His dad owns the house she lives in—"

"The one who won't do any improvement on it?"

"That's the one. So… you know. Every time I went up there… got…." His voice broke. Oh hell. Bobby's voice broke, like his heart hurt. "Got fuckin' awful. 'Cause Jessica wanted sex, and then Keith wanted his goddamned blowjob, and my mom was all 'Baby, go play with your friends!' and I just wanted to spend time with *her*. Because coming down here wasn't that easy, and I just wanted my mom, right? So when I broke up with Jessica, I got to break up with Keith—but he keeps swinging by my mom's house and saying things like 'We've got to get your boy back up here.'"

"Like hell!" Reg rubbed his stomach. "I feel… oh God. Bobby, he made you?"

"Yeah." That one word, and it sounded so hopeless.

Reg reached over and grabbed for his hand, and Bobby helped him out. "That sucks." Oh God. "I mean, that's *terrible*. I'm…. What an asshole! I want to rip his nuts off!"

Bobby let out a weak laugh. "Well, you may get to meet him, but I'd rather you not. My mom still has to live in that damned town."

It was Reg's turn to grunt. He knew this reason. He got sacrifice for people. But… but this?

"Would she want you to—"

"No—but she doesn't know I'm gay either."

"Are you ever going to tell her?" Reg asked, wondering. Who did they hold hands in front of? Not V—not with the way she went off about whoever the people on TV were going off against. Not in public, because both of them were still learning that they could touch at all, much less in front of other people. In front of friends?

It was complicated, and Reg wondered if *that* was why it hadn't occurred to him to have a relationship with a man before this. Complicated was way above his pay grade.

"I wanted to," Bobby said, and something in his voice made Reg ache. "I wanted you to come with me."

"I... how would I leave V?" he asked. First thing—always.

"I asked Trey and Lance," Bobby said, but he didn't sound proud. "I sort of did some work on the apartment for them. They said they could stay with her in February, early. And the snows should be less deep by then, because I don't have any chains. Does that sound like it would work?"

"You're asking me?" Reg felt a little bewildered. "Because I have such a rocking social calendar that once you had V taken care of, I might go on a cruise or something?"

"No." Bobby sighed. "I mean, I *am* asking you. But mostly to be selfish. Because I just... I'm going to come out to my mom, Reg. And I'm not doing it because of you, or for you—but you're who I'm coming back to if it goes really fucking wrong."

"Well, yeah, of course," Reg said, without irony. "Because if that's what you need, that's what I can do for you."

Bobby squeezed his hand. "Also...."

It wasn't like him to hesitate. "Also what?"

"My mom's a good mom. I just... you haven't seen a good mom a lot lately. And if she doesn't freak out at the gay, I thought... you know."

"You want your mom to... take over for me?" Reg asked, tickled for some reason.

"I want you to feel cared for," Bobby said. "Even if it's just for a little teeny bit of time."

Reg grunted. "Maybe come out at the beginning," he said practically. "That way, if she seems all nice and then gets mean to you, I won't get attached."

"That's a really good idea," Bobby said sincerely. And then he did that thing they just agreed they weren't ready to do in public, but they were in the car so maybe it didn't matter.

He took Reg's knuckles to his mouth and kissed them, with just a little bit of tongue.

Reg whined in his throat. That was no goddamned fair. None. They were going to his house to watch TV and read and for Reg to pretend he didn't want Bobby so damned bad, with a two-and-a-half-day window in front of them where he wasn't supposed to screw around.

This wasn't usually a problem. It wasn't. But Bobby's hot breath and slick tongue—on his knuckles, of all places—was making him stiff and drooling while he was driving the goddamned car.

He wasn't going to make it unless he kicked Bobby out of his house for the next two days.

"Want to get some popsicles at Target?" Bobby asked after he relinquished Reg's hand. "That way we can have dessert and you don't have to worry about eating heavy."

"Yeah," Reg answered, conveniently ignoring the idea of kicking Bobby out of his house so he could work in two days. "That sounds great."

DINNER WAS chicken broth for him and heartier soup for Bobby and V, and their evening found them in front of the television, Bobby and Reg reading, Veronica's voice rising and falling in response to the news guys, who were preaching to the lost.

They gave V ice cream afterward, but Bobby had a popsicle in solidarity, and then they put V to bed.

Bobby yawned and stretched, smiling sleepily as he stood up and began to turn off lights. He'd bought a nightlight for the bathroom, Reg had noticed, so he didn't have to leave the kitchen or the porch light on but nobody stubbed their toes in the darkness.

Together they turned for the bed, Reg's cock a swollen, aching thing in his pants, and he wondered when he was going to tell Bobby to go home, or sleep on the couch, or… oh God. Bobby went into the bedroom first, and all Reg could notice in the shadows was his back.

He'd been doing butterflies and other back exercises, and after he pulled off his sweatshirt, Reg could see the smooth hills and valleys of his distinct muscles under his shirt.

"Wait," he whispered, thinking if he could just look, he'd be okay. "Just...." Maybe just touch. He lined up along Bobby's back and wrapped his hands under Bobby's armpits, tugging on his shoulders so Reg could place a line of kisses.

First along the bare skin of the back of his neck, the touch of his lips to the salt under Bobby's longish hair sending a charge through Reg's body straight to the pit of his balls. Oh! He couldn't just stop!

His tongue flirted with the crew neck of Bobby's T-shirt, and Reg yanked on it so he had more access to smooth, bare Bobby.

Bobby let out a quick breath. "Reg... what are you doing? I thought you had to—"

"Mine," Reg whispered, although that was stupid. Bobby had spent two miles in traffic telling Reg about the first guy he'd ever wanted to touch him like this, and it wasn't Reg.

But that wasn't what mattered right now. What mattered was Bobby letting his head drop forward, rounding the pretty curve of his spine, making it easier for Reg to plant kisses. Just a few more. Reg tugged the shirt up and spanned his slender waist, rubbed his face against Bobby's shoulder blade like a cat, before kneading Bobby's pecs, marveling at how tight and bulky his chest had become in the past few months.

"Reg, uh—" He was going to remind Reg—no sex, not tonight.

"Just more," Reg begged. He kneaded some, pinching Bobby's nipples, tugging lightly, wanting to taste but needing the full-body contact right now.

"Nungh!" Bobby bucked, grazing Reg's erection with his backside, and Reg slid a hand beneath his waistband to pin his hips. There. Right there. Reg bucked up against him, now that he was still, his cock straining through two layers of denim to wedge itself in the crack of Bobby's ass.

Bobby whimpered a little, twisting his body so Reg's grip slipped and he could feel the silken tickle of hair.

"You sore?" he whispered. "Sexed out? Sensitive?"

"Not much—ah...."

In Reg's palm. It needed to be there. Reg gripped it, hard and full, stroking shortly, and Bobby made more helpless sounds. "Reg!"

"I want it back," Reg told him, sure he wasn't making any sense but needing to say it anyway. "Never had a mine before."

He slid around to Bobby's front, and Bobby stopped him, taking his mouth in a kiss, overwhelming him, his own mouth hot and almost angry, dominating Reg, telling him what was good, what was right about the two of them together.

Reg gave back. He wanted *his* back. Someone else had touched it, played with it, done things to it, and Reg never had something good. He wanted this good thing back in his arms, back in his body.

His good thing needed to be outside and inside him, right now.

Bobby groaned and shuddered, his cock spurting a little in Reg's hand. "Reg, you can't—"

"My good thing," Reg muttered. "Mine." He lowered his head to one of Bobby's nipples, knowing they were sensitive and needing Bobby to not talk so much and just let Reg do this. His body craved—just—oh, Bobby's nipple popped in Reg's mouth, tickled his tongue, and Bobby tugged on the short strands of Reg's hair.

"Reg… Reg, I'm sort of on a peak, really—"

Reg pulled back reluctantly. "Good," he breathed and sank to his knees, fumbling only a minute for Bobby's belt and fly before shucking the whole works down.

Bobby's cock didn't so much flop as unfurl, and Reg took it in one hand and stroked while flicking his tongue over the head. Soap and water, even dryer sheets—Bobby's skin needed to be licked some more before it even tasted like Bobby's skin again.

Good.

Reg let his mouth fill with spit and slurped hard on the head. Bobby let out a startled cry, and his knees gave a definite wobble.

"Reg?"

But Reg had no words. The only explanation he had in his head was that he wanted Bobby back, which was stupid, because Bobby hadn't gone anywhere. All he knew was that—*pump*—if he didn't get—*suck*—Bobby's taste in his mouth—*slurp*—he would fly apart at the seams!

Ah….

Bobby's bitter spurt of precome flooded his taste, and Reg swallowed, hoping it was like an antidote to the fire of need that rushed his body.

For a moment he could breathe, but Bobby bucked and shuddered, and Reg swallowed again. It wasn't going to be enough.

"Turn around," he rasped.

"Reg—"

Reg didn't bother with more words. Instead of turning Bobby around, he scooted behind him and bent him over the bed.

Taste. Taste him.

He spread Bobby's cheeks and licked without fear. Soap again. Fabric softener. Bobby had done his damnedest to clean away the remnants of the job. Reg probed with his tongue, and Bobby opened for him easily, already stretched and loosened from his day's work.

"Reg," Bobby gasped, moaning into the coverlet. "What're ya—"

Reg licked some more, harder, until Bobby tasted like skin, like Reg's spit, like human being. Bobby collapsed against the bed, shaking.

"Can you?" Reg begged, resting his cheek against Bobby's nether cheek. "Can you? I need… God, Bobby. I ain't never needed like his before. Can you do it again tonight? Tell me no, and I'll… uh, go beat off in the bathroom or something. But can you?"

"Please," Bobby whispered. Something in his voice, something broken, told Reg he needed this too.

Reg stripped in record time, and by the time he was naked, boots thrown in opposite corners of the room, Bobby was in the center of the bed on his knees and elbows, head resting against his clasped hands, ass presented out, waiting.

For a breath, Reg looked at him in an agony of indecision. He wanted… wanted…

Had to have.

He didn't remember mounting the bed or slathering the lube—but the slick, tight embrace of Bobby's asshole clenching around him—*that* shocked him to himself, brought him boiling to the surface of his skin, snarling.

Bobby moaned softly, shaking under his onslaught, and Reg pulled him up by the shoulder, wrapping his arms around Bobby's chest and thrusting into his ass like a great devouring machine.

Soft grunts filled the air, both of them keeping their voices subdued for V's sake, and the slap of their flesh together echoed loudly. Bobby clenched Reg's hands at his chest, and he reached behind to tug Reg's hair. For his part Reg bit his neck, his shoulder, his back, scraping with his teeth.

Bobby's hands, work-roughened and strong, grounded him, kept him from flying apart, from yelling too loud and drawing blood.

He needed those arms, long and muscular, wrapped around him.

Pulling out was an agony, but he did it anyway and whispered, "Turn around." Bobby, who knew how to give an order, did exactly that, holding his thighs up, spreading them, lifting his hips.

Reg shoved pillows under his ass, remembering how to be thoughtful, and then he was back inside, Bobby's body welcoming him again.

Bobby's cock lay across his lower stomach, engorged but not straining, and as Reg pulled back to slam forward, Bobby dropped his thigh to grab it. With his first few strokes, Bobby's asshole clamped tighter, and Reg let out a gasp, thrusting forward again. Bobby's noises were breathy, sensitized, like every touch blurred the boundaries of pleasure and pain.

Reg remembered what it was like to have sex after a scene, when your body was sexed out but your soul was still empty. With a quiet roar, he thrust forward harder, trying to drive out the emptiness, hit the note of pain, make Bobby's body sing so Reg could drink his fill of this beautiful, smart, strong boy in his bed.

Every stroke both quenched his thirst and stoked the fire higher.

Bobby gave a low cry, and his back arched almost violently. He stroked his cock slowly, hard at the tip, and he oozed come, milking his body dry.

God, that was sexy. It was why they filmed the come shot, so you could see the body do something wonderful. Reg's own orgasm rushed up on him, and he groaned and shook, flying apart like he'd tried so hard not to do.

His howl of completion rumbled out from his stomach and contracted all the things—taint, gut, nipples—even the muscles in his neck contorted, and he threw his head back and sobbed as he climaxed so hard he thought he'd bring the house down on his head. One more thrust, and again and again and….

"Oh *balls!*" he swore, falling sideways and trembling. He pulled out of Bobby, still spurting, and before Bobby could even move, he scrambled down the bed to pull that amazing cock into his mouth and taste, and taste, and swallow.

Bobby groaned, sliding out of Reg's mouth and rolling to his side, and Reg flailed, trying to anchor himself to something, anything, because he was going to bounce off the ceiling, for fucking chrissakes, he really was.

AMY LANE

"Sh." Bobby rolled back over, reaching around to grab the back of Reg's neck and hold him still. "Stay there."

Reg nodded, held in place by Bobby's will and the firm, not painful, grip on his neck.

Bobby moved some more, until he was lying on top of Reg, their wet groins mashed together. Instead of frotting or grabbing or any of the sex things, though, Bobby just kissed him gently, opening his mouth and going in. Every time Reg's body gave a sharp tremble, Bobby kissed him harder, longer, the kissing the main thing, not a buildup to something else.

Reg moaned, and then softer and softer, until when Bobby pulled away, Reg lay limp against the quilt, freezing except for where Bobby was touching him.

"Sorry," Reg breathed, one last hard shudder racking him. "So sorry."

"Sh." Bobby kissed him again, and then again, finally rolling over to his side and taking Reg with him until they were face-to-face. With some wiggling and squirming, they kicked the quilt down to the bottom of the bed so Bobby could pull it over their shoulders, but he stayed close, close enough that their chests touched when they both breathed in at the same time.

Finally Reg's breathing returned to almost normal. He groaned and pushed his face into Bobby's chest. "Goddammit, I'm going to have to call Dex."

"Yeah," Bobby murmured. "I wondered about that. What happened?"

Reg shook his head. "I... I don't know. I just needed. Just needed you. That's never—that's never happened to me before. Not even when I was a kid and I was made of jizz. I don't understand. I just... it was like, today, when I saw you in the hall. It was like you got taken far away from me, and I needed you back."

"Mm." Bobby rubbed his palm along the outside of Reg's arm. "It's the job, Reg," he said after a painful moment. "Someone else touched me. It made you mad."

"Yes!" Oh my God! The words were like an explosion in his head, all the words—painful words—like *jealousy* and *faithfulness* and *cheating* rolled into his heart. "Wait—how come... I mean, I've never felt that before. Jesus, Bobby, how come I've never thought of that before?"

He was starting to shake again, and Bobby hushed him until he calmed down. "Maybe this is special," Bobby whispered. "Maybe I'm special to you."

"Yeah." The word seemed to hurt Reg's throat. "I knew that."

Bobby closed his eyes softly, and when he opened them, they were bright and shiny. "I don't want to be with anyone else. Does that help?"

"Even that guy?" Reg asked, because this had seemed to make the wound worse. "Keith Gilmore? What if he—"

Bobby shook his head. "No. Blackmail, Reg. I had sex on film today. For money. And I don't feel dirty. *Keith* made it dirty."

Oh! Reg's eyes burned. "Did I?"

"No." Bobby kissed him, almost chastely, like a big brother, on the lips. "No."

"This is so confusing," Reg admitted. "But you... like this. You feel... bigger." He grimaced. "Not your dick, but that thing—ain't getting any smaller." He closed his eyes and leaned his forehead against Bobby's chest. "Just... just you. In my heart. You're bigger than I've had. It's like... like my heart has to get used to your size."

Bobby let out a little laugh. "Fair enough. But maybe... you know. Try to find the words before we have to call our boss again and say we had sex when we weren't supposed to."

"Augh!" Reg was suddenly so contrite he almost couldn't stand it. "I just mauled you all over your body, and Dex is gonna kill me, and—"

"Sh...." Bobby kissed his forehead, and Reg took a deep breath. "Good. Like that," Bobby urged. "Ain't nothin' bad gonna happen tonight."

REG WENT in to talk to Dex while Bobby was working on his phone with Kelsey. He asked for John at first, because he was used to John being in charge, but Dex gave a tired smile.

"John's got sort of a family thing going now. He'll be back in a month or two. Right now I'm what you got."

Reg shrugged. John had been looking pretty strung out the last time Reg had seen him—greasy hair, bad complexion. Reg knew the signs—a lot of his friends from high school had made themselves crazy on drugs. If John was doing rehab, good for him.

"You're good," he decided. "I, uh... well, I've got a shoot in two days, and I sort of...." The blush caught him by surprise. "Uh, need another day."

Dex's eyebrows shot up. "Do I want to know why?"

"So I can test with the window?" Reg thought that would be obvious.

"I figured that," Dex said impatiently. "Why would you blow your abstinence? I mean, what's it been—ten years? If you didn't think with that thing when you were a kid, I don't know why you'd let it do the talking now."

Reg scowled. "Sometimes it's the smartest part of my body, you ever think of that? I've never had anything mine before, and… well, I wanted something—some*one*—mine."

Dex's obvious frustration eased, and he took a deep breath and sighed it out. "Yeah. Yeah, Reg. Believe it or not, I'm getting that right now. Like, personally. It's… it's a different way of thinking, right?"

Reg nodded soberly. Dex once asked him if he'd do a gig just for business. Reg and Dex had gone into a hotel room full of horny businessmen and fucked them into a coma. Twelve hours later they walked gingerly out with nothing more than a signature on a paper and a shit-ton of hickeys. Dex had upped the percentage on Reg's royalties since that week, which had more than paid for Reg's time, but Reg wondered. Would either of them do that again?

Reg thought about Dex and Kane, touching each other casually at the Christmas party, looking at each other with diamonds in their eyes.

No. They wouldn't.

"We're… we're changing," he said, feeling stupid.

But Dex shrugged. "Yeah. Yeah—growing up, maybe. It's about time."

Growing up. Would that mean doing something besides fucking his way through life?

"God," Reg moaned, burying his face in his hands. "I am *so* unprepared."

Dex let out a bitter laugh. "Yeah, well, join the club. I'll push you guys back a day. Lance won't mind."

Reg wanted to brighten—he liked Lance. But then he remembered: he liked Lance.

Was that bad? To like the guy he was going to fuck for money?

He wanted badly to ask Dex, but he couldn't figure out how.

Dex picked up on something, though. His weary expression softened. "It gets harder as we get older," he said softly. "It should. I mean, sex should mean something. We don't think that when we're nineteen and we can fuck anything."

"I like Lance," Reg said. "He's not who I want to be with. Is that bad?"

"No," Dex responded immediately. "His heart's not gonna be involved. He knows yours isn't. You like working with the guy. As far as porn goes, it's perfect."

"Perfect?" Reg admitted it—he was reaching for straws. He didn't expect Dex's expression to turn bleak.

"You don't want to... to have a scene with someone you really care for," Dex said. "I mean, it's complicated enough as it is. But this way, you know sex is sex and loving someone—that's different. It's more important." Dex's full mouth twisted wryly. "So, like, you know—apparently more important than your abstinence window?"

Reg had the grace to look away, embarrassed. "Yeah. Like more important than my abstinence window," he admitted.

"Well, it happens. Ready to tell anybody who the lucky girl is?"

Reg squinted at him, confused. But then, he'd been telling people for years—*years*—that he was mostly straight. Why *wouldn't* Dex think it was a girl?

He fought the urge to look out of Dex's window, where Kelsey was sitting with Bobby, helping him set up his bank account so he could pay his mom.

"No," Reg said, wishing he could put a cold cloth on his forehead and have somebody bring him ice cream. V used to do that, he remembered plaintively. Before their lives became a constant battle over whether or not she should take her meds and what the people on TV were saying, he used to come home from a scene and tell his sister he'd had a bad day at work. She'd bring him dessert and put a cloth on his forehead and let him have the television.

But he didn't have her to do that anymore, and he couldn't explain to Bobby why he was confused—not yet—and pretty much, Dex was making things better and worse.

"Well, I'd be glad to meet her when you are," Dex said kindly. He looked out at Kelsey and grimaced. "'Cause, seriously. This place needs more women, you think?"

Reg grinned at him—it was a funny joke, right? Gay porn place, needing more women. But he liked Kelsey—he liked women in general— and he had to agree.

"I thought you guys were gonna keep working on the het, right?"

Dex rolled his eyes. "It's doing some money," he admitted. "I just need to get better at directing it."

Reg stood up, because he had to do one more thing before he could collect Bobby and go home. "You will," he said with confidence. "You know what makes porn good. It's not always the sex or the putting the thing in the place."

"What is it?" Dex said, but like he had his own answer and just wanted to see what Reg's would be.

"It's the people like each other," Reg said thoughtfully. "You were right—it's the perfect working situation. Your job is to like who you're with and make that person happy. I'm a fan."

Dex grinned then. "Glad to hear it." He shook Reg's hand, like they *were* grown-ups and not just talking about being grown-ups, and Reg walked into the back to take his blood test for his window. And then he went up front to collect the guy nobody knew he was sleeping with and everybody thought was a girl.

They went to the big hardware store afterward—they'd brought the truck, and Bobby was going to fix the leak under Reg's kitchen sink, of all things. Reg hadn't even known there'd been one, but Bobby said he could smell it. He bought wood and stuff too, because Bobby said there was rot down there. On the way back, Bobby asked how his talk with Dex went.

Reg grunted—a habit he was getting from Bobby.

"He wasn't too mad. Said he'd set it up with Lance to put off the shoot for a day—I got my blood test before I got you."

"You told me that," Bobby said mildly. "I'm glad he's not too mad. So, Lance?"

"He's a friend," Reg said with dignity. "You're not going to tell me I can't have sex at work with friends, are you?"

Bobby snickered.

"That didn't sound good, did it? I just mean—"

"Don't worry about it," Bobby said gently. Because they were in the truck, maybe, he reached over and patted Reg's knee. "You get along with all the people you work with. And that's just how we'll deal, okay? It's work. That's what we'll call it to my mom, that's what we'll call it to ourselves. Someday we'll find another job, that's all."

Reg could breathe again. Bobby managed to not freak out like Reg had—which on the one hand was totally unfair, but on the other hand,

Bobby had done *his* freak-out way earlier, so maybe it was kind of even. Either way—they had a way to look at work and talk about work that wasn't going to break them.

That's all Reg wanted.

Well, Dex's kindness helped.

"So," Bobby asked, "do you want me to stay tonight? Or would it be better if I left?"

Reg took a deep breath. He knew what he wanted, but that meant he was going to have to be a grown-up.

"Stay," he said. "Please."

Bobby squeezed his knee before putting both hands on the wheel. "Course."

THEY WENT to bed around ten o'clock, Bobby wrapping those long arms around him and kissing the back of his neck softly. His hands stroked the bare skin of Reg's hard stomach absently, and Reg held his breath, waiting to see if it would get sexual.

It didn't, and Reg had just settled down, thinking he could sleep like this, protected, cared for, when his phone rang.

It was Ethan. Kelsey's ex-boyfriend—and Dex's too—had trashed Kelsey's place, and could Reg please come help with the cleanup?

Bobby was half-dressed with boots and his jacket and work gloves before Reg even got off the phone.

Yeah. He got it now. The guys at work were their friends. Reg and Bobby would go to their rescue in the dark of a cold winter night—but the bed they got called out of to do that was theirs, and theirs alone.

Cautionary Tales

THE ONE thing Bobby learned from cleaning up Kelsey's place was that relationships could get ugly—but then, he already knew that.

He and Reg got back to Reg's place at the small hours of the night after putting the plywood up in the windows. Bobby remembered the name of a glazier—one of the guys he'd worked with back in Dogpatch who lived in Sacramento now. He gave the guy's name to Ethan so Dex could make the arrangements to fix Kelsey's house—

But Bobby didn't think she'd be back.

He looked around the place, after they'd picked up the broken glass from the windows her ex had smashed in, and wondered if she'd had any investment in living there. The warm, funny girl who'd spent the entire day trying to catch Bobby up to the twenty-first century seemed to be missing.

After the police had gone, and Dex had bolted out of there in a panic for yet another emergency, Ethan took Kelsey home, and Bobby showed Reg how to tack the plywood in place so it wouldn't rip out a chunk of drywall when the window guy got there.

"This is a nice house," Reg said wistfully, and Bobby thought maybe any place that wasn't falling apart was nice for Reg.

"Your house has more books," he said. He was getting used to Reg's quiet smiles, the ones that told him he'd touched Reg somehow, made him feel special.

Riding that high of helping Reg feel special was not getting old or tarnished in any way.

The next day, after they got to be muscle for even *more* Johnnies drama, Bobby went back to Reg's house and flopped exhaustedly on the couch.

"No housework today?" Reg asked, yawning.

Bobby looked over at V, who was doing her usual spacing-out-at-the-television thing. God, he wished he could hold Reg, just in the privacy of

Reg's home. "Nope," he said, shaking his head. "In fact, I think I'm going to use your room and call my mom."

"I'll go get us some dinner," Reg said. It was already eight o'clock, because they'd gone back to Kelsey's house and closed it up, then helped her get out of her rental agreement. Bobby thought wistfully that it would be a good place to bring his mom, but he figured he should stick to the plan of the cheap apartment that let him save more money and get her input.

"You have a mom?" Veronica asked unexpectedly, glancing up.

"I do," Bobby said, keeping his voice pleasant. He'd wondered often how it must feel for someone so small to constantly be surrounded by her brother's big, bulky friends, so he tried to tone his whole... body down.

"Does she scream at you?" V asked, darting a glance at him.

"No!" Bobby answered, startled. "She misses me. I left her to find a job so I could help her with rent."

"Did she give you presents?" V asked, sounding wistful. "Our mom didn't."

"Yes," Bobby said, voice soft. "That's how I knew to leave presents for you and Reg."

She swallowed and looked away. "Somebody wrecked Reg's books. That's too bad."

Bobby gaped at her. Somebody? *Somebody?* But then, this was the most contrition he'd seen from her—about anything—since they'd been introduced and he realized she'd stabbed her own brother because he'd been trying to give her the meds that kept her from going off the rails.

"Wasn't one of our better days, no," he said, hoping understatement would defuse things. "Hurt Reg real bad."

V tugged at her cuticle. "Reg takes things too seriously," she said after a minute. "Always did."

Bobby squinted at her, unsure of her motivation. "It's a good thing he does. He's kept a roof over your head, food in your cupboards, gotten you to your doctor's appointments—"

"No one asked him to," she snarled, putting her finger in her mouth and ripping the cuticle off completely until it bled. "Meddling. I'm a grown-up—why's he need to get in my face about shit? Everybody, trying to keep me in this shitty little house—who the hell are you anyway, you faggot?"

Bobby knew his eyes got big.

"Excuse me," he said and walked into the kitchen. "Your sister's off her meds again," he told Reg.

Reg had been with Bobby over the last two days, picking up broken glass and helping other people manage their messy lives. He was exhausted, and it showed in the droop of his jaw, the quiver of his lower lip.

"I… I got nothing," he said. He closed his eyes and then opened them again. "Wait! I got something! She's got a doctor's appointment tomorrow! They texted me this morning when we were on Kane's lawn." His entire body shuddered. "Wait… I don't have a scene tomorrow, right?"

Bobby frowned. "No—you would have if you'd done your regular schedule, but not now."

"But… but she has them every two months." Reg started counting on his fingers. "And then we go get medication. I put it out for her from the bottles, but she should have needed a refill by now."

"Yes, I know that." Bobby was intimately aware of V's medication rituals by now—he'd had to give her the pills on occasion when Reg had been at work.

"No," Reg muttered. He frowned at Bobby. "You don't understand. Usually I know there's an appointment coming because the pill bottle levels go down. But we went to the appointment last time, and they told me her prescription would last as long as it needed to, and she's got another appointment tomorrow and we have full levels in the bottles and…."

Reg clapped his hand over his face and then went to root through the cupboards. He came out with three full bottles of pills.

When he opened them up and shook one into his hand, it disintegrated. "They been doing that," he said flatly.

"I don't understand." Bobby knew he should be getting this, but it seemed so simple. A child's gambit, but Reg, trying desperately to keep his sister normal, had missed it.

"She put them in her mouth," Reg muttered. "And pretended to swallow."

"But that episode—right after Christmas—wouldn't there have been more?"

Reg shook his head. "Not if she was trying to hide—"

The sound of the back door slamming was like a shot in the night.

"Oh shit!"

The two of them tore through the house, through the hallway, and through Reg's bedroom, where the only back entrance sat.

Reg's backyard was mostly mud and weeds, surrounded by a rickety fence that Bobby had put on his list of things to do when the weather got a little better. They heard Veronica swearing as she disappeared over that rickety fence, and Bobby hurried to vault over it while Reg ran through the side yard to intercept her coming out of the neighbor's gate.

It was a good plan, and probably would have worked, but the fence—which could hold V's weight just fine—crumbled under Bobby's heavier bulk, and he slammed through three rotting boards and support struts, landing on the ground with a fuck-ton of familiar pain.

"Oh Christ!" he moaned, rolling over. "Oh Jesus. Fucking Jesus!" In the light from the neighbor's yard he could see the nail sticking through the back of his hand. With a wrench, he grabbed the board at his palm and yanked, growling pain through the frosting night.

Reg was there in an instant. "Oh my God! Bobby! Are you okay!"

"Where'd she go?" Bobby looked around wildly and realized he had a pain in his shoulder too.

Reg shouted, "Hold still!" and a curiously queasy sensation rolled over him as Reg pulled a giant six-inch sliver out of the meat of his shoulder.

"*Gah!* Oh fuck! Oh fuck oh fuck oh fuck oh fuck! *Jesus!*"

"I'm sorry, Bobby!" Reg cried, staring at the bloody splinter in his hand. "I'm sorry. Man, I'm sorry. We need to get you to the ER—that's a mess. You need a tetanus shot and some antibiotics and—"

"Reg, where's your sister?" Bobby almost sobbed. "We've got to find her, man—she attacks people with *knives*!"

Reg wiped his bloody hand over his eyes. "Okay," he said, nodding, like that all made sense. "Okay. Go get in the truck. I'll take you to the ER and call the mental health people. They... they've dealt with this before."

"Your sister has just up and taken off before?"

"Her medication wears off!" Reg shouted defensively. "I'm sorry! I don't got a handbook! I got 'V's okay' and 'V's batshit crazy'! Right now she's batshit crazy, and you need a doctor, and having them come get her is all I got!" A sob tore loose from his chest. "And I'm sorry. Man, I'm fuckin' sorry. You—you shouldn't be getting this bullshit. I'm so fuckin' sorry."

Bobby was going to throw up, or scream, or cry.

He reached out and grabbed Reg's shoulder with his good hand instead. "It's a plan," he panted. "It's a good plan. Don't be sorry. Let's get in the truck so you can call the doctors on your sister. But first, I gotta puke."

Pain washed over him, and a wave of black nausea followed. Tossing his cookies on the frosty grass was almost a relief. They got to the truck right when a man ventured out of the house next door, skinny legs sticking out of his bathrobe, wispy hair scattered over his head, and a big scary gun in his hand.

"Who's there?" the guy shouted. "What the hell's going on in my backyard?"

"Sorry, Mr. Simpson!" Reg called, opening Bobby's door for him. "My sister got away again. Keep everybody inside—the mental health people'll be out!"

"If she's not careful, she's gonna get shot!" Mr. Simpson shouted back. "Crazy bitch—she needs to be put away!"

"So do you!" Reg shouted back, helping Bobby into the cab. "But we let you stay there with your fifty zillion cats and everything!"

The door slammed shut, and Bobby leaned his head against the window woozily, thinking *Oh. That's where the cat pee smell came from.* It had been bothering him since he'd first been to Reg's place, since Reg and V didn't have a single goddamned cat.

Reg got into the driver's side, and Bobby handed him the keys. The truck started right up, and Reg pulled out of the residential neighborhood, driving as fast as safety would allow.

Bobby regretted not putting his seat belt on, though, when the truck screeched to a halt.

Reg threw the thing in Park, leaped out the door, and made a flying tackle on the shadowy figure on the lawn next to them. He had a struggling V in a three-point restraint in short order, and Bobby made it out of the truck in time to watch him strip her shirt over her head and bind her wrists behind her back with it. He yanked her up, wearing her bra and her sweatpants, and hauled her into the truck while Bobby got back inside.

"You can't fuckin' keep me here!" she screeched. "You fuckin' retard! You didn't even know I was spitting those pills up! How in the fuck do you think you can keep me there, you faggot?"

She wiggled something awful, but Reg had bound her up tight, and Bobby had no choice. He leaned his head against the window and blanked her out, the fear, the pain, all of it, relegating it to a haze in the distance.

The bay to the ER was a relief, because Reg opened the door and the noise stopped. He helped get Bobby into a wheelchair and said, "I'll find you."

As the nurse wheeled Bobby into check-in, he heard V's screaming, and then he realized he heard the most disturbing thing of all.

Reg's silence.

Reg's absolute and complete silence as he dealt with that rage, that confusion, that misplaced hatred, and tried to fix someone who had been broken before he'd been born.

TWO HOURS later, Bobby's hand was wrapped, his shoulder was stitched, his upper arm ached with tetanus shots and antibiotic shots and vitamin shots, for all he knew. He sat in his cubicle in the ER and wished desperately he could grab Reg's hand or his shoulder or something and calm him down, because he was becoming unglued.

"They took her off!" he raged, pacing the thin strip between the curtain and the bed. "They took her off her meds. That's why she put them back in the bottle—so I'd think she had a full prescription when we weren't gonna get no more this next time. She went in two months ago and said she hadn't been taking her meds for a week! And the doctor, who's probably more retarded than me, goes, 'Yeah, sure, you seem fine. We'll just not give you any more *anti-fucking-psychotics* and let you back into the world with your brother, who doesn't know!' Because... because I got no idea! Why the fuck would they do that, Bobby? Why in the holy mother of fuck would they do that?"

Bobby stared at him, at his red eyes and his complete confusion. A ball of rage hit Bobby's chest, and he stood up, grabbing hold of the IV tower and taking the papers Reg was waving right out of his hands. "Where am I going, whose ass am I kicking, and who do I have to fucking kill to figure this shit out?"

Later, he'd wonder at his luck, because the overworked intern who'd fucked up two months ago was actually working that night. He shouldn't have been. Bobby didn't know which time the guy was out of his element, filling in for a position he wasn't qualified for in the least, but he didn't actually care either.

"You took her off her meds?" he snarled, catching the guy by surprise as he did his charts. After stalking through a maze of corridors that Bobby was already lost in, Reg had gestured to the man, a young, thin thirtyish guy who looked like he hadn't slept in months.

The guy closed his eyes. "She reported that she'd been off them for some time—"

"And you believed her?" Bobby asked, his voice shaking in anger.

"There was no reason to doubt—"

"No reason?" Bobby's voice rose. "*No reason*? Do you have any idea what happens when you send her home like that? *Do you have any idea what we've been through?*"

"The hospital can't afford to have patients on drugs that aren't necessary," the doctor said primly—but he couldn't meet Bobby's eyes, and his hands shook as he ran them through his unruly dark hair. "I didn't know. I had no way of knowing—"

"Her brother has her conservatorship papers," Bobby said. "You didn't think maybe you should discuss this with *him*?"

"Well, you know, she said she'd tell him…."

Bobby just stared at him and shook his head. "Jesus. Everybody looks up to you people, and I'd rather be in porn. At least when you're fucking with someone, they know why and they get something out of it. What happens now?"

"Well, f-f-first we assess the situation—"

"The situation is that she's been terrorizing her brother since September, and she finally ran out of the house and into the night in a T-shirt and bare feet. We're exhausted," Bobby said, looking apologetically at Reg. "We can't fucking sleep. I keep trying to fix their house, but I can't, because if I leave so much as a hammer behind, I'm afraid she's going to drive it through my skull. Her brother hasn't left the house for longer than a day's work in *years*. And *you* thought it was a good idea to wean a woman who has been on antipsychotics since she was a teenager without even a how-de-fuckin'-do. Have I assessed the situation?"

Bobby was snarling in his face, and the guy was almost in tears. It wasn't fair—Bobby wasn't proud of himself, but fucking Jesus.

"She needs… she needs to be admitted," the guy muttered.

"No!" Reg protested. "No—Bobby, I promised!"

"For how long?" Bobby said, holding his hand up to calm him down. "How long will she be in captivity or whatever?"

"She's not a zoo animal!" the doctor protested. "It's a perfectly reputable mental health facility that's designed to get patients to respond to a schedule, take their medication regularly, and function in the outside world."

"It's a filthy place that stinks of cigarettes and pee!" Reg retorted. "And you never fucking feed her there! She says so!"

"Reg?" Bobby intervened. "I mean, your sister isn't exactly a reliable witness. Maybe if *we* take her food once in a while…."

"Bobby!" Reg had reached the end of his rope, and Bobby had nothing in him for appearances. This time, when he held up his hand, it was to pull Reg forward so they could stand, forehead to forehead, and Bobby could be real.

"Baby," he rasped, "you need a break. A month's break. To see what life is like when you're not trapped in the house with your sister. And your sister needs someone *not you* to drug her up. To test her levels. To get her into a routine that doesn't include the goddamned news channel. It's not forever." He turned reluctantly from Reg, who was openly crying now. "Right?"

The doctor nodded, gnawing on his lip. "No. Not forever. We can admit her for a month, reassess her then, and see if she can go home."

"Okay?" Bobby asked, nodding, *willing* Reg to say yes. He felt weak and stupid. He hadn't predicted this. He'd done nothing to prevent it. He couldn't protect Reg from this decision. And right now they were exhausted from other people's problems, from the storms of their own hearts, and from just a goddamned awful two days.

"She can't go home tonight, anyway," Reg told him, relaxing with a sigh. "They totally sedated her. Martians could invade and she'd keep snoring."

"Thank God," Bobby murmured. "Good. You can come meet my mom. I can replace your goddamned fence. We can repaint her room again. It'll be okay."

"Okay," Reg agreed. Bobby pulled him closer so his face was buried against Bobby's chest.

"Okay."

He had no idea if it was going to be okay. He felt like the world's biggest fraud, because he was so lost on okay at the moment. But he wanted to be back at Reg's house, tucked in his bed, finally able to sleep.

An hour. An hour of paperwork, of nurses fussing over him, of finding a pair of scrubs since his sweatshirt and T-shirt had been torn to ribbons. An hour of reassuring Reg and double-checking with the doctor who had already proven less than reliable, and finally an hour of signing paperwork so they could get the fuck out of there.

Bobby remembered filling out the papers for health insurance and thinking, "Oh yeah. That might be nice." He'd never been so grateful for "nice" as he was as he and Reg left Kaiser to get back in the truck. Reg pumped the heater as soon as they got in the cab, because it was mid-January and cold as balls outside.

They were quiet on the way back, until Bobby had Reg stop for food. In-N-Out—very necessary right now.

"Thank you," Reg muttered in the quiet of the idling engine.

"For what?" Bobby had taken painkillers, but whatever had been in the IV was wearing off. He missed it. That drug had been his friend.

"Not telling the doctor I couldn't take care of her anymore."

Bobby sighed and tilted his head back. "This… this might not work. You know that, right?"

"No," Reg mumbled. Then, louder, "No. I wish I did. I wish I could look in the future like you did. My sister disappeared, and I thought, 'Find her! She'll get cold!' and you thought, 'Find her! She'll hurt people!' And I was, like, 'No she wouldn't!' And then I remembered. She would. She has. She's hurt *me*. How dumb—"

"Stop it," Bobby snarled, done. "You're not dumb. You're overwhelmed. And you did fine. You were going to call the mental health people before you spotted her. I was impressed."

"Thanks." Reg sighed and let the truck creep up a space. Late-night drive-thru was always damned slow. "But… but you still think this might not work."

"Yeah, but Reg, that's not you. It's not. *I* can't deal with this situation. Hell—the doctor couldn't deal with this situation, and he's had *years* of fucking useless education to tell him how to deal with this situation."

"I still don't know why he'd do that," Reg muttered, flummoxed.

"Yeah, well, maybe he was like us. Maybe he'd been on rotation and was somewhere he had no training to be and no sleep in fucking forever. They're not gods. They're just like we are—doing their goddamned best. And if she can outmaneuver everybody's goddamned best, maybe she… you know. Shouldn't be in a place where we're all she's got. You think?"

Reg shook his head, wiping under his eyes, because he was exhausted too. Finally they were in a place where he could pay, and he handed Bobby a large chocolate shake and took his own, strawberry.

"Mm…." Bobby swallowed and enjoyed. "We're going to have to work out forever for this, you know that, right?" He took another swallow. "And don't you have a scene in two days?"

Reg nodded. "Yeah. Me and the enema bottle are gonna be good friends." He took another drink and swallowed. "But sometimes, you just fucking need a big-ass shake."

That sounded wise as fuck to Bobby.

REG SLEPT in, but Bobby couldn't.

He sat in bed for a while, arms wrapped around his knees, making a mental list of things he was supposed to do that day.

He was supposed to wait tables, but looking at the way Reg curled in on himself, the idea of leaving him alone was just too painful.

He *needed* someone. He just did. Bobby could rattle around his apartment, walk around the city, find a world outside himself. Reg wasn't as limited as he thought—Bobby firmly believed that. And his limitations weren't "being smart," as he said. His biggest limit was that the world he'd built for himself, when he was young and ignorant and unprepared, was really small. Bobby couldn't hold that against him. He'd just left a town full of people who thought Dogpatch was the center of the world. Reg wasn't any different.

But if Reg was going to have a bigger world, he needed a Bobby to help him find it.

Today, he needed Bobby to help him see beyond this empty house.

Bobby kissed his cheek and thought yearningly that he'd love to just stay in bed, hold Reg's naked body, make love in the gray cold of the winter morning. But Reg had a scene tomorrow, and that wasn't going to work, and Bobby was too practical to mourn over stuff he couldn't change.

He put his nose in the hollow of Reg's shoulder and breathed deeply, letting the warmth and maleness wash over him.

With a sigh he wriggled out of bed and wrapped a tattered afghan around his shoulders. He'd gone to bed in the scrubs the nurses had rounded up, and his sweatshirt and jeans were too torn up to save. In addition to the shoulder and the hand, he had some scrapes on his knees and shin that had smarted during cleanup as well.

He would need to go get clothes from his apartment sometime that day, but first, coffee.

After he'd started the pot and downed his first mug, he settled down at the kitchen table and called his mother.

He wasn't planning to tell her much, but, well, moms.

"Sweetheart? You okay? You don't usually call me at work."

He cursed himself, because he should have thought of that. "No," he said, voice quiet. "I'm fine. Just don't want to wake my friend up. We, uh, cleared some dates so we could come visit."

"Oh, that's nice!" She *hmm*ed a little, and he assumed she was checking her calendar. "I have to work this weekend, but next Saturday and Sunday I can have off free and clear. How's that?"

"Perfect." He and Reg could go out dancing. They could let the hickeys and the beard burn of someone else's sex fade off their skin. They could have sex with *each other* every morning for a week, as loud as they wanted.

And they could go see his mom without all the stuff that was hanging over their heads now.

"Are you sure?" she asked kindly. Someone said something to her in the background, and he heard her say "It's my son" through the muffled receiver. "You sound… odd. Sad. Are you okay? How's your friend? The one with the sister."

"Sad," Bobby said, because that was the only word he had. "She's in observation right now, at a mental health place where they try to get them back on their med schedule."

"Oh, honey." She muffled the receiver again. "It's important, okay? Consider this my break." Then, back into the phone, "What happened?"

"I'm messing up your work," Bobby said, suddenly undone by her concern, by her effort to put him first. She'd done that their entire lives— even when the old man was beating on her, she'd done her best to make sure

Bobby came first. "We'll come up in the morning, first thing. Weekend after next. Me and Reg. You'll like him, Mom. I swear."

"Okay, hon." She sounded puzzled. "Good—"

"Wait! Mom—has Keith Gilmore been by lately?"

He heard a heavy breath on her line. "Yeah, hon. Actually…." Her voice dropped. "Yesterday morning, I went to leave for work and two of my tires were flat, which was weird because I'd just had them checked at the gas station. And Keith Gilmore came driving down the road, asking if I wanted a ride. It was really strange, Vern—he had no reason to be there. I told him no thank you—we have the generator out in the garage, you know."

"Yeah. The air compressor still works, right?" It had the last time Bobby had needed it.

"Oh yes. I filled up my tires and got to work just fine, but I swear— there was no reason at all for him to be down that road unless he thought I was going to need help."

Bobby grunted. "Good job, Mom. Seriously. But, you know—keep avoiding him if you can, okay?"

"What's going on with him? Do you have any idea?"

Bobby let out a breath. "Yeah. I do. And… and I don't want to tell you over the phone while you're at work. Can you just wait until I get there? And not tell him?"

"Yeah, honey." She sighed. "I miss you. Call me in the evenings sometime. We can watch TV together or something. I swear, I hadn't realized how in the middle of nowhere this place was until you were gone."

"Mom, I've got an apartment down here. It would be small and cramped, but I spend most of my nights with friends. Would that be enough?" He closed his eyes and tried to decide if he wanted her to say yes or no.

"Let's wait until the summer," she said gently. "It's easy to hate this place in the winter. If I'm still hating life here in the summer, then yes. Yes, if you don't mind your mother as a roommate, I'd love to."

"It might not be just me," he said hesitantly. "I might… I might have a friend who wants to room with us." *If he decides to leave his sister in hell so he can have his own life. Oh Jesus, this is not going away.*

"That would be fine, hon. You're sort of a picky roommate, you know. No dishes in the sink, no creaky stairs—if your friend can deal with you, I'll deal with her."

"Him," Bobby said without thinking. He cringed, but his mother corrected herself with "Him" without missing a beat, and he realized she took friend to mean just that—friend.

He was going to have to be plain and clear with her—and like he'd said, not now.

"Okay, then," he mumbled, needing to be off the phone. His body and wounds ached, and he longed to crawl in next to Reg, but what he wanted to do was off-limits for a whole other day. "I'll talk to you later, Mom. See you in a week or so."

"Bye, Vern. I can't wait."

He ended the call and rested his forehead against his palm. A week and a half. He didn't know how Reg or Lance or any of the other guys at Johnnies could deal. He missed his mother in his life so bad his stomach cramped with it.

He heard the creak of footsteps behind him, and warm hands rested on his shoulders. "Your mom?" Reg asked softly.

"I miss her." The yearning lessened, somehow, now that Reg knew. He felt the hesitant kiss on the top of his head.

"That's good. Not that you're sad, but that you have someone to miss."

Bobby nodded and rested a bandaged hand on top of Reg's.

"You know," Reg said softly, his voice a little fractured, "I don't have the faintest idea what I should do today."

Bobby smiled and turned around, resting his temple against Reg's hard-planed stomach. "Go to my place so I can get clothes," he murmured. "Work out." He'd already called in to his waiting job. "Go see a movie. Come home and read or watch TV."

"Mm. Sounds okay. What do we do tomorrow?"

Bobby looked up at him and smiled. "Tomorrow is your scene day. Whatever you want. And the day after that too. But after that?"

Reg looked down at him soberly, hanging on his every word. "Yeah?"

"I'm going to take you apart. I'm going to lay you out on the bed and play with your body until you scream jizz. I'm going to buy things I've seen on my phone and use them on you and watch your face as your body forgets it ever knew another cock but mine. And when you are crying from coming out your eyeballs, I'm going to go back and do it all again. 'Cause I have you to myself for a while, Reggie, and I want your body to remember every goddamned minute."

Reg's arms convulsed around his head, and he let out a low moan. Bobby's cock ached fiercely in his shorts, and over the cacophony of his injuries and his heartsickness, that shit felt good.

These months, turning himself into a finely tuned sexual machine, and all the heartache and the uncertainty and the drawbacks that came with the job, and he wanted him and Reg to hit the open bed and see what they could do.

"You suck," Reg whimpered, bucking fruitlessly against the back of the chair.

"Not today," Bobby promised darkly. "But soon."

The Moon

REG'S SCENE with Lance went really well.

Reg couldn't explain it—maybe it was because Lance seemed more responsive under his hands, or because his breath—which was usually bright with mints—was a little more subdued but more wholesome. But Lance moved like sex was his drug. Reg topped, and when Lance came, he kissed Reg like Reg was a lifeline, and Reg kissed back the same way.

But when they were done kissing and the scene was over, they both rolled apart and lay panting on the bed, and Reg didn't feel any need to do the soft touching, the running his hand up and down Lance's arm or kissing of the shoulder or the neck that Bobby spent so much time doing.

"That was great!" the camera guy said, and Reg squinted at him unhappily. This guy was new—Dex had hired him since John had disappeared—and Reg and Lance had done their jobs like the professionals they were. But Reg had gotten the feeling this guy was freaked-out with pretty much everything they were doing. He just didn't get close enough to the body parts to be filming real porn.

"Shower scene?" Reg asked, and the guy gave them a blank look.

"I'm thinking that's a no," Lance said, popping Reg on the flank. "Let's go clean up. You doing anything today?"

Reg grunted. He felt energized, not tired like good sex sometimes made him feel, and he wasn't sure he wanted a quiet day today. "I gotta ask Bobby," he said. "He was still a little sore this morning. Did I tell you he fell through the fence chasing my sister down the street?"

Lance stared at him. "No. No, you did not. But if he's up to it, how 'bout call him up and have him meet up for lunch." He appeared to think about it for a moment. "I'm hungry," he said, sounding like he was surprised. "I'm hungry, and I want company. How's that?"

Reg grinned. He didn't want to think about V. The doctor had called the day before and told them to give her another week in the interim hospital while they got her behavior under control. Reg didn't know what this meant, but Bobby's face had darkened when he heard.

"It means she's in restraints," Bobby said, like he knew this would hurt but had to say it anyway.

Reg's chest had frozen, and for a moment he imagined himself in the corner, rocking back and forth like he had as a kid, helpless and terrorized and feeling like somehow he'd brought all this on his own head.

"It's not your fault," Bobby had said, maybe reading his mind. "She did this, Bobby. She lied, she pretended to take pills for two months, and she manipulated the doctor. And yeah, she's sick, but that part—that part she did. She stopped taking her medication when she knows what she does without it. You promised her, baby, but you can't do it all by yourself, and she wasn't helping."

"She'll take the medication in the health facility," Reg said, because he couldn't imagine making the decision that came with that not happening. "Then she can come back here."

Bobby let out a sigh, and they both let the matter drop, and now Reg was excited. He had a rare free moment—he was going to treat this like a holiday, not the scary beginning of a new way of life.

Lunch was fun.

Reg picked Bobby up and brought him to the restaurant. Bobby and Lance suggested something sort of upscale and interesting, but Reg saw a barbecue place near the Golden 1 Plaza, and he was *starving*. He ate too much seasoned beef while he and Bobby told Lance about Bobby taking out the fence. Lance's eyes got really big when Reg told him about having to tackle V running down the road in the dark, and *then* he got pissed when Reg told him about the doctor.

"He did what?" Lance said weakly.

"He took her off her pills," Bobby said, voice grim. "Could he do that?"

Lance let out a growl. "Well, obviously he did." He shut his eyes tight. "Guys, I've done a psych rotation for about six weeks. The end. I haven't taken a lot of classes in it—not my specialty. But I can tell you, a month or even two in a facility might not be enough."

Reg swallowed a bite and remembered his determination not to think about it. "She'll be okay," he said, giving Lance a brief smile. "Don't worry. Me and V, we take care of each other."

Lance nodded and rubbed his stomach. He hadn't eaten a lot, but then he rarely did. "I'm going to go use the bathroom—I'll be back."

Bobby stood too and sent an intense look at their friend. "I'll come with you," he said, squeezing Reg's shoulder. "Reg, you can have the rest of my portion if you want. I'm full."

Reg smiled sunnily up at him and took the last of his rolls and meat, while Bobby stalked grimly next to a very uncomfortable-looking Lance.

Reg was going to not think about that. He wasn't going to think about why Lance looked so guilty and Bobby looked so mad, and he wasn't going to think about how everybody thought V wasn't coming home.

He just flat-out wasn't going to think about that.

He was going to go home to Bobby, and they were going to have sex that night, and sex the next morning, and sex—just *their* sex—as many days as possible for the next month or two.

He was a simple guy, he told himself desperately. He couldn't be expected to handle anything else.

TWO DAYS later, simplicity was a beautiful thing.

After their workout and a light lunch, Bobby went outside to get some things to fix the fence. By the time he got in the house, swearing about needing to change, it was pissing down rain, and Reg was hunkered down with a book, enjoying the sound of the rain on the roof, the clean smell, the quiet in the house.

No *Fox News*. No V muttering to herself. The living room had been straightened and vacuumed, the dishes were washed and put away, and all Reg had to do was figure out how the heroine who lived back in the American West was going to save the ranch. Bobby had read this one—he said she was resourceful and brave, and Reg liked that story best.

He was deeply engrossed in the book, so at first Bobby's warm hand massaging his neck was simply pleasant—a luxury he wasn't used to yet, something he'd only done with this one human, that made him feel wonderful without being too exciting.

Reg tilted his head back and closed his eyes, while Bobby very gently pulled the book from his hands and set it down on the battered coffee table. Reg kept his eyes closed and nibbled on his lower lip as he recognized the tender darkening of the mood.

"You, uh, get dried off?" Reg asked, and Bobby's response was to lift Reg's hand and spread it over his hard, bare abdomen.

"Took off my wet clothes."

Reg grinned and looked up at him, just to see his slightly crooked front teeth in a wicked smile of his own. "All of them," he said, rubbing a circle on Bobby's stomach. How had he never noticed how silky a man's stomach could be, how pleasing the feel of taut muscle under smooth skin?

"Even my socks," Bobby purred. "And you're overdressed."

Reg crunched his upper body off the couch so he could take off his shirt, and Bobby tackled his belt and jeans. In less than a minute, they were both naked, *in Reg's living room*, which made Reg shiver because it felt sinful.

There was nobody in the house but *them*.

"Here," Bobby murmured. "Stand up."

Reg was confused until he found himself behind the couch, arms braced, while Bobby slid soft lips down his shoulders, the back of his neck, the back of his arms.

"Mm...."

Bobby's hands weren't idle either. He was so big, his hands spanned so far, that they practically encircled Reg's tight waist, and his touch was just firm enough to not tickle Reg's ribs as Bobby stroked him.

"Nipples?" Reg begged, feeling pathetic, and Bobby's chuckle made him shiver.

"Impatient?" he asked.

"Yes." Oh my God—"*Yes!*" as Bobby pinched sharply. He started to sweat, shaking, as Bobby kissed down his spine.

"Spread 'em," Bobby ordered, and Reg did, feeling open and vulnerable. Bobby took advantage of him, skating his fingertips down Reg's cleft, between his thighs, along his taint. The touches were just hard enough not to tickle, just soft enough to leave Reg aching for more. Bobby was using Reg's hip to balance as he worked his sorcery, and the print of his hand felt burned into Reg's skin.

Reg's breaths were coming fast and hard, and all Bobby did was touch him. Lightly.

The touches grew stronger, broader, and Bobby's warm hands on Reg's asscheeks were a welcome relief.

"Fucking now?" Reg begged.

"Licking now," Bobby returned playfully. Reg let go of the couch and just leaned his torso on it, exposing his ass and lifting to his toes, legs spread as wide as he could.

He was rewarded by the wet heat of Bobby's mouth, his tongue, dragging down his cleft, licking circles around the target, until Reg pleaded shamelessly.

"Please, Bobby... please... something. My cock, my ass, don't care, just... just don't tease me no more. Don't.... Augh!"

One finger—one—penetrated him, and Reg almost cried. "Yes! No! That's not enough!"

He clenched hard on that finger, knowing his muscles there were tight from use. Bobby pushed past the resistance, and the burn intensified. Reg moaned.

"You want more?"

"Yeah."

The snick of a lube bottle sounded, and Reg didn't even want to know where he'd been hiding it. The pressure in Reg's asshole increased, another slick finger pushed in, and Reg's eyes rolled back in his head. "Yesssssss...."

But it was still not enough.

"Bobby?"

"Yeah?" A third finger, and Reg wanted to sob.

"You got a giant cock, man—don't you wanna fuck me?"

Bobby kept his fingers where they were and started working them in and out. "Yeah, sure," he breathed, his breath teasing the whorls of Reg's ear. "But I wanna see you fly first."

Reg rested his face on his hands and wiggled his ass, partly in time to the thrusts and partly in pure stinking need. Bobby stayed to the side of him, fucking his ass slowly with his fingers, and then, oh God, reaching around with his other hand and.... *Oh please... please....*

"One lousy finger!" Reg hollered, utterly helpless, utterly aroused. "Jesus—grab it. Hard. Stroke it. Don't tease it. Please, Bobby—please! Please!"

Bobby whispered in his ear. "No."

"*Gah!*" Reg howled into his cupped hands, super stimulated in the back, barely stimulated from the front, his body shaking uncontrollably. "*Bobby!*"

226

Bobby's low chuckle set every nerve ending on fire, and all the teasing fingers disappeared. "I can suck you off," Bobby whispered. "I can get down on my knees in front of you and swallow your come. Or I can fuck you. Choose, baby—but choose wisely."

There was no choice. "*Fuck me!* Oh, fuck me fuck me fuck me fuck me—please, please, please—*yes!*"

Oh, Bobby's cock was a thing of beauty, especially as it battered its way into Reg's ass. Reg let out a real sob, dropped his hand down to his own much neglected member, and let Bobby seat himself.

"Ready?" Bobby asked, gliding his hands up and down Reg's ribs.

"Yeah." And Reg gave himself over in that word. No more fighting what Bobby wanted, no more trying to get his own way. He trusted. Bobby would take care of him. Bobby hadn't failed him yet.

Bobby pulled out slowly and then thrust firmly back in. Reg's entire body went weak, conceding, submitting, just as Bobby said, "Good."

What followed was a little like being turned inside out and then put back without the awful stuff you didn't know was inside you.

On one level, it was just fucking. Magnificent fucking. Bobby slammed his cock in and out of Reg's body hard and fast and beautiful, and Reg could barely keep up with it. He was practically limp with submission, but that didn't mean wave after wave of excruciating pleasure didn't crash over him, tossing him about in a storm of shocked nerve endings and sensation.

But as he grabbed his cock and squeezed, too overwhelmed to even stroke himself off like he'd done since he was a kid, he could feel the *more* to this. This thing Bobby was doing to him—this left that thing he'd done in front of the cameras in the rearview. This was all over his body. Bobby had drawn him out, made him beg, pulled the things he needed to the surface of his skin, and then *gave him what he needed*. Reg was an exposed nerve, and the one person, the *only* person who could touch him with pleasure, with generosity, was the big country kid behind him, fucking him with the giant dick.

Bobby wrapped an arm around Reg's chest and kept pumping his hips. Reg could smell him—plain soap, rain in his hair, fabric softener, male skin—and knew suddenly that it wasn't the dick size, or even the fucking.

It was the man.

He was too far gone to moan or groan or even whimper. His breath wobbled out, and without even another squeeze to his cock, his entire body, from the arches of his feet to his ears, for God's sake, tensed, a giant ball of painful pleasure, before he snapped hard, like a big rubber band, and came and came and came.

Behind him Bobby groaned loudly in his ear and clenched his arm so tight Reg's ribs creaked. He bit Reg's shoulder, the sting of teeth making Reg spurt harder, and gave a gigantic shudder.

Reg could feel him.

Hot come, pulsing inside his body, something he didn't think would register anymore, given how long he'd whored his ass out for money and kicks.

This was different.

This was a mark, a possession, and as Reg's eyes fluttered closed and he tried hard not to swoon on the back of his own goddamned couch, he recalled the past two days.

They'd had sex, soft, hands skating, brief climax sex, since Reg's last scene and the lunch with Lance. Reg had thought sure—Bobby did the jealousy thing once. He was so much smarter than Reg. He didn't need to lay a claim or mark Reg—he'd grown up.

But now, half fainting, physically exhausted from half an hour of balls-out sex, dripping Bobby's come from his asshole and coated with his own come all over his hand and his forearm and even his stomach, he realized the truth.

Bobby had been waiting.

Bobby wasn't more grown-up than Reg. Wasn't over the jealousy thing. He was *just like* Reg.

He just bided his time better, that was all.

Reg was poured across the back of the couch still when Bobby withdrew, the absence of his body in Reg's leaving a big ache, a hole, like a missing limb or something. He could have stayed there for hours, come running down his upper thighs, shivering in the sudden cold, but then Bobby did an amazing thing.

He put one arm under Reg's knees and the other under his shoulders and *picked him up*. Like a kid.

"I weigh one sixty, solid," Reg mumbled, rubbing his cheek against the smooth skin of Bobby's chest. "Jesus, kid, how much are you benching?"

"More than I was when I moved here," Bobby said. He put Reg back in the bed they'd left that morning so they could go work out, crawled in after him, and pulled the covers up.

Reg turned into his chest and began to lick the sweat off his pecs and his nipples in a hazy, desultory way. His entire body tingled.

"You were jealous," he said, surprising himself. "Me, my scene. You been waiting two days to just... just...."

Bobby's arm lay under his shoulders, and Bobby crushed him against that amazing chest. "Take back what's mine."

"How do you do that?" Reg asked. "I've been everybody's boy for so long... how do you just make me... yours?"

He expected Bobby's laugh, low and filthy, and a crude joke about his member, but that's not what he got.

"I love you," he said, blowing Reg's mind. "I don't know if any other boyfriend, girlfriend, whatever, has said that, but that's how I feel."

Reg couldn't breathe. Those words? Who said them? Those were wedding words. Engagement and diamond-ring words. Since when did men say those words after screwing around?

He shivered, and Bobby pulled him closer. His eyes stung, no matter how much he squeezed them shut.

"That would make me yours, then," he croaked.

Bobby dropped a kiss in his hair. "I hope so."

"How do you say those words?" he asked, feeling stupid in ways he didn't think he could.

"When you're ready, you'll say them," Bobby said. He sounded a little uncertain, a little sad.

"I won't leave you hanging," Reg mumbled, but his eyes were already closed, and his body was practically not even his anymore. "I'll say them."

"You already did," Bobby whispered, and before Reg could argue, he'd fallen fast asleep.

Old Business

IN EARLY February they threw duffel bags in the back of the pickup, locked up Reg's house—new fence and all—and took off for Dogpatch.

They'd visited V the day before, and she'd sat sullenly, eyes averted, at a cheap Formica table. The place was every bit as bad as Reg had feared—scuffed beige walls, cracked green tile and all. On their way in, Bobby had seen a frantic young man with quarter-sized gauges in his ears and face and neck tattoos begging a dead-eyed girl with bandages on her wrists to please, for the love of God, just talk to him.

Inside the visiting room proper, people sat at crappy cafeteria tables in folding chairs, or in the battered, duct-taped couches. Everyone had an attendant with a clipboard. Some of the groups were actively engaged in conversation, and some of them were sitting in cold silence, but the attendants—casually dressed in jeans and T-shirts and tennis shoes—all looked around alertly, like whatever the situation, it could change in a long breath.

The stink of cigarettes, ammonia, and vomit was thick enough to cut with a steak knife. An attendant—a thick, muscular woman with a steady smile for Reg and Bobby and a flat-eyed assessment for V—brought V in from the sleeping quarters.

She looked like hell in rumpled pajamas Reg had brought from home. Her hair lay piled on top of her head haphazardly, and Bobby had needed to work to not recoil at the smell.

"She's not bathing," the attendant told them matter-of-factly. "She's afraid people will steal her clothes."

"You want my fuckin' clothes," V snapped at the woman.

"Got my own, thanks. Sit down and behave, Veronica. Your brother and his friend came to see you."

V snarled, "What the hell you doin' here, retard?"

Reg had bit his lip. "I just wanted to see how you were, V. If you were taking your meds yet, you know. So you could come home."

"You want me to take my meds? Fucking poison! Get me the hell out of here!" V half stood, slamming her fists on the table, and the attendant sighed, stood up from her folding chair, and grabbed V by the elbow.

"You may want to try again next week," she said with resigned cheerfulness. "Her regimen had to be started practically from scratch."

V was hustled out, and Bobby stared at Reg.

His full lips were parted, making him look vulnerable and young, and his almond-shaped blue eyes that Bobby had found so appealing from the beginning were wide and dazed. The blank devastation on his face did things to Bobby's chest he wasn't sure would heal.

"Next week," Reg said weakly to the air. "We'll work at getting her home next week."

"Sure," Bobby said. *Another week for you to maybe think of option three. Come on, Reg. It can't be me.*

That night Bobby made dinner, a recipe he got from Kane because he could cook and didn't snap at Bobby if he didn't know the difference between sage and basil, like Tommy did.

Reg ate it and thanked him shyly, his front teeth worrying his bottom lip like he did when he was embarrassed. Bobby had kissed him then, dirty dishes on the counter, backing him against the wall until the shyness burned away and he leaped up, wrapping his legs around Bobby's waist so Bobby could carry them both to bed. Face-to-face this time, Bobby up on his knees at the end, watching Reg's head tilt back and the utter abandon wash over his face, cleansing him of the worry.

Bobby shuddered in climax and collapsed next to him, studying Reg's face in the borrowed light from the kitchen.

Maybe it was the fading acne scars, or the way Reg angled his chin out into the world like he was taking every hit directly without question, but the soft light made his features look delicate—poignant, even.

He grinned at Bobby, teeth glinting softly in the faint glow, the corners of his eyes crinkling up just enough to remind Bobby that he would be thirty next year. Bobby had always known that Reg had a special magnetism that had made him one of Johnnies' mainstays, but here, in the dark, in Bobby's bed and Bobby's bed alone, Bobby could see a beauty the cameras could never capture.

"You're very good to me," Reg said in that quiet moment.

"I want the world for you." Bobby kissed him then, trying to drink that simple beauty into his soul. Even when they eventually dressed in sweats and went back to finish the kitchen, he knew he'd failed somehow.

He would always need another kiss, another taste, another moment.

He wasn't sure how that happened, how the "I love you" had happened nearly two weeks before, how he'd found the patience to wait to reclaim Reg, to wait for the "I love you" in return. Reg took his time, maybe. Bobby had to learn to take his.

And now, clearing Auburn, heading toward Truckee and beyond, Bobby couldn't help taking sideways glances at that deceptively pretty face as Reg made the connection between the mountains that had lived in the horizon his entire life and the topography that surrounded him now.

"This is amazing," he breathed. "There's snow on the ground. Can you see that? No wonder you told me to bring all my warm clothes."

"I went and bought chains last week, just in case we need 'em," Bobby said. He'd been planning to wait until after the snows, just to spare the expense, but the weather people kept predicting a long wet winter—he wanted to see his mom before April.

"This road is amazing—this is I-80? I mean, it's right out our back door, right? And it leads here? That last curve, we could look down and see all of Auburn and Sacramento to boot. You lived here? That's super cool!"

The roads were more than clear. Bobby reached across the bench seat and grabbed Reg's hand. "It felt like a cage," he said quietly. "But then, you know, turned eighteen, graduated, found the key. Like you."

Reg fell quiet for a moment. "This is more like a visitor's pass," he said sadly. "I don't think there *is* a key."

Bobby grunted and refrained from saying that there had to be a key or his sister was going to shred Reg's sleek little body by dragging him through the bars.

"Dogpatch is in a little valley between mountains," Bobby said. "There's a branch of the river going through the middle, and lots of pastureland. It's still pretty high up, but it's not, like, on a mountaintop, you know?"

It was Reg's turn to grunt. He followed it up with "I guess I can see how that would feel like prison. But seriously—can you see stars at night?"

Bobby let out a small smile. "Yup."

"So, see? Already better'n Sacramento."

232

"We should take a trip to the sea," Bobby said, letting excitement build up in his stomach for it. "I mean, I've been a few times with my mom." His eyebrows drew together at the memory. "And once with my dad. I really loved it there."

Reg was still looking through the side window, trying to gaze upward to see the tops of the trees. "Let me get through this first, Bobby," he said, obviously tempted to roll down the window and stick his head out. "I still gotta meet your mom. I can't believe you really think that's such a good idea."

"Here, Reg. I'll pull over in town, and you can look up at all the trees while we fill up. And did you bring all the books we've read?"

"Oh yeah. First things I packed."

Bobby smiled, glad he'd brought gifts. "She'll love you. She'll even have books to give back."

THE ONE thing Bobby had noticed since he'd moved away was how much younger his mother looked when she smiled at him on his return.

This time, though, she *literally* looked younger. "Mom!" he laughed, as he swung out of the truck. "You dyed your hair!"

She grimaced. "Yeah, yeah. Well, you send me money, and suddenly I don't have to worry about feeding you, and I've got time to do foolish things."

"Not foolish," he said, liking the subtle blonde/brown she'd chosen. "Looks good. You look way younger."

She frowned up at him and played with his hair. He'd left it long but taken Kane's advice and gotten a trim. It fell around his ears in layers now, and when he slicked it back for a scene, it looked tousled on purpose by the time they called "cut."

"You look older," she said, biting her lip. "And slicker. Not that it's bad, mind you, but even your boots are new."

Bobby shrugged. "Well, you know. People tip better when you look good."

She appeared to be appeased by that, but Bobby felt a hollow spot under his breastbone. How often was he supposed to lie to her about this?

"Well, your friend must get great tips," his mom said, laughing as Reg grabbed all the luggage from the back. "Hold up there, son—let Vern help you."

Reg stumbled on a duffel strap, obviously confused. "Vern—sorry. I gotta remember you call him that. We call him Bobby, 'cause, you know, Roberts." Bobby had made him practice that, and it came out real good. He grinned from behind his mom's back and gave Reg the thumbs-up.

Bobby's mom harrumphed. "That's a likely story. He's hated the name Vern since he was a baby."

Bobby nodded emphatically as he went to help Reg with the duffels. "I'm saying."

"Reggie," Reg said, rolling his eyes. "It's not even Reginald. I think my mom got Reggie and Veronica from some sort of comic as a kid." He paused. "Don't know where she got Queenie."

"Archie, though, for you and Veronica!" His mom clapped her hands, delighted. "That's wonderful."

Bobby looked at Reg and winked. "That's easy for her to say. Her name's Isabelle."

Reg smiled, full force. "Pretty name for a pretty lady," he said as she turned to lead them into the house. Bobby bumped shoulders with him, because God, they were making it work, and that alone made him happy.

"Vern said you two wouldn't mind sharing his bed," Mom said as she walked through the door. "So I'll let him show you around. I made stromboli for lunch—I hope that's okay."

Reg looked at him in confusion, and Bobby said, "It's like an all-meat pizza baked in a croissant bun." He looked ruefully at his mom. "It's apparently designed to make us fat."

"Well, look at you—you're both built like racehorses. A stromboli isn't gonna kill you."

"I hope not," Bobby said, feeling gratitude in his bones. "Because seriously, anything we don't have to cook is the best."

He ventured into his room—which had a few more big plastic boxes of needlepoint supplies than he remembered. He used one to put his duffel on and had Reg put his on another one. They were like coffee tables in the front room—moveable furniture.

His mom watched them from the doorway, a half smile on her face. "Do you guys cook together a lot?" she asked, but not judgy-like.

"Reg has a big kitchen," Bobby said, keeping it casual. "My apartment has a minifridge and a hotplate."

"Bobby brings groceries over," Reg said guilelessly. "He'll cook for me and, uh...." His face fell. "My sister. She's not at home now—but he cooks for us a lot."

"That's nice of him," his mom said, a quizzical smile on her face. "I didn't know you liked to cook."

Bobby gave her a half smile. "Well, you know. You do such a good job of it, why would I need to do it here?"

She nodded, but thoughtfully. "Speaking of, let me go put lunch on the table."

She left, and Reg looked at him in agony. "I forgot to give her the books!"

"Later," Bobby told him. "After lunch."

Reg nodded and pulled out the bag—Bobby had bought one of those pretty recyclable grocery bags so it would be more like a gift. "Okay. It's going good, right?"

"Great, Reg. Why wouldn't it?"

Suddenly Reg was standing close—perfect distance, from Bobby's POV, but Bobby understood.

"'Cause we don't want her to... you know," Reg whispered.

Bobby stared at his open door. "Maybe," he said quietly. "Maybe not. Like I said—see how the weekend goes, okay?"

Reg nodded unhappily. "Yeah, sure. But this is a real nice place, Bobby. You may want to think twice about getting kicked out."

Bobby resisted the urge to look around the crumbling little mother-in-law cabin Frank Gilmore rented out for the price of a mansion. It *wasn't* a "real nice place." It was, in fact, just as cramped and out of repair as Reg's place.

The one difference—and one difference only, that Bobby could see—was that his mom lived there, and she'd greeted them both with a hug and pizza in a bread crust.

Well, who'd want to risk that, right?

"SO, REG," his mom said as they sat down to steaming platefuls of pizza pastry and salad, "Bobby didn't say what you do for a living."

They'd talked about this too. "I work for John Carey Industries," Reg said dutifully. It was the company name that appeared on the check to help give the employees privacy. "It's, uh, sort of a small media business. I hold lights and help them set up scenes and stuff."

"What sort of scenes?"

And this was the one thing that was an out-and-out lie. "College students making commercial products." But not much of one.

Isabelle looked at Reg quizzically. "What sorts of products?" she asked, eyes narrowed.

Bobby took over. "Anything they want—the company pretty much just provides the equipment."

His mom fixed her eyes—clearly set on "bullshit detecting"—squarely on Bobby. "Do you work there?" she asked.

Bobby shrugged. "Couple times a month. It's where me and Reg met."

"That's nice," she said, eyebrows still doing that thing that said she knew Bobby had spent his Friday night out drinking with friends behind the Frostie after the football game and not at someone's house like he said. "It's nice that you two boys just sort of hit it off."

"Yeah," Reg said, taking a bite of lunch. He closed his eyes. "Oh man. Bobby, you gotta try this—it's amazing."

Bobby did and had to agree—Mom's cooking wasn't getting any worse.

"This is good, Mom. You'll have to give me the recipe."

"Sure. So, Reg—you got a girlfriend?"

Reg took another bite and closed his eyes. "Nope. Mostly my sister keeps me busy. She's sort of crazy. Most girls don't want to hang around when she's there."

"That's a shame," his mom said, her eyebrows untangling long enough for some honest concern to show through. "That doesn't allow for much of a life of your own."

Reg avoided Bobby's eyes too. "Is there any milk?" he asked out of the blue. "I'm sorry to trouble you—this is just so awesome, I'd love a glass of milk to wash it down."

"How silly of me," she said, moving to the fridge.

Bobby met her eyes then, because usually milk would have been the first thing on the table. She used to complain that Bobby sucked it out of the refrigerator through his pores as he walked by, and she hadn't stopped buying a gallon of it when he visited.

236

She looked levelly back at him as she reached for it, her mouth pursed in suspicion.

"I'll get the glasses, Mom." He stood up belatedly, and she waved him down.

"No, no, not at all. So, Bobby has told me your sister's sort of a handful. How have you managed so far?"

"The guys from John-uh-Carey." Reg carved off another bite and nodded before he took it. "There's a few of us who've been there awhile."

"That's really nice of them," she said. "What about—"

Reg was starting to sweat. "Mom, stop it," Bobby said, keeping his good humor in his voice. "Reg is going to think you don't like him."

And oh, God bless his mom. "I think he's a very nice young man, honey."

Reg looked up guiltily and swallowed. "I'm not that young," he confessed. "I'm twenty-nine, actually. Bobby's way younger than I am."

"That doesn't seem to have stopped him," she murmured, and now Bobby was sweating. He stayed that way—sweating and uncomfortable—for pretty much the rest of lunch.

HE HELPED his mother do the dishes while Reg took a walk outside. Bobby directed him to the west side of the house, where he could see the horse pens of Frank Gilmore's stable.

"Don't go in the pen," Bobby warned him, pulling out a little bag of carrots from the fridge. "But if you hold the carrot like this"—he demonstrated on his palm—"they'll nibble it out of your hand. But only if you hold your hand flat—otherwise they'll bite."

"Can I pet them?" Reg asked, wide-eyed. Bobby smiled, remembering Reg hadn't ever seen a horse up close.

"Like this," he said, holding his palm gently to the bridge of Reg's nose, cupping his forehead. "Firm-like. They like that. But don't give them any flesh to bite, okay? They like to explore that way. I got dragged by a snotty little pony when I was a kid—"

"Those scars under your arm?" Reg asked guilelessly, butting his face up against Bobby's palm. Bobby worked hard not to wince and look at his mom to see if she thought there was anything odd about Reg knowing that. Well, hell—they worked out together, right?

237

"Yeah," Bobby confirmed, moving his hand and looking only at Reg. "There. Just be careful. Move slowly. They're big animals—and they can be like really big dogs, but they can also be like those hippos in the documentary." One of the things they'd watched since V had gone to the hospital.

"Yeah," Reg said seriously. "Gotcha." He took the carrots and smiled.

"I'll be right out there. If you see anyone, tell 'em you're my friend, okay? But remember—Vern Roberts, right?"

Reg grimaced. "Yeah. I don't think I'll ever get that right. You'll always be Bobby to me."

He turned around then and waved briefly at Bobby's mom before setting out across the icy meadow that separated the Robertses' yard from the more developed parts of Frank Gilmore's land. Once or twice a year, Frank would mow this big meadow and sell the hay, so he did keep it seeded nicely—not too many thistles. Bobby had always yearned for a dog, but by the time his dad had moved away, making that possible, his mom had been desperate for money. He'd started helping Frank Gilmore at fourteen for money under the table.

"He going to be okay?" his mom asked as she packaged up the leftover stromboli and put it in the fridge.

"Yeah," Bobby said, watching as Reg turned his face up to the sky and the mountains around him in wonder. "He just needs a direct explanation sometimes, you know?"

Reg kept walking, and Bobby turned toward the table. "I'll go out with him when we're done here."

"Funny how he knows about your scars," she said mildly. "*I* don't even know about that one on your hand."

Bobby held up his hand, where the puncture wound was scabbed over and healing. "Fell through Reg's fence," he muttered. "Spent the last week and a half putting it back together." He didn't like thinking about that night—or the pain in his hand as he'd worked. He hated getting hurt.

"That's fascinating. And now I know. But so does Reg."

"Well, we work out a lot together," Bobby returned, but inside, he hated himself. He could do this, he realized. He could dance with words and keep quiet about what was really happening in his life for as long as she lived. He could see himself, getting an apartment for the two of them and staying some nights at Reg's house and making up a mystery girl and basically living his life in one big frightening shadow.

But he remembered that moment, stomping down on the tenderness he'd felt for Keith Gilmore, and how hard it had been to see himself as someone who could love again, with Reg.

He didn't want to be that person.

"And we sleep together too," he added, looking at her and hoping she'd get it.

Her eyes widened, but her mouth quirked sideways. "I wasn't going to ask...," she said, inviting conversation in the time-honored mom way.

"I... I never should have dated Jessica," he said, feeling that wrongness in his bones. "It wasn't... honest."

His mom swallowed and shrugged. "It's not like we live somewhere easy for that," she said roughly. "Not sure how you could have been open about that and lived through high school."

Bobby's throat ached and his chest felt swollen. "Probably couldn't," he said with an almost hysterical laugh. "How did you... did you guess?"

His mom shrugged again and turned toward the sink. Her eyes were red, and he could see the glaze of tears trembling at her chin, but the two of them weren't big on demonstration. He started clearing the table, stacking the dishes on the counter next to her.

"Just a hunch," she said, answering him without the electric wire of pain between them. "Your voice when you talked about Reg on the phone. Your pain about his sister. You never sounded that way about Jessica." She gave a half laugh. "You didn't even sound that way about Keith."

Oh God. "Mom, about him—"

"He still says he's marrying Carla," she said gently, looking over her shoulder.

"I wouldn't have him if he stripped naked, painted his dick rainbow, and joined the Pride parade in San Francisco," Bobby snapped. "I... I tried to break it off between us, and he got ugly. It's one of the reasons...." He let out a sigh and set down Reg's milk glass with an unhappy thump.

"Why you moved away," she said, like she was putting things together.

"Yeah. I'm sorry he's been scary here with you. I just—I couldn't see him anymore." He gazed out over the meadow toward the fence, smiling a little as Reg held his arm way out in front of him, carrot on his palm. "I guess I know what it's like to be honest with someone now, mostly. And... after that, you can't go back, you know?"

"I know what you mean about not going back," she said, starting on the plates. He grabbed a spare washcloth and went to wipe the empty table. "My boss has hit on me plenty of times in the last five years. I never took him up on it because he's just like your father. I have to work for the asshole—I'm not going to take that bullshit home."

"Good," Bobby said forcefully, turning back toward her. "You need to get out of here. There's more than just your bullshit boss and people like Dad out in the world."

His mom nodded and stared out the kitchen window. "Keith Gilmore."

"Why would you date Keith—" Bobby shut up as he looked back out the window. "Oh fuck. Oh fuck—fuck no fuck no fuck no—"

He was still screaming "Fuck no!" as he turned and hauled ass out of the house.

Needing More, Needing Better

"So you're Vern's friend?"

Reg looked up to where that smooth country-boy voice came from and took a step back from the peaceful brown horse with the white splotch between his eyes. Reg didn't know the horses' names, but this one had trotted up to Reg like it was used to good things from this side of the fence, so Reg believed they could be friends. "Yes, sir, I am. Just up visiting."

"He used to come here and feed the horses all the time." The stranger was pretty—stringy muscles, hazel eyes, a big white smile with brackets around the mouth, and a square jaw.

"He hasn't mentioned it," Reg told him truthfully. But then, Bobby didn't talk much about home. "He did like the horses, though."

"Bobby and I used to pet these guys all the time, after we baled hay for my daddy." The guy—dressed like Bobby dressed, in a denim jacket over a hooded sweatshirt, with work gloves and a baseball hat—reached out and casually patted the animal Reg had been feeding.

His motions with the horse were so gentle, for a moment Reg didn't put two and two together.

"Wait," Reg said, unable to keep the information to himself. "That would make you Keith Gilmore, right?"

Keith stopped patting the horse. "What has he told you about me?"

Reg swallowed and glared at him. "He told me everything," he said angrily. "He won't do that for you no more."

Keith took a step back; then his handsome, full-lipped face contorted, and he reversed that. "And who's gonna stop him? You? You think you're enough to keep him from doing that? I gotta tell you, your boy craves cock, right? He'll ditch you in a fast minute to take me down his throat—he just forgot how good it was—"

Reg laughed. It wasn't a good laugh—it sounded like V's laugh when she was angry and off her medication. "That wasn't good. You think what he gave you was good? I can tell you right now, if he didn't want to, it was the worst blowjob in history. You're just too dumb to know it."

241

"I'm dumb?" Keith gaped at Reg like nobody had ever said this to him before. Well, lucky Keith Gilmore—Reg was going to hear it for the rest of his life.

"You can't make someone love you," Reg cried out. "You certainly can't do it by shoving your dick down their thro—"

He ducked the first punch because his body was a well-oiled machine. He dodged the curious horse and walked right into the next punch because he wasn't used to horses and had never been in a fistfight in his life.

The third punch hit him square in the face, and his knees buckled. He went down onto the frosty ground, pulling his legs up to his chest and wrapping his arms over his head and hoping it would be over soon.

Keith got a kick in to his ribs, and one to his back, and that was when Reg heard Bobby roar.

"Get your damned hands off of him!"

The flurry of kicks stopped, and Reg pushed up to his hands and his knees in time to see Bobby level a haymaker at Keith Gilmore that had him crumpling to the ground—or would have, if Bobby had let him. He grabbed Keith by the lapels with both hands, threw him back against the fence post, and slugged him hard and fast, in the jaw, in the stomach, in the side of the face. Keith tried to block, but Reg had been watching over the past months as Bobby went from stringy country kid to well-built human powerhouse, and *that* was the Bobby who was working his friend over.

Reg had to stop him.

"Bobby!" he screamed, grabbing hold of his left hand and hoping he weighed enough to slow Bobby down. "Bobby—stop it! Stop it! You're gonna fucking kill him!"

"*He touched you!*" Bobby screamed, face contorted with rage. "He fucking touched you! It's bad enough, what he done to me, but he *touched you*!"

"I'm fine!" Reg shouted back. He hurt. His face hurt, his stomach, and his back where he'd been kicked, but Bobby hurt inside, and this wasn't going to make it any better. "I'm fine! He'll leave us the fuck alone now!"

"He touched you," Bobby half sobbed. He reached out to touch Reg's cheek, and his thumb came back with Reg's blood, mingling with Keith Gilmore's. "He hurt you."

"You fucking faggots!" Keith mumbled, sagging against the fence. "I'm gonna tell my dad you're a faggot, Bobby, and he's gonna evict your mama, and you're gonna be fucked."

Bobby turned to him, such cold fury on his face that Reg was afraid for a minute. But Bobby didn't hit him again—didn't touch him, not even when he stumbled to the ground.

"My mom knows who I am," Bobby said through his teeth. "I'm not afraid of what you can tell her. She knows. She knows about me, she knows about you—and the only way she says something to another living soul is if you raise a finger to anyone I fucking love. You think about that, Keith. You tell your daddy to evict her, and it's out. You, me, the goddamned barn, your filthy uncle and his rancid cock cheese—I'm telling *everybody*, including Carla. You want to live in this town, fine. But unless you leave my mother the hell alone, you're going to wish you were dead here, just like I did."

Keith spat blood onto the ground next to him and let out a sound suspiciously like a sob. "You... you're just gonna... gonna go? I didn't mean anything to you at all?"

Bobby shook his head and wiped his eyes with his bloody fist. "Yeah. Sure. When we first started, I thought you were great. But you took away my choice, man. And all that great turned to horseshit, and you didn't see it."

Keith let out a broken sob. "You think I got any choice?" he asked. "You think my daddy wouldn't fuckin' kill me if he knew what we did?"

Bobby shook his head, and Reg wrapped an arm around his shoulders. "C'mon, Bobby," he said gently. He hurt. Bobby's knuckles were bleeding. They needed Bobby's mom. They just did. In ways Reg couldn't even fathom, they needed that nice woman who served them weird pizza.

"Get out of here, Keith," Bobby called over his shoulder. "This place turned what we had to shit. It'll keep eating another piece of you, and more, and more, until there's nothing left."

Reg urged him a couple more steps then. And a couple more. And some more. And by the time they were halfway across the meadow, Reg looked back and saw Keith had pulled himself up. He was standing, arms around that sweet brown-and-white horse's neck, sobbing.

"He gonna be okay?" Reg asked between sobs, forgetting for a minute that this was the guy who had just kicked at him as he huddled on the ground.

"No," Bobby said bluntly. "He hasn't been okay for maybe his whole life." He looked back and then shook his head, wrapping his arm tighter around Reg's shoulders until Reg winced. "Are *you* going to be okay?" he asked.

Reg wrapped his free arm around his own stomach. "I might have to... I'm sorry...." Pain, put off from the panic maybe, roiled up under his ribs, and just that quickly, he was down on his knees, throwing up on the icy stubble of the meadow.

BOBBY GOT him back to the house and made him take a warm shower. He put on boxer shorts and lay down on the bed while Bobby and his mom took stock of his bruises and put ice packs on them.

"There was no blood?" his mom asked Bobby for the fiftieth time.

"Not when he got sick, Mom. I think he just got gutshot."

"I'll be okay," Reg mumbled. He grimaced up at Bobby. "Can I not be in my underwear around your mom?"

"Deal with it," Isabelle Roberts said bluntly. "You've got bruises all over your body, sweetheart. Let me make sure they get iced, okay?" With that, she turned toward the kitchen, presumably to get another ice pack.

"Sorry I'm not a good fighter," Reg mumbled, feeling stupid. "You were a real good fighter out there. I was surprised."

Bobby had taken his own shower, and he crouched down by the bed and smoothed Reg's hair from his eyes with bandaged knuckles. "You didn't live through grade school if you didn't learn to beat the hell out of people," he said with a shrug. "Didn't hurt that I bulked up, but I know how to throw a punch."

Reg half laughed. "V always protected me," he said softly, remembering. "Until I started at Johnnies, I was just always so small."

Bobby grunted. "It's easy for me to forget," he admitted after a moment.

"Forget what?"

"How much she gave you," Bobby said, leaning over to kiss Reg's temple.

Which reminded him. "You really told your mom?" Reg asked, heart full of wonder.

"Yeah."

"She was okay with it?"

Bobby shrugged. "Didn't kick us out. Still seems to like you okay. We'll call it good."

Reg smiled and closed his eyes. It was only three in the afternoon, but they'd given him some pain relievers, and he felt like a little nap. "That's amazing," he mumbled. "Make sure she knows I love you too."

He heard Bobby's breath catch, but his eyes were closed. He could only feel the kiss on his temple and the rasp of the bandage as Bobby dragged his knuckles gently across Reg's cheek.

HE WOKE up about two hours later and made his way creakily to the bathroom, being careful to hit the water. No blood—he checked.

Bobby's mom showed up in the doorway as he was making his way back to bed.

"You okay?" she asked, and he grimaced.

"I need my sweats." He was still in his boxers, and it wasn't right. Besides, it was cold up here.

"That's fine. You can get them out of the bag, you can wear them."

Reg made his way to his duffel bag and started sorting through his clothes. He had to balance against the wall to get one leg in his sweats, and she made a sound of impatience and came around the bed to help him. Embarrassed, he gave them to her to hold while he put one foot, then the other, into the fleece. Then she pulled out a clean T-shirt and a sweatshirt for him to wear.

"Where's Bobby?" he asked, feeling a little lost.

"Fell asleep in front of the TV," she said with a half smile. "Afternoon nap, I guess, just like he was a kid."

Reg frowned. "I don't remember if I ever took them or not."

"Your mom could tell you," Isabelle said, holding the sweatshirt by the hem. Reg put his hands in, and she pulled it over his head. He was so grateful too, because his chest, his back, his core—everything ached.

"No, she couldn't. She took off a while ago."

"That's too bad." Isabelle tugged the sweatshirt down and straightened the shoulders. "My parents died when Bobby was young. I felt so alone. It's hard, you know? Taking care of someone else with no help?"

Reg nodded emphatically. "Yeah. I was lucky. The guys from work—"

"John Carey Industries," she said suspiciously.

"Uh, yeah. They help."

She just looked at him, and his face heated as he looked away. "Look, I know you're trying to get me to say something, but it's a real place, and I don't know what you want me to tell you." He scratched behind his ear, which was his tell for lying, but she didn't know that. It's why he didn't lie that often—he was really obvious about it.

Her mouth twisted, and one of her eyebrows shot up. "Mm."

He closed his eyes. "You're really going to have to ask Bobby… uh, Vern," he said weakly.

She rolled her eyes. "Well, it's obviously not theft, fraud, or gambling," she told him dryly.

"Oh yeah. I'd suck at all those things."

To his surprise, she laughed. "Okay, then. Whatever you guys are hiding, at least it's honest work. And you're both too healthy for it to be drugs, and you are obviously too sweet to be mob muscle. I'll wait for Vern to tell me."

"He thinks the world of you," Reg said, throat aching because now he knew why. "He just… you know. Wants you to be proud." Reg looked around at the house, thought of all the things Bobby would want to do to it to make it nice. "Wants to get you someplace better."

She looked around too and shrugged. "His dad and I lived in some really awful goddamned places before we ended up here." *Sigh.* "This was supposed to be the place he turned it all around. Stopped being mad at the world. Stopped yelling, stopped hitting. So many promises. In the end, best thing he could do for us was leave."

Reg thought of Bobby, ready to throw that last punch—and not. "Bobby's better'n that," he said soberly. "He tries real hard. Even when he screws up, it's 'cause he's learning." Heartbeat. Thought. Memory. "We're both learning."

She sat down on the bed and patted the space next to her. He sat, because his body was too stiff not to, and she scooted toward the head so they could talk.

"Is this your first relationship with a man?" she asked, head cocked.

He grimaced. "Uh, yes and no?"

Her laugh again. He liked how she laughed—it made the lines at the corners of her eyes seem kind and not old. In fact, it made her whole long face lighten up—it became oval-shaped and smooth. Her son was a really pretty boy, and his mother was a really pretty woman, especially when she smiled. It hit Reg then—hard—she was Veronica's age. Oh, he was so much older than he should be.

"I fooled around a lot," he said frankly, feeling stupid. "Bobby was the first person to say 'Hey, this is a relationship, and we can do this.'" He swallowed, because that kiss in the rain had seemed magical, and so out of reach before it had actually happened. "It was hard, I think. For both of us. To figure out that's what we were doing."

"Mm." She nodded. "Not just fooling around."

"God—no. There was no fooling around for us until we knew what we were doing. Weirdest thing I've ever done in my life."

She laughed again, leaning back comfortably against the headboard and pulling her knees up in front of her. Her feet were bare, and he stared at her naked toes.

"You should get a pedicure," he said. "I like those—I don't get the colors on my toes, but they make my feet all smooth."

Her eyebrows went up, showing him Bobby's round hazel eyes. "You get pedicures?"

Oh shit. Oh shit oh shit oh shit. He got pedicures before he had *scenes*, because sometimes the guys sucked on your toes, and it was just not nice if your feet were all gnarly.

His face heated again, and he gnawed on his lower lip. "Uh, yeah. I like, uh, smooth feet?" He was scratching behind his ear again, and what he was starting to think of as "Bobby's Mom's Bullshit Face" was staring back at him.

"Sure you do," she said, mouth pursed in a droll little *O*. "I'm going to let it slide, then, okay?"

"Yeah. Sure." Reg smiled toothily, and she scrubbed her face with her palms the way Dex did sometimes. Oh good. He got Dex's moods. This should be easy. "Oh! Hey—I almost forgot. We brought you something."

Reg got up, restretching all his stiff muscles, and walked around again to his duffel bag. "We brought you books. We've been reading them ourselves— first me, then Bobby, and then we thought we'd bring them to you."

He handed her the bag, which was all dolled up with flowers, and she smiled as she reached for it. "That's wonderful!" She started going through the bag, her expression growing more and more bemused with every book. "But, uh, Reg—these are all girl-and-boy romances."

Reg shrugged. "They didn't have any other kind at the used-book store. Bobby's got a new phone now—he says we can buy books on it and stuff, and that there's boy/boy books, but I gotta figure out how to use my phone like that." He reached into the bag and grabbed one of the paperbacks. "I like books this way," he admitted. "It feels real like this."

"Me too," she said. "Oh! Amanda Quick! I love her books!"

"I like those." Reg flipped through the book. "The girls were really awesome. Brave and smart and stuff." He looked at Bobby's mom and bit his lip. "They probably wouldn't have let themselves get beat up by the bad guy."

"No. But then, they probably *would* work hard to keep their mentally ill sisters home with them instead of someplace they didn't like."

Yeah, he was going to make his lower lip raw, but he couldn't help himself. "But I'm supposed to be the hero," he apologized. "I'm supposed to have the house and the servants and the people who can take care of her." He sighed. "Bobby had to have stitches when he fell through the fence chasing after her."

"I saw the wound on his hand," she said, head cocked to the side. "There was more?"

"On his shoulder," Reg said glumly. "He's been fixing the fence after work for the last week or so."

"Hm," she said. "That's expensive."

Reg shrugged uncomfortably. "Well, he's got two jobs. Waiting tables and stuff."

"Yeah." Thankfully she changed the subject. "Reg?"

"Yeah?"

"You ever think that maybe the reason women read romance books is not so we can dream of a rescuer?"

Reg frowned. "None of the women in those books seemed to want one of those."

"Right. What they really wanted was a work partner so they could rescue each other."

Reg sighed. "Then you need to get Bobby to read some more of those books. I can't even rescue myself."

She stood and patted his shoulder. "Maybe you'll figure out how. I'm going to go fix dinner. You should wake Bobby up and watch some television."

He smiled at her. "Sure. Thank you. You know. For being nice."

It was her turn to bite her lip. "Anytime, Reggie. I mean that."

He thought she was just being polite—he really did.

But he went and shook Bobby awake, and they turned on the TV and found a movie—*shit-go-boom style*, as Bobby said, and Reg was right on board that shit. Bobby was sitting on a battered corduroy couch, and he pulled Reg into the V of his legs and wrapped an arm around Reg's chest.

Reg toyed with his battered knuckles and the scabbing hole that was his closing wound. "Did you reopen your shoulder?" he asked anxiously.

"No," Bobby said, kissing his temple. "I'm fine."

They paused for a moment to watch the heroes kill people and run through some obstacles and kill more people. Sometimes TV was just so easy. "I feel stupid."

"You shouldn't. You wouldn't have dreamed of hitting him. You wouldn't think he'd attack you."

"But I just laid there," Reg mumbled.

"Remember when I got hurt?" Bobby reminded him. "You tackled your sister on the way to taking me to the ER? Hard-core, baby. You just need to know what's coming, and you do fine."

In the kitchen, Bobby's mom let out a breathless little shriek, and then, loudly: "John Carey Industries my *ass*!"

Bobby cringed, and Reg looked over his shoulder in horror. "Do you think she—"

"Got out the laptop and looked it up?" Bobby supplied. "Yup. That's Mom."

Reg sighed and tried to pull away.

"Where are you going?"

"To pack," Reg told him resignedly. "It's a real shame too—I think she liked me for an entire minute."

Bobby held him tighter. "She'll still like *you*," he said, his voice sounding like it was laughing. "It's me she's gonna yell at. Wait for it…."

Sure enough, she stomped into the living room and stood in front of the television.

Reg closed his eyes. "Oh God."

"Porn?" she asked, hands on her hips.

"Yup," Bobby replied laconically.

"Both of you?"

AMY LANE

"It's where we met," Bobby said, arm still around Reg's chest. "But we haven't done any scenes together, if that's what you're worried about."

Reg opened his eyes and saw that she was glaring at Bobby but seemed to have forgotten him entirely.

"Vern Carl Roberts—"

"Mom, are you going to make us leave?" he asked simply.

"No! But are you seriously—"

"Then maybe go back into the kitchen, calm down a little, and talk to us about it during dinner. I'm serious, Mom. My body hurts, Reg looks like he's gonna disintegrate, and my knuckles feel like they're on fire. If we could maybe, just for the next hour, pretend like I'm still your kid and this ain't a big deal."

She let out a sigh. "You *are* still my kid, and this *is* a big deal."

"Sorry," Reg squeaked, wishing he could burrow behind Bobby like a cat or something.

Her mouth twisted as she noticed he was still there. "You are killing me," she said on a sigh. Then, to her son, "You are so lucky he's... he's frickin' *him*. Because he could be the only thing saving you from getting your ass whupped with a shoe."

With that she stomped back into the kitchen, and they both winced as they heard her throwing around pots and pans.

"Is she going to be mad all night?" Reg whispered.

"Not if we bring out the cookies and chocolate we brought her," Bobby said, with undue optimism, Reg felt.

But the movie, in all its inanity, beckoned. Just as Reg lost himself in it, he realized Bobby was right. They still had a roof over their heads. She was still cooking them dinner. And she seemed to like him, even if she was apparently pissed at Bobby.

UNLIKE LUNCH, dinner started out to be a grim and silent affair. Bobby's mom did a lot of glaring, and Bobby did a lot of eating and pretending his mom wasn't glaring.

"So, uh, flat spaghetti with white sauce?" Reg said encouragingly into the silence.

250

"Fettuccine Alfredo," Isabelle said with a tight smile. Then she shook her head and sighed. "How old were you," she asked, "when you started working for John Carey Industries?"

"Johnnies?" Reg shrugged. "Bobby's age. Nineteen. McDonald's wasn't cutting it for property taxes, and V couldn't work anymore. I was, uh"—Reg tried hard not to scratch behind his ear—"on a website and saw an ad. John was real nice to me. It felt like, you know. The one thing I could do. I mean, besides McDonald's, but they yell a lot."

"Oh Lord," she muttered. Then she turned to Bobby. "So?"

Bobby sighed. "The construction guy was a sham," he said baldly. "I didn't have a place to stay. I was crashing on people's couches and showering at the Y, Mom. What do you want me to tell you? Dex—he's our other boss—spotted me when I was bussing tables. Gave me their card."

"What were you doing?" she asked skeptically. "How do you go from bussing tables to having sex for money?"

Bobby appeared to think about it. "Mostly I was just wearing really tight jeans," he said, and then he caught Reg's eye. "The ones with no rips in the knees?"

Reg grinned. "Oh yeah. I like those ones. They show off your...." He swallowed and went back to his white spaghetti. "They make you look good," he mumbled.

"You were wearing tight jeans?" Her head was still cocked, and Bobby finally had the grace to look uncomfortable.

"I don't know, Mom. It's not like I mail-ordered what was in them. You changed my diapers—you know what's there."

Her eyes got big, and Reg could see it. Right there. The moment when Isabelle Roberts recognized that her son had a special talent she might never have even thought of.

"I'm not sure if that's why God gave you that," she said weakly.

"Well, it must be. Because I've been able to keep an apartment and send you money," he said frankly. "I've been able to help Reg fix his house, and keep medical insurance. I mean, sure. I'd love a construction job, or cabinetmaking or something—but I'm not trusting that shit until you are the hell out of Dogpatch."

Reg was still looking at his white spaghetti, but he knew Bobby was looking at him when he said the next part.

"And the people I've met there—not all of 'em are gay, Mom, but they're all real nice. They took care of Reg here for years before I came along."

"Bobby…." Her voice was pained, but for the first time, Reg thought maybe Bobby was right and they wouldn't be driving back to Sacramento in the dark.

"He's got his health insurance for his sister through them," Bobby was saying firmly. "Maybe if I get a construction job and I make a little more money, we can find something else he can do that will pay as much without…." Reg looked up this time in time to catch Bobby's gaze. "Without people yelling at you," he said with a little smile.

"I didn't like that part," Reg said, smiling back.

"No. You do okay at Johnnies," Bobby told him. "People are good to you. They help with V." He closed his eyes. "We'll figure something out for later." Then he turned back to his mom. "This isn't forever," he said softly. "But right now, it works for us."

"Dear Diary," his mom said flatly, "today my son told me he was a sex worker, and I almost fainted with pride."

"Dear Diary," Bobby returned just as flatly, "today I got my mom out of a shitty little town where my ex-boyfriend couldn't stalk her and sabotage her car, *and* my boyfriend got to know his sister wasn't wandering the street with a shopping cart. Wasn't Christmas, but it wasn't bad."

Isabelle looked away, her throat working. "Do you have any idea how many doors this job will close?" she asked. "How many things you can't do?" She turned back to him. "Work as a teacher. Adopt kids. Do you think they'll let you do those things?"

"Maybe not," Bobby said softly. "But I've got six films already out. If those doors are closed, they're closed, Mom. What matters now is where we go from here."

She scrubbed at her eyes. "Where *do* we go from here?" she asked.

Bobby looked around at the decrepit house. "Keith Gilmore isn't going to let this go," he said softly. "I think where *we* go from here depends on where *you* go from here. I think you should move out in the next week. You can stay at my apartment—it's not great. We'll put the furniture in storage for a couple of months, and maybe, in the summer, we'll find a new place."

For a moment, Reg wanted to protest. A new place? Why couldn't Bobby move into *his* place?

And then he remembered. V was there. She hated Bobby. He couldn't ask Bobby to move into that situation. Bobby could stay the night a lot, but... oh Lord.

"Maybe V'll be feeling better," Reg said weakly, staring at his plate. "I... someday, you know. You and me, maybe."

"Yeah," Bobby said quietly. "I'd like that. But right now, my mom can't stay here any longer."

"I have a job here," Isabelle said worriedly. "I can't just bail on that—not after seven years. George Foster may be a sleazy control freak, but he gave me a job when I had no skills and a child and an arm in a sling."

Bobby nodded. "Two weeks' notice? Maybe commute the second week. Reg and I are still free next weekend. We can do the moving then."

"Dex has got a truck," Reg said helpfully. "And Kane has the big Navigator. Ethan and Jonah can help, but, you know. Jonah's not as big as Ethan."

Bobby let out a low chuckle. "Jonah'll be fine. We'll get everyone to help. I'm telling you, Dogpatch won't know what hit it."

"Wonderful," his mother muttered. "What am I supposed to say to these guys? 'Hi, I'm glad to meet you, so nice of you to seduce my son into porn'?"

Bobby scowled. "They're good guys, Mom. How about 'Hi, I'm glad to meet you!'—just like you said to Reg, okay?"

"Yeah," Reg said, nodding. "That was real nice. I gotta tell you, it's been a long time since I met a mom."

Isabelle closed her eyes. "Vern—goddammit. How could you... what are you... augh!" She stood up then and went to the stove, where two pies sat on the counter. One was obviously homemade apple, and the other was sort of a silky-looking chocolate mousse cream. She pulled out a pie slicer and cut about a third of the chocolate one off, then threw it on a dinner plate before grabbing a fork and coming back to the table.

Reg and Bobby stared at her.

"Bobby, do you guys eat dessert for dinner a lot?" Reg asked, because that seemed to violate one of the fundamental rules he'd always read about in books.

"No," Bobby said, round hazel eyes wide. "Never."

"Should you and me—"

"No!" Bobby and Isabelle both snapped, and Reg would have been hurt, but even he could tell they were snapping at each other. Bobby turned toward him and gave a weak smile. "This is a mom thing right now," he said carefully. "I think, you know, this is what happens when I'm too big to beat with a shoe."

Reg nodded and gave her a tentative smile. "Good, because this white spaghetti is really amazing. Maybe Bobby can make it for us sometime."

Isabelle nodded and shoved a giant forkful of chocolate in her mouth, closing her eyes as it went down. "Sounds great," she said, taking a deep breath, almost like a smoker taking a drag. "I'll give him the recipe. But not right now." With that she shoved another forkful of pie in her mouth, and Bobby and Reg finished their white spaghetti in peace.

Moving In, Moving Out, Moving In

"YOU'RE AWFULLY quiet," Bobby said, piloting the full truck back through the snow.

"Tired," Reg told him, scratching the back of his ear.

"Yeah—sorry. That bed was really narrow." There was something else going on—Bobby could feel it.

"Just different." Reg yawned. "And... and I'm wondering. When you'll get tired of dealing with my sister and leave me."

Bobby kept the steering wheel steady and tried to catch his breath. "No," he said harshly. "No."

"But... but I want her home. And you're not going to live with me if she's home," Reg said, sounding sad.

"Well, no." Bobby had to be honest. "But sometimes we just need a place to sleep, Reg. You think of that? We'd need two places so at least one of us can get some honest shut-eye?"

Reg grunted. "Yeah, okay." But he still sounded unhappy.

"Do you *want* me to leave?" Bobby's whole chest ached.

"*No!*" Reg reached over and squeezed his knee. "I just don't know how to make this last, is all. You're bringing your mom to your apartment. That's a change." The back of Bobby's truck rattled with stuff he was going to unload into his front room.

"Well, yeah. But I'll be spending more time with you. That's a good change."

Reg nodded and leaned over to kiss his shoulder before straightening up. "Okay. Yeah."

He didn't mention it again, and Bobby relaxed—mostly. They were both waiting for the other shoe to drop, but neither of them knew who was holding the shoe.

THE NEXT weekend, Ethan and Jonah and Dex and Kane drove up to Dogpatch to help his mom move in the snow.

Dex was honest—the snow was most of the reason they were there. Kane had gone all-out and bought his niece, Frances, a little snow-bunny outfit with tiny mittens and little shiny snow boots. Bobby was actually glad it had snowed a little between visits, because he didn't want to disappoint the little girl.

Bobby had met Ethan's boyfriend already—and liked him—the day they'd kicked Frances's mother off Kane's property. Jonah was about Reg's height and thin, like Reg would be if he hadn't been working out for over ten years, except with curly sand-colored hair and enormous gray eyes. He was also funny, smart, and humble, and Bobby could listen to him and Ethan talk about anime and geeky movies forever. He couldn't participate—he didn't know those things—but listening to their banter wash over him was a treat.

He'd never been happier that his clumsy, stupid overture with Ethan had failed. Boy, how many people would that have fucked up?

The two trucks and the SUV caravanned up the hill together, stopping in Truckee to put on chains and following Bobby carefully when he turned off Highway 80 to take the winding path toward Dogpatch.

They passed the town sign, and Reg answered his buzzing phone.

It was Kane. "Oh my God! Bobby, you said that was the name of your hometown, but I swear to God, I thought you were making it up!"

Reg and Bobby laughed all the way out to Bobby's mom's house, which sat in the middle of a big meadow of snow now.

"Frances'll get to see it," Reg said wistfully. "I bet V would like to see snow."

Bobby bet V would like to see anything but the inside of the institution she was in now—but by all accounts she was starting to take her meds again, so maybe, in another month or so, he could go back to sleeping with one eye open.

He'd been making up for the uncertainty—and the loss of his apartment—by having as much sex with Reg as possible in as many rooms of the house as they could manage.

The results had been highly satisfactory—if a little destructive. For example, they didn't need to put his mom's kitchen table into storage, because Reg and Bobby had been eating on the couch for the past three days. Apparently Reg's old table hadn't been up to the "Bend over, I want you right here!" fantasy that occurred in the books they'd been reading, which was too bad.

It was a good fantasy. The next time, they'd used the counters and been out nothing but a little bit of 409.

Bobby's contemplation of bending Reg over the kitchen countertops again was called to an abrupt halt as he pulled up in his mom's driveway and saw the brand-new Ford F-250 dwarfing his mom's little Toyota.

"Shit," Bobby muttered in disgust.

"Who in the hell is that?" Reg asked, antennae perking up.

"That would be Frank Gilmore."

"Is Keith with him?" There was a little bit of apprehension in Reg's voice, and Bobby didn't blame him.

"He's in the truck, see?" Bobby said, nodding to Keith lying with his head on the headrest, so immersed in his iPod that he didn't even see them pull up. "Keith isn't gonna act up," Bobby said. "The important thing is not to out him."

"The important thing is not to get pounded," Reg said glumly.

Bobby growled low in his throat. It was *terrifying* how much he'd enjoy pounding Frank Gilmore, but he always swore he wouldn't be that guy.

Frank's truck was parked about three car lengths back from his mom's Toyota, in prime *get in the way* space. Bobby solved that by pulling around it and driving on the meadow on one side of the gravel drive, pulling the truck until it was right in front of his mother's front porch. There was enough room on either side for the other two vehicles coming up the drive.

Bobby hopped out of the truck and told Reg to stay where he was.

"I'm not a kid," Reg snapped, sliding out on his side. Bobby sighed.

"I never said you were. I just don't want—" Frank Gilmore walked around his truck then, spitting mad.

Frank was an older, shorter version of Keith, his thinning gray hair slicked back from his head, although his almond-shaped eyes and dimpled cheeks were still handsome. But Bobby had never warmed to Frank, no matter how much work he'd given. For one thing, he paid shit—baling hay for eight bucks an hour was no way to support yourself *or* your family. But for another, he was rattlesnake mean, even to Keith. Jessica had always been his princess—sweet and a little bit oblivious to how hard he worked to screw people over. But Keith had just been a strong back to him, a way to flaunt his prowess over the town. Keith had been his minion, the farthest reach of his already long arm.

Oh, Bobby hated him so.

"So, decided to grace us with your presence, Vern? I'm surprised you even remembered where your mama lived."

"I know where my mom lives," Bobby said evenly. "I just don't know what you're doing here. She paid you up for the rest of the month. You don't need to be here to help her move."

"Now you just wait a minute. Your mama's leaving me here without a tenant in the middle of winter—how'm I going to make that money back up?"

Bobby shrugged and waved at Kane, who was heading down the drive, so he'd know where to park. "I don't know and I don't care. I just want my mom the hell out of here, that's all."

"Wait a minute," Frank snapped. "Who's going to fix all the damage done to that place? You two owe me money to fix the floors and the windows!"

Bobby turned to his mom, who was standing behind Frank, hugging her arms around her ribs and crying.

"Reg, go check the house," he snarled, right before he grabbed Frank Gilmore by the jacket front and forced him back against the side of the truck. "What did you do?"

Frank smiled ingratiatingly. "Now, not my fault your mama knows how to party, is it?"

Reg came trotting out, looking distraught. "The back windows are smashed in, Bobby. There's glass all over the boxes. And someone went in there with a crowbar and punched holes next to the toilet—it's leaking all over the place, and there's a fucking mess!"

Kane pulled in right next to where they were standing, or Bobby might have lost his temper. But Dex was in that car, and Kane's niece, and he was damned if they'd see him turn Frank Gilmore to hamburger.

Dex slid out of the passenger side of the Navigator and came walking toward them, while Kane turned the SUV off and got Frances out the other side.

"What seems to be the problem here?" Dex said calmly. Well, Bobby had seen him, sleep-deprived and half out of his mind, "calmly" deal with a family situation about twice this ugly. Dex was the right guy for this job.

"This guy and his son broke my mom's windows and punched holes in the floor—"

"I didn't do it," Keith said, almost desperately, coming out the driver's side of the truck. "Vern, it wasn't me. My dad had his buddies do it—I didn't know."

Bobby turned his head toward Keith and saw bruises—fresh ones—swelling his face. He grimaced.

"Oh, Keith." Then he turned back to Frank. "You useless piece of horse, uh, crap...."

From behind him, he heard his mom go, "Baby?"

Kane walked around Bobby and Frank and said, "Yeah—you Bobby's mom?"

"Yes—who is this?"

"This is my niece, Frances. Bobby said there were horses?"

Bobby's mother masked a sob. "Would you... would you like to see the horses, Frances?"

Oh, Kane. He looked like a gorilla—shoulders as wide as a tank, forehead still bruised and eye still red from the drama a couple weeks back—but that boy was smart in ways Bobby couldn't even name. His mom and Frances both started across the meadow, and Bobby felt the warmth of Dex and Kane behind him.

"So, now that we can say the word 'shit,'" Kane said pleasantly, "what horseshit were you just feeding Bobby here?"

"That woman can't take care of a house by herself," Frank hissed. "My boys came in to do an inspection—"

"And terrorized a woman by herself," Dex snapped. "Where's the lease?"

"What?" Bobby asked, looking over his shoulder.

"What?" Frank Gilmore asked, sounding stupid.

"Let me see your paperwork, Mr. uh—"

"Gilmore," Bobby supplied.

"Gilmore. Let me see it. I want to see what rights you have versus what rights Bobby's mom has. And then I want to see what you violated."

"Keith!" Frank screamed. "Get out the papers! They're in the truck! Let these assholes see what kind of laws they're violating!"

"You entered her premises without permission," Dex said smoothly. "You're already in the wrong. Let me see how many other rules you broke."

He pulled his phone out of his back pocket as he peeled off from Bobby's shoulder and Reg took his place.

"You go, Dexter," Kane said sincerely. "You're in for it now—he's getting out his phone. You got no idea."

Bobby's arms were starting to ache from holding on to Frank Gilmore's jacket. He let one arm down and shook it out, and was going to grab the coat again when Kane growled, low in his throat, and Frank visibly recoiled against the truck.

Bobby lowered both his hands, and he, Reg, and Kane just *stood* there, staring Frank Gilmore down. Ethan pulled in, driving Dex's truck, and he and Jonah slid out and took in the situation.

"Where's Frances?" Ethan asked, his voice, loud and deep, resonating.

"Across the field with the horses," Kane supplied. "Jonah, you want to go join her and Mrs. Bobby's Mom?"

"Do you idiots know how mafia this looks?" Jonah asked, and Bobby had to choke back a grin.

"He broke all the windows in the house and is trying to make her pay for them," Reg said, visibly upset. "It was a real nice house, Jonah—she's a real nice lady."

"Oh." Jonah's voice softened, and he sighed. "Yeah, sure. I'll go on mom detail."

"Moms like you," Ethan said, all earnestness. "You have a good one. It matters."

"Yeah, fine. I'll go make nice with the parent. You guys be good." From the corner of his eye, Bobby could see Jonah, slight form bundled in an old down coat, curly hair under a stocking cap, and hands safe in fleece gloves as he trundled through the foot or so of snow toward the other end of the field.

And then Ethan was looming behind Reg, all of them staring down poor Frank Gilmore, who was starting to acknowledge he was in trouble.

"Jesus, Vern—who *are* all these fuckin' guys?"

Kane snickered, and Bobby rolled his eyes. "These are people I work with. They came to help my mom move. They didn't expect to beat the crap out of a douchebag, but I'm pretty sure they'll adapt."

"No," Keith moaned. "Vern, don't. Don't beat him up. You know what he's like—"

"Keith, man, you gotta move," Bobby said, glancing at him briefly. "This piece of shit is not worth your loyalty."

"Yeah, don't hurt him," Dex said absently, coming out from the other side of the truck. He had a sheaf of papers in one hand and a phone up to his ear. "Because if you hurt him, he can't pay her damages."

"*What?*" Frank sputtered. "I'm not paying that bitch—" Everybody— all the giant bodybuilders standing at Bobby's back—moved in about six inches closer. "That woman," Frank amended quickly. "I'm not about to pay that woman *shit*."

"Keith?" Dex asked, like Keith was the guy holding the lights at a shoot. "Did Mrs. Roberts break her own windows?"

Bobby locked eyes with Keith Gilmore, daring him to lie about this.

"No," Keith whispered.

"Did she poke the holes in her own floor?"

"No." Keith closed his eyes.

"Now, I'm not even going to ask you who did," Dex said reassuringly, patting his shoulder. "It doesn't matter. See, this is a classic rental agreement— every apartment complex in the world has one. It says that asswipe over there—"

"Frank," Bobby ground out.

"Yeah, asswipe—he's liable for pretty much everything. Do you know what that means, asswipe?"

Bobby had to grin at Dex—he was good at this shit. Then he went back to scowling at Frank Gilmore.

"It means I have to pay," he growled.

"Why, yes. Yes, it does. And it also says that Mrs. Roberts here paid first and last month's rent, doesn't it?"

"Yessir?"

"So if she's paid up for next month, that's one month too long. So I'm just going to rip this up here"—Dex pulled out what was probably Bobby's mom's check and ripped it into confetti before putting the confetti in his pocket, but he kept talking while he was doing it—"and mostly, you guys can leave. I mean, we'll have her stuff in an hour, hour and a half, most, and all we have to do is leave the key under the mat."

"You can't do this!" Frank howled, and Dex grunted.

"Oh yeah. Totally legal. In fact, hold on right there." He held up his camera and took a picture of all of them, huddled around Frank, and Frank, looking pathetic and small, once-honed body rounded and stocky. Then Dex strode into the house, long legs confident, wide shoulders swinging like he did this shit all the time. Well, Bobby had seen him in action—he sort of did.

He came back in a few moments, still fiddling on his phone. "Okay now, so I've got a lawyer, sort of a catch-all type of guy, and I'm sending him the pictures. We've got two eyewitnesses that say the damage wasn't caused by Mrs. Roberts, and we've got pictures of what damage there was—*and* we've got pictures of the guys and you, and nobody's hurt, and nobody has so much as a hangnail. So there you go. Can't hurt anybody, can't wreck anything in the house, and can't give Bobby's mom one more goddamned bit of trouble. In fact, the most you *can* do is get the fuck off the property and let us do our thing."

"Fine!" Frank hawked and looked for a place to spit, but nobody was moving. Watching him swallow was both really gross and really gratifying.

Kane stepped aside just far enough to let him pass, and he sidled by, his back scraping the side of Bobby's truck.

"You'd better be out of here by the end of the day," he snarled. "Or I'm gonna make—"

"What?" Dex said, nose still buried in the papers. "She has until next week. What are you going to do?"

"I'm gonna tell everybody in town her boy's a faggot, and he's got a whole passel of faggot friends—urk!"

Kane had decided not to let him through. "I. Don't. Like. That. Word." He punctuated each enunciation with a little shake; then he looked at Bobby. "Could it hurt your mom? You know, if he goes to town and uses that word?"

"She put in her notice," Bobby said, eyes on Frank. "She's commuting up to Truckee for a week, which is gonna suck, but then she's looking for another job." Bobby gave a small, mean smile. "My mom doesn't have to ever visit this pissant town again, Frank. But you do. You're stuck here. And that's fine. You just keep throwing your money around and being the king of Dogpatch. I don't give a shit. I'm living somewhere else now, where when I walk down the street, nobody knows me or gives a shit who me or my family are." Bobby looked up at Keith again. "It's liberating. Free as a goddamned bird."

Keith nodded. "Dad, let's go."

"Shut the fu—"

"There's a little kid out there with Bobby's mom," Keith said, his voice uncharacteristically strong. "What are you going to do? Mow down all these people in front of a little kid? They got a lawyer. Not a Dogpatch lawyer—someone outside. And they're right. Why are we here anyway? It's a rental property—why does it matter?"

"I let that woman stay here when she couldn't keep her man—and she had nothing!" Frank snapped. "This? This is how she repays me?"

"She paid you in rent!" Bobby protested. "Jesus—what else did you want?"

Frank gave him a narrow-eyed glance that told Bobby a whole lot about how strong his mom was, and where Keith Gilmore had learned to be a blackmailing motherfucker.

"I hope your dick falls off," Bobby said, feeling his entire body go cold.

"Cold bitch never put out—*oolf!*"

"Kane! I told you—don't hurt him!"

"Just his ribs," Kane said mildly. His jaw was clenched, though, and his eyes narrowed. "Maybe his kidneys. I don't like men who bully women."

"None of us do," Ethan said, his usually warm, happy voice locked up and hard. "I think it's really important that he knows that. Do you know that, Mr. Gilmore?"

Frank was still doubled over, clutching his ribs or his kidneys or whatever. "Yeah," he managed. "I think I got it."

"So yeah," Dex said, folding the rental agreement up and putting it in his pocket. "You'll get back the papers with her signature on them when she's done working. You can't rent the place out before then. So, you know. Maybe don't go down to Truckee and tell stories, 'kay?"

"Keith, start the truck!" Frank wheezed, and this time Kane let him go.

They all watched as Keith executed a wide, destructive three-point turn. If Bobby's mom had planted flowers this year, he would have decimated the beds, but she'd given up on that a couple of years past.

"That was exciting," Kane said, not even rubbing his hand for show. "Can we move shit now? My blood's all up. I need to work out."

"Yeah, sure," Bobby said numbly. He looked up to where Jonah and Frances and his mom were still petting horses. "Let's get as much done as we can before they come back. If I know my mom, it's all labeled and shit."

HE KNEW his mom.

Most of the books and needlepoint supplies were going to Bobby's apartment. Most of the furniture was going to the storage cube he'd rented nearby. Everything else had been boxed and labeled, including dishes and clothes, and Bobby thought woefully of the stuff he'd put in boxes to take to Reg's.

"God, that apartment is small," he murmured. "We really gotta figure out where we're gonna live."

Reg came up to his side and bumped his shoulder. "You guys make enough—maybe just a better apartment?"

"Yeah," Bobby said with a sigh. "Two bedrooms. That way she has someplace to put her needlework if I move out." It would give him and his mom something to do after V came back, Bobby figured. Because he was going to need a break from V, even if he loved spending most of his time with Reg.

"When," Reg said hopefully. "*When* you move out."

Oh God. "Sure. When."

It was as close to a lie as he ever hoped to tell Reg, but he consoled himself with the thought that there was a way to be found.

IT TOOK them less than an hour.

Part of that was because there were five of them, and the other part of it was that all five of them were freakishly strong.

"Jesus, Kane—put the couch down!"

"But Dexter, look—one hand!"

"Great—but it's gonna crack in two if you don't let Ethan and Reg get the ends."

"Bummer. I want a try."

Bobby grinned at Ethan. "You break it, you bought it. Twenty bucks at the Goodwill, I'm pretty sure."

Ethan looked speculatively at the couch as Kane brought his other arm up and tried to decide how to lower it, now that he was exactly in the middle.

"I think I'll keep the money, move the couch, and have the contest in the gym with witnesses. Here, Dex—you get one side and I'll get the other. Kane, squat so it's in a good place."

Kane crawled out from under the couch, crowing with pride. "Looked pretty good, right, Dexter?" He stepped up to Dex, who put the couch down so they could rub noses.

"Yeah, baby. Looked great. Maybe only do that where Frances can't see, okay?"

"What's she gonna bench?" Kane asked, entranced. "We could make her little barbells, with stuffed animals on each end, right? Like, buy her a baton and some duct tape and—"

They kept talking while Dex and Ethan lugged the couch out, and Bobby and Reg rounded up the last of the boxes. His mom and Jonah were walking across the meadow as he deposited them in Dex's truck. Frances was sleeping in her arms. Bobby took in the way she held the little girl, tight and sweet, and thought sadly that she probably would have been a good mom with lots of kids, and a happier mom if she'd had a man she wanted to have those kids with.

"Here," Kane was saying after Bobby slammed the tailgate shut. "I'll take her. We'll be leaving in a few, and we need to get her in the seat." He gave Bobby's mom an earnest look. "It's hard getting her in there in the snowsuit, right? It's all squishy. But once we bought it, she wanted to wear it up here. I swear, Dexter and I froze the whole way so she didn't melt."

"We had a snowball fight," Isabelle said, keeping her hold still. "She had so much fun."

Kane grinned, and Dex walked from the truck to lean over his shoulder to brush Frances's cheek with his gloved fingers. "Aw, sleeping bunny. Did we pet the horses?"

"Forever," Jonah complained good-naturedly. Ethan—per usual—was all over him as he walked up, hanging over his back, mauling him in hugs. Jonah turned around and hugged him, staying snug in his arms. "Seriously, Kane—she kept saying, 'But they don't have scales!' You gotta get some normal animals, man!"

"Lizards are normal!" Kane defended. "It's the furry things that're weird."

Bobby came over to his mom and put his arm around her shoulders. "You gotta give her back, Mom. We can stop for lunch in Auburn if you want—she should be awake then."

His mom gave a small smile. "Well, I understand your friends are about to be neck-deep in babies. Maybe they'll need a sitter."

Kane took Frances this time, although Bobby's mom's eyes still looked pretty bright. "Are you kidding? Most of our *friends* still need a sitter. You guys get a decent apartment, you'll be neck-deep in giant goombahs who need a mommy."

Isabelle looked around at all of them, obviously surprised. "Vern," she said faintly, "you haven't introduced me to your friends."

THEY ATE in Auburn, and Bobby and his mom treated because everybody else had put themselves out to help. After that Ethan led the way to the apartment, while Bobby and Reg unloaded the furniture into the storage unit. By the time they got to the apartment, everybody else had gone, and Isabelle was sitting at the little table, looking around bemusedly.

"Your friends are really nice," she said, nursing a fresh mug of coffee. It was the only appliance Bobby had bought.

"They really are," Bobby said, setting the pizza he'd bought on the table. Reg got some milk out of the refrigerator, and they sat down to eat. "Wan'som?" Bobby asked through a mouthful.

"God, Vern—we only ate about four hours ago. Give me some time. I've got a question, though," she said, sipping her coffee again. She looked happy there, in front of the boxes of all her possessions.

"Yeah, sure." Bobby swallowed and smiled invitingly. "Hit me."

"How come none of your friends know you're a couple?"

Reg choked on his pizza until Bobby had to thump him on the back.

HIS MOM insisted he spend the night at Reg's—told him frankly that she'd rather be alone with the strange night sounds in the cheap little apartment than see Bobby sleeping on the couch with his feet hanging off.

She also told him that she felt free there, and she wanted to see what that was like.

Bobby thought that was probably closer to the truth.

They walked into Reg's house and turned on the lights and adjusted the thermostat, before hanging up their coats and pulling off their boots to shake off the cold. Bobby was standing, hand on the coat hook by the front entryway, when Reg walked in and wrapped his arms around Bobby's waist. Bobby lowered his lips and kissed the top of his head, holding him close and enjoying the warmth of his body.

"Mm...." Bobby closed his eyes. "I needed this all day."

"Me too." Reg took a deep breath and let it out. "Why don't we do this in front of other people?"

Bobby kept his eyes closed. He'd known this was coming as soon as his mom had asked the question. "I don't know," he said. He was picturing the thousand-and-one touches he'd seen that day. Dex, looking over Kane's shoulder at the baby, close enough to rest his hand in the small of Kane's back. The way they'd rubbed noses, like nobody else could see. Ethan, hanging on Jonah like a giant floppy spaniel who would need pets forever and ever, and Jonah turning around to pet him.

"It's just... this thing... I mean, we can't touch in front of V," Reg said softly. "But it's more than that. It's private."

Bobby didn't want to say it. Didn't want to think it. "I think it needs to become public before I move in."

Reg tightened in his arms, but Bobby didn't let him go.

"I'm not breaking up with you," he said, voice harsh. "And I'm not giving you an ultimatum. But Reg—Reg, I know who I want to be. I know who I want *us* to be. And I know it's going to take a while for you to put your finger on it. But when you do, let me know, okay?"

"Don't break up with me," Reg whispered.

"Right back atcha," Bobby told him, holding him tighter.

"Don't give up on me."

"Not going anywhere."

Reg pushed up in his arms then, taking his mouth, and Bobby responded right back. The quiet evening Bobby had in mind melted away in the heat of Reg's hands on his body, in the franticness of his touch.

Bobby put a hand on either side of his neck and touched foreheads. "Easy," he whispered. "Easy."

Reg nodded, trembling, and Bobby turned him toward the bedroom, close and dark, where they touched all the time, and both of them knew the rules. Their clothes hit the floor in a jumble, and Bobby laid Reg down, feet in the air, and grabbed the lube from under the pillow.

"Fast," Reg begged, naked, stroking himself, shameless. "Just... fast."

Fast and now, Bobby knew. Because they'd both heard it, what could be the death knell of them, the thing that could break them apart. *It's got to be you, Reg,* Bobby thought as he stretched Reg, slicked him up, made him ready. *You've got to do it. I can't help you.*

Reg groaned, shaking, and Bobby thrust in. For a moment Reg's grip on his cock was completely overwhelming, as he'd prayed it would be. Oh yes—it was them. It was only them. It was Bobby and Reg, and they were the bright light in the center, and the universe whirled around them. Bobby began to thrust, letting that light wash over him, letting their pleasure become the only thing that mattered.

Beneath him Reg shook, he trembled, he screamed Bobby's name and *only* Bobby's name. There was nothing between them, not flesh, not doubt, not family.

Reg's back arched so hard he came off the bed, his impossible angle hitting Bobby just right. Bobby cried out, groaned, and fell forward, coming that quickly, too quickly, because the white light would fade, would drain from them like come, and they would be left, just their heartbeats, alone in the darkness of an uncertain world.

A Different Normal

V CAME home in late April—and John came back to Johnnies about two weeks earlier.

Reg would remember the dates as seeming to be so close together, because life without V and John had become the new normal before then, and although he missed them both, the new normal was really so wonderful he didn't have a way to put words to it.

Bobby and his mom found a new, better apartment with two bedrooms. It wasn't too expensive, because his mom was finding work. She had a job with a temp agency, but finances were solid since Bobby was working two jobs. His mom still wasn't awesomely excited about one of them. Bobby told Reg that she frequently tried to feed him extra during his three-day abstinence, and Bobby spent a lot of time boxing up leftovers to give to the street people who could be seen searching the dumpsters in their neighborhood, but she wasn't mean about it either. In fact, she was pretty nice to his friends as a whole. She had Dex and Kane over for dinner, as well as Ethan and Jonah, and Lance and the other guys from the flophouse.

Bobby said she'd never had so many people to cook for, and between his two jobs and the temp job, they were making enough money for her to cook.

There were also about ten million craft stores in Sacramento, Bobby said—Reg wasn't sure about his math—so the number of boxes in the spare room had gone up as well.

And most of the time it *was* a spare room.

Bobby would finish waiting tables and come over to Reg's and work on the house. He completely replaced the fence and dug out the backyard to plant grass seed. By April they had a nice carpet of grass in the back, some starting in the front, and he'd replaced the floors in the hall and was taking measurements for cabinets in the kitchen.

"Do you know how to make cabinets?" Reg asked apprehensively. It seemed like someone who knew how to make cabinets should probably not be in porn.

"No," Bobby said, frowning as he wrote the measurements down on paper. "But I know how to install them. I'd need you to pitch in on the having them made, but we could rip them out and replace the flooring, then put in the new ones."

Reg had looked around his crappy kitchen with big eyes.

"I got no idea how to do all that."

"Well, I do—but it's going to take two of us and…." Bobby bit his lip and grimaced, and Reg knew what he wasn't saying.

He didn't want to do it with V there.

Well, Reg couldn't blame him. Did they have, like, boarding places for people with schizophrenia? So, like, she could go live there for a month, like a vacation, while they had hammers and saws and whatnot all over the house so they could fix the floor and install the cabinets?

Probably not, Reg reflected glumly.

So Reg just said he'd help pay if they could manage to do it, and Bobby found other things to fix. By the time April had rolled around, they'd repainted V's walls—the same color pink, but without the graffiti—and Bobby was replacing baseboards and window treatments, and that seemed like it was going to take him a long time. The thing *Reg* noticed, though, was that every time he replaced a window treatment—like with blinds or curtains or something—the whole rest of the wall looked like crap.

Reg figured painting the house was going to be their thing in June, because Bobby should be done with sealing the house to help the air-conditioning and heating by then.

He liked helping Bobby.

He remembered all the times he'd ended up screwing around with someone because he couldn't think of anything better to do. Bobby would take him to movies or to the bookstore, or to live music in downtown, and Reg loved that.

But the other times, the times they weren't fooling around—and there were lots of the fooling around times; Reg narrowly avoided blowing his abstinence more than once—they spent fixing the house. Reading. Watching television.

Sure, they hung out with friends separately. Reg went to Ethan and Kelsey's house a lot. She was getting close to having the baby; she needed him to bring lots of stuff. Bobby hung with his mom. But most of their time was together, and it was awesome, and Reg didn't want to fool around with anybody else because that meant he couldn't spend time with Bobby.

Apparently being in a relationship was that easy.

But it sure did make porn hard.

"Uh, Reg," Dex said blankly. "Do you have that thing out for a reason?"

"Yeah, Dex," Reg said. "I'm fluffing, right? When you're done with the lights?"

"Been done for about ten minutes, buddy. We're waiting on you."

Reg looked down at the thing in his hand. He'd been petting it for the last ten minutes, but it didn't see Bobby anywhere, so it didn't think it was going to get any use.

"Uh...," he said, looking at his cock and feeing stupid. Sex. On camera. He'd been doing it for eleven years. He looked over at "Chris"—and again, he didn't feel so bad about his shitty porn name situation—and back at his dick.

Chris was a sweet kid, blond, blue-eyed, sort of like a young Dex, complete with baby fat around the chin. But the older Dex was stacked and ripped, and he had this sort of dangerous self-knowledge around the eyes. Reg could probably bang Dex now, if Dex still did scenes, and like Lance, they'd shake hands and walk away, like guys on a bowling team.

But this new guy, Chris....

Reg looked back at his dick.

"I suck cock like a dream," Chris said sweetly. "Man, I seriously converted the quarterback at my junior college. He totally plays for our team now."

Reg grinned at him and stripped off his pants before folding them to stash on the shelves. He followed up with his shirt and grinned at the angel with the apparently filthy mouth. "Wanna start there?" he asked Dex. "Him deep-throating me? I bet I could get it up *then*."

"Sure," Dex said easily, kicking back. "Go to it!"

It worked. Chris's mouth was everything advertised and more, and they laughed a lot while they were fucking. But when they'd finished up and had filmed the shower scene—which had ended up with Reg fingerbanging the kid against the wall, because he had a sweet ass too—Dex waited until he was coming out of the locker room to pull him aside.

"So, Reg."

"Yeah?"

Dex rolled his eyes. "Anything on your mind?"

Reg tried a grin. "You know me better than that," he said.

"No." Dex shook his head. "You don't get to pull that shit on me. What's up?"

Reg shifted his weight from one leg to the other. "I don't know. Guess, you know. Got that thing out and it was expecting someone else."

That got a laugh, and Reg was glad. He was getting better at eliciting a laugh from people—it was worth trying. "Anything else?" Dex asked quietly.

Shift. Shift. Shift. "My, uh, sister's coming home next week," Reg said, gnawing on a cuticle. "You know. Don't know how much longer me and someone else got."

Dex looked away and sighed. "Reg…," he said, in that pained tone of voice Reg knew by now.

"No." And he couldn't smile about this. "Thanks for filming the scene, Dex. You did a real good job."

"Wait a sec!" Dex waylaid him with a hand on the arm. "About filming scenes. You think, maybe, not your thing anymore?"

Reg gnawed on another cuticle because the first one was bloody. "You think of something a guy who barely finished high school can do that gets him health and dental, you let me know," he said honestly. Oh God—he was gonna be thirty. "And I'm not great with animals. I mean, I know Tommy's at PetSmart and stuff, but I may get a dog someday, and that's gonna be the end of it, you know?"

Dex nodded, looking sober and a little sad. "I hear ya. Look, just hang on, okay? I've got a thing I want to do. John's coming back in a couple of days—I think he'll help. It's so, you know, guys who work here have maybe something to do when they're done working here."

Reg smiled, but even he recognized the bitterness. "That sounds real nice and all, Dex, but we both know those plans are for other guys. Not me."

He turned away then and walked out. Bobby was waiting for him with a special meal he'd cooked all by himself, and movies, and generally some peace and quiet. Reg, who used to be able to go out and fuck himself raw after a scene, thought peace and quiet with Bobby was about the best dream a guy like him could have.

"I WANT to go back to the place."

Reg stared at his sister, uncertain. "V?"

She looked better. Her hair was pulled back from her face in a ponytail, and she was clean, wearing a pair of jeans and a sweater that fit. He'd asked her doctor—the one who'd been assigned to her as she'd climbed rung after torturous rung of mental health institutions until she got to the one that said she could be released and taken home—and he'd said she'd never stop wearing long-sleeved shirts, even in the worst of the summer.

Damned bugs crawling out of her skin. She would believe that until she died.

"I had a boyfriend there," she said accusingly. "I don't know where they'll put Kevin after this. How am I supposed to find him?"

"You could write him," Bobby said, and Reg's heart beat triple-time, he was so relieved. Oh, thank God for Bobby, who had dealt with the acres of paperwork and legions of doctors, taking careful notes the entire time.

Reg had signed everything—his name was on the conservation—*conservatorship*—papers, so he was legally in charge. Somehow, being legally in charge felt worse and harder now that V had been inside a hospital she apparently didn't hate and wanted to go back to.

"I could write him?" she asked, suddenly curious.

"Yeah." Bobby grabbed one suitcase by the handle and stepped forward to take hers. She yanked on hers, keeping it in her possession, and he shrugged and started up the stairs. "We have the address of the care home in about sixty different places here. You write him a letter, we get an envelope and address it, and we send him a letter. Then he has your address, and he can send one back."

"That's a good idea," Reg said in an undertone, and Bobby winked at him. It wasn't until he winked that Reg realized how much he'd been dreading this moment, with V home. He'd almost seen Bobby just ditching her at the door and saying "I'll see you around." But that wasn't the case at all, and Reg could suddenly breathe again.

It wasn't over. It wasn't over. V was here, and Bobby was here, and maybe Reg didn't have to give her up after all.

"I'll do that," she said, following Bobby upstairs. "Thank you." She smiled briefly at Bobby, who inclined his head in *you're welcome*. Oh, that was encouraging, wasn't it? "Make sure my pill is ready in two hours, Reg. They said I have to keep to a real strict schedule, remember?"

Reg remembered. The week before, the doctor had briefed him on the different medications she took three times a day. He'd written it down and put it on the refrigerator and then put everything in the little weekly pack they'd gotten at the drugstore. The regimen was longer and more complicated this time, but V swore it helped her keep the voices at bay while letting her function without the cloud around her brain.

"Yeah, V. I've got an alarm and everything. We don't want any bad shit to happen."

She turned to him, brown eyes troubled, biting her lower lip. "I don't always remember when it does," she said honestly. "But no. You gotta know that, Reg. I don't want to hurt you."

Reg smiled and bit his lip at the same time. "I knew that, V. Me and Queenie always knew that. You wanted to keep us safe."

V looked sad then. "I miss Queenie," she confessed. "I… I liked having a sister. And the babies were sweet."

Reg sighed. He'd gotten a letter from Queenie over Easter, with pictures of the kids—five of them now. He'd shown it to V during their last visit, and she'd wept hard and begged him to have her visit.

Queenie didn't respond to his letter. Reg guessed she didn't know what to say. For a minute he thought about Bobby's mom and how excited she'd been to hold Frances. He'd been there the night Dex and Kane went over for dinner. She'd bought toys for the little girl to play with, and after dinner, she'd held Frances on her lap so she could do her hair. Reg wondered, for maybe half a minute, if he could do the same thing, have Frances visit, but in that half a heartbeat, he saw the way V was *without* her medication.

He didn't want his friend's kid to see her like that.

"I'll see what I can do," he lied, his throat dry.

"Thanks, Reg." She smiled a little and yawned. "I'm going to go lay down now, okay?"

Reg nodded and watched as she followed Bobby up the stairs. "I'll wake you up when it's time to take your medicine. We'll have lunch."

"What's for lunch?" she asked, animated for the first time.

"Spaghetti with salad." He and Bobby had made the sauce from scratch.

"That sounds nice. Thank you."

They disappeared up on the landing, and Bobby came back down in a few moments, smiling tentatively.

"So. That was good," he said hopefully, nodding.

Reg nodded back. "She remembers Queenie more now that she's on her meds."

"Well, you know. All men here, Reg. Maybe she'd like to meet my mom?"

Reg gave a half smile. Bobby's mom—the cure-all for everything the Johnnies guys might have. "No," he said softly. "No. I don't trust this to last. I don't.... I mean, she likes me now. What happens if...." He wasn't making any sense.

"The guys still like you," Bobby said, drawing near. He gave an instinctive look over his shoulder, making sure V couldn't see him as he pulled Reg into his arms. Reg's heart shrank into his gullet as he realized they would have to do that *forever* while she lived here. Living to the alarm, making sure she had her medication every time, making sure he and Bobby never touched when she could see, and that Bobby only stayed the night if she went to bed first and that she never realized any of Reg's friends were gay and that Dex and Kane could never bring the baby and neither could Chase and Tommy, or Kelsey, or—

He couldn't breathe.

Bobby's arms tightened around him, and Bobby soothed him, breath after breath, as he tried to pull himself together. Oh God. Oh God. This was his life, and he'd promised, he'd promised her, and he'd signed the papers, but he'd never seen, until right now, how much of himself he'd signed away.

It took Bobby the better part of an hour to calm him down, until he could breathe again and talk in sentences. But he couldn't put words to what panicked him so bad, because all the words were disloyal and painful and things he'd never voiced before, not when he was sixteen, not at eighteen, not at nineteen when he'd decided to whore himself out.... Oh God... oh God... he'd fucked for a living for most of his adult life, and he was doing it, had been doing it, for someone who would never know what price he paid and would hate him if she did.

Bobby had to fix lunch and set her pills out, and Bobby kept her company when Reg retreated to his bedroom, distraught, unable to think, unable to do anything but sit and watch television, letting the mindlessness

275

hypnotize him as he'd been mesmerized into trading his adulthood for family, when he'd never had much of either one.

In late afternoon, Bobby brought him a plate, sat him up, and made him eat.

"She's reading," he said quietly. "Not watching the news. It's something you've read before. Maybe you can come talk to her about it in an hour."

Reg nodded and took a bite of spaghetti. "Sorry," he said, voice broken and wretched. "I don't know what happened."

One corner of Bobby's wide, wicked mouth turned up. "It hit you, is all," he said. "What you've given up your whole life. What you had for a couple of months. What you're giving up again."

Reg nodded and forced himself to take another bite. His scene had been five days ago—he was still hungry. "How come?" He took another bite and swallowed, then clarified, because Bobby was still looking at him gravely in the long shadows of the April afternoon. "How come I never thought about it before?"

Bobby reached out and stroked his cheek. "Maybe 'cause I'm here. And you can't have me when we're out there in front of her."

Reg shoved another bite into his mouth. "God, I'm dumb. I mean, *so* dumb. How can you love someone this dumb, Bobby? How can you just stand there and watch me fuck up my life and struggle to figure shit out, and I'm slow. I'm so goddamned slow. How can you—" His voice was rising again, and Bobby stopped him, scooting closer and wrapping his arm around Reg's shoulders, kissing him softly on the temple.

"Not stupid," he said. "Not stupid. Slow isn't bad. Slow is just… taking your time. Not doing what everyone says because they're saying it. Figuring out for yourself what's right."

Reg nodded and tried to center himself again. "Porn is getting to be not right," he admitted, voice shaking. "How is that? How can I be fucking the whole world one minute and just… just wanting one person the next?"

Bobby's laugh was dry. "Four months, Reg. I kissed you almost four months ago. I touched you six months ago. Think about that. We've been snuggling like this for half a year. That's growing time, right there."

"Two goddamned inches," Reg said sourly. Bobby had started out six foot three, and now he was officially six foot five. His chest looked narrow again, although he was working out like a boss. It was in-fucking-sane.

Bobby chuckled shamelessly. "Yeah. Both of us. Growing."

"What am I gonna do?" Reg asked, the pain in his chest congealing.

"Mm...." Bobby thought for a moment. "How 'bout come out to the couch and sit between my legs while we read, like you do. If she says something nasty, tell her it's how you and me are. Sometimes I think it's the label she doesn't like—not the people. When your head's confused, it's the label that's easy."

Reg grunted. Well, yeah. *He'd* been all caught up on labels too—but then, he was so bad with words, with matching them to concepts, that labels were all he had.

"We can sit together," Reg said. Small things. Like he'd done all his life. He could grab for small things. "Okay. It's not so bad, then."

He could breathe. He could breathe. One breath at a time.

V WENT to bed on time, without putting up a fight with her meds. She didn't watch the news and, in fact, talked to Reg excitedly about the Regency romance she was reading.

And Reg had a terrifying realization.

"They're so stupid!" she laughed. "All this fuss over whether they sleep together! Making the two of them get married. Why don't they just tell the world to fuck off?"

"Well," Reg said, remembering what Bobby's mom had told him. "It was a different time back then. Women were... well, their virginity was a big deal. So they had to protect her honor."

And V had laughed, long and jarringly, about how virgins were boring and how it was all about a book title and how nobody cared if they were doing it.

And Reg stopped talking, let Bobby take over, while he dealt with the fact that it wasn't just when she was *off* her meds. On the whole, V's mind, once sharp and quick and on point, with As in high school and junior college, and promotions at work and everything, had deteriorated over the last eleven years.

She didn't understand the book. She didn't understand the time period. All the things Reg and Bobby had needed to look up on the internet, she didn't remember. In particular, she didn't remember the simple human trick of putting herself in another person's situation and thinking about how they might feel.

He would look back later—much later—and realize that the mourning started then. But his heart was so sad, so shattered, he couldn't sort the pieces of it yet. Not then. Not a month later when his world fell apart.

All he could do was try to spread the pieces on the table and bleed.

HE WAS emotionally exhausted that night—but he needed. It was like he was internally hemorrhaging, and he needed Bobby inside him to keep him alive.

They got to the dark of their bedroom, and all the quiet talk between them died. They undressed in silence, Reg taking off his underwear and tucking them under his pillow while Bobby opened the window to the side yard, letting a soft breeze and the smell of the neighbor's cats waft in.

By the time Bobby turned around, Reg was sitting on the bed naked, waiting.

Reg looked into his lover's eyes and opened his mouth suggestively. He was empty. He needed. Bobby would fill him.

Bobby slid his own boxers off and threw them near the head of the bed—the easier to find them when they were done—and let his cock unfurl.

It was thickening as Reg watched, but it wasn't huge. Not yet. Reg mouthed it, taking the whole thing in. His gag reflex had been long ago burned away, too many cocks shoved to the back of his throat. But he was glad now, taking the whole thing into his mouth, his lips tight against Bobby's pubic hair.

Bobby swelled, lengthening, fattening, taking all the room in Reg's mouth, penetrating his throat, and he swallowed, swallowed again, then pulled back with a tightened tongue and palate, lips over teeth, his suction strong and hard as he exposed the great club of a penis, wet, glistening, blood throbbing under the surface, and prime.

Bobby moaned softly and massaged his scalp under his hair, and Reg thrust his head forward again.

"Such a sweet mouth," Bobby said softly. "Let me know if you want my mouth on *your* cock."

Reg just shook his head. His own cock was swelling but not urgent. He wasn't aching for Bobby's touch—he was aching for Bobby's *use*. He needed to be of service tonight. He needed to be ravished.

He kept sucking, again and again and again, pulling off to slap his own cheeks with Bobby's member, harder and faster, until Bobby grunted and smeared precome on his face.

"Want it hard tonight?" he whispered, making sure. He was always so tender with Reg—making sure Reg wanted to be hard-fucked, that was something he'd do.

Reg nodded and kept slapping, glad, so glad when Bobby shoved him back and turned him over, putting him on his hands and knees.

The cold drizzle of lube shocked him, and his cock finally began to ache. Then Bobby's fingers, two at first, because Reg could take it, thrusting in and out until Reg grunted *yes*.

Three next, long, slow strokes, and Reg just squatted on the bed, grunting like an animal, needing this, needing to be a sex puppet, needing Bobby to mold him to use.

Another finger, almost a fist, stretching him to pain. He shoved his palm in his mouth and howled, screaming, shoving his ass back. He'd take a fist tonight, when he'd never taken one before, anything, anything to fill the sudden void of self-knowledge, the terrible, terrible ache of his wasted youth, the promise he'd never had a chance to understand before he'd pissed it away.

Bobby pulled his fingers out, and Reg howled louder with the emptiness, until Bobby shoved inside him, battering, hard, unapologetic.

Reg needed him so bad, he half sobbed into his own cupped hands.

Bobby fucked him savagely, short, hard thrusts while Reg shuddered, clenching, trying to capture that behemoth inside him.

Don't leave me. Don't take it away.

He bore down, using all his muscles to tighten up, to burn, to ache, and Bobby's pop across his ass amped him up higher.

"Let me in, Reg," he hissed. "Don't clench me out."

Reg whimpered, releasing, and the savagery diminished, replaced with speed and smoothness.

Pleasure flowered in Reg's gut like a betrayal, but he couldn't stop it. Warmth, joy—all the things he and Bobby had been to each other in the last four months washed over him, rinsing away the desperation. He lay, facedown, ass up, while his entire body shuddered, loosened, relaxed in release, and Bobby pumped, hot and full, inside him.

Bobby draped over his back until his knees gave way, and he sprawled, legs open, come running down his balls. Bobby stayed on top of him, pressed him into the mattress, limp as a come rag.

Their breathing evened out. "I'm sorry," Bobby breathed. "I'm sorry. I wish I could do this for you. I wish I could make these decisions. I wish I could fix this inside you. All I can do is just be here. Be whatever you want. It's all I can do."

"Love me," Reg begged. "Love me."

"I already do." Confused.

But Reg had no words for the fear, the emptiness of the pieces of his heart. "Love me," he whispered again. "Just love me."

Bobby pulled his hair back from his temples and kissed his ears. These were things he'd never thought of doing in bed, not until Bobby. These were love things. It was the only way he knew the word at all.

The Blindside

BOBBY HUDDLED in the back of the hospital room as the rest of the Johnnies gang fawned over the baby boy cradled in Tommy Callahan's arms.

Yeah, kid was cute, Bobby wouldn't argue. Reg stood next to him, happy, involved, taking part in the banter, but for once Bobby was aware, painfully, that they weren't touching.

In this room, with these people, it should have been natural.

But the week after V had gotten home, she actually caught them kissing in the kitchen, and the peals of her raucous laughter still rang in his ears. Men. Kissing. She thought it was hilarious now.

On the one hand, he was glad she wasn't launching after him with a piece of crockery, but on the other?

He and Reg couldn't touch in Reg's home unless they were in bedroom, alone.

They couldn't touch in public because neither of them was comfortable with that in public. They could touch in Bobby's apartment, but Reg couldn't spend the night there. Their entire lives were boiled down to the moments they were alone in the dark of Reg's bedroom.

Bobby saw that happy family and wanted to take Reg's hand so bad, his stomach ached with it. Reg said, "Oh yeah, my sister has lots of these things. You need to support the head," and Bobby had a sudden vision of him, heartbreakingly young, holding the absent Queenie's child. Knowing Reg—hell, seeing the dynamic between him and V—he'd probably been responsible for those kids too.

All that responsibility for oh, so long.

Bobby could see him fray at the edges, the life he'd been leading coming into direct conflict with the life he realized he wanted, and Bobby could do nothing.

When Reg had a meeting with John later that week and came home glowing with the promise of being able to do something else, anything else at Johnnies, Bobby almost cried.

"So you'll be...."

281

"Going to shows," Reg crowed, hopping on both feet while Bobby dug out the old planters in the front lawn. Bobby handed him a spare shovel so he'd have something to do.

"Like movies?" Because Bobby had already seen a lot of porn—more than he'd ever dreamed of, as a matter of fact. He really didn't want to watch his friends fuck anymore.

"No, like, say there's a celebrity night at Gatsby's Nick—that dance place you took me to."

Bobby smiled. That had been a good night, Reg bouncing around like a cork in the wake of the music. They'd touched then, in public, and the sky hadn't fallen over their heads.

"Okay, so you'd be the celebrity?"

Reg wrinkled his nose. "No. *You* would, or Lance, or any of the new guys. And we'd bring posters and shit, and the guys would sign them and give away DVD collections. So apparently the front desk gets, like, calls asking for guys to come out, and usually it's been Kelsey calling 'Hey, any goober wanna do a thing?' around the office, first come first serve. But they're gonna give me my own phone line in the corner of Dex's office, and I'm going to book events and go there with the guys and make sure everyone treats 'em right and, you know. I mean, if the guys wanna sell ass that night, that's up to them, but if someone wants to buy and they're just there to sign? I mean, we're all built, but I get to be in charge of saying 'don't touch that.' And they want to advertise online, so I get to surf websites and see who advertises porn and how much it costs and shit. I mean, John's gonna teach me, and so is Dex, and mostly I'll just pick up the slack for them, but…." He bit his lip, and for the first time since V had come home the month before, Bobby felt something besides soul-sucking anxiety from him.

"It's new," Bobby said, smiling with encouragement. "It's new, and you're… you're free. You don't have to do scenes anymore."

The smile that washed over Reg's face, the relief that washed over his body—oh God, it let Bobby breathe again.

"I was having a really hard time getting it up," Reg confessed quietly, like this was shameful. "Bobby, I'm sorry—the only guy I wanna bone is you."

Bobby laughed, setting down his shovel and walking in to hug him, public or not. Reg dropped his shovel too, and for a moment, the two of them stood in the hot May sunshine, sweaty and happy, holding each other like lovers, like the whole world could see.

There was a noise at the front door, and V stuck her head out just as the two of them flew apart, grabbing their shovels and standing up to work some more.

But inside, Bobby was rejoicing, hoping, praying.

Something had happened to Reg that he hadn't expected—something good. Something he'd earned. He was growing.

Veronica asked nightly when she could go back to the other hospital, the one with her boyfriend in it, until Reg had started to ask if they could bring her in to visit. So far the answer had been no—Kevin hadn't been doing so well since V left—but that knowledge, that the worst things that could happen—V being in the hospital, Reg being out of porn—could also be the good things that could happen, was starting to build inside him.

Bobby started to wonder what it would be like to move all his stuff into this house, to rip out the cabinets, replace the kitchen floor.

He liked living in the apartment with his mom fine—in a way, it was like living in Dogpatch, except he and his mom talked openly now, even when she was trying to talk him out of Johnnies. She didn't yell at him, she didn't suspect him of things—they just talked.

But he didn't feel like it was home.

Reg's house felt like home now, but it was one he wasn't welcome in. They all knew that.

V stood on the porch now, practically vibrating. "It's time for my pills!"

"No, it's not," Bobby said calmly. He pulled out his phone. "See? Pills in an hour."

"It's wrong," she snarled. "I feel like shit. Get your lazy ass in here and make my lunch!"

Bobby and Reg met eyes, and he could tell the good feeling brought on by Reg's sudden change in fortune had just dissipated like cloud vapor in the ninety-degree heat.

"V, that's not nice," Reg said, trying to be conciliatory.

"Fuck you both," she sneered. "Faggots."

And she turned into the house and slammed the door.

"Oh fuck," Bobby muttered.

"It's gotta be this last week," Reg said, both of them analyzing every exchange with her. Yeah. The last week, their quiet evenings had turned into the news station blaring again. This was the first time she'd been overtly hostile, but her body language had become more aggressive.

When she'd first come back, she'd smiled sometimes, said *please* and *thank you*. But she didn't now.

Bobby took a deep breath. "I'm going to go put the shovels in the back of my truck," he said thoughtfully. "I think you and I need to spend the rest of the day cleaning the house."

Because they needed to find her stash of pills, and count them, and make sure she got what she needed today.

Because they *both* knew where this was heading if they didn't.

THEY HUNTED.

They searched her room, her closet, under her bed. Bobby felt like a total asshole when he opened her box of feminine protection—but then he found the little repository of pills. He thanked his lucky stars it was in the box and not with the used product in the trash.

"Nine doses," he counted grimly. "Reg, call the hospital and tell them she's missed nine doses." He glared at V, who was sitting unrepentantly at the table and chewing her dose for the day without water. The pills in the box had been spat out into the glass—and then fished out after she finished the water.

"That's just what I saved," she snarled.

"Why *do* you save them?" Bobby asked, curious. "I mean, if you flushed them, we wouldn't have any evidence at all."

Her eyes flickered. "Well, last time it was so Reg'd forget the doctor's appointment and wouldn't figure out I wasn't taking them."

Bobby had figured that out in the hospital. "But now?"

She picked a cuticle. "'Cause I do okay without 'em. But if I stop doing okay, I want them there to take."

Bobby stared at her and tried to process that. "You think this is doing okay?" he asked, making sure. "You're not nice without your medication, V. You scream shit at your brother. You're mean to people. You deliberately hurt their feelings. He can't sleep when you don't take your medication— he's afraid you're going to hurt him. You understand that, right?"

"He keeps me trapped here," she said, eyes bright. "Like a prisoner."

"He takes you shopping, out to eat," Bobby said, at a loss. "But he's worried—"

"Worry worry worry," she snapped. "I'm not a little kid."

"No!" Bobby snapped back, done. For a brief shining moment, he'd seen the kind of life he and Reg could have. "You're a mentally ill adult, and you're abusing your little brother, just like you abused him when you made him sign your papers!"

That seemed to take her back. "But… but I did that for *him*," she said, suddenly in tears. "He was sixteen! They would have put him in foster care. I'm the one who kept him safe!"

"Well, now I have to keep him safe from you," Bobby cried. "And you're not helping me one goddamned bit!"

"Well, you people should let me do what I want to do," she replied, starting to rock back and forth. "Just let me do what I want to do. Stop thinking about the past. Just let me do what I want. I'm not a little kid. I'm not stupid. Just let me go."

Bobby looked at her, feeling helpless, wondering if Reg could get out the cuffs *right now*. Reg came back from the bedroom, phone still in hand, and sighed.

"What?" Bobby asked.

"Two things. One, I reached out to Gatsby's Nick, and that was Dex. I did it—they want us to show up. I booked my first gig."

"Seriously? Oh wow! Go Reg!"

"Yeah—and he took me off the other schedule."

Bobby gaped at him, so happy in his heart he could burst.

"What's the other?" he asked, remembering that Reg had been in there to talk to V's doctor.

Reg gave a little chin-nod, and Bobby started toward him before V interrupted.

"You two, always plotting. You and your filthy little secrets—what's he even *doing* here, Reggie? Why's he making me take these fucking pills? I was good to you when you were a baby. Why are you trying to keep me drugged!"

"Fine!" Reg burst out. "Doctor says you can either take your pills and be good, or you can go back to the first place. Not the good place with Kevin—we don't get that place anyway, not when I can take care of you.

No—you go back off your meds now, you gotta go all the way back down the ladder, to the place that stinks like vomit and piss and cigarettes and we don't even get to talk to you without an enforcer. *That's* what I was gonna tell Bobby. So it's on you, Veronica. You can take your meds, behave, and let us try to get you in touch with your boyfriend, or you can be a god-awful bitch and end up there." His voice broke a little. "That's what we got, V. That's where we are. I know you don't like the pills, and I know you don't like your life. But I don't got nothing else. I'm trying—I'm trying to make a better life for all of us, but it's been damned hard when every breath I take is filled with whether or not you're gonna fuckin' kill me in my fuckin' sleep!"

Veronica caught her breath like he'd slapped her and triple swallowed in rapid succession.

She had been, Bobby realized sickly, keeping the pills lodged somewhere so she could spit them out later.

"You hate me," she sobbed, throwing herself away from the table. "Everyone's fucking against me. I hate you all!"

Bobby met Reg's bleak gaze.

"I'll go," Reg said softly. "I know where the handcuffs are."

A WEEK. A hard one.

Bobby had a scene in the middle of it—but he didn't want to leave Reg alone. He stayed the night, reading on the couch until six in the morning so Reg could sleep, and then went to wait tables before going home to crash at his mom's. Reg got up, took care of V, went in to Johnnies, and came back to give her medication during lunch. Bobby got there, and they were a team for dinner. They were both cranky and tired—and hungry for each other's touch but afraid to set V off.

The night after Bobby's scene, Bobby stayed up to read until around midnight. Then he set the book down and crept into Reg's room. He called softly first so he didn't startle Reg, then came to sit on the side of the bed.

"What?" Reg mumbled groggily.

Bobby put his hand on the back of his neck, keeping him still, and then swept his palm down Reg's bare arm, taking in the toughness of the muscle, the smoothness of the skin on his shoulder.

"Just want to touch you," Bobby whispered. "Remember, that's how this all started? With touch?"

Reg *hmm*ed in his throat. "I wanted to take you," he confessed, voice strained. "I get so… so mad when you have a scene. And I hate that feeling, but I'd hate it worse if I didn't have it."

Bobby nudged him to his back and kept stroking, from his throat, down over his chest, over his abs. "I'm sorry," he said, genuine regret filling him. "Johnnies… it worked for me. It worked for me when we first got together. But if it's not working for you—"

Reg shook his head, and Bobby could see his shy smile in the dark. "Maybe a little while longer. Maybe until we know this thing I'm doing works." He ducked his chin. "I really want to promo an event with you in it."

Bobby laughed, and Reg covered his eyes. "It's dumb! I know it's dumb! But… but you are so…." He pulled his hand away from his eyes and cupped Bobby's cheek. "So beautiful," he said, biting his lip again. "So hot. And I love that I'm not the only one who sees that. I love that the world sees that. I… I know that you bring home something that only I get. And for now, that's enough. When it stops being enough—"

"You'll tell me, right?" Bobby asked anxiously. God help him, he'd been the invisible kid from Dogpatch for so long. Being Bobby on Johnnies, having the whole world look at him, being beautiful, being sexy, fucking like a god—it felt powerful.

He felt powerful.

It had taken him a while to figure out why—why he loved his one scene every three weeks or so. Why he didn't want to actually *be with* anyone but Reg, but why he wanted to *fuck guys* as long as the camera was rolling.

But now that he knew, he'd like to keep it.

Not at the cost of Reg, though.

He'd seen enough shitty human connections, even at nineteen, that he knew to treasure the ones that were wonderful.

"I'll tell you," Reg said softly. "I'll tell you when it gets too hard." He rubbed his thumb across Bobby's lips—a tender, grown-up gesture from a man who'd tried hard to find his inner adult this last year. "I'll tell you when it's getting in the way."

Bobby smiled and lowered his head for a kiss. Reg responded, and the kiss kept going. Not urgent. Not *fuck me now*. Just a gentle build, their mouths in the night, their hands on each other's skin. Bobby pressed him against the bed, wanting more—not more sex, but more kissing, more touching, more *them.*

Eventually their clothes came off, and their final coming together was in each other's fists, but that was secondary. They never stopped kissing, never stopped touching—

Never stopped loving, with all they had learned.

Bobby held Reg for a long time after Reg fell asleep and before he got up and dressed, going to sit watch in the next room, because he just… just didn't trust the well-being of the man in his arms to the sister who wasn't able to care for him the way she probably wanted to.

They *had* learned a lot since October—both about each other and about themselves.

Would it be enough?

Please God—let it be enough.

AT THE end of the week, they asked Skylar and Rick to come over and sit with V while Reg went and manned his first show—but they were under strict instructions to act like they were in the closet.

Skylar had rolled his eyes and said, "Yeah, just like the rest of our lives in front of my parents. Awesome."

"Really?" Bobby grimaced. "You're going to keep visiting and tell them you're friends?"

Skylar shrugged. "Well, they didn't take 'boyfriends' too well, right? And seriously. How often do I see them? Once a year? I mean, not everybody can be Mrs. Bobby's Mom."

"Vern," Rick said maliciously. "*Vern's* mom."

"And what is *your* real name?" Bobby asked, showing all his teeth. "Because *my* mom is starting to call me Bobby 'cause I like it better."

"Yeah," Rick returned, needling. "But doesn't that make you Bob Roberts?"

Skylar chortled. "Dude! Burn!"

Bobby let out a mock growl. "Skylar, what's his real name?"

"Gaylord," Skylar said promptly.

Bobby's whole body went transcendent with joy. "*Really?*"

"It is not!" Rick protested. "It's Derrick."

"Hunh." Bobby wrinkled his nose.

"Yeah, I know," Skylar agreed. "It's the epitome of anticlimax. So, no holding hands or having sex in the living room. Anything else?"

They were standing in the newly seeded front yard, under the shade of the single tree on the side, and Reg and Bobby looked at each other. "You need to give her meds," Bobby said. "You remember where. You've done this before, right?"

Skylar keened. "Really? That again?"

"Well, she'll pretend to take them—but you need to make sure she really does."

Rick grunted. "Aces."

"Sorry, guys," Reg said, looking way more embarrassed than he had in the fall. "I'm... I'm sorry."

"No—it's okay," Skylar said, and Rick wasn't far behind. But as the two of them, dressed in their best jeans and athletic-fit Johnnies shirts, got into the truck, Bobby's heart sank a little further.

It was a lot to ask.

Anybody.

BOBBY WENT with Reg for moral support and to make sure Lance and the other headliners had their posters and water and someone to escort them to the back if they needed a break.

He didn't expect to be popular himself—nor for Reg to provide him with promotional posters and a corner along the back wall where the signing was happening as sort of a surprise.

"Sign them," Reg said with grin, handing him a Sharpie. "You're hot, they connect with you. Go!"

So Bobby took his own turn, saying things like, "You like the scenes? That's awesome. It's great of you to watch!" And it didn't matter who was asking him to sign—men, women, old, young, waxed and young or furry, paunched, and grizzled. He was just so happy he'd done something they liked, meeting them felt like an incredible honor.

Finally, though, Reg called an end to the event but promised the guys would be out on the floor for a good half hour to dance. He grabbed Bobby's hand then and hauled him to a quiet corner, and even though the music was loud and rocking, Bobby pulled him close and started to drift in small circles. They were both hot and sweaty, but it didn't matter. They were flushed with excitement, thrilled to be there, happy with the triumph of what Reg had accomplished.

He'd organized the gig, the crowd had loved it, the guys felt appreciated—and the manager of Nick himself had come out and thanked Johnnies for showing up. He'd even asked them if they could make it a monthly thing, now that there was someone in charge of promotion.

It was a win—and Bobby was so proud of Reg, he couldn't stand it.

In spite of the crowd and the excitement, he lowered his head and took Reg's mouth, letting his pride fill them.

Joy exploded behind their eyes like stars.

THEY WERE exhausted when they got back to Reg's house, though, and grateful that Rick and Skylar were ready to take off for the flophouse, where they could, in Rick's words, actually look at each other without hearing the *F* word.

That sobered them both, and Bobby could see Reg's neck droop as they turned the lights off and went to Reg's room.

"She's going to have to go back in," Reg murmured. "I don't know how—I mean, she's not good enough right now to put her in the good place, or even to agree to go. I…."

Bobby pulled his back flush with Bobby's front and dropped a kiss on top of his head. "Maybe call a social worker?" he said softly. "Tomorrow?"

"Yeah," Reg sighed. They took separate showers a few minutes later, but for that moment, Bobby didn't want to let him go.

They fell asleep quickly, in boxer shorts and nothing else because it was hot. They were tired and distracted, and Bobby forgot his resolution to sleep with one eye open.

He didn't wake up in time.

One minute he was fast asleep, and the next minute he was sitting up in bed, watching as V swung a shovel at her brother's head.

Bobby lunged, throwing himself on top of Reg as the blow fell, taking it on the back of his shoulder. He screamed and continued to roll, coming to his feet and standing in front of Reg with his arms out, warding off V and the wild swings from the shovel.

"What are you faggots doing in my house?"

Oh Jesus.

"Reg! Reg, grab the phone and call the police! We need some fucking help!"

She swung again, sideways, and the shovel, dirt encrusted and sharp, ripped a slice across his stomach, even as he tried to wrench it out of her hands. Behind him he heard Reg scrambling for the phone, and he clenched his scream inside.

"Did you get this out of my truck?" he asked, trying to dodge, trying to protect Reg, trying not to hurt V all at the same time.

"Shut up! Shut up! All the fucking people, screaming at me all the fucking time!"

Oh Jesus. Jesus, she almost caved his skull in with that last one. His ribs were on fire, and his arm ached from one of her first blows, and he was running out of room. With a concerted effort, he woke up and timed his grab with her thrust, yanked the shovel out of her hands, and handed it backward to Reg to guard.

She screamed—and then, oh holy God, reached for the knife tucked into the waistband of her pajama bottoms, and Bobby swore. He'd never even *seen* that knife. Where the hell had it come from? He grabbed at the bed, coming up with a throw from the top, which he whirled around his arm and used as a shield.

She got through once, twice, but Bobby knew he was bigger, knew he was stronger, and the second time the knife ripped through the sheet around his arm, he yanked it out of her hand, and then, hating himself, he backhanded her, cracking her across the face, and throwing her into the far wall.

As he straddled her, held her hands behind her ass, put her in a three-point restraint, he could hear her sobbing, hear her curse the strangers in her house...

Hear her call for Reggie, her little brother, because he disappeared in the night.

In the distance sirens blared, and behind him Reg fell to his knees, phone still in his hands, and cried.

"Bobby," he said, sounding young. "I'm bleeding."

Bobby turned toward him in horror, seeing the dirt on the side of his head, the blood in his hair from where the first blow, the blow Bobby had slept through, had landed, just as Bobby had sat up in bed.

291

"Oh God," he whispered. He couldn't get up, couldn't risk that he'd let her up, let her hurt him again. "Come here, Reg. Come here and lean on me. They'll be here in a minute. Just one more minute. One more."

Reg leaned up against him, his back to Bobby's sore side, and that's where they were as the cops broke in, guns drawn, and both of them had to lift their hands over their heads.

They obeyed slowly, and as the police helped V up, asking her if the two of them had hurt her, Reg toppled sideways in a dead faint, and the ambulance arrived soon after.

THE COPS wouldn't let him alone.

One of them hopped in the ambulance with him and Reg and battered the two of them with questions while the medics worked until Reg started to cry.

"Make him stop, Bobby. Make him stop. My head hurts, and she was so still, and calling my name. Make him stop, Bobby, please!"

"But sir, we don't understand—"

"She's mentally ill!" Bobby snarled. "She's mentally ill, and we got her from the adult care home a month ago because she stopped taking her meds, and she stopped taking them again and lost her shit. Can you just leave us alone!"

"What we don't understand, Mr. Roberts, is what you were doing there."

"He's my boyfriend—do you need me to draw you a picture?"

"So, you two were engaged in...." The cop was middle-aged and worn, white with a sort of permanent sneer on his jowls.

"Young folks call it sleeping, sir," Bobby snapped. "You may have heard of it."

"That residence is not the one you gave the officer on the site," the guy said, relentless.

"I haven't moved in yet," Bobby told him, feeling like this was too private for words. "Veronica obviously doesn't like me."

Reg started to cry some more, and Bobby nudged the paramedic aside as the ambulance jounced down the road. "Sorry," he whispered, looking at the bruising on Reg's face and hating himself for falling asleep. "I didn't wake up in time. I thought I did. I thought I stopped her. I didn't realize she got you first."

"Hurts, Bobby," Reg said. "I'm so weak. It hurts."

"You're not weak, baby. You called the cops. You were hurt and bleeding and you called the cops."

"She got you," Reg moaned. "She got you too."

The medics had already wrapped Bobby's arm on scene and tried to tend his stomach. They'd managed to irrigate it but told him they'd need to wash it more thoroughly before stitching it.

"Yeah, but we're both tough. We're both tough, okay?"

"Yeah, you looked pretty fucking tough when you were sitting on a helpless woman," the cop snarled, and Bobby lost his temper.

"*She almost killed us!*"

"Okay, okay—but if you think I'm bad, wait until the social workers get hold of you. And don't think I don't want to help them out. You two, carrying on when a respectable woman lived under the same roof. Fucking perverts."

Bobby stared at him, realizing that here was the hatred he'd feared his whole life in Dogpatch, smacking him in the face when he'd least expected it in Sacramento—and he didn't care.

"I'm not talking to you anymore," he decided coldly, turning his shoulder away from the cop. He'd managed to snag his cell phone and a pair of jeans on the way out of the house. "Reg, baby, hold on. I'm gonna call Dex. He's got that lawyer guy. We need some fucking help."

Reg nodded sadly. "Where's my sister? Do you know?"

"We took her to booking," the cop said. "You assholes said she tried to kill you."

"Oh Jesus." Bobby closed his eyes. "*Mentally fucking ill.* She needs the psych ward and restraints. Get her out of jail, you asshole. Fuck. Just fuck." He pulled out his phone and dialed Dex's number. "Dex?" he said weakly into the phone. "Dex? Yeah. Bobby. No, the gig went fine but...." He grabbed Reg's hand and clung. "We need some fucking help."

THE COP kept up, relentless, in the ambulance, in the hospital. A social worker arrived—nobody Bobby knew—while Reg was being triaged in a curtained chamber. A nurse was injecting Bobby's wound with lidocaine, and Bobby's world became a whirlwind of questions, of insinuations, of accusations, while Bobby listened to people ordering tests for Reg and tried not to whine like a baby about his own hurts.

"So you just woke up and she was beating you with a shovel?" the cop said for the umpteenth time.

"How is it Mr. Williams got care of his sister?" the social worker asked.

"Yes—she got it from my truck. I was landscaping. And their mom left when he was a kid. V sort of tricked him into signing her conservatorship papers."

"She tricked him?" The social worker was an older woman, looked like she'd seen the wars. Well, if this was her job, Bobby imagined her whole life felt like a war.

"He was sixteen! She told him that hospitals were real shitholes, and he loved her, so he faked their mom's signature to say he was taking care of her."

"But he's not sixteen anymore," the cop said. "He knows better now!"

"Have you *been there*?" Bobby snarled. "'Cause we were. We went to the shitty one to the better one to the better one, and I gotta tell you, they don't seem all that awesome to me!"

"No, they're not nice places," the social worker soothed, but she had a sarcastic edge too, like what did he expect? "So your friend, he's been trying to keep his sister out of them. Do you have any proof she's been skipping her meds?"

"Yeah—we figured last week. We've been forcing her to take them—"

"Forcing?" the cop sneered. "'Cause I'd want to hit you with a shovel too!"

"I wanna hit you with a fucking shovel right now, and I haven't had so much as an aspirin! *Fucking ouch!*"

"Sorry," the nurse apologized. "I'll go get you some painkillers when we're done here."

"Answer the question, junior. What's it look like, this 'forcing' her to take her medication?"

To his relief, the social worker came to his rescue. "Exactly what you think it looks like, Officer. The only difference was her brother and his friend holding her down and keeping her calm instead of a bunch of strangers with handcuffs and a straightjacket and a needle full of Demerol. Managing the severely mentally ill isn't for the weak."

Bobby wasn't expecting tears to start, but that did it. "Reg tries so hard," he said.

294

"Yeah?" the cop came back in his face. "Your little buddy tries hard? That's pretty fuckin' weak, considering from what I can see he's a retard who can't keep his dick in his pants!"

Later, Bobby would think back to that moment, to his kneejerk reaction, wondering if he gave the cop the opening he needed. But then, all he knew was that his vision went red, like it had when he'd backed off with Trey, when he'd been hitting Keith. Except this time he was in pain, and panicked, and angry, and this guy had just used the biggest, scariest word in Reg's world.

"*He is* not *retarded!*"

Bobby didn't make the conscious decision toward violence, but it took two cops and a three-point restraint to pin him to the ground.

"Nice!" the cop howled in his face when they'd jerked him up. "Nice! We got you on assaulting an officer! Do you feel like a big man now, not jumping on a hundred-pound woman?"

"She's *dangerous*!" Bobby sobbed desperately. "She's *sick*. And he can't do it. He wants to do it—he's worked his whole life to take care of her, but he *can't*. It's killing him! And it's killing *me*. I don't care what you think of me, but don't let her go home with him again." He caught his breath, aware he was crying and shouting and—oh fuck—Reg was right on the other side of the curtain. "She'll kill him," he whispered, pressing his face against the floor. "She'll kill him without me. She's killing him slow as it is."

The social worker crouched in front of him, sudden compassion on her face, but Bobby didn't care. She was the enemy.

"Are you saying he's incapable?" she asked, her voice loud in the sudden silence. "Are you saying your friend is too impaired to offer good care?"

He knew what she was asking. "He's smart," Bobby said, his breath coming in shuddery pants. His open stomach wound stung on the floor. "But she's so cunning. She's going to kill him."

"Honey, this won't work unless you tell me he's incapable. Is your friend capable of taking care of his sister?"

He heard it—Reg's betrayed voice on the other side of the curtain, calling his name just as he said, "No."

HE DIDN'T remember much after that. They rewashed and stitched up his stomach wound while Reg sobbed and cursed his name, hidden from view.

When they were done, the cop yanked him roughly up, and he begged to go see Reg, to talk to him, to explain—but the cop said he needed to be processed for assaulting an officer first.

It didn't matter.

Bobby heard the final things he was shouting. *"Fuck you! I don't fuckin' need you! Fuck off, Vern Roberts—your promises mean shit!"*

The words rang through his head as he was taken to the local jail, arrested, and processed. They gave him his one phone call before they threw him in the cell, and he paused for a moment, trying to decide.

In the end there was only one person he could think of who would make sure both Reg *and* Bobby were taken care of.

Dex was coming for Reg. Bobby needed his mom.

SHE CAME to get him in the morning, and for a moment he couldn't meet her eyes. Then Dex walked in behind her, and he wondered if he could die, right there, melt into the floor.

"Did you see him?" Bobby asked desperately. "Is he okay? They wouldn't let me see him. They wouldn't let me talk to him."

Dex nodded, looking tired. "He's got a major concussion and some stitches." He grimaced. "He was pissed at you, so I told him he'd have to do his observation time in the hospital."

Bobby groaned. "I... they asked me if he was capable," he said, the shame biting him deep. "It was yes or no. And all I could think was—"

"Nobody was capable," his mom filled in for him. Her hands fluttered at his shoulders. "Honey, you don't even have a shirt on."

"She attacked us in our sleep," he said. He looked at Dex, begging for forgiveness. "Nobody could take care of her—not one person or two. We needed help, and he wouldn't ask for it, and I could either...."

The holding cell had been quiet. Basic cinder block, six other guys, three of them drunk. Bobby was built like a tank and apparently looked badass. Nobody touched him.

But nobody talked to him either.

Now he realized it was a good thing he hadn't talked. One word about what he was talking about and he'd be dead, because his voice would break, and he would have been crying in the jail cell like he wanted to cry in his mother's arms.

"You could tell them the truth or send him home with his sister like a time bomb," Dex said on a sigh. "I get it. What I *don't* get is where assaulting a police officer comes in."

They were walking out, down a long hallway, toward daylight. Bobby blinked at the daylight, his eyes feeling sore and sensitive and small.

"He... when they busted in, I was sitting on her, her hands behind her back, my elbow on her shoulder. I... she's tiny, Dex. It looked like I beat the hell out of her. But the cop wouldn't listen. He kept trying to get me to say I beat on her. And the social worker was there, asking me if Reg was capable, and the cop called him retarded and—"

Dex grunted. "Yeah. I get it. Not retarded. Your arraignment is in three days. We got you out on bail now, and I've got the lawyer working on the particulars. John's friend in Florida might have a take on it too. He's sort of a shark. We'll see what we can do about no jail time, okay?"

"Yeah," Bobby said, voice rough. "Jail I could do."

He looked out to see where they were taking him and realized Dex's truck was parked at one of the meters nearby. Thank God. He was shirtless and bandaged and looking like a thug from a movie. He'd rather get on his knees and give someone a blowjob on the lawn than look like a violent offender released from jail.

But he was going... to his mom's apartment, he thought mournfully.

Not home. But somewhere safe.

"Thanks," he said to Dex as he felt a strong hand on his elbow, helping him up into the back of the cab. Dex helped his mom up too, and Bobby leaned back in the jump seat and wished for death. Sleep. Oblivion.

Anything to drown out Reg's pitiful voice as Bobby'd been dragged away.

Dex got in and started the truck immediately, pumping cold air into a destructively sweltering June morning. He turned in his seat before putting on his belt.

"Bobby, I know it feels like... like the end of the world right now."

"Yeah." Bobby closed his eyes and fought tears again. They'd been lurking, apparently, all night. He only needed some safety to set them free.

"But Reg, he's got the biggest heart in the world—"

"And I just broke it, Dex," Bobby said, eyes still closed. "He thinks I think he's... he's retarded, and it may be a medical word, but it's his worst goddamned fear. That he's not smart enough, strong enough to take care of his sister. And he just heard me tell the world he's not. Trust me. He's better off without me, if he thinks I don't respect him."

Dex grunted in frustration. "I get that you're feeling low, okay? But don't give up. Please? He's…. John and I worried about Reg a long time. Guys grew up, grew out of Johnnies, and Reg just kept on, because he couldn't think of anything else to do, but I saw the changes. Didn't know you were a couple until *last night*, but I saw them." Bobby grimaced because he sounded damned bitter, but Dex kept talking. "You made him think beyond that. You gave him faith to do that. Don't… don't discount that, okay? Just give him time."

"Sure." For a moment he hoped Dex's lawyer would lose in court. That after the arraignment he'd be put in jail for a year, maybe two, and he could spend a year beating the shit out of people—or blowing them—just to stay alive.

He'd never have to think about the thing he'd done, the way the red haze had blown over his eyes and taken his life away.

"I mean it, Bobby," Dex snapped, and Bobby's eyes shot open. "Don't give up. You got a month, you hear me? A month—you and Reg get a month to cool off, and then I fucking intervene. I'm not shitting around here. I got John in a good place, Ethan in a good place, Chase and Tommy are good. Kelsey's due any minute, but she's good. All my people, Bobby. You and Reg are the last. I'm not letting you blow this for me. Me and Kane are fucking exhausted, and we need a year of rest."

Bobby found himself smiling, even as Dex turned around and did his belt, then took off into the visible heat rising from the pavement.

Okay, so he needed to figure something out, or Dex would fix his life. Deal, then.

Some sleep, a trip to court, some loose ends, and Bobby could get to work.

Full Circle

HE TOLD Bobby to fuck off.

Not just once, but twice. The second time, Bobby had tried to come into his hospital room, looking like hell—and damned contrite—and Reg had lost his shit, screaming and carrying on even after Bobby left.

The nurse had needed to sedate him, and when he woke up, John—John, fresh from rehab John—was there to scold him for being an asshole.

"Can't you see that kid is breaking his heart over you? I got no idea why, but he seems to think you're special."

"So special he said I was retarded and I couldn't take care of my own shit!"

And John—his friend, who had always been so exquisitely gentle with him—had growled. "Everybody needs help, Reg. And you know what? You can't save someone just because you want to. Trust me. I spent ten years doing blow, trying to wipe out the memory of the one guy I couldn't save. You know what he did to pay me back for all that useless wanting?"

"I got no idea," Reg said, stunned. As far as he'd been concerned, John was like a teacher—he didn't have a personal life. Even rehab had been like one of those seminar things teachers were always talking about but Reg could never picture.

"Jumped off a fucking bridge and killed himself," John said succinctly.

Reg stared in horror. "That's fucking *awful*!" The sedative was still wearing off, and he had a confused picture in his head of V jumping off the bridge over the Sacramento River and trying to fly.

"Tell me about it. And he left me to clean up his mess." John's hair was clean these days, and he was filling out. He really looked like an all-American boy now. No more drugs.

"Poor John," Reg said, feeling genuine sorry. "You're a good guy. Didn't deserve that."

299

"No," John said softly, settling down a little more comfortably into the wretched hospital chair. All the guys had whined about this model—apparently it was like sitting in a plastic cage. "I didn't. And you didn't deserve your sister."

Reg bit his lip, eyes smarting. "She was so good to me when we were little," he said, willing someone, anyone, to understand.

"So was Tory," John said back, and Reg saw pain in his eyes. Honest, grown-up pain.

Reg's pain was just that flavor.

"What happened? I mean, with V it was schizophrenia, but—"

"People can't always hold their own burdens," John said softly. "And they can either ask for help and accept it, or they can throw their burdens on someone else's back and watch them drown too. Tory did that second thing—so much pain and so many drugs, right?"

"V wouldn't… wouldn't take her drugs," he said, remembering a talk he and Bobby had once about irony. He'd never understood that until now.

"Either way," John said softly. "It's taking responsibility for living in the real world. You can try all you want, Reg, but you can't do that for someone else."

"He thinks I'm stupid," Reg whispered.

"He attacked the cop who called you stupid," John told him.

Reg closed his eyes, his head hurting more. "Nobody told me that."

"Well, you should know. He was coming in to tell you he's doing fifteen days in jail—it was almost three years, but I know good lawyers."

"He's going to jail?" Reg tried to sit up, but God, his head—it was gonna pop the fuck off his shoulders.

"Two weeks, Reg. So two weeks in jail. You got three more days in the hospital. You may want to use that time to think about what's important here. From what the social worker told *me*, all he was worried about was you not going home with your sister alone."

"Jail," Reg moaned, eyes closed. "I told him to fuck off. I screamed at him—oh God."

John smoothed his hair back from his head, like Bobby did sometimes, like his sister used to. "He'll understand, Reg. He will."

"But I'm still so mad!" What kind of person did that make him, that he heard Bobby saying "No, he's not capable" in his head over and over again.

And every time it echoed, he saw Bobby being kind, fixing his kitchen, bringing him books, *possessing his body*, and he thought *He doesn't see me as a person. I'm like the house. I'm a project. How can he love me when he wants to fix me?*

And all the good parts of the last year became a lie.

"He thinks I'm... I'm substandard! I'm not... I'm not enough!" And that was the thing he was maddest at. The lie, the terrible, hope-bringing lie, that Reg could be enough to keep his household in order. Enough to love.

"Oh, baby," John said, his green eyes narrowed with frustration. "Don't you see his biggest fear is that he's failed you?"

"It wasn't his fault she got the shovel from his truck," Reg said, because they'd both slept through it. God—they hadn't even heard the door opening.

"Well, your sister's pretty smart, Reg."

"No, she's not." Reg's eyes burned at this too. "She used to be smart about people. Used to care what they thought, what hurt their feelings. She doesn't know how to do that no more."

John let out a breath. "Then she's not as smart as you. What do you think Bobby thought when he saw you bleeding? How do you think he felt when he realized they might send you home with your sister and not him?"

"That she'd kill me," Reg said dully. She would have. She hadn't even seen her brother at that point. He'd been as much a stranger to her as she was to him.

"Maybe he'd rather you hate him than have that happen."

"Yeah."

Reg had fallen asleep then, and when he'd awakened, Ethan and Jonah had been there instead of John. They'd played Uno with him that night, and after they left, something in his chest and back felt like it unclenched. It wasn't letting go—he couldn't yet—but maybe, when his hands didn't hurt so much from holding on too tight, it was a possibility.

Lance brought him home after his three days in the hospital, and he walked past his Camaro in the driveway and into his house expecting the worst. But the guys had cleaned up—the lamp that V had shattered, the bloody sheets, the prints of cop boots—all of it was gone.

Looked like his house again—the new bathroom, baseboards, window treatment, hall floor, all glaring brightly against the old, crumbling parts, but his.

That's okay—Bobby'll fix the—

He put a hand to his aching head and moaned softly.

"What's wrong?" Lance asked, going to the cupboard for a glass. "You need a pain pill?"

"I told Bobby to fuck off," Reg said. "And now he's in jail."

"Yeah." Lance brought him the pill. "Sort of a low-rent move, Reg."

Yes. Yes, it had been.

And he wasn't sure if it was one somebody could forgive.

He wiped his eyes with his palms, and again, and again. Lance stood, pulled his face gently to his middle, and let him cry.

But Reg knew, a dull certainty in his stomach, that this was all they would do. There'd be no sex, no fucking. Because they used to do that for comfort, but now it would hurt more than help.

As he wept on his friend's stomach, he thought bitterly that putting off being an adult for most of his life had saved him a shit-ton of pain.

HIS HEAD got better, and he went back to work.

Booking gigs got easier, and he started doing things like putting out a sign-up sheet for the guys and coordinating it with guys who had scenes coming out. In short order he had a calendar full of events for the next two months.

Some of them needed his presence. About two weeks after he got back to work, he and John drove to San Francisco to escape the bone-crushing heat, and they and four other guys did a signing at a huge, busy nightclub. Reg was glad John was there—he shook hands and danced and laughed a lot—but Reg mostly made sure everybody had what they needed and were taken care of. The guys were new—they stayed at the club that night to do blow and get laid, John supposed—but John and Reg drove back together. John dropped Reg off at two in the morning and shook his hand.

"Nice job, Reggie. You did Johnnies proud."

Reg nodded and looked behind him at his completely empty house. No worries about V tonight. No asking someone to sit with her. No checking for meds.

But no Bobby waiting either.

"Thanks," he said, trying to smile. "I'm glad I could do a good job for you."

John pursed his lips and sighed. "He gets out tomorrow."

Reg swallowed hard. He'd had updates from various sources—Dex, Lance, Skylar—who all told him about Bobby in jail. Apparently a whole batch of guys went to visit him on visiting day, which had made Bobby laugh because, two weeks? What was two weeks? But nobody had invited Reg to that party. Reg wasn't sure he would have gone.

"What am I supposed to say to him?"

"Maybe let him talk, Reg. He knows what you think of him. You're the one who isn't listening."

Reg nodded, backing away from the car to slam the door shut. He made his way across his creaking porch, sweat still running down his spine. He wondered if he bought the materials, could he get some of the guys to come help him fix his house?

But it wasn't the thought of how hard it would be that stopped him.

It was the sudden grief that it would be anybody else's job.

KELSEY HAD her baby the next day. Reg went on visiting crew, not just to see her and the baby but on the hopes that Bobby would be there.

He wasn't, and nobody there had talked to him.

Reg congratulated Kelsey, gave her a baby gift he'd bought on the way, and went home, feeling like a coward.

That night Bobby sent him a text.

How are you?

Should ask the same. I'm sorry about jail.

Jail was my bad. I'm sorry about everything.

Reg just stared at the phone. What was *everything*? How exactly did one define "everything"? Was "everything" what Bobby said? Was it how he felt? Was he sorry about Reg's sister? About leaving when Reg needed him most?

Reg didn't answer, and Bobby didn't press. Reg couldn't text about it. He couldn't talk about it. He was slow—he always had been. For once in his life, he was going to have to sit in his house and listen to the silence and let his heart and his brain whirr slowly, telling him things in their own time.

It would be easier for them to move if he wasn't afraid they were muffled by the hurt, like a car engine in shaving cream, but he didn't have a cure for that.

Done and Raw

BOBBY MANNED the grill at the company picnic, grateful that the heat had broken. Behind him his mom set potato salad, watermelon, buns, and condiments on the picnic table, pulling them out of a giant ice chest she'd rented for the occasion.

It had been Dex's idea to pay Bobby's mom to help cater—he'd given her a budget and a week to gather supplies. Bobby had helped, telling her that a lot of the models were health conscious and there should be lots of fruit-and-veggie trays and soy dogs and whole-grain buns. He'd helped with the shopping, the prep, the transportation—hell, pretty much the whole thing, since Hazy Daze had written him off with the misdemeanor assault conviction.

He'd like to say he was doing it all for his mom, because she'd been fucking awesome in the last month. She'd put up his bail and even given Dex's lawyer a small fee, all they could afford. She'd visited and called, and when he got out, she'd been there to pick him up.

The first thing he'd done was go get tested at Johnnies—not because he'd had prison sex, he was quick to assure Dex, but because he wanted to prove he hadn't.

He had a fading bruise under his eye and a broken nose to prove he'd defended himself a couple of times—and walked away when the defending was done.

Jail had been awful. Not the small concrete cell of the movies—or even his detention tank—but a big open area, divided into smaller quads. You found your bed, you minded your business, you didn't talk to anybody, you threw a punch back when someone threw at you.

But Bobby walked away knowing one thing.

He controlled his temper. His temper didn't control him. Never fucking again.

If he could walk away from someone who wanted to bend him over in the laundry room, after doing no more than laying the fucker out flat, he could walk away from a cop, from an enemy, from a friend out of line.

That red haze in front of his eyes never had to scare him again, because he had it by the balls.

It was a hard lesson—but then, it was one he'd needed, apparently, and not one he was ever going to need again.

And his mom never asked about the incident. She never reprimanded him. Never told him she was disappointed.

She didn't even object to Johnnies anymore. Apparently the prospect of three years in jail versus the two weeks he'd served had converted her quick.

So Bobby should have been doing the work for the picnic for *her*—but he wasn't.

He was doing it for a glimpse, a spare word, a chance to talk to Reg.

Most of the guys were on his side—not that he thought of it as a side. Most of the guys told him that Reg just needed space. He asked what Reg was doing with his time, and they'd told him that he went home. The end.

Bobby wondered if he was just listening to the silence, wondering what his life could be without his sister there.

It was why he hadn't pressed.

Because Reg's sister had been his world. His entire life had been twined up in keeping Veronica fed, clothed, and on her regimen. Having that taken away? Must have been bewildering, and while Bobby never thought Reg was stupid, he also knew Reg wasn't *quick*. It was going to take a while.

Patience.

Their courtship had been slow. They'd danced around each other for months. They'd figured things out, one fumbling step at a time.

If Bobby wanted Reg back, he was going to have to give him room—just enough—so Reg knew Bobby trusted him to make a decision, make a good one, without pressure.

This was important. Bobby didn't want to fuck it up.

But God, he was hungry to see Reg.

"Reggie!" Bobby jerked his head around at the sound of his mom's voice. She'd thrown her arms around Reg with no hesitation, and Bobby swallowed at his tentative return of the hug. "It's so good to see you," Isabelle said, holding his hands and smiling at him. "I've been so worried."

Bobby watched as she touched the still-healing bruised part of his temple with gentle fingers. "Bobby couldn't think of anything else but you."

Reg gave her a brief smile and turned away. "It sort of sucked," he said gruffly.

God, he'd lost weight. Bobby knew he'd been working out. Trey or Lance met him every morning, both of them a little less thin but a little happier as time went on. But neither of them had been feeding *Reg*, and it showed. His hair had grown out, curly and a little vulnerable to the side of his widow's peak. The circles under his eyes were practically blue in the bright sunshine, and that kind, irrepressible smile was dim, on auxiliary power now.

He must have sensed Bobby's scrutiny, because he glanced up. For a terrible, wonderful moment, they stared at each other, soul to soul, and Bobby could see the sun for the first time in weeks. Reg's fingers went up to his own cheek to mirror the healing cut under Bobby's eye—a reminder of his worst fight—and then fluttered down. A look of profound sorrow crossed his face, so deep, so painful that Bobby had to fight for breath.

Then he turned away and spoke into the silence that seemed to have encompassed the entire picnic.

"Uh, anyone seen, uh, Dex?"

"They're at the zoo," Isabelle said. "All the babies and daddies and uncles—John took them." Bobby knew she was counting the minutes until the babies came back. He was glad she had them in her life—but just as glad he wasn't the baby provider too. Right now, her attention on Reg, she looked around at the rest of the guys—and some of their boy- and girlfriends—and smiled. "But that's okay. There's plenty of folks here."

The flophouse roommates were all sort of gathered in a group around Kelsey. Kelsey's baby was with Ethan and Jonah at the zoo, which Bobby thought was pretty damned funny, but Kelsey was taking the moment to kick back in a soccer chair and enjoy the shade. Skylar and Rick were playing off each other as always and making her and the others laugh. Reg gravitated to them, and Lance looked up over his head at Bobby in question.

Bobby nodded. He didn't want anybody to be mean to Reg, to make him feel unwelcome because of Bobby. This wasn't that kind of fight. This wasn't a take-sides thing. This wasn't Bobby *against* Reg.

This was Bobby *fighting to keep* Reg.

Lance nodded back and turned to Reg and smiled, and Bobby went back to grilling soy dogs. Which smelled nasty. He was going to eat one of the big whole-beef ones his mother had brought, with no apologies either.

He managed to lose himself in the grilling, compartmentalizing all his grief, all his hope for something better, when he felt a tap on his shoulder.

He turned around and met a handsome man about John's age, with dark hair, a trimmed goatee, and blue eyes. He had a few scars around his mouth, his cheek, but it did nothing to detract from his cool good looks, and the snappy linen suit in the California heat added to the appeal.

"Are you Bobby?" And a really sexy Southern accent, Bobby thought bemusedly.

"Yes, sir. You are...."

"Galen," he said, extending his hand. "Galen Henderson."

Bobby held up his hands, grease- and grill-stained, and grimaced. "I wish we could shake," he apologized. "I'm sort of all crappy. But thank you. Seriously—John's lawyer said you're the reason I'm not rotting in jail still. You wouldn't even let my mom pay you. I can't thank you enough."

Galen's mouth twisted, and he kept his hand out. "I'll shake your hand any day," he said softly, and Bobby had no choice but to wipe his hand on the ass of his denim shorts and take it. "I'm just sorry I couldn't do more. If I'd been here, maybe I could have kept you out entirely."

Bobby smiled tightly. "I had shit to learn," he said, his voice gruff. "Two weeks was plenty of time to learn it, but it needed to happen."

Galen tilted his head. "What is it you learned, young Mr. Roberts?"

Bobby shrugged and looked around. His mom was still putting stuff out on the table, and everybody else was talking to Reg. He hadn't talked about this to anybody, and it was suddenly pressing against his chest, begging for release.

"My whole life I was afraid of being my old man," he said. "Beating the shit out of people because it's the only way I could think of to deal. Having to pin Reg's sister felt like the worst thing I've ever done, and she was trying to kill us. When I attacked that cop, all I could see was red. But two weeks in jail and I know I can walk away. I got muscles, and I got build, but I got common sense too. I know how to use it."

Galen's smile was unexpectedly pretty. "You, sir, are a force to be reckoned with. I'm proud to have helped in your defense." He gave an almost courtly bow then, and Bobby remembered why Galen hadn't been there for the arraignment.

"Weren't you in Florida?" he asked.

Galen nodded. "I was. Like you said, some lessons you have to learn, even if they're painful."

"What lessons did you learn?" he asked, suddenly hungry to hear he was not the only one living life by touch.

Galen gestured to the cane Bobby hadn't seen, leaning up against the table, next to two suitcases. He must have come here from the airport, Bobby realized in surprise.

"I learned the difference between accepting help and living with a crutch. And now I can do one and not the other," he said, a slight smile on his lips.

Bobby grinned. "You are way too smart for me," he decided. "But I sure am glad you're here. I bet John will be too."

"Your hot dogs are burning," Galen said dryly, and suddenly Bobby had something else to do.

But he did have a moment, about half an hour later, to see Galen and John's first kiss, after John got back from the zoo.

For a moment in time, Bobby didn't exist. Nothing existed but these two souls, reconnecting, learning the feel and taste of each other all over again.

Bobby watched them, entranced, and swallowed.

He wanted that. He could have that. He could have that with *Reg*.

He found out later that Galen had stayed in Florida to finish rehab, to learn to walk without the cane, to make himself worthy of a life with someone he thought was wonderful.

And then he'd come to claim the love he deserved.

That day, Bobby left soon after the last of the plates were cleared. He helped his mom put stuff in the truck and said a quiet goodbye to Dex and John. He had a scene next week and some playdates planned at the flophouse, so he knew he'd be seeing everybody again.

Reg managed to stay as far away from him as possible, the entire time. But Bobby wouldn't forget the look they'd shared.

That look—that was everything.

It said that love was there for the claiming. Bobby just had to choose his moment, his time, his place.

He began to make plans.

A WEEK later, after his scene—some kid named Chris who had almost passed out on Bobby's cock, he'd been so excited—Bobby stepped into Dex's office. At first he'd been worried that Reg would be there, but Kelsey was back on the receptionist desk part-time until they could find someone full-time and permanent, and she told him Reg would be out talking to the manager at a new club, so he was safe.

"Hey, Dex?" He smiled tentatively, and Dex turned away from his editing computer and swiveled his chair around.

"Take a seat," he said, then looked over his shoulder. "Want a cookie?"

Bobby blinked. "Is this part of the service now?"

Dex shook his head and fished a tin from his desk. "No. Kane has been on sort of a kick, now that it's not hotter than balls. He keeps trying out new recipes, and I swear to Christ I'm gonna get fat. Help a brother out here and eat some goddamned carbs for me, willya?"

Bobby laughed and snagged three. "You're the best boss ever," he said after wolfing down a little disk of heaven. "And it would totally be worth getting fat if you could eat these every day."

Dex eyed him dispassionately. "You only say that because you just turned nineteen and you still have the metabolism of a fucking Trojan. I swear that kid's entire purpose in life is to watch me grow love handles."

Bobby smirked. "Well, he wants something to hold on to," he said mildly, and Dex grabbed two more cookies and set them on the desk in front of him.

"Work *those* off, smart guy. What can I do for you?"

Bobby finished his second cookie and took a deep breath for courage. "I think this thing with Reg has gone on long enough."

Dex sighed and stole one of his cookies. "Word. He's... he's starting to say you'd be better off without him. I think... I think he's depressed. No sister. No boyfriend. He's hit that groove, you know?"

Bobby swallowed, the cookie turning to sawdust in his mouth. "The one where you think you suck and everybody would be better without you and how can anybody love a fuckup like you are?"

The cookie tin came out again, and Dex dealt them another round.

"You been there too?" he asked quietly.

"I got the condensed version in jail," Bobby told him, eyes level. "And then you know what?"

"What?"

"I fought off the third guy who wanted to be my daddy and decided I really was the belle of the goddamned ball."

Dex guffawed and clapped a hand over his mouth. "That's fucking awful," he said when he could talk.

Bobby shrugged. It was partially true. "It was a shitty situation, Dex. He never should have gone through it. I know I wasn't up to it, but I did my best. How's his sister?"

"Climbing the ladder again," Dex said, referring to the institutions she would get transferred to, one after another, until she got to one with a marginal amount of freedom.

"When's she going to be back where she was?"

Dex let out a breath. "According to Reg, she's got another two months. She had to do a long stint in the one for violent patients—no visitors, no outside stuff—because, you know—"

"She tried to kill us."

"Yeah. I guess she's actually showing remorse for that now, but then, every time they switch her drugs, she forgets what she did."

Bobby tilted his head back and groaned. "Mental health shit is so fucked-up," he muttered. "Seriously. They gotta give those places more money. They've got to have better places. I just... he never would have tried so long if she'd had better places to go."

Dex nodded soberly. "But it's out of his hands now—and he's made his peace with it."

"Really?" And until he asked, Bobby had forgotten how hungry he was for the answer.

"Why?" Dex looked over Bobby's shoulder, like he was checking for Reg to just appear. "What did you have in mind?"

Bobby outlined a very simple plan, and Dex grimaced. "Do you think he'll agree to go back in the game?"

"You did," Bobby reminded.

Dex smiled slightly. "Your eyes were so goddamned wide."

Bobby winked. "I'm still a country boy at heart, Dex. Not all the dick in the world changed that."

"Yeah." Dex's smile was reassuring. He was as married as a guy could get, but he didn't regret a goddamned minute of his past. "Okay, country boy. Am I going to be losing you after this?"

Bobby shrugged. "We'll ask Reg. If this works." He smiled, and it held all the hope he could summon. "He really does like to watch me fuck, you know."

A week later, Dex's laughter, warm and a little dirty, gave him the confidence to walk into the scene room and take his shirt off and pretend this was like any other scene.

When Dex left the room, Bobby looked over to Reg, tired, small, huddling in on himself without his usual cockiness, and thought *This is it. He needs me. It's time to take him back.*

Breaking the Circle

REG CUDDLED into Bobby's chest, suddenly understanding the entire purpose of being there on the shoot with Bobby.

"Dex set me up!" he said, feeling betrayed.

Bobby nodded, unbothered. "He helped me out," he said, those strong arms around him still. Then he closed his eyes. "God, Reggie—it's been two months. Are you ever going to forgive me?"

Reg rested his cheek against Bobby's bare chest. "I'm old," he said, because the thought had been nagging at him, haunting him for the last week. "You... you and me—maybe we're just better off—"

Bobby kissed him then, mouth warm and sweet, hard like a man's, demanding.

God, he was so good at giving Reg a center, a thing to do, a place to be, a person to strive for.

Reg opened to him helplessly, all his trepidation washed away in the heat of his body. In the heat of his kiss.

"What's it gonna be?" Bobby whispered again. "I want you back. I want *us* back. I went to sleep with the man I love and woke up with nothing."

Reg feathered a touch along the healing scar on his stomach. "How can you... look what she did," he whispered. Then, even more horribly, "You went to *jail* because of me!"

Bobby shook his head and cupped Reg's chin between his fingers. "I'll say this once out loud, and it's important. I went to jail because of *me*. Because I got violence in me, Reg. You were there to pull me off Keith Gilmore, but I needed to hold myself back off that cop, and I didn't."

"You were under—"

"Extreme duress," Bobby said, sounding like he'd recited the words a thousand times. "It's why it was two weeks and not three years. But even if it was three years, I woulda gotten out and come looking for you. I woulda written you letters, embarrassing ones, like in the books we read, because you're who I would be thinking of the whole time."

Reg nodded, closing his eyes tight, listening to Bobby's heart beating in his chest. "I would have broken my heart and died if I couldn't see you for three years," he said, all the missing him of the last two months washing over him.

"What's it gonna be?" Bobby asked again.

Reg looked around at the pretend bedroom, where so many people had fucked each other raw for fame and money.

"Not here," he said wretchedly. "I don't... I don't want to do it here."

Bobby half laughed into the hollow of his shoulder, and his chest shook. Reg was going to ask if he was crying when he realized that he, *Reg*, was the one whose eyes were burning, the one who couldn't catch his breath.

"Can we go—" Bobby started out, and Reg interrupted.

"My house," he said, voice broken. "You drive, Bobby. I... I don't even want to be in the car without you."

They dressed and slipped out of the room. As they went, Reg gave a last look around, at the wretchedly uncomfortable bed and the laundered thin sheets, the tape marks on the floor and the mirror that had witnessed a thousand orgasms or more. He was done with that room. He had no business in there, not as a model. Not anymore. Bobby had known that—so had Dex when he'd asked.

Reg knew it now. He'd found a different life.

It was something he wanted to tell Bobby as Bobby drove, jaw clenched, eyes narrowed, toward Reg's house.

"The guys kept telling me I was stupid," he said after a few moments of tense silence.

"They shouldn't have—"

"No!" Reg interrupted. "I was. I was stupid. About you. About what I heard you say. And afterward, you were going to jail, and I...." Reg closed his eyes. "I felt so bad, Bobby. You have no idea. My sister was in crazy-person jail and you were in regular jail, and I was in the hospital because I was useless. Just fucking useless. And how was I supposed to tell you I still loved you, when I was the person who let all that happen? How was I supposed to make that better?"

Bobby sighed, and some of the tension left his face, his arms, his hands on the wheel.

"Baby, none of it was your doing."

"But it was," Reg surprised himself by saying. "I… I should have let her stay, in the spring. I should have grown up and realized—she couldn't be my big sister anymore. She hadn't been for years. The kids we were—she wouldn't have wanted me to take care of her like that, not for as long as I did. We were…." He swallowed hard, because this was a new word to him. "We were *terrorized* by our mom. And then she grew up to do the same thing to me." Oh God. This hurt. "I should have let her go, Bobby. And I didn't. And she almost killed you, and she ended up in the shitty place. And it was my fault. I just—"

"Stop." Bobby reached across the seat and squeezed his knee. "Just… being mad at yourself kept you away from me for two months. I'm the violent criminal, Reg, and I just let it go. You need to let it go."

"I'm sorry," Reg said, the words freeing. "I got mad because I thought you weren't treating me like an adult. But an adult would have made that decision sooner, and I'm sorry."

Bobby let out a half laugh. "Growing up happens to us all," he said softly. "Are you going to kick me out?" he asked, surprising Reg.

"No!"

"Are you going to wake up one day and blame me for your sister being gone?"

And Reg saw where he was going. "No," he said soberly.

"Do you forgive me for saying you couldn't do it?" Bobby's voice throbbed, and Reg could hear it—the pain of that decision. The pain of admitting Reg couldn't do it all.

"Do you forgive me for not admitting it sooner?" Reg asked. He felt like Bobby had more to forgive.

"Done," Bobby said softly. "Done that night, waiting for my mom in jail. All the good things I love about you—they had a part in not wanting to let V go. It's why I had the balls to do what I did today. Because you don't give up."

Reg found himself wanting to laugh forever and ever. "*I* don't give up?" he chortled. "*I* don't give up? Oh my God, kid! Last year this time, I thought I was *straight*! You damned near cuddled me into falling in love!"

Bobby chuckled. "Well, we use the gifts God gave us."

"No," Reg said, suddenly sober. "God gave you a ten-inch cock, Vern Roberts. You gave yourself kindness. And…." He struggled for the words.

"Don't-give-up-ness. And forgiveness. And that thing you do where you fix my house when nobody's looking. All the good shit—that's you."

"Cock helps," Bobby said, but his lips were quirking, and Reg knew he was kidding.

"I can buy the cock online," Reg said, not kidding even a little. "The Bobby that comes with it—he's got to be mine in his heart or it's no good without him."

"I am," Bobby said softly. He pulled up to Reg's house and turned in his seat before turning off the motor. "I am. Baby, I was waiting for you, was all. Your whole life changed in one night."

Reg swallowed and felt his shame cut deeply. "I'm sorry I told you to fuck off," he said, voice rasping. "I'm sorry I felt so bad about it I couldn't even look at you."

"I'm sorry I broke your heart," Bobby said, cupping his cheek. "Because I know you heard me say you couldn't do it, couldn't take care of her, and…." His lower lip wobbled. "You trusted me, and I let you down."

"No." Reg trapped his hand. "You were doing the grown-up thing when I couldn't. I was the one who let you down. I'll never do it again."

Bobby nodded. "It's okay if you do," he said softly. "It's okay. You don't have to be perfect. You don't have to be all grown-up at once. I didn't fall for Dex or John. I fell for you."

Reg smiled, feeling it glow from the inside out. "Damned if you didn't." And then Bobby pulled him in for a kiss.

THEY MADE it into the house, and a lot after that was a haze, a blurred whirl of clothes coming off and Bobby's hands on his skin while he grabbed for as much of Bobby as he could manage.

Finally Bobby backed him up against the wall, hands held over his head. "Breathe," he commanded, chest laboring. "Breathe. Not so fast."

"Want it all now," Reg demanded, forgetting all those resolutions about being a grown-up.

Bobby smiled, slow and wicked. "You'll get it all—but not all at once."

Reg reached down and squeezed him through his briefs. Big. Thick and long. "You are bigger than your cock," Reg said, closing his eyes and breathing in the heat and the vague sawdust smell that made up Bobby Green.

"Yeah," Bobby whispered, teasing his ear, nibbling on his lobe. "But the cock has its place."

Reg chortled—and tried not to let his knees buckle. "My ass, right?"

Bobby sucked hard on his neck, making him whimper, and let the flesh out of his mouth with a pop. "Yeah, Reg. It's going up there."

"Oh, thank Go-awd?"

Bobby dropped to his knees on the floor of Reg's room, shucked his briefs, and sucked the head of his dick into his warm, skilled mouth.

Reg gave a soft shriek, a happy sound. Oh hell—he'd been too depressed to even beat off these last two months. His dick was prime, aching—

"Oh my God, Bobby, gonna—maybe don't—wanna wait a... *Jesus!*"

His orgasm scalded, ripping a hole through his soul, his heart, his gut. He slid down the wall, trembling, pulling out of Bobby's mouth with the last spurt. Bobby stayed on his knees and grinned down at him, Reg's come striped across his chin, running down his neck.

"You look pleased with yourself," Reg said, laughing weakly.

Bobby's eyes grew dark, and he leaned in close. "I missed your taste," he growled. Reg leaned forward, licking his chin first before taking his mouth, tasting himself on Bobby's lips. Bobby shifted, and Reg slid all the way down the wall, lying flat on his back on his own floor. He brought his knees up, spreading wide so Bobby could thrust against Reg's nakedness, still clothed in his underwear.

"Skin," Reg begged. "Please?"

Bobby groaned and pushed smoothly to his feet, extending his hand. Reg saw him for a moment, looming tall at his six-foot-five-inch height, shoulders spread, eyes glowing with promise. Larger than life, that was his Bobby, but then he took the offered hand and levered up, right into his arms.

And suddenly he was a part of that greatness, touching it, enveloped by it, skin to skin.

Bobby took his mouth again, and he found himself on his own bed, sprawled and sex-drugged, while Bobby rooted for the lube in the dresser.

Bobby came back and kissed him, then broke away, shoving two fingers into his mouth. Reg sucked, closing his eyes because he knew where those fingers were going—*yearned* to feel them penetrate.

"Spread your knees," Bobby whispered, pulling back.

Reg did, looking at him with what even he knew was worship. Bobby used a wet finger to toy with his rim, circle, push through the puckered hole, and Reg's knees fell even more open.

He wanted this. Wanted it so bad. He held his ankles to his ears, knees to his chest, while Bobby kneeled beside him and fingered his rim.

"You are so prime," Bobby whispered, sounding awed. "Just begging for me?"

"You have no idea," Reg whispered, tilting his head back and closing his eyes. His entire body floated in the dark for a moment, and then the penetration in his ass became a bright spot, glowing orange. Bobby widened the circle going in, and the spot became a ring, burning, aching, glorious and red.

A little lube cooled it, and then the ache resumed, spread, two fingers, scissoring wider, and Reg groaned. He shoved his body down and pulled back, down and back, wanting more.

"Easy." Bobby planted his other hand on Reg's chest. "I want to make sure you're ready."

Reg opened his eyes and reached over to stroke Bobby's cock. Iron-hard and damned long, it wept at the end with so much attention.

"I will always be ready," Reg told him. "All of you. All those guys that came before? That was their job. Making sure I was ready for someone as big in his heart as you are." He squeezed hard and stroked slow, enjoying the way Bobby tilted his head back and groaned. A spurt of pre scalded his wrist, and Reg kept looking up at Bobby as he let go and brought his palm to his mouth so he could lick it off.

Bobby grunted and pulled his fingers out of Reg's ass.

"Need!" Reg begged, arching up, and Bobby captured his hand, sucking on his thumb and forefinger, scraping the underside with his teeth.

"When we're done here," Bobby whispered harshly, "you're gonna stretch me. And then you're gonna fuck me. And you'd better make sure I'm big and wide as the world. 'Cause all I want to do when you're fucking me is scream and come."

Reg moaned, wanting all the things at once.

"All I wanna do now is scream and come," he admitted. "C'mon, Bobby—I'm ready. Fuck me."

Bobby positioned himself between Reg's thighs, and Reg felt him, pressed up against his sphincter, battering his way in. He tilted his head back and bore down, forcing his body to swallow Bobby's girth in one gulp, sighing in surrender as that titanic member breached him.

It filled him completely, gave Reg shape, gave him substance. The throbbing of Bobby's cock became Reg's heartbeat, and the smooth stroke of him inside became Reg's breath.

Bobby pushed, relentless, sure, and rested, seated deep in Reg's body.

Reg's breath stopped, and he peered up at Bobby through the dim light of his room.

"I gotcha," Bobby promised, and Reg nodded, reassured.

"Then take me," he urged.

Bobby pulled back and thrust in hard, and Reg saw a train behind his eyes, hurtling, forceful, climbing, climbing, climbing, building every peak until it reached the top of the world.

Reg's breath caught for a moment, he opened his eyes to see Bobby's head thrown back, his eyes squeezed tight as he fucked hard and sure—

And the train plummeted to earth on the rails while Reg screamed with the thrill of the ride.

THEY RESTED for a moment, and Reg thought *This is when we have round two*, because once was never enough for Bobby to fuck.

Bobby surprised him then.

"You look tired, baby," he said, kissing Reg's temple.

Reg was going to say he wasn't so old he couldn't go again, but a yawn caught him by surprise.

"I ain't been sleeping good," he confessed, tired enough to use "ain't."

"Sleep," Bobby whispered. "I'm going to go get a drink."

"Mm." Reg closed his eyes, then spoke from behind the falling curtain of unconsciousness. "Don't wash me off. Want you inside me."

"Good."

"Gonna top next round."

"Good. I want you inside me too."

Reg smiled a little and rolled to his side. "Don't leave," he whispered. "I can survive if you do, but it would hurt to live."

Bobby wrapped a sweaty arm around his shoulders. "I'm not going to leave," he said.

"Ever," Reg stressed. "Gonna live here."

"Damned straight."

"Okay, then."

And it was enough. Wasn't the promises in the books—not the hearts, not the flowers—but it was all Reg had never dared to dream of. He could sleep, secure in Bobby's warmth, and wake, knowing Bobby would be there too.

It was so much more than Reg had ever thought life could hold.

Building

"I'M GOING to get some water," Bobby whispered, waiting for Reg to mumble "Okay." He didn't want Reg to wake up alone, but he was too excited to sleep.

He slid on his briefs and padded across the house in the long shadows of a late-summer afternoon. He felt hot in the barely functioning AC, but he also felt revitalized—reborn. A cool shower, some Gatorade, and he and Reg would be able to keep going all night.

He longed for it—every cell in his body sang that once wasn't enough. Not now.

Maybe not ever.

He'd gulped his second glass of ice water when the smell reached his brain. New paint. Huh.

He followed his nose up the stairs, making more notes about fixing them, carpeting them, carpeting the landing, fixing the banister, and hey, maybe getting a dog.

Reg could have a dog now. God, he'd be good with a dog—something big and steady, unshakable.

He got to the top landing and ventured into the lion's den—and paused. Reg had cleaned it out.

The bed, the dresser, the computer. The place was bare, right down to the floorboards, which only needed some sanding and some stain to be a real handsome floor treatment, and Reg had taped tarps around the edges.

He was trying to paint.

Yeah—he'd made about six mistakes that Bobby could see. Hadn't taken off the baseboards first, hadn't taped around the window ledges, was using a roller with too high of a concentration of paint, and seemed to be using all-weather paint as well, which was why it had smelled so strong.

But the mistakes didn't matter.

What mattered was that Reg was fixing up Veronica's room.

What mattered was that he could make his own beginnings, with or without Bobby.

Bobby was so proud of him, he almost cried.

He was looking around, making a list in his head of things Reg might want to know—or that they could do together—when Reg came padding up.

"You disappeared," he mumbled sleepily.

"Looking at this thing you did," Bobby said simply. "Good job, baby."

Reg smiled a little. "Not as good as you could do it."

"Doesn't matter." Bobby shrugged. "It's your house—you took charge. You did great."

"Our house," Reg said soberly. "I'll put your name on papers, like with V. Needs to say ours."

Oh. Bobby bit his lip. "I been waiting for that," he admitted. "It's had good bones all along."

"But you fix it up so pretty," Reg said, smiling enough to glow. He blinked then, and his smile went shy. Sultry. "God, you look good."

Oh yeah. Bobby had known. They weren't over yet. Not by a long shot.

"Wanna shower?" he asked. "Nice cool shower?"

"Yeah," Reg said. "You first. I'm gonna hydrate."

Bobby laughed, low and dirty, and pinned him to the wall that wasn't painted yet with a hungry kiss.

They had to wash that wall again when they were through—and *then* they showered.

And hydrated.

And by God did it all again.

BY THE beginning of September the heat *still* hadn't faded, so Bobby was fixing the porch in the early mornings. His residuals from his porn videos were enough to pay expenses, so he hadn't found another job yet. He was too busy fixing the place up.

They'd completely redone the top floor, bathroom too, including painting over Reg's original paint job, which Reg didn't seem to mind in the least. They were going to ask Bobby's mom if she wanted to move in, but she seemed to really love her apartment, and her new independence, and even her new job, taking over as the receptionist for Johnnies now that Kelsey had a new position helping their *non*-porn-related industries. Apparently Bobby's mom was doing all the Dex things—making sure the guys had enough to eat and a safe place to stay and the numbers of the counselors and doctors they might need if something came up.

She seemed to be really happy, Bobby thought in admiration. She sat behind the desk and worked her needlepoint and fielded calls, and for some reason, the guys really adored her. For that matter, so did the few girls on the roster. He never thought of a middle-aged woman being in high demand behind the desk of a porn company—but he remembered Dex saying something about all the guys needing mommies.

Apparently she was the mommy everyone had needed. He was proud of her—and damned glad she wasn't living up in Dogpatch with Frank Gilmore anymore. She even got grandbabies, in a way, because she was de facto babysitter when Ethan and Jonah needed the time off.

So she wasn't going to take the top floor, which meant Reg could put in bookshelves and a weight set and some exercise machines—just so they didn't have to go in to the gym *every* day. And he bought a computer desk and set up a computer. Bobby was going to figure out how to play games on it—Reg did so good on everybody else's game console—but that's not what he wanted it for.

He used it for research, to look up the things he didn't know, to look up places he'd never been. He used it for work too, now that he was getting booked out months at a time, and learning some of the things Dex did to promote the guys and give them as many options to make money as they needed.

With the walls painted ecru and a throw rug under the computer and mats under the weights, it looked as different as it could from V's pink prison of madness, and Bobby thought that did Reg's heart a world of good.

V had finally gotten to a permanent facility—a decent one, thanks to Reg's health insurance and her own social security. She could check herself out for two-hour time blocks and walk to the store or take in a movie—even just walk around the neighborhood without an escort. In return, she had to be there, morning, noon, and night, to take her medication, and submit to blood-test levels once a week.

They'd visited her, taken her out to lunch, and Bobby thought that while she was just as disconnected as she'd ever been—still wore long-sleeved shirts to keep the bugs from coming out—she was also a little more lucid.

For example, she knew Bobby was Reg's boyfriend, and the word "faggot" hadn't once made an appearance.

Reg had been so happy after that visit, so relieved he wasn't abandoning his sister, that Bobby had needed to just lie on the bed and hold him while he babbled. He talked about trips to the park with her when they were little, and the way she'd looked after Queenie's first two children, and the way she'd always been the smart one.

Bobby had never been so grateful for intervention of any sort as he was for the intervention of that social worker, who had taken their small family in crisis and helped get V to a better place. It was worth two weeks in jail, just for her happiness and Reg's peace of mind.

All in all, Bobby was pretty content as he hauled out the materials and started to build the framework for the new porch. They'd worked out early, Reg was at Johnnies, and he basically had about six hours before the heat got too intense, and he could get enough of the porch framed out and built to walk on, just for today. He didn't have a scene for another three weeks, so he and Reg could spend the afternoon inside having loud noisy sex, or they could go to the pool at the gym and swim laps. Both options sounded good, although Bobby was rooting for the loud noisy sex, just because you couldn't go wrong with that.

Ever.

He worked quickly and competently, idly watching the crew hired to flip the house next door as they did their thing too. He saw a lot of ugly rugs come out, as well as a lot of warped floorboards and baseboards, and some warped drywall as well.

Yeah, the people next door had owned a lot of cats. Apparently they'd inherited some property up in the hills where there wasn't a cat limit, and Bobby wished them well in their version of Dogpatch. It was good to know there were people who could be happy out there—as long as it wasn't Bobby or his mom.

He was just nailing the last board into place in the interim walkway when he saw the foreman of the crew walking across the newly seeded lawn, pausing at the brand-new, unstained porch steps Bobby had just erected.

"This here's good work," he said. In his fifties, with sandy-brown chin scruff to match his bird's nest of hair and a faded blue baseball hat, the guy struck him as tough. Stringy, probably strong as an ox, he wore blue jeans and a tan T-shirt with faded blue chambray over it.

His work boots were of the highest quality—and still beat to shit.

Bobby had respect for those boots, even though he didn't know the man.

Who let out a low whistle as he surveyed Bobby's work.

"That there, son, is some prime workmanship. That is a thing of beauty."

Bobby allowed himself a small smile of pride. "Thank you, sir," he said, glancing up before going back to hammering in the next nail with one blow.

"You got an outfit you work for?" the guy asked, and Bobby paused and sat up on his knees, grateful for the pad underneath.

"No, sir."

"I seen you out here a lot. You got a job?"

Bobby's lips twisted. He figured he knew where this was going, but he wasn't going to work for no place that didn't like who the fuck he was.

"Yes, sir."

"Doing this?" The guy used his hat to gesture to the framed porch.

"No, sir. Fucking for money."

Oh yeah. He would enjoy the memory of that nice man's gray eyes bugging out of his head for years to come.

"Really."

"Yes, sir. Johnnies. Gay porn. My boyfriend works promotions."

Eyes weren't getting any smaller. "*Really?*"

"Yes, sir."

And then a wonderful thing happened. The man's long, weathered face was taken over with a tremendous, riotous smile.

"That's *amazing*. Wait 'til I tell my nephew. He's in college, and he thinks I don't know anyone cool. He'll get a kick out of that. You got any posters you could sign?"

Bobby half laughed. "I can have Reg bring some home. Be happy to. You'll be here tomorrow?"

"Be here for the next two weeks." The guy looked the porch up and down. "You wouldn't want a second job, would you?"

Some of Bobby's glee leaked away. "Last time I worked construction… well, the guy wasn't so ethical," he said, hating that story, that time, the year before.

"I'm as honest as they come." The guy reached into his wallet then and pulled out a card. "Here—I'm going to tuck this in your tool chest, okay? Says Charlie Swanton. Look me up. I'm reputable, and union. I'm telling you, son—I've trained a lot of guys on the job, but I've never seen anyone as young as you are with this sense of workmanship. It's a thing you can't teach. I'd love to have you with my outfit. We'd let you have time off for your other job and everything."

Bobby knew his own eyes widened. "Really?"

Charlie Swanton lifted a shoulder. "You were straight up with me, man. I can't object to that. I'm just damned impressed."

Bobby pursed his lips and nodded, thinking about Reg's cabinets they could replace, and furniture and siding for the outside and...

And a job that wouldn't depend on his complete fuckability.

"I've got a record," he said baldly, his voice shaking with a little bit of shame. "Just so you know."

"What did you do?" Charlie asked, surprised.

"A cop called my boyfriend a name. I sort of saw red."

Charlie sucked air in through his teeth and whacked his thigh with the baseball hat a couple of times. "Your temper do that to you a lot?" he asked, like this was important.

"Not after jail time," Bobby said. "You learn a lot about defending yourself and walking the hell away."

Charlie's tension dissipated. "Then you're welcome to work for me anytime. You talk to your boyfriend and call me up. You don't even need to work full-time. I'm just saying—your work ethic, your ability, we could pay you union wages and health and dental, plus workman's comp." He grinned then, showing even teeth. "You get unemployment in porn?"

Bobby chuckled. "You do. Never know when you're gonna break your wiener, right?"

Charlie guffawed and turned to leave. "You'd better call me, kid. I want to hire you already."

"I'll talk to Reg," Bobby agreed. In his heart he knew he wanted to. Charlie's outfit was where he was supposed to have ended up last year. "Part-time might be best at the beginning."

"I can totally do that."

Charlie left, and Bobby finished the walking part of the porch, retiring to shower right when Reg got home.

He got out, and Reg was making a giant pitcher of lemonade, which about made his day.

So did Reg, in his jeans and tight T-shirt, standing in front of the counter.

Bobby drew near, plastering his front to Reg's back, and started to kiss his neck.

"Mm… that's nice."

Bobby thrust up against him through their clothes. "That's nicer."

"Yeah. Wait 'til I get this in the fridge," Reg told him, laughter in his voice. "We're gonna need it to hydrate later."

Bobby laughed, low and filthy. "Yeah, we will."

Reg looked out the window. "The crew next door is closing up too. Gonna be too hot for them, you think?"

"Yeah. They offered me a job, by the way—good to see they don't work through the stupid hot part of the day."

Reg cocked his head. "You gonna take that?"

Bobby kissed his lips over his shoulder briefly. "Help us buy siding for the house," he said practically. Then: "And when I'm ready to quit porn, it's a good outfit."

Reg smiled a little. "Not quite yet," he said.

"Still like watching me fuck?" Bobby asked, liking his voyeurism.

"Yeah." Reg turned in his arms. "But I'm getting more jealous every scene," he said seriously. "Soon."

"You give the command," Bobby murmured, taking his mouth for a quick, teasing kiss. "I'm yours."

"God, you really are." Reg closed his eyes and took Bobby's mouth harder, with all the tongue. He pulled away, breathless. "Best damned thing to happen to me ever."

Bobby grinned and kissed him some more. It was mutual. It was forever. It was as close to heaven as the world would allow, and he would grab on to it with both hands.

AMY LANE is a mother of two grown kids, two half-grown kids, two small dogs, and half-a-clowder of cats. A compulsive knitter who writes because she can't silence the voices in her head, she adores fur-babies, knitting socks, and hawt menz, and she dislikes moths, cat boxes, and knuckleheaded macspazzmatrons. She is rarely found cooking, cleaning, or doing domestic chores, but she has been known to knit up an emergency hat/blanket/pair of socks for any occasion whatsoever or sometimes for no reason at all. Her award-winning writing has three flavors: twisty-purple alternative universe, angsty-orange contemporary, and sunshine-yellow happy. By necessity, she has learned to type like the wind. She's been married for twenty-five-plus years to her beloved Mate and still believes in Twu Wuv, with a capital Twu and a capital Wuv, and she doesn't see any reason at all for that to change.

Website: www.greenshill.com
Blog: www.writerslane.blogspot.com
Email: amylane@greenshill.com
Facebook: www.facebook.com/amy.lane.167
Twitter: @amymaclane

AMY LANE

CHASE IN
SHADOW

Johnnies: Book One

Chase Summers: Golden boy. Beautiful girlfriend, good friends, and a promising future.

Nobody knows the real Chase.

Chase Summers has a razor blade to his wrist and the smell of his lover's goodbye clinging to his skin. He has a door in his heart so frightening he'd rather die than open it, and the lies he's used to block it shut are thinning with every forbidden touch. Chase has spent his entire life unraveling, and his decision to set his sexuality free in secret has only torn his mind apart faster.

Chase has one chance for true love and salvation. He may have met Tommy Halloran in the world of gay-for-pay—where the number of lovers doesn't matter as long as the come-shot's good—but if he wants the healing that Tommy's love has to offer, he'll need the courage to leave the shadows for the sunlight. That may be too much to ask from a man who's spent his entire life hiding his true self. Chase knows all too well that the only things thriving in a heart's darkness are the bitter personal demons that love to watch us bleed.

www.dreamspinnerpress.com

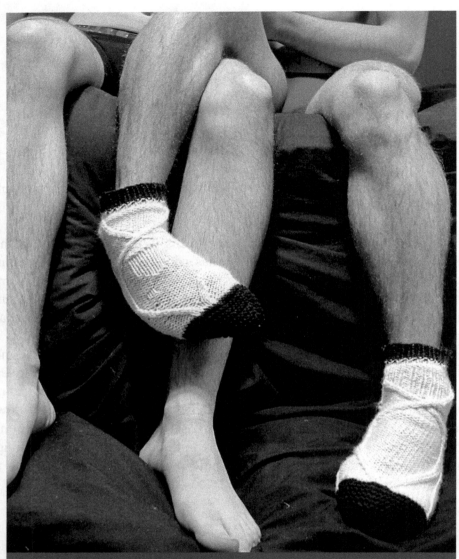

Amy Lane

**Super
Sock Man**

A Johnnies Story

Donnie's crush on his sister's roommate, Alejandro, has gone beyond childhood dreams—and it's driving Donnie insane! So when Donnie gets a chance to house-sit for his sister and Yandro, Donnie doesn't feel alone. He's got all his vivid fantasies to keep him company! Can a little dumb luck—and a little help from a magical homemade gift—help Donnie's fantasies come true?

www.dreamspinnerpress.com

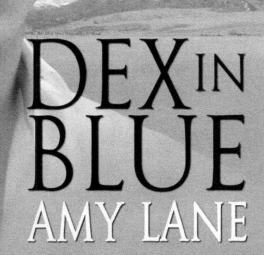

DEX IN BLUE

AMY LANE

Johnnies: Book Two

Ten years ago David Worral had plans to go to college and the potential for a beautiful future in front of him. One tragic accident later, he fled to California and reinvented himself as Dex, top porn model of Johnnies.

Dex's life is a tangled mess now, but the guys he works with only see the man who makes them believe even porn stars can lead normal lives. When Kane, one of Dex's coworkers, gets kicked out of his house, the least Dex can do is give him a place to stay. Kane may be a hyperactive muscle-bound psycho, but he's also a really nice guy. What could be the harm?

Except nothing is simple—not sex, not love, and not the goofy kid with the big dick and bigger heart who moves his life into Dex's guest room. When they start negotiating fractured pasts and broken friends, Dex wonders if Kane's honest nature can untangle the sadness that stalled his once-promising future. With Kane by his side, Dex just might be able to reclaim the boy he once was—and if he can do that, he can give Kane the home and the family he deserves.

www.dreamspinnerpress.com

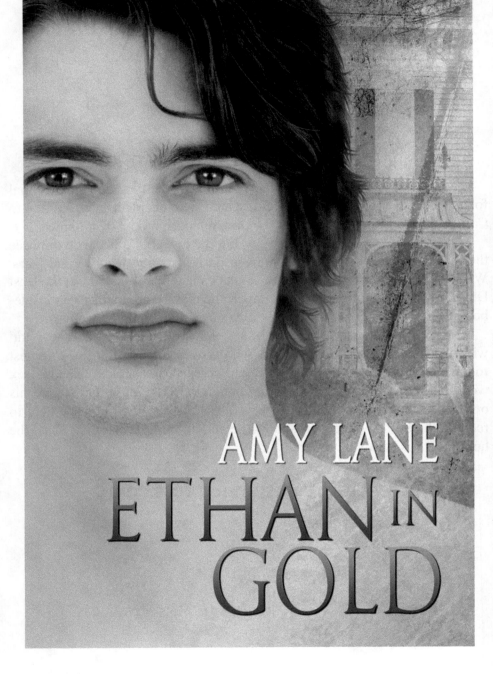

AMY LANE
ETHAN IN
GOLD

Johnnies: Book Three

Evan Costa learned from a very early age that there was no such thing as unconditional love and that it was better to settle for what you could get instead of expecting the world to give you what you need. As Ethan, porn model for Johnnies, he gets exactly what he wants—comradeship and physical contact on trade—and he is perfectly satisfied with that. He's sure of it.

Jonah Stevens has spent most of his adult life helping to care for his sister and trying to keep his beleaguered family from fraying at the edges. He's had very little time to work on his confidence or his body for that matter. When Jonah meets Ethan, he doesn't see the hurt child or the shamelessly slutty porn star. He sees a funny, sexy, confident man who—against the odds—seems to like Jonah in spite of his very ordinary, but difficult, life.

Sensing a kindred spirit and a common interest, Ethan thinks a platonic friendship with Jonah won't violate his fair trade rules of sex and touch, but Jonah has different ideas. Ethan's pretty sure his choice of jobs has stripped away all hope of a real relationship, but Jonah wants the whole package— the sexy man, the vulnerable boy, the charming companion who works so hard to make other people happy. Jonah wants to prove that underneath the damage Ethan has lived with all his life, he's still gold with promise and the ability to love.

www.dreamspinnerpress.com

BLACK JOHN

AMY LANE

Johnnies: Book Four

John Carey is just out of rehab and dying inside when he gets word that Tory, the guy who loved him and broke him, has removed himself from the world in the most bitter way possible—and left John to clean up his mess.

Forced back to his hometown in Florida, John's craving a hit with every memory when he meets Tory's neighbor. Spacey and judgmental, Galen Henderson has been rotting in his crappy apartment since a motorcycle accident robbed him of his mobility, his looks, and his boyfriend all in one mistake. Galen's been hiding at the bottom of an oxy bottle, but when John shows up, he feels obligated to help wade through the wreckage of Tory's life.

The last thing John needs is another relationship with an addict, and the last thing Galen wants is a conscience. Both of them are shocked when they find that their battered souls can learn from and heal one another. It doesn't hurt that they're both getting a crash course on how growing up and getting past your worst mistakes sure beats the alternative—and that true love is something to fight to keep if your lover is fighting to love you back.

www.dreamspinnerpress.com

CPSIA information can be obtained
at www.ICGtesting.com
Printed in the USA
FSHW021950270819
61490FS

9 781640 802568